QUANTUM LEAP
PULITZER

A NOVEL BY

L. ELIZABETH STORM

**BASED ON THE UNIVERSAL TELEVISION
SERIES *QUANTUM LEAP*
CREATED BY DONALD P. BELLISARIO**

BOULEVARD BOOKS, NEW YORK

Quantum Leap: Pulitzer, a novel by L. Elizabeth Storm, based on the Universal television series QUANTUM LEAP, created by Donald P. Bellisario.

QUANTUM LEAP: PULITZER

A Boulevard Book/published by arrangement with MCA Publishing Rights, a Division of MCA, Inc.

PRINTING HISTORY
Boulevard edition/June 1995

ISBN: 1-57297-022-7

BOULEVARD
Boulevard Books are published by The Berkley Publishing Group, 200 Madison Avenue, New York, New York 10016. BOULEVARD and its logo are trademarks belonging to Berkley Publishing Corporation.

PRINTED IN THE UNITED STATES OF AMERICA

10 9 8 7 6 5 4 3 2 1

This one is for my father, who was there in '72 and said he'd end the war. Maybe he did, maybe he didn't; what really matters is that he came back.

And in memory of my mother (October 22, 1973), who knows where I was on that day twenty-one years later.

ACKNOWLEDGMENTS

There may be many reasons you're reading this book. But here are a few more:

Ginjer Buchanan, who gave me my first chance; absolutely and without question the Editor from Heaven.

Kris Aasmo, who gave me a second chance—when it *really* mattered.

Dr. Omar Omland, who gives so much by listening.

My sister, Patricia, and my brother, John, who got me through some long nights.

Charles and Stephen Willard, the best research assistants in the world.

José Rivera and Dave Walp, who founded a company where my dream could flourish.

All the people at Horizon Data Corporation who, in one way or another, gave me help, ideas, suggestions, or an occasional kick in the butt when needed.

All those without whom *Quantum Leap* would not be real, especially, in this case, Mr. Dean Stockwell.

And above all, Syd, who alone knows how much of this story is mine; and how much is hers. Rule Numero Uno, kid: we did it!

PREFACE

In July 1970, the U.S. Army declassified a photograph for publication. The picture of an American POW being held captive in Vietnam won the Pulitzer Prize the following year.

By March 1973 all living American POWs from that conflict were reportedly brought home.

In 1974 an Army reconnaissance photograph of a field near the Cambodian border showed the SOS, cut in the grass, of a recently captured American POW. *Operation Phoenix* was organized a month later as a covert Joint Forces Operation made up of members from each branch of the armed services and overseen by a select Senate subcommittee. Its objective: to free American POWs still alive in Southeast Asia.

PROLOGUE

Dr. Donna Elesee closed the two-hundred-page volume in front of her, her mind whirling with abstract mathematics and quantum mechanics. She ran a hand through her hair and glanced at her watch: it was after midnight. And she was finally tired enough to sleep.

For four years she'd had only one goal: to bring her husband, Dr. Sam Beckett, home. The Retrieval Project, funded as part of Project Quantum Leap, was her priority; and the two-hundred-page addition to that program—a new theory on what kept them from being able to retrieve Sam from time, and a recommendation for updates to the computer that "ran" the Project—was her latest presentation to the Committee. They hadn't been convinced enough by her findings to warrant allocating any further resources to it. Donna rubbed her eyes and stretched, realizing she was going to have to bite the bullet and ask Al Calavicci to pull some strings. Again.

Her office, devoid of almost all character, sat beneath the earth of the New Mexico desert, an isolated refuge from the tumultuous activity that took place above her in the rest of the Project. In the four years since Sam had first Leaped and she had buried herself in this office, she'd never bothered to decorate it; somehow, it seemed, that would be admitting to herself that her husband wasn't going to come back very soon, and that she would be working down here a long time.

She turned to the pictures on her desk and sighed. Two pictures, the only sign of personality in the room.

"Good night, Sam," she said, as she did every night. "When-ever you are." She pulled in a deep breath, then spoke into the air. "Ziggy?"

"Yes, Dr. Elesee." The sultry female voice of Sam Beckett's hybrid computer filled the room.

"Has he Leaped yet?"

"No, Dr. Elesee."

Donna looked back at the picture of her husband. "I love you, Sam," she whispered. Perhaps, as he shifted through time, he would hear that. And remember.

Donna looked at the other picture, the picture of her father, Colonel Edward Wojiehowitz. It was the only picture she had of him, and it seemed to belong here. The image was frozen in time, frozen in memory. He'd given her the picture the last time she'd seen him, the night before he left to fight a war that never was. The night before he never came back.

For Donna, her father would be forever forty. He would be forever handsome. And he would be forever missing in action in Vietnam.

It wasn't often that she still felt the open wound of never knowing what had happened to him. But tonight, just for a moment, she did. "I miss you, Dad," she whispered.

She fingered the petals of the yellow rose she kept in a vase between the pictures. Then, as she did each night, she shut off the lights in the office and left the room.

DAY 1

Sunday, June 15, 1975

CHAPTER ONE

The plane had landed. The passengers had departed. The lieutenant hefted his garment bag over his shoulder and searched the crowd for other naval uniforms. He saw none. He moved through the security gate and started for the baggage claim. That was when he saw it: the dress white uniform of an ensign in the United States Navy.

The lieutenant swallowed and took a deep breath, walking toward the young man who had not yet seen him.

"Ensign?" The kid turned, startled.

"Lieutenant?" The young man smiled. "Welcome home, sir."

"I have a bag," the lieutenant said. He could hardly believe how young the kid was; he couldn't believe he had once been that young.

Young. In uniform. And at war . . .

"Yes, sir, of course."

Sir. The lieutenant swallowed tightly and took a deep breath as the ensign began moving toward the baggage car-

5

ousel, assuming he would be followed.

The kid was suddenly nervous. Quick, jittery movements and a gaze that moved too quickly away from the lieutenant's eyes had replaced the first smile of welcome. The kid was ready to wet his pants.

The lieutenant followed him to the baggage area and waited nearly four minutes for his solitary duffel bag. It was out of place on the conveyor belt, a single military bag among scores of brightly colored satchels and overnight cases and a collection of more businesslike suitcases. The lieutenant swept it up quickly and pulled away from the crowd. The press of people was making him feel sick.

"The car's this way, sir," the ensign instructed, and the lieutenant followed without comment. The ensign led him through the maze of Dulles International Airport toward the short-term parking lot. As the lieutenant stepped out of the terminal, he stopped, stared around him, and closed his eyes. The ensign moved back to his side and stood quietly for a moment.

"You're home, sir," he said quietly. "You're really home."

Washington in the summer. He had forgotten how beautiful it could be. Gentle winds gusted from time to time; people walked through the parks with their arms around each other; the tidal basin was clear and quiet. The ensign hadn't tried to make conversation as they'd walked to the car, nor after they began driving. "I'm supposed to take you directly to Bethesda," the young man had said, and when the lieutenant merely nodded once in assent, he began driving without another word.

The ensign chose the more scenic route to Bethesda, off the I-495 beltway that circled around the Washington metropolitan area. The traffic in the District was heavy but it moved well. And the lieutenant watched everything that passed the windows.

"My wife?"

The question seemed to startle the kid.

"Uh, they told me she's been notified, sir."

It was another minute before he could ask. "When can I see her?"

"I—" The kid swallowed twice. "I'm not in charge of the arrangements, sir. I'm sorry, I don't know."

The lieutenant sighed and looked around the car. "Radio work?"

"Oh, yes, sir. Uh, here." The ensign turned the knob and music came screeching out. The kid seemed flustered and quickly turned it down. "Sorry, sir, I was listening to it on the way to the airport."

"What *is* that?"

"Uh, disco, sir."

The lieutenant nodded and listened until the end of the song. The ensign turned back to the road, still not meeting his charge's eyes, still moving nervously.

"Beatles."

"Sir?" The kid paled at the word.

"The group. The Beatles. Are they still popular?"

The ensign sighed with relief and said, "Uh, they broke up, sir. In '71."

Past history to the ensign; today's news for the lieutenant. He wanted to ask more, but the kid looked like he might pass out.

"You okay?"

"Oh, yes, sir, I'm fine, sir."

"Look, no one's called me 'sir' for years. How 'bout you drop it for now?"

"Yes, si . . . uh, if you want."

The lieutenant almost smiled. "I'm not going to fall apart, Ensign, you don't have to worry about that."

"I know, si . . . um, I know."

"Well, it sure isn't the heat making you sweat."

The kid clenched the steering wheel and licked his lips. "My father . . . died in '68."

"In 'Nam?"

"Yes, sss— Yes. He was . . . captured."

The lieutenant stared at the young tormented profile next to him, seeing his own recent past come to life in the boy's grim determination not to let go of the small amount of control he still had.

"And?"

The ensign drove silently for another block. When they came to a stop light, he said, "I'm afraid you'll want . . . to talk about it. And I'd rather not hear . . ."

The lieutenant smiled and let out a quiet, bitter chuckle. "Relax, kid. It's over, it's past. This is what counts now."

The ensign turned hesitantly and looked the lieutenant in the eye. "Thank you, ss— Thank you."

"You're gonna choke on that word if you can't say it, aren't you?" the lieutenant asked. He waved his hand in a circle. "Well, then, go ahead, make yourself comfortable."

"Thank you, sir."

The rest of the drive was silent, but the nervous tension in the car was mostly gone. The lieutenant watched the people and cars that passed them, noticing how little of everyday life was familiar to him now. The music, the clothes, the cars, the Congress, the president. Everything had changed. Everything was stranger than where he'd come from. Stranger than what he'd called home for almost a decade.

8

"Sir?"

The car had stopped. The tower of Bethesda Naval Hospital loomed above them. The lieutenant took a deep breath and got out of the car, reaching behind the seat to rescue his bag.

"Uh, sir, before we go in . . ." He waited. The ensign's discomfort had returned. "Uh, I'm supposed to take your dog tags, sir."

The lieutenant stared at him, not comprehending at first. Then voices in his memory came back, deals, exchanges, bribes. He took a deep breath, pulled his only identification over his head, and handed it to the young officer.

He had agreed to the terms.

The ensign took him in, walked him confidently through the maze of hallways and corridors, and finally stood at Outpatient Registration, waiting until a clerk noticed him. The smell of sterility in the hallways made the lieutenant's stomach knot; he hated hospitals.

"I'm Ensign Davalos. Dr. Meyers is expecting me."

Curious, the lieutenant thought. They were dead serious about the routine after all; *his* name wasn't mentioned to the secretary. It was the ensign who was expected, not him. It was funny in a perverse way.

The secretary checked a log on her desk and nodded. "Room 2485, Ensign. Down the hall, take the elevator to the second floor, turn right. It's at the end of the hall."

The ensign nodded and gestured the lieutenant to follow him.

All military hospitals look the same, smell the same, feel the same. The smell of fear and alcohol, the clacking of shoes on shiny linoleum, the ugly lights that hung from the ceilings and made everyone look sick. The lieutenant followed the ensign to room 2485. The kid knocked and a voice inside the room called to enter.

The office was spare and plain. Government-issue bookshelves, desk, chairs. No carpeting on the floor and one of the overhead lights was burned out. The room was dark and full of paper.

"Lieutenant Doe? I'm Nathan Meyers."

The captain behind the desk stood and extended his hand to the lieutenant. Dr. Nathan Meyers was in his fifties, the lieutenant estimated. Dark brown hair going gray, wrinkles around his eyes. He was fit, his handshake was firm, and there was something comforting in the stability he offered. This was not a man who would want to pick his brain for information, or psychoanalyze him until hell froze over. This was a military officer, a naval officer, a man trained to do his work and get on with the next task.

"Welcome back, Lieutenant," he said, and gestured his guest to sit in the chair across from his desk. He turned to Davalos and said, "Thank you, Ensign. That'll be all."

The lieutenant turned to the ensign, sorry to see him go. He managed a half smile.

"Good luck, sir."

The door closed quietly and the lieutenant turned to the physician.

"Can I get you some coffee, Lieutenant?" he offered. The lieutenant shook his head.

"My wife," he said. "When can I see her?"

A hesitant second too late the doctor sat down and said, "We've got a mountain of paperwork here, Lieutenant. I'm sure that can wait."

The lieutenant's congenial attitude left so fast it startled Meyers. He planted his fists on the desk and looked down on the senior officer. "When can I see her?" he repeated very slowly.

The man met his eyes for a few seconds, then lowered his gaze slowly to the desk. "I guess there's no easy way to tell you."

The knot in the lieutenant's stomach tightened and he felt a familiar rush of terror.

He waited. He was good at that.

The doctor looked back up. "Lieutenant, your wife . . . has remarried."

The lieutenant stared. The words didn't make sense. A horrible taste of panic started in his mouth and he swallowed it out of habit.

"When?"

"In 1969. She—you were listed as MIA. By the time we got word you were still alive—she'd had the Navy declare you 'presumed dead' and remarried."

Slowly the lieutenant sank down to the chair. He said nothing. The memories, the hope, the love—it was all gone. Everything he'd come back for was gone. The deals he'd made were worthless now.

For years he'd clung to that one small hope: one day he'd come back to her.

It had kept him alive.

It had kept him sane.

He wasn't sure how to breathe anymore.

"Did—did you tell her I was back?" he asked. The words fought the choke hold in his throat and came out cracked and twisted.

"Yes."

"Where . . . is she?"

Dr. Meyers fidgeted with the papers on his desk. "Actually, Lieutenant, the Department of the Navy will have to give you the details—"

"I want to know where she is!" She was life and sanity and everything he had.

He had to find her.

Meyers met his eyes and sighed quietly. "I don't have that information, Lieutenant, I'm sorry. I'll see what I can find out for you."

The lieutenant stared at him, not believing, even yet, that what the physician said could be true: the world he'd clung to was gone.

She was gone. She hadn't believed he'd come home. She hadn't believed he could survive what they'd done to him over there.

"There's some preliminary stuff we have to get out of the way now," the doctor said, "but we can wait on the rest until later. There's a room set aside for you. Once we get through these papers, you can rest if you like."

The lieutenant slowly focused on the noise across the desk and opened his mouth to respond. But there was a snake churning in the pit of his stomach, winding its way through his chest and up into his throat. He couldn't get a word out. He swallowed and felt the muscles in his throat spasm with the effort.

"I'm sorry, Lieutenant."

He couldn't move. Whatever wasn't being devoured by the snake simply wasn't there. There had been a time, almost two years ago, when the pain had been so bad that everything else had stopped existing for him. He remembered lying very still, not moving anything, not breathing, not blinking, so the pain wouldn't find a part of him that wasn't being consumed and attack it. He remembered the bloody stench of the hootch where that pain had become a god and he had almost obeyed its death wish.

The thought of coming back home to her had kept him

alive. One more minute, one more hour, one more day. One more year.

He didn't feel the tears on his face. But some part of him had cracked open, and he had to be alone. He stood and headed for the door.

"Lieutenant, you can't leave now. We have to get—Lieutenant!"

He walked down the corridor, saw it spinning around him. He found the elevator and punched the call button. He heard voices and saw men running toward him. He stepped into the elevator and waited for the door to close.

The voices came closer, became louder. His vision blurred as the door enclosed him in the compartment: small, confined, familiar. He pressed one button, then another. Then he sank slowly to the floor, huddled in the corner, and cried.

"Admiral? Are you awake?"

Ziggy didn't sound like a computer. Her voice was human, sultry, petulant. And it intruded at the worst possible times.

Al Calavicci kept his eyes closed, ignoring the call for a few seconds as he tried to wake up.

"I am now." He surrendered to the inevitable and swung his legs over the side of his bed. He sat on the edge, rubbing his eyes. "What is it, Ziggy?"

"I've located Dr. Beckett." Ziggy stopped and waited for the admiral to pull the details from her proverbial teeth. It was only one of Ziggy's more endearing idiosyncracies.

"Well? Where is he?"

"Bethesda, Maryland."

There was a tone in Ziggy's voice that Al didn't like. "And?"

"Dr. Beeks is in the Waiting Room now. Dr. Beckett has Leaped into a naval doctor stationed at Bethesda Naval Hospital."

Al stood up and began dressing. He glanced at the clock on his night stand and grimaced: 0330. Couldn't God, or Time, or Whoever, Leap Sam in at a decent hour for those who had to monitor him?

"On my way, Ziggy. Have someone make up some coffee, will you?"

"Dr. Beeks has seen to that, Admiral."

The Command Center was bustling with activity. Gushie, the head programmer who seemed never to sleep, was updating Ziggy's information on Sam's Leap, presumably finding all information local to Sam's current location. Next to him, Dr. Tina Martinez-O'Farrell generated the handlink that would contain the most up-to-date information Ziggy could give him. They were comparing notes as they worked, a scene as familiar to Al as his own quarters; of course, he had never understood how Tina could stand so close to Gushie, whose infamous halitosis was usually noticeable even across the console.

Al let his gaze wander over Tina's slender form, enjoying the view, appreciating the tight red sweater she was wearing. But when Tina was working, she never seemed to notice if he was in the room. Off duty, of course, was another story. At least, it had been until recently.

He must have screwed up again, and so far Tina wasn't telling him how; these days, she wasn't telling him much of anything, in fact.

To the left of the table-high console at which Tina and Gushie worked was the door that led to the Imaging Chamber. Al headed for the console, checked that the Chamber was on-line, and pressed his palm onto the identi-scanner for Ziggy.

"Here."

He turned in time to catch a mug filled with hot coffee that landed abruptly in his hand. He smiled gratitude at Verbeena Beeks. The elegant black psychiatrist's expression, usually comforting and serene, held his attention. He took a sip of the coffee, surprised at how fresh it was, and kept his eyes locked on her, waiting. She wasn't volunteering anything.

"What is it?" Al asked, wondering if Verbeena had started taking lessons from Ziggy: *How to Irritate People in Three Easy Steps* . . .

"Let's talk." She turned and went toward her office at the other end of the hall. Reluctantly Al followed, drinking coffee as he went, still trying to wake up.

Dr. Verbeena Beeks hadn't settled for the Project-supplied furnishings that littered the rest of the complex. Once Sam Beckett had Leaped, changing forever the original purpose and intent of the Project, Verbeena Beeks had found herself in the unenviable position of counseling anyone on the Project who needed the help, and providing indirect counseling (through Al) for Sam when needed.

Naturally she wanted an office that encouraged people to come in and feel comfortable. So she replaced, at her own expense, the metallic desk, the uncomfortable chairs, the gray metal filing cabinet, the overhead lights. She had turned the office into a warm, richly colored haven with leather chairs and settee, a walnut-veneer filing cabinet, oriental rugs, and brightly colored abstract wall hangings. It was a mix of traditional and contemporary that made most of her charges feel comfortable.

Al took the seat across from Verbeena's mahogany desk

15

and waited until she had poured herself a cup of coffee.

"So?" he launched. "What's wrong?"

"Sam's Leaped into Bethesda Naval Hospital," Verbeena started. She waited, as if expecting some reaction.

"So Ziggy said. A doctor, right?"

Verbeena nodded, watching him with a look that made him squirm.

"Bethesda Naval Hospital. June 15, 1975," Verbeena said slowly. "According to Ziggy, you're a patient there."

"Oh, hell." Al did a lousy job of covering. He shifted his gaze away from her and ran a hand over his face to wipe away the memory. She spoke before he could begin a covering lie.

"Ziggy says that, according to your official Navy medical records, you *weren't* a patient at Bethesda in '75. In fact, you were *never* a patient there."

Al swallowed. "Then why does Ziggy say I'm there now?" he asked, grasping at a straw. It was too late, he knew. His reaction had been too unguarded.

"She's picked up *your* brain waves along with Sam's. Want to tell me about it?"

In the instant between her gentle invitation and Al's response he regained control of himself and the situation.

"I can't."

"Can't or won't?"

"Can't."

"You don't remember it?"

"I can't, Verbeena, so just leave it alone, OK?"

Verbeena drank some of her coffee. "Alright, you don't have to tell me. But Ziggy needs to know."

"Like hell she does!" His vehemence caught Verbeena off guard, and Al realized the sentiment had to have seemed

16

misplaced to her. "I mean, it doesn't matter. It has nothing to do with Sam's Leap."

Verbeena was watching him carefully. "Well, Gushie's still feeding local data to her, but she can't figure out what Sam's there for. And aside from a patient whose record shows he was never there, she's having a hard time coming up with a hypothesis."

"Trust me, Verbeena, Sam's Leap has nothing to do with me."

"How do you know?"

"Because I know, OK? There's nothing there that needs to be fixed. It isn't me." He took a sip of coffee, then asked, "Who'd he Leap into?"

"A Chinese man—"

"Not Xiao!"

For an instant the panic returned and he looked away. He turned to her only when he was back in control.

"Yes, a Weizheng Xiao," she said.

If Al could have left the room, he would have. But he'd stopped running away from himself a few years ago and he'd stay at least enough to complete the conversation decently.

"He was your doctor?" Verbeena prompted, a clear "I knew it!" to her question.

Al said nothing for another minute. "Sam's not there to change anything that happened with me." He wasn't looking at her. He stood and headed for the Control Room. "He's not there because of me." His cup of coffee sat forgotten on her desk as he left.

CHAPTER
TWO

Sunday, June 15, 1975, 12:13 P.M.

The first moment of disorientation was familiar. It left quickly. Dr. Sam Beckett looked around, found himself in an office, seated, and not being assailed by anyone at the moment. There was a patient chart open on the desk in front of him. The rest of the desk was neat and orderly, almost compulsively so. It was rare to Leap into a new situation and not instantly have to respond to someone or something demanding his attention.

He checked out his new surroundings. From the diplomas and certifications on the wall, he found himself in the person of a Weizheng Xiao. Harvard, class of '61, board certified in psychiatry. There were no pictures in the room, and no mirrors either, but at least he could guess he was a Chinese male. He looked at his left hand, but there was no wedding ring. And the lack of pictures in the room seemed to confirm that he was a childless bachelor.

Given how hard it usually was to find out who and where and what he was from Leap to Leap, this one was going pretty well.

The sound of sirens beckoned him to the window, and he found himself looking down from three floors up over the Emergency Room entrance. An ambulance pulled in and was lost from his view.

Judging from the trees, he was probably on the East Coast, he decided, and more than likely it was spring or early summer. He turned back to his desk and found a calendar.

June 15 or 16, 1975: the calendar showed two days, and he couldn't be sure which day it was. But he'd narrowed the field considerably. And given the date, he estimated he was probably in his late thirties, assuming he'd graduated Harvard on schedule.

He heard the Door slide open and turned around, surprised and pleased.

"Al!" This was turning into a dream Leap: he knew who he was, when he was, roughly where he was, and now Al was here, sooner than usual, to fill him in on the rest of the details. The all-important *why* being primary.

But Al's expression, not to mention his color, left Sam with a sudden sick feeling.

"Hi, Sam," Al began, punching the handlink as he spoke. He was looking nervously around the office, as if afraid someone might see him. The Observer seemed to have dressed hastily; his colorful outfits were always co-ordinated, at least in his own eye, but Sam had learned over the years to "read" Al's costumes. What he wore now—a dark blue shirt with silver threads shot through it, deep blue slacks, and a vest splattered with both colors—was unusually restrained. Coupled with the Observer's obvious discomfort, Sam took a deep breath and prepared himself for the worst: someone was going to die.

"What's wrong?"

The question brought a guilty look to the Observer's face and his gaze continued to dart around the room. "Oh, uh, nothing, really."

"Nothing," Sam repeated. "Al, you look like you're going to jump out of your skin. What is it?"

Al took a deep breath and rubbed his hand over his face. He looked at Sam.

"Well, it's, you know, the Leap. There's a little . . . problem, Sam."

It was a phrase he hated. Sam closed his eyes and shook his head. He turned away from Al and stared back out the window. "Is it Ziggy?" he asked.

"Uh, well, no, not exactly."

Al's hesitancy made him turn back. The handlink squealed rudely and Al shook it, irritated.

"Then what is it?"

"Well, you're, um, you're a doctor, Sam. And you're stationed at Bethesda Naval Hospital in Maryland."

"Maryland," Sam repeated. He'd been right about being on the East Coast. He waited but Al wasn't continuing. "And?"

"And, it's June 15, 1975," Al hedged.

"*And*?"

"And, uh, well, Ziggy isn't sure why you're here yet."

"OK, so—why are you here?"

Al took a deep breath and pulled a long drag from the cigar in his right hand.

"Uh, well, there's a—well . . ." He let out a sick little laugh that Sam knew well. "There's a patient here that—aw, hell."

"A patient," Sam repeated. "Something happens to one of my patients?"

"No, no, that's not—I mean—" Al took a deep breath,

20

let it out, and faced Sam squarely. "I'm a patient here, Sam."

There, it was out.

Sam said nothing for a moment, still not comprehending Al's discomfort. Of course, it was tricky to come into contact with a past version of Al, or of himself, for that matter. But it had happened before, at least twice. Maybe more, Sam couldn't be sure. And in each case the disaster they had imagined looming on the horizon had never materialized.

So why did Al look like a malaria victim?

"OK, you're a patient here. So?"

"Well, the thing is, Sam, uh, it'd be a good idea if you, you know, just kind of avoided me. I mean, the past me. You know. While you're here."

Sam nodded slowly, still not understanding. Al wasn't coming clean yet. He didn't say anything; the silence would drag it out of Al better than a question.

"Look, Sam, it's just—it'd be a good idea if you just kept a low profile until we know why you're here, OK?"

"A low profile? Who am I, Al?"

"Oh, uh, your name is Wendell Xiao, you're a naval doctor—"

"Wendell?" Sam asked, glancing back at the medical degrees hanging on the wall.

"Yeah, well, you're a second-generation American. Graduated *cum laude* from Harvard in—"

"1961, I know," Sam interrupted. "So why do you want me to keep a low profile? I mean, what happened to Wendell in the original history?"

"Oh, uh, nothing," Al said, staring at the readout on the handlink. He punched a few buttons, bringing out a pre-

21

dictable squeal, and shook the small machine. Sam waited through the ritual patiently.

"Wendell Xiao married in '78, he's got two kids, he's retired from the Navy. He lives on the Cape." There was a sneer in the last sentence. Sam smiled.

"Well, then, it must be someone else, right? So, get Ziggy to figure it out."

Al pressed whatever was on the handlink that opened the Door, and stepped backward. "Yeah, I'll—I'll get Ziggy to figure it out. In the meantime, Sam—"

"I'll keep a low profile," Sam promised. The Door slid shut on the malaria victim and Sam shook his head.

"Doctor?"

The office door opened as he continued to stare at the spot where Al had disappeared, wondering at the man's discomfort. A woman in a nurse's outfit stuck her head in cautiously.

"Yes?"

"That patient is awake. You wanted me to tell you when he woke up."

The woman might have been reasonably attractive, but she looked tired; creases around her eyes were filled with smudged mascara, and her lips were pale and dry as if she'd been licking them a lot. Her reddish-brown hair was touched with gray in wisps that strayed from beneath her cap. But all in all, she seemed harmless, possibly even friendly. He couldn't read her name tag from across the office, and she showed no signs of actually coming in, so he smiled, unsure of himself.

"Uh, the patient?"

" 'Lieutenant Doe,' " she prompted.

Sam fixed a stilted grin on his face and nodded, uncomprehending. "Oh, uh, Lieutenant Doe."

The nurse cocked her head and wrinkled her forehead. "Are you OK?"

"Oh, yeah, yeah, I'm fine, I just . . ." He didn't finish the sentence.

The nurse gave up her distance and came into the office. She reached across his desk and held up the chart that had been lying open in front of him when he'd Leaped in.

"You're supposed to do the evaluation," she reminded him. He took the medical chart from her hand and opened it.

"Right, the evaluation. I just—I just need a couple more minutes to go through the chart," he said, his forehead wrinkling as he leafed through the pages. Every one was stamped TOP SECRET. "Lieutenant John Doe" must be some hotshot, he thought.

The nurse was watching him, not certain. "Well, tell me if you need anything else," she said, and started toward the door. He had the feeling she was expecting him to say something more, but he couldn't think of anything else to say.

"Yeah, thanks." She closed the door behind her and Sam sat at the desk to read over the chart.

He knew he had a medical degree; it had come in handy once or twice on his Leaps. But having a medical degree and having a degree in psychiatry were entirely different. He wasn't comfortable with the idea of plodding through another man's psyche without training. Or help.

The chart wasn't organized like any other medical chart he could remember having handled. To begin with, there was no registration form, no in-processing documents at all. The patient history was also missing. There were references to some classified documents that, presumably, the real Wendell Xiao had seen. The front of the chart contained a list of all personnel who were authorized access to Lieutenant Doe: they included a Dr. Nathan Meyers, himself—Wendell, three nurses, three nurse's aides, and a Captain Robert Barrows.

He skimmed quickly through notes scrawled by Nathan Meyers earlier in the day and gleaned little insight into the patient; the man was admitted for "a routine physical and psychological evaluation for continued active duty." Sam was familiar enough with military procedures to know that, in the Navy, in 1975, no psychological evaluation was "routine." Dr. Meyers's notes indicated that Wendell Xiao was scheduled to do a psychiatric evaluation this afternoon.

The patient had been sedated and started on a dextrose and water IV at 11:00 A.M. And there had been a bevy of blood tests; one taken earlier in the day had shown a dangerously low blood glucose level. There was no indication that he'd been admitted for diabetes or hypoglycemia, however, and no indication as to what had prompted the sedation. Once more Sam found himself frustrated by the apparent assumptions in the record.

Something disagreeable was going on with this patient, and Sam began to wonder if *this* was why he was here.

He took a deep breath and left the room. His office was at the end of a sterile white corridor. Fluorescent lights dangling from the ceiling did nothing to warm the place up. There were no pictures on the wall, not even something inspirationally Navy, no decorations anywhere that he could see. He glanced again at the chart, noted the room number, and figured it must be on the bottom floor.

The corridor ended at an intersection. Sam turned right and saw two closed, unmarked doors on his left. The nurse sat at a table stationed outside a single-door elevator. There was a phone on the table, along with some papers and a couple more patients' charts. She glanced up as he came around the corner.

"I'm going to go see the patient now," he said. It sounded lame and the look on the nurse's face confirmed his awkward feeling. He was close enough that if he had stopped to stare, he could have read her name from the name plate on her uniform, but he had the feeling that would look even more conspicuous.

"Bottom floor, right?" he said, punching the button for the elevator. She stared at him as if he'd jumped out of a petri dish, then shook her head.

"Basement," she suggested, not very patiently. "Are you sure you're feeling OK?"

"Oh, sure, I'm feeling fine. I just . . . didn't get a lot of sleep last night."

She nodded, not believing him, and watched him disappear into the elevator.

The description of "Lieutenant John Doe" in the chart was spare: Caucasian male, forty-one, five-eight, 115 pounds. The man could stand to gain some weight, Sam thought. Black hair, brown eyes. No other descriptive features listed. No date of birth. No place of birth.

He got out of the elevator and found himself in another bleak hall, this one in the bowels of Bethesda Naval Hospital. Exposed pipes in the ceiling and peeling paint on the walls indicated that patients weren't commonly housed here. Even for a military hospital, it was grim.

The corridor was filled with mechanical noises, and as he began walking he found the source of some of them. Conveyor belts ran along the ceiling, crossing the hall between the rooms of the laundry facilities. Farther down, the entire left wall was replaced by floor-to-ceiling metal refrigeration units; he could see shelves and racks full of bread and milk and other food inside. He kept walking, checking the room numbers against the one on the chart: 0351.

He found a room with a "Private" label on the door and knocked. There was no room number on the door, and no answer, so he opened the door gingerly, peering in. The room was empty, but it was set up for a patient. A hospital bed, bed tray, and a dirty-orange, plastic-covered chair occupied the windowless room. Another door, half opened in the room, led to what looked like a small, barely functional bathroom.

Sam closed the door and wandered farther down the hall. He opened the next door and again found it empty but ready for occupancy. The third door, near the end of the corridor, across the hall from the women's locker room, bore the magical number. He knocked, received no answer, and opened the door.

"Lieutenant John Doe" wasn't just awake: he was pacing. Dressed in a standard blue-and-white hospital gown and pants, his feet bare, he paced the small, ugly white room, pulling the attached IV pole along like a recalcitrant dog on a leash.

As Sam entered, Lieutenant Doe's back was to the door, and the sound of it opening didn't stop his deliberate stride. It was even, measured, rhythmic. The man's dark curly hair was too long for regulations, Sam thought, and the way he squared back his shoulders as he walked was familiar. The hospital gown, tied loosely at the neck, swung open to reveal a series of scars lacing the man's deeply tanned back.

It occurred to Sam that he couldn't remember having noticed the scars before. And in that instant a hundred small, subconsciously noted signals congealed into a single conscious realization: Lieutenant John Doe was Lieutenant Albert Calavicci.

Sam cleared his throat by way of introduction, grateful at least that the future Al had warned him. Sort of.

"Lieutenant?"

Lieutenant Al Calavicci finished his eight steps away from the door to the bedside, turned, pulling the tipsy IV pole, and faced his visitor.

My God, he's so young, Sam thought. He turned away, looking unnecessarily through the chart in his hand, and took a deep breath.

"Who the hell are you?" The anger in Al's voice belied the trapped look in his eyes.

"Oh, um, my name is Xiao. Wendell Xiao. Dr. Meyers wanted me to see you."

Al slid the rolling bed tray open and pulled out a wrapped cigar. It was on the edge of Sam's tongue to tell his "patient" not to smoke in the hospital. But Al's hands were shaking and Sam swallowed the admonition.

"See me? See me for what?" Al demanded. He managed to unwrap the cigar and bite a small hole in the end, but a search through the bed tray yielded no matches.

Instinctively Sam patted his pockets and was surprised to find a half-empty pack of cigarettes and a lighter. He stepped into the room, offering the light.

Despite the openly friendly gesture, Al pulled back at the approach, a reaction he caught in himself. He reached forward and took the lighter. "Thanks," he grunted.

The cigar lit, the lighter returned to its owner, Al began again the systematic, rhythmic pace across the room.

"So?" Al said. "What are you here for?"

"Uh . . ." Sam was certain that Al would not respond well to being told he was there to do a psychiatric consult.

And Sam was equally certain *he* wasn't up to doing one. "Well, Dr. Meyers wanted me to . . . talk with you. You know, just to get some background stuff."

Al turned and stared at Sam, his eyes narrowed.

"You're a shrink," he said, speaking around the cigar between his teeth. Oddly, it was comforting to see Al puffing on it; it was the only thing familiar about his friend at the moment.

"Well, yeah." Sam glanced around the bare room. He couldn't exactly leave right away. He had to make an attempt at sounding like a professional, at least for a few minutes. He'd have to find a good reason to be taken off the case as soon as he left the room.

He found another of the ubiquitous orange plastic chairs behind him and took a seat.

"But since I'm new, maybe you, um, could fill me in. On what's going on." It was worth a shot; the future Al sure wasn't talking.

"Fill *you* in? What the hell are you talking about?" The anger that had been smoldering behind Al's eyes came out. He pulled the cigar from his mouth, jabbing the air with it. "You're the bastards that made this deal, remember?"

"Deal?"

"Look, stop screwing with me, OK? Nothing in this bargain said I had to sit back and let a nozzle like you psyche me out. So you can take your medical records and ink spots and Freudian slips and shove them!"

The brief tirade finished, he stuck the cigar back in his mouth and turned to pace the room.

"You're angry," Sam said. It sounded like a psychiatric thing to say. But it stopped Al in his pace. He turned around.

"Angry? Why the hell would I be angry? I'm free, right?

Home sweet home. And in six weeks I get to start a *wonderful* desk job pushing papers around the Pentagon! And what's more," he added, stabbing the cigar like a knife at Sam, "I've been dead since 1969!"

An unfinished sentence in the chart, half overlooked, came back to him: *"The patient was informed of the events leading to his wife's remarriage in 1969..."*

"Oh, boy."

The cryptic note suddenly made sense. But even as it did, something else stopped making sense.

Sam licked his lips. "You just found out—about B... your wife."

Al blew smoke. "Look, it's over!" he snapped, waving his hands in a broad, all-encompassing gesture. "The whole damn thing is over, right? So why don't you just leave, OK?"

Sam stood up; it was the best chance he'd have to get out without looking like he was trying to escape. And he had to talk to the future Al. He had to find out what was going on here before he said anything more. He glanced around the room.

"Yeah, well, why don't we talk later. Uh, have you had lunch?" he asked, remembering the reason for the IV. Al gave him a look that made him realize food was the furthest thing from his mind.

"I'll—I'll see that someone brings you something."

He didn't wait for a response. He opened the door and stepped into the cold corridor. He closed the door behind him and leaned back against the wall, shutting his eyes.

"Are you *sure* you feel OK?"

He opened his eyes. The nurse from upstairs was watching him anxiously. He was close enough to read her name badge unobtrusively: Lieutenant Farraday. Sam wanted to ask her first name, but there was a familiarity in her manner that told him Wendell probably already knew it.

She had fixed her makeup and tucked the graying wisps back under her cap. And Sam reevaluated what he saw. She was much prettier, and somewhat younger, than he'd originally thought. Without intending to, he looked her over and smiled; she'd be perfect.

"Yes, yes, thanks. Um, listen, do you think you could do me a favor?"

Her eyes crinkled with a wary smile. Sam realized she must have heard that line before.

"Could you get A . . . the lieutenant something to eat?"

"Oh," she said. There was almost a hint of disappointment in her voice. "Of course. Is that all?"

"No. See if you can hunt up a TV. And maybe a radio and some books. Oh, and—a lighter," he added reluctantly.

She folded her arms over her chest, drawing Sam's attention there. The phrase "big kazooms" came unbidden into his mind and he cleared his throat, embarrassed.

"Is *that* all?" she asked again, her tone different this time. "Would his majesty like anything else? A red carpet, maybe, or some caviar?"

Sam chuckled. "No, I think that'll do for now. We'll save the caviar for tomorrow."

She shook her head patiently and went off on her errand. Sam watched her until she turned the corner, then started for the elevator, his thoughts returning to the confusing, angry conversation with the past Al.

There were too many missing pieces from the medical record in his hand, and apparently as many missing pieces in his own memory. There was one thing he did remember, a memory that was clear and fresh and one he was certain of. He remembered a Leap, at least part of one, and he knew that what he remembered was true . . .

San Diego. Tuesday, April 1, 1969

He had just survived an undercover operation that had netted him and his partner two drug dealers. He was in the locker room back at the police station when Al showed up, teasing him about how good he looked in high heels. Dressed as a hooker, Sam waited through the jokes for the data from Al that he needed. But as Al stared at the handlink, his joking attitude disappeared.

"What's wrong?" Sam had asked, seeing Al's face turn a strange color that almost matched the mottled green of his shirt. Al was staring at information that Ziggy was pouring through the handlink.

"Sam, you're here to stop a woman from making the mistake of her lifetime," he said, not facing Sam as he spoke. He was transfixed by what he saw in the palm of his hand.

"What woman?"

Al began a small, four-step pace in front of Sam. "Her name is . . . Beth. And her husband's an MIA. A naval pilot whose A4 went down in the highlands over two years ago. And she thinks he's dead."

"But—he's not," Sam concluded.

"No. The VC have got him. He's in a cage near Cham Hoi. And he's going to be repatriated in '73. But Beth won't be there waiting for him."

It hadn't been until much later that Sam had realized Beth was Al's wife. And in the hardest moment of Leaping he'd ever faced, he had told Al he couldn't help him. He couldn't break the rules, he said. He wasn't there to give Al and Beth a second chance.

He had believed it at the time.

He punched the button and the elevator door opened. He

pressed the third-floor button and the door shut.

But above and beyond all the insinuations and assumptions in the medical chart was one overriding problem: the years were wrong. How could Al have only *just* found out about Beth? He said he'd come back from Vietnam in 1973.

And that was two years ago.

Admiral Al Calavicci watched the single door to the Chamber slide shut. He stood on the ramp, his back to the rest of the Control Center, not moving, trying to shut down the sudden onslaught of memories.

He was safe inside. Not out here, not with them. *He should go back in. He'd be safe there: safe, alone. Maybe it* was *dark and wet and cold. But at least* they *couldn't touch him in there.*

"Al?"

He turned and saw Verbeena watching him oddly. He pulled out a smile and fixed it reassuringly on his face.

"Are you OK?" she asked carefully.

Don't make a sound. Don't make a sound.

"Fine," he said. He moved down the ramp and took a deep breath. He gave Tina the handlink, not meeting her eyes, and headed for the elevator.

CHAPTER

THREE

Tess Conroy stared at the paper in her typewriter, the final paragraph of her article still resisting her. She grabbed the pack of Camels on the desk next to the old Olivetti, lit one, and puffed it until a slow red burn started at the end.

Freelancing being what it was these days, she had been lucky to get her "Fourth of July" pitch accepted by *Cavalcade* magazine. As Sunday newspaper magazines went in Washington, *Cavalcade*'s reputation was unsurpassed. Her last story for the magazine, "Terror on the Highways," had been published nearly a year ago, and it had been a long dry season with little to inspire her since then. Now, as she worked the summary for her article on firecrackers and childhood burns, she was determined that this article make the editorial staff of the *Cavalcade* come back for more.

But something was holding back the words, something she couldn't figure out. She slid down in the old chair she'd salvaged from a yard sale and stared up at the picture on the wall above her typewriter.

"Why can't I write this?" she demanded of her icon. It stared back at her in silence. In the last couple years she'd started talking to that damned picture as if the key to her inspiration and creativity lay in the face that looked back at her.

Sometimes, she almost believed it did.

Tess tapped the cigarette on the edge of her ashtray and sat back up. The four-footed, rolling chair slid along the bare wooden floor and Tess grabbed the edge of the desk to pull herself back. The chair was torn at the edge and always ripped her stockings. But today was Sunday, she was wearing jeans, and the chair was still more comfortable than the old plaid sofa she'd saved from a scrap heap two years ago.

The phone rang and Tess lunged from her chair, racing to the living room and grabbing the receiver. The phone fell off the brick and board shelf unit with a loud clamor onto the floor.

"Damn," she swore. She lifted the receiver to her ear. "Hello?"

"Tess? It's me, Jackson."

Tess picked the phone off the floor. It had left a dent in the wood where the bottom edge had struck first. She rubbed the small gouge and grimaced; her landlord wasn't going to be happy with any more damage to the apartment. She took the phone to the couch and sank into it, squirming into a familiar, if awkward, position to avoid the springs that had started to poke through.

"I'm throwing a party tomorrow night. Wanna come?" the voice on the other end asked.

"Tomorrow?" she repeated. "Monday night?"

Jackson Fellows, whom Tess wouldn't quite call a friend, laughed. "Sure. Best way to prepare for the week ahead!"

Tess sighed and glanced around the apartment. A week's

worth of dirty laundry sat on the floor near the front door, waiting for her to take it down to the laundromat. And in the kitchen, which she couldn't see from here, a five-day pileup of dishes lay in a molding heap, waiting to be washed. And then there was the story, her deadline . . . Of course, that was nearly done.

She reached across the shelves next to the sofa to grab her cigarettes. She lit another one and asked, "Anything new?"

"Nope."

Tess let out a stream of smoke. "Too bad."

"Are you just using me for my information?" Jackson demanded. Tess smiled to herself.

"Yes." And when the harsh laugh of response sounded in her ear, Tess shook her head; if he didn't want to believe the truth, that was his choice.

"So does that mean you won't come?"

She sighed. "What time?"

"Uh, people'll start coming over around seven," he said, and she heard the pleasure in his voice. It was obvious that Jackson had more than a friendship in mind, and that wasn't an impression she'd intended to give him.

"Just a few dozen of my closest friends," he added. At least, if there were a lot of people there, it wouldn't be as unpleasant as it had been the last time. And given Jackson's circle of friends, there was always the chance that one of them might tip her to the story of the decade. Without that hope, all the work she'd put into cultivating her friendship with Fellows would go to waste.

"Want me to bring something?"

"No, everything's covered. Got the booze, got some grub. Got some *women*," he added suggestively, itemizing the fundamentals of a good "Jackson Fellows Party."

"Well, I'll drop by. Thanks for the invite."

"Sure. See you at six?" he tried.

"Not a chance," she said, trying not to shudder.

He was quiet for a moment. Then, his voice lowered, he said, "Aw, come on, Tess. It wasn't that bad, right? I mean, the way you were—"

"Look," she interrupted, getting up from the sofa and sucking hard on the cigarette, "I told you. We can be friends, but nothing more, Jackson. Not now, not later. And if I get over there and the place isn't crammed with people, I'm leaving. That's the deal."

There was another moment of silence. "Yeah. Okay, see you tomorrow." He hung up and Tess stood with the sound of the dial tone ringing through the room for several seconds.

How the hell could he make *her* feel guilty after what he'd done?

She decided not to worry about it right now. She went into the kitchen, ignored the mounds of dishes in the sink and on the counters, and opened the refrigerator. She pulled out a bottle of Coke and took it back to the desk.

"After the burns, after the shock, after the therapy and the scarring," she began to write, *"it's too late to be sorry. After the damage is done, it's too late to wish you'd insisted the fireworks be watched from a distance. This year, more than three thousand children will be burned and scarred for life by—"*

She stopped writing and looked up at the picture above her desk. She met the eyes that stared from a frozen past. "Too heavy-handed?" she muttered. Then, a second later, she tore the paper from her typewriter and crumpled it into a ball she tossed backward; she missed the trash can by a yard.

When the phone rang again, she didn't race to answer it. She got up, bringing her cigarette with her. "Conroy."

"Miss Tess Conroy?"

"Yes?" This sounded official, she thought. She glanced at her watch. At one thirty-something on a Sunday afternoon?

"Miss Conroy, I'm Kelly Fulham, calling from the editorial desk at *Cavalcade*."

Why, Tess wondered, did bad news always come on Sunday?

"I'm afraid," the sexless voice at the other end began, "we won't be able to publish your story in the July second issue."

By silence, Tess knew, she'd get more information than by probing. She mouthed the cigarette and waited.

"We've just concluded a meeting and—well, we've decided to go with another angle this year."

"What angle?" Tess asked, wondering why there'd be an editorial review on Sunday.

"We'll pay you, of course," said Kelly Fulham, the patient harbinger of bad news, ignoring her question. "And if you'll submit the story, we might consider it for a future—"

"What angle?" Tess repeated. She was damned if she'd be cheated out of the publicity the Fourth of July issue would give her.

"You've heard of the Woodcock Commission?"

Tess stamped out her cigarette. "The one investigating the MIA issue?"

"That's it," Kelly answered. "Seems to be a lot of interest in the POW/MIA angle right now, so we decided to capitalize on that."

The calm response to market pressure, Tess thought. Not that she could blame them.

"Do an angle on the boys who never came back," Kelly continued. "The ones who weren't accounted for. Those who fought and gave their lives, that sort of thing."

Tess was grinning, an ear-to-ear, almost painful grin. She glanced at the icon.

"Have you got a personal angle?"

"We have several stories we think—"

"How about the civilian angle? How about," Tess added, sinking happily onto the sofa and avoiding its broken spring, "the story of a civilian who died over there? Someone who gave her life to get the story America wanted to hear. The story America needed to know?"

There was a moment of contemplative silence and Tess chewed her lower lip, waiting.

"What did you have in mind?"

Tess took a deep breath and let it out quietly enough not to sound like a sigh. "Margaret Dawson," she said. She leaned forward excitedly, as if Kelly Fulham were seated across from her, not miles away in a Washington office. "She died in a sapper attack in 1970. She was one of UPI's best photojournalists. Her work's appeared in—"

"I know—I knew . . . Maggie," said Kelly Fulham, suddenly interested. There was a pause that told Tess she'd just hooked herself a live one. "What . . . angle were you thinking about?"

"Well," Tess launched, trying to control her eagerness, "I've done some research on her last days. Talked to some of the people who knew her. And—I heard her lecture once in college." That wasn't really an answer, Tess realized, but hell, she was thinking on her feet. Almost.

This time, the pause wasn't as encouraging.

38

"Tell you what," Kelly Fulham said. Her voice had dropped. "Come by here in two hours, we'll talk about it. The deadline's still going to be the same, though."

Tess nodded, not that Kelly could see that. "I'll be there," she said calmly, stifling an exultant crow.

Her mind was churning with ideas even before she hung up the phone. God, what an opportunity! She went back into her study and and scrutinized the red-matted image on the wall.

"And you thought it was a waste of time," she scolded, waggling a finger at the mute photograph.

There was, of course, no response.

Sunday, June 15, 1975, 3:15 P.M.

Sam Beckett survived an agonizing afternoon, led by Lieutenant Farraday, seeing patients he was supposed to be familiar with and hadn't a clue about. The first, a young ensign fresh out of the Naval Academy, had tried to kill himself two days before. The next, a captain about to be transferred to Germany, was suffering from acute depression over the recent loss of his parents in a plane crash. The third, a lieutenant who'd just been transferred from San Diego, was "exhibiting conduct unbecoming an officer."

Sam spent the day moving from one abnormal personality to the next, feeling alternately uncomfortable and guilty. He didn't have the first idea about what to do to help these people, and it was obvious most of them needed help. While some of them were here only because they'd overstepped some naval standard of acceptable conduct, most of those he saw were in need of real attention. They needed their doctor, Wendell Xiao, the real Wendell Xiao, not a quantum physicist who looked like Wendell Xiao.

He waited anxiously for Al to show up again. After lunch, he became concerned that the Observer hadn't returned. By the time the day was over, he was angry. Why didn't Al at least come back with an update, even if there wasn't much news? He didn't usually stay away this long, not at the beginning of a Leap. At least, Sam didn't think so.

"This'll be the last of them," Lieutenant Farraday said, handing over a chart on an ensign suffering from schizoid depression.

The shift had ended, but Farraday had hung around, guiding him through the final hours with a cautious watchfulness that told him he wasn't acting enough like Wendell Xiao to make her comfortable. He read through the chart in his hands.

"Doctor," Farraday began, after Sam had checked the list of medications for the third time, "you seem . . . distracted."

Sam grimaced. "I was just thinking about A . . . uh, Lieutenant Doe," he explained. For most of the day, he'd kept his mind off the problem of the past Al, holed up in the basement of the building. He'd been too busy earlier to devote any time to the many questions Al's presence here raised. But he wanted to check on him again, at least once, before he left for the night, maybe find out something about what was going on. But given Lieutenant Calavicci's earlier anger and Sam's own lack of information, he wasn't looking forward to the encounter.

"Were you able to get those things for him?"

"Well, I found a radio and a cigarette lighter." Lieutenant Farraday pushed a strand of hair back under her cap.

"And I ran out and got a couple novels. Spy stuff, you know."

"How'd he seem to you when you took them in?"

"OK, I guess. He was doing calisthenics." Her face wrinkled in disgust.

Al hates calisthenics, Sam thought. *And he didn't invite you to join him.* It was depressing. While he disapproved of Al's attitude toward women and sex, he was more concerned now with the apparent lack of interest in either. Even marriage had never stopped Al from looking, inviting, or reminiscing.

Farraday was watching him again, her head tilted to the side. The angle made her look much younger. Then she glanced at her watch.

"Coming? I still have to brief the next shift when we're done here."

"You go ahead," he said. "I think I can manage."

She shrugged and stepped into the elevator while Sam searched through the stack of patient charts for John Doe's.

"Oh, I almost forgot!" She put her hand on the closing door and held it open. "Dr. Jansen called, said he has a meeting all day tomorrow. Asked if you'd cover for him."

He found the chart and turned around. "Jansen?" he repeated. "Cover? Isn't there . . . someone else?"

"Well, I think they're overstaffed in maternity."

It wasn't funny. The way he felt, an obstetrician would do these guys more good than he could. But he said, "OK, I . . . guess I'll have to."

"Guess so." She let the door close.

Sam opened the chart, wondering as he read through Meyers's notes if he should write his own: *"What the hell is going on here?"*

He shut the chart without adding his comments and

41

pressed the button for the elevator. Maybe tomorrow he could get some answers from Nathan Meyers.

Sunday, June 15, 1975, 3:24 P.M.

Captain Robert Barrows was less than ten minutes late for his meeting, but those had been a critical ten minutes. He could tell that the moment he entered Senator Blackwell's obscenely small office. The looks directed at him from Lieutenant Commander Stern, U.S. Navy, Colonel Wainwright, U.S. Air Force, and Senator Elwood Blackwell, himself, were unforgiving. Had the expressions been guns, they'd have been loaded. And cocked.

"Sorry I'm late," Bob started uneasily, slipping into the empty chair near the senator's desk. He avoided facing either the elected official or the Air Force representative, and turned instead to his only known ally.

"What'd I miss?" He leaned back, folding his fingers together as he rested his elbows on the arms of the chair.

"We were just discussing Nathan Meyers's unexpected departure." Dennis Stern had a sense of humor that matched his physique: lean and well honed. His sharp, young features twitched with sarcasm.

"I just got back from Alexandria Hospital," Barrows explained. He shot a quick look at the senator. "Nathan's wife went into premature labor this morning."

"*Nathan?*" Senator Blackwell repeated. "You know Dr. Meyers, too?" At sixty-five, Elwood Blackwell still possessed a commanding presence, when he chose to use it. His hair was a dark silver, combed back to cover a balding area toward the crown. His eyes, equally dark silver, but set far apart on his wide face, gave him the impression of always being half startled. He had a round, fleshy mouth that was constantly chewing something—a pencil, a toothpick, a swizzle straw—and left people with a first impression that the man was nervous. It was an impression he let them hold on to as long as possible; it took them off guard when they discovered they were wrong. But his voice, a sonorous drumroll that came like distant thunder into the room, was by far his greatest asset.

"I thought we agreed," the senator said as he turned from Bob, "that this was to be a completely sterile operation."

Colonel Jerry Wainwright, the Air Force's best excuse for an intelligence officer, squirmed in his seat under the senator's long gaze.

"Mr. Senator," he began politely, "nothing in Washington is that sterile."

The senator waited and Wainwright was forced into a defensive position.

"Captain Barrows and Dr. Meyers are only recent acquaintances." He glared at Bob for confirmation. Barrows sighed.

"That's true," he agreed, unwillingly supporting Wainwright's claim. He glanced over at his enigmatic naval colleague, then added, "Mutual friend introduced us."

"And," Wainwright added, "Meyers was the best physician on staff for this operation." Then, shifting his enormous bulk in the chair, the colonel turned to Barrows. "What's his status?"

Bob shook his head. "Don't know. Best guess, he'll be off the operation. At least for now."

"Then," said the senator, pulling a half-ground pencil from his lips, "we better keep the other two in France a couple more days."

43

Stern nodded agreement. "They're not in the best condition."

"Worse shape than Calavicci, that's for sure." Wainwright's unspoken accusation scraped Bob's nerves.

"Meaning?" he demanded. He unfolded his hands and laid them on the arms of the chair, hunching forward in the seat. He was tired of Wainwright's insinuations. He caught the warning look from Stern and ignored it.

Wainwright turned a nearly triumphant look at the senator, then looked back at Barrows. "Meaning, Captain," he started, much too sweetly, "that I've talked to the others. And they confirmed what our sources told us."

For a few seconds Bob held his breath, not aware that he was doing so until he let it out. He tried to meet Dennis's eyes, but the younger man had found something else to stare at: his feet.

"I don't believe it."

"Lieutenant Calavicci has been accused by his fellow POWs," the senator pointed out, not unhappily. "We must at least investigate the charge."

"Al wouldn't—" Bob stopped, partly because of the expressions in the room—loaded, cocked, and aimed—and partly because of his own doubts.

"We've been hearing this story almost from the start," Wainwright kindly reminded him. "I believe an investigation is in order."

Bob took a deep breath to control himself. It had taken him years to relearn how *not* to respond to an implied threat.

"Look, he trusts me. Let me go to the hospital and talk to him. Alone."

That was the wrong thing to say. Dennis shot him an appalled look and the senator responded by slowly leaning forward, an effect like flowing volcanic ash.

But it was Wainwright, still inexcusably satisfied, who said, "You and Calavicci were in the same camp in 1970."

"He saved my life!" Bob responded sharply. He added Blackwell into his gaze. "Several times."

"I don't think it would be wise," the senator calmly refused.

"Who's with Calavicci now?" Dennis Stern's quiet, objective question was a relief.

"The psychiatrist," Bob said, sitting back in the chair. "Xiao."

"Have you talked to him?" Wainwright asked.

Bob had heard that Wainwright intimidated men under him, and having worked nearly a year with him now, he could understand why. Had he been less certain of himself, he'd have responded to the implicit criticism in Wainwright's question.

"Not yet."

Short, quick glances were exchanged: Wainwright to Blackwell, Blackwell to Stern, Stern to Bob.

"Perhaps," Wainwright suggested, "an amytal interview might shed some light on—"

"A what?"

"Interrogation," Stern interpreted. His dark blue eyes held an unheeded warning.

"Interrogation!" Bob shot from his chair and took one step toward the colonel. "Dammit, Wainwright, this man's a returning POW, not a criminal!"

"He's been accused by his fellow POWs of collaborating."

"He's not a traitor!"

"He didn't *want* to come back!"

Wainwright's accusation silenced Bob. He focused on

45

controlling his urge to strike the man.

"He was willing to give his place to someone else," he said at last. He turned to the senator. "That's not the same."

"We have only *his* word for that altruistic gesture," Blackwell countered.

Bob slapped his palm on the senator's desk. "He's not a traitor!"

"An amytal interview should clear up that issue."

"You don't need a truth serum!"

"Would he lie to protect himself?"

Bob stepped back and sat down. *"Rule numero uno, Bobby..."*

He didn't answer.

"I believe," the senator began, "an investigation would be appropriate." Then he gnawed for a moment on the pencil. "There's to be no coercion."

"Amytal is not coercive." The colonel locked gazes with the politician, and Barrows caught the look: the humanitarian order and its acceptance were for the benefit of the others in the room with them. For the record.

"Air Force Intelligence does have the prerogative to investigate all suspected collaborations," the senator reminded them. "Ever since the Navy botched that Alley case back in the fifties, it's been the Air Force's responsibility." He was looking from Barrows to Stern. "You boys are free to tag along because of the nature of this operation. But you're not to interfere. And—" He hesitated in order to pick a splinter from between his teeth. "You're to give Colonel Wainwright your full cooperation."

Bob waited. He glanced at Stern, who sat in his silent shroud of detachment.

46

"And if he's guilty?" Wainwright's lust for a hanging was obvious.

"Then we'll deal with it. Quietly." The politician finally stood, and so did the rest of them. "If he betrayed his own men," he continued, "we need to know that. But for the sake of this operation, no one else should." He looked, in turn, at each of the men in his office. "Especially not the press."

CHAPTER FOUR

Oh be kind to your web-footed friends,
For a duck may be somebody's mother.

Impatient anxiety betrayed Tess Conroy as she tapped a Sousa march on the leather portfolio she held in her lap. She glanced at her watch, continued her drumming, and watched the caldron of activity that made her own blood simmer with passionate longing. The newsroom of *Washington Life* was an adrenaline rush of hysterical dialogue, pounding typewriters, phones that were always ringing, and stale coffee swigged into desperate mouths. She watched it all from the chair near the door to Kelly Fulham's office, where the frantic reporter she'd introduced herself and her purpose to had hastily stashed her.

Be kind for they live in the swamp,
Where the weather is cold and damp.

48

Tess's piano-trained fingers danced out "The Stars and Stripes Forever" while she tried to sit still.

"Denny! Get a crew down to Seventeenth and D. There's a hold-up in progress."

The shout was almost lost in the cacophony of unco-ordinated sounds that cried through the air. Tess watched as men and women rose in a flurry to answer the battle cry, grabbing recorders and pens and cameras and heading out of the smoke-filled room.

"Miss Conroy?"

The voice above her pulled Tess from the fantasy she'd momentarily indulged in.

"Kelly Fulham." The woman who stood over her extended a freckled, ink-stained hand and waited as Tess nervously shifted purse and portfolio, stood, and took the offer.

"Pleased to meet you."

With no more introduction, and no further indication of civil preludes, Kelly Fulham strode into her office, waited until Tess followed, then pushed the door and let it slam shut under its own weight.

"I'm sorry, but I haven't much time this afternoon." Kelly Fulham was much younger than Tess had imagined from her voice. She couldn't have been much more than thirty-five, and her dark red hair only accentuated her pale face. She wore no makeup and her eyes, sunk back into hollows, weren't large or dark; it was easy to lose sight of them against the camouflage of freckles.

She opened a deep drawer in her desk as Tess, taking the chance, sat across from the woman in the claustrophobic office.

"I know I've got it here," Kelly mumbled, rummaging through the drawer. Tess glanced around the crowded room

49

and noticed a familiar Olivetti sitting on a roll-away cart near Kelly's paper-crowded desk. She felt a surge of professional camaraderie.

"Here!"

The woman pulled an overstuffed manila folder from the drawer, leafed quickly through it, and tossed it on the desk with a trajectory that left it almost in Tess's lap.

"That's my file on Maggie Dawson. Smoke?"

"I'm sorry?"

The editor grabbed a half-empty pack of Benson & Hedges that lay tucked beneath a stack of papers nearly seven inches high, and held it out. Tess waited for the pile of papers to topple now that their precarious support had been removed, but they didn't.

"Cigarette?"

"Oh." Tess took one, accepted a light, and murmured, "Thanks." Then, with the sense that she was engaging in a hostage exchange, she set her own portfolio on the desk in front of Kelly. "That's my file on Margaret Dawson."

Kelly blew out a contrail of smoke and opened the leather cover. "You did a story for us last year," the woman said, idly glancing through Tess's comparatively slim notes.

"Yes. It was about the oversized rigs on the highways and the dangers—"

"I read it," Kelly cut her off. She closed Tess's portfolio and looked up. A long ash dangled from the end of her cigarette. "That's why you're here." The woman used her cigarette to gesture, and Tess found her eyes locked on the ash. "Look at that."

The ash didn't fall.

Then, realizing the woman didn't mean the cigarette, Tess followed her gesture. She opened the folder and found a haphazard, hastily collected assortment of pictures, articles, notes, and interviews.

If my apartment were a file folder, Tess thought, *it would look like this.*

"The Army claims Maggie died in a sapper attack on April 7, 1970," Kelly said. "She didn't."

Tess sifted through the unorganized assortment of information, finally focusing on one piece in particular.

"What's this in here for?" She held up a photograph that seemed out of place. Kelly took a drag that made Tess think she'd just switched to tobacco from something far more potent.

"That was Maggie's last photograph." Finally, as Tess tapped her ash into the ashtray on the desk, Kelly followed suit.

"I know this picture," Tess said. "It won a Pulitzer, right?"

"Yeah." Kelly stamped out her half-finished cigarette and pulled out another one. "But not for her."

Tess's gaze drifted away from the picture in her hand to the mound of papers in front of her.

"Turn it over." Kelly's command snapped Tess's attention back to the picture. She flipped it in her hand and read the carefully typed paragraph.

This picture of an American POW in Vietnam raised the country's awareness of the brutality of an undeclared war. As in Korea, American POWs, with no protection from the Geneva Convention, were subjected to inhumane treatment, coercion, and torture. While some Americans registered their protest to the war, marching placards up and down Pennsylvania Avenue, other Americans, like this one, could only wait and hope for freedom. —July 1974

"Did you write that?"

Kelly exhaled smoke. "No. Wish I had." She leaned forward and grabbed the picture from Tess's hands. "Pretty good, though, huh?"

Tess nodded, finished her cigarette, and waited.

"The Army says Maggie died at the SEAL base she was at," the editor started, cupping the lighter to the end of her cigarette. "They said she never went on that mission."

"What mission?"

"*That* mission." Kelly gestured with her head to the picture. "After the Army released that picture, they released some of the details surrounding it. Most of the information's still classified, but it seems our boys in green were out on a search and rescue. They were after those POWs."

"And you think Maggie took this picture?"

"I know she did." Kelly put the picture on the desk. "That's not military film. I finagled a look at the original and had an expert analysis done on it years ago. It was taken with the same kind of film that was in Maggie's cameras. And the Army doesn't use that kind of film."

Tess's heart began to beat a little faster. "So why are they covering it up?"

Kelly's wide lips spread into a narrow grin. "Would you admit to taking a woman along on a dangerous mission if she ended up getting blown to pieces at the end? *And* you screwed up your mission?"

Tess shook her head, but it was apparent Kelly was on a roll, so she didn't interrupt her.

"Just between you and me, I knew Maggie pretty well. We grew up in the same neighborhood, went to school together. She knew what she wanted and she went after it. And, frankly, it didn't often matter what she had to do to get it."

Tess cleared her throat, remembering the lecture she'd heard Maggie give a few months before her death; journalistic integrity had been the subject.

"If Maggie was on that mission," Kelly continued, her eyes narrowing a little as she watched Tess, "I'll bet you anything I know what she did to get on it. Probably another reason the military won't admit she was there."

For a moment Tess wasn't sure she followed Kelly's train of thought. Then she did.

"You think she—you're not saying she'd—"

"Hell, Conroy, the woman was like a cat in heat when she got wind of a story!"

Tess blushed and cleared her throat again. It wasn't that she hadn't heard of women who traded their bodies for information, but Tess had never thought highly of those who did. One of the problems with Jackson Fellows, she realized, was that he seemed to assume that Tess was just that kind of reporter.

"Look, if Maggie went on that mission, she knew the risks. If she got killed on that mission, she died doing what she loved most. I got no problem with that. What I've got a problem with," Kelly said, stamping out the cigarette in her hand and reaching for another, "is that no one in the Army or the Navy has the balls to admit that they let her go on that mission. And they stole credit for her Pulitzer to keep their own butts out of the sling." She offered the nearly empty pack to Tess.

"And—that's the story you want?" Tess lit a cigarette and glanced at the mounds of papers and pictures in front of her, and the photograph that lay apart from the rest. She fingered it, picked it up, and waited.

"That's the story I want." Kelly pointed to the folder. "You can have that for backup, but most of it's pretty old.

Most of my sources on that are probably gun-shy by now.''

"Why don't you write it?" Tess asked, wondering where the impulse to shoot herself in the foot came from.

"No time." Kelly tapped the cigarette and glanced at her watch for emphasis. "And I'm too close to the story to do it right. Too pissed at the Army and Navy to be objective." She paused, her eyes searching Tess's expression. "Think you can do it?"

"I have until—"

"Wednesday."

Tess felt her eyes open wide with astonishment. "I thought the deadline—"

"Wednesday," Kelly repeated. "If you can get it to me by close of business, I'll see that it's the cover story."

Tess stopped breathing. "The cover—" The awe-inspiring words wouldn't quite come out. Her mouth dried up and her hand began to shake.

"Twenty-five hundred to three thousand words," Kelly said. "And—probably two or three photos."

Tess forced air into her lungs and nodded.

"Okay," Kelly said. She smashed her cigarette into the overcrowded ashtray and made a small gesture with her hands that indicated she was finished. Wordlessly, Tess killed her own cigarette and grabbed the folder, the papers that had been hastily strewn over the desk, and the Pulitzer Prize–winning photograph. She put her portfolio on top of the stack and stood with it.

"This is—this is really a great—"

"You're losing time," Kelly suggested, not unkindly but definitely impatient.

"Right. Thanks." Under other circumstances, Tess would have felt uncomfortable leaving so abruptly, but abruptness seemed to suit Kelly Fulham just fine. Tess stag-

54

gered out under the weight of Kelly's obsessive research and floated on the hope of fame.

Sunday, June 15, 1975, 3:48 P.M.

Outside Senator Blackwell's office, Wainwright held a brief meeting to map the next step. At 1700, he, Barrows, and Stern would convene at Bethesda Naval Hospital.

"What about the psychiatrist?" Wainwright demanded of Dennis. "Can we count on him?"

"The guy's as clean as they come. No connections. He doesn't ask questions. He does his job. And he goes home. Alone. And he doesn't know a soul connected to this operation."

"Is his conscience likely to give him any trouble about using amytal?" Wainwright pressed, glowering down at Barrows with a kind of pleasure. Dennis tried to ignore the look.

"Far as I can tell, the man's conscience is defined by his orders. He got his psychiatric training through the Navy, he still owes them a few years. I don't think he'll squawk too loudly, not as long as his future's still ahead of him."

"Good, that makes it easier." Wainwright looked briefly at each of them, adding, "And just remember, gentlemen. As far as this phase of the investigation goes: I call the shots."

Dennis and Bob Barrows wandered toward their cars in silence. In the parking garage Barrows asked Dennis to join him across the street for a sandwich before they left for the hospital.

"I have some chores to take care of," Dennis declined. "I'll meet you at Bethesda."

Barrows hesitated, then turned unhappily toward his own car. Dennis watched him leave and was sorry he couldn't join him; Bob was a decent enough man, and he'd given up more than any of them to stay on this operation. But now that even the other POWs had called Calavicci's activities in 'Nam into question, Dennis was concerned about Bob's occasionally rash actions. It might have been a good idea to feel him out before the "interview." But he didn't have that choice.

When he left the garage, he was surprised by how hot and humid the day had turned, and as he sped along the parkway he listened for a weather report on the radio. Summer in Washington was like being in the armpit of the United States, he thought, listening to the gloomy prediction of hot, humid weather and probable thunderstorms for the next three days.

Twenty minutes later, at the site of the most infamous political scandal in recent times, Dennis checked through security and took the elevator to the well-known sixth-floor apartment.

"I expect there's been some development or you wouldn't have risked this," his host said, opening the door and ushering Dennis in. The lieutenant commander removed his cap and waited uneasily in the foyer. The apartment was decorated with either real or excellent reproduction Louis XV furniture. One wall was completely covered with a glass mirror, doubling the apparent size of the room. The dark-framed portraits on the opposite wall were of men Dennis suspected might actually be related to the man who greeted him.

"Drink?" his host invited, moving to a wet bar in the living room and dropping ice from a silver ice bucket into glasses.

"Scotch and soda," Dennis decided. Not too strong, but strong enough to brace him for the next few hours.

Dennis decided that one of the men pictured in the room was most certainly related to the man who handed him the drink; the resemblance was too striking.

"My father," the man said, following Dennis's gaze. "I was elected to his seat when he retired." The man stroked his carefully trimmed, dark beard, then walked toward the balcony and Dennis followed.

"Blackwell's authorized an amytal interview," the naval commander started. "I have to be there, so we'll have to make this brief." He took a sip from his drink and followed his host's stare out over the expensive view of the Potomac River and Arlington.

"We're in for one hell of a storm," the man observed, not meeting Dennis's eyes. The commander waited and finally, with a half turn of his head, the man asked, "Why amytal?"

"Because even Barrows couldn't swear that Calavicci'd tell the truth without . . . encouragement."

The tall man chuckled without humor. "Who would?"

"Wainwright wants a scapegoat," Dennis reminded him. "One way or the other, he's determined to get one." He hesitated before adding, "And I think Blackwell's still got some reservations about keeping Barrows on the operation."

"Do you?"

For the first time, Dennis's host turned to look directly at him. The man had a disconcerting habit of staring at his prey with an almost hypnotic gaze.

"No."

"What if I told you that *Cavalcade* is going with a POW/MIA issue for the Fourth of July?"

Dennis felt a little queasy and put the glass down on the black wrought-iron table nearby. "Are you certain?"

His host tilted his head slightly to indicate his displeasure with being questioned, then stroked his beard again and looked out over the water. "If Barrows leaked this to the press—"

"That's the last thing he'd want," Dennis interrupted, wondering suddenly if Barrows's motive for inviting him out earlier had anything to do with this. "If the press gets hold of this, Wainwright shifts to Plan B and Calavicci is publicly crucified." His host winced at the analogy, but didn't object to it. "I'll talk to him, though," Dennis promised.

The tall man nodded, still staring over the balcony. He was, Dennis thought, particularly pensive today. The air around them grew heavier with impending rain.

"When Blackwell and I were in Saigon last year, finishing up the negotiations," the man said without preamble after several seconds, "I finally began to understand his motives for being involved in this." Again, he half turned to Dennis. "He's not interested in getting our men out. He's interested in normalizing relations with Vietnam." The drink in his host's hand disappeared rapidly after that statement and Dennis wasn't sure what kind of sign that was. "Blackwell's constituency would benefit if we lifted the trade embargoes."

"Well," Dennis tried, lifting his own glass and taking a cautious sip. He ran his hand through his hair as the wind suddenly swept across the balcony and blew it in his eyes. "Not everyone's motives are as pure as ours," he observed with a touch of sarcasm.

His host let out a breath, not quite a sigh. "What you need to keep in mind, Dennis," the man said very quietly, "is that Blackwell cannot lose in this situation. Whether this first experiment works or not," he continued, his eyes locked on the rapidly approaching storm that darkened the horizon, "Blackwell has set up methods for the Vietnamese to account for all our men over the next several years. It'll be a slow process, but in the end, everyone *will* be accounted for."

Dennis found the man's somber attitude peculiarly disturbing: normally, his tall colleague was an ebullient, philosophical man, perpetually evaluating whether the glass was half full or half empty. Something had happened.

"Accounting for all our men is what we're after, isn't it?" Dennis asked carefully.

"There are men over there we know are still alive. Bringing them home *alive* is what we're after."

As the man turned to look at him directly, heavy drops of rain began to pelt the balcony.

"Blackwell and Wainwright can't lose," the reincarnated image of Abe Lincoln explained, making the point excruciatingly clear. "With or without a scapegoat, with or without the press getting wind of this. So keep that in mind, Dennis. And make sure Barrows keeps that in mind. Nothing good can come of challenging them at this point. Better to give them a little slack now and ensure that we get another chance at this than force them to cover their own butts and shut everything down."

They moved off the balcony as a crack of thunder punctuated the man's orders.

"I have to get going," Dennis said. He felt more than a little queasy now. "I have a prisoner to interrogate."

CHAPTER FIVE

A patient with multiple personalities, Sam Beckett decided, should have more than one chart and should count as more than one patient. Still concerned that his guide from the future hadn't yet returned, Sam put his last patient's chart back on Farraday's desk in the corridor and pressed the button to call the elevator. The door opened on Admiral Calavicci, half sunk into the floor of the old elevator, visible only from the waist up.

"Al." Sam caught his surprise and shook his head.

The hologram glanced around and adjusted his image until he was level with Sam.

"Where have you been?" Sam got in, pressed the button for the basement, and leaned back against the wall.

Al looked a little surprised by the question. "What? Oh, well, it's taking Ziggy a little while to figure out why you're here, that's all." He was wearing one of his favorite outfits: red trousers and fedora, white shirt, a vest that was mottled black and red in the front, and silver in back, a slender silver tie and silver shoes. It generally meant he was relaxed. The change in Al's mood and behavior didn't make Sam comfortable. It was too drastic, too sudden, too unexplained.

"So what does Ziggy say?" Sam prompted. Al played a familiar tune on the handlink and shook his head.

"She doesn't know. She's checked out all of Wendell's patients, and they all pretty much have the same ending: their careers are either over or stalled, and those that don't end up paper pushers retired."

"Well, what about after they retire? I mean, what happens then?"

Al stuck the cigar between his teeth, reading the information from Ziggy. He shrugged after a minute. "Well, none of them end up killing themselves or anyone else. Some of them go through a couple divorces. Some of them end up drinking, a couple are just fine." He looked up, waving his cigar in the air. "But unless you plan to stick around for the next ten years, it has nothing to do with any of them."

"Well, maybe it's a patient who isn't here yet," Sam suggested. "Have Ziggy check—"

"Ziggy's checked all of Wendell's patients for the next three weeks. *Nada.*"

Sam sighed and watched the indicator in the elevator sink.

"Did you ask Ziggy what the chance is that it has something to do with 'Lieutenant John Doe'?" He heard the sharpness in his voice and regretted it the moment he saw Al's expression.

"It doesn't."

"Did you ask Ziggy?"

Reluctantly Al punched a few buttons and stared at the

link. Sam couldn't see his eyes, but then Al shrugged, not quite looking at him.

"See, like I told you. It doesn't have anything to do with me." The handlink squealed.

"Jansen!"

"What?"

"Is there a Dr. Jansen on staff here?"

Al quickly input the information and nodded. "Yeah, Captain Adam Jansen, he's a psychiatrist."

"I'm supposed to cover his patients tomorrow."

Al was already ahead of him. Sam watched the older man coax the information from the handlink.

"Bingo!" Al beamed with success and relief.

The elevator doors opened, but neither man moved immediately.

"There's a kid who was admitted today, Ensign Terry Martin. He was in a car accident and—" Al sighed and read, "It killed his wife. They'd only been married six months, poor kid."

"And?" Sam stepped into the doorway of the elevator to hold the door open.

"And when Jansen did an evaluation on him, he thought the kid was dealing with it."

"But he wasn't."

"No. A week after they release him from the hospital, he's gonna kill himself. Ziggy says there's a . . . 68.4 percent chance that's why you're here."

"Okay, okay. Al, I'm not a psychiatrist. Am I?"

"No. Look, all you do is ask a few questions, take a few notes, and listen a lot. For a day or so, you can handle it, Sam. You go talk to this kid tomorrow, get him to accept that he's not responsible for his wife's death, and you're outta here."

"Al, I'm not Dear Abby, and these aren't frustrated housewives. These men need help, real help."

Al gave him the "So what do you want me to do about it?" look, usually followed by a capitulated solution.

"Alright, I'll have Ziggy check into their records and see if maybe she can give you some help. Feel better?"

"A little."

Sam stepped out of the elevator, expecting Al to follow. He turned around, aware that the hologram was not floating along with him. Al stared into the corridor with dread. Sam walked back and caught the elevator door just before it shut.

"Al?"

"What are you doing down here, Sam?" he asked. His voice was harsh and quiet.

Sam leveled a long, serious look at his friend. "What's going on here? With you? I mean—the past you." It was awkward trying to differentiate between the two times of one man.

Al put his cigar in his mouth and met the stare. "Don't worry about it, Sam. It has nothin' to do with why you're here. So just don't worry about it."

He still hadn't moved from the elevator; in fact, he'd backed into it, almost pressing his immaterial form against the wall that would go right through him if he actually tried.

Sam took a deep breath. "You told me you came home in 1973, Al," he said. "So how can you just be coming home—now—in 1975?"

"When did I tell you I came home in '73?" Al asked suspiciously.

Sam gave him a look. "April Fool's Day, 1969."

Al lowered his gaze, not quite staring at the handlink or anything else. He shrugged.

"Slip of the tongue."

"Look me in the eye and tell me that." Sam waited; Al might have tried to fool him or lie to him many times, but Al had never been able to look him in the eye and get away with it.

Al looked up, taking a deep drag on the cigar. "I came home in 1975, Sam, OK? Don't get involved."

"Involved? Al, in case you forgot, I'm sort of 'filling in' for your regular doctor. I can't *not* get involved!"

"Sure you can. You're Wendell Xiao. You go home, you have dinner, and you mind your own business." Al was waving his hands in the air, the smoke from the cigar and the glow of light from the handlink adding to his already peculiar expression. "You convince Ensign Martin that he shouldn't kill himself, and by tomorrow night, you're history."

Al started punching the sequence that would open the Door, and Sam lunged to try to stop him.

"Al, don't—"

Too late. The Door closed and left him alone in the corridor.

He started down the hall, looking again through the chart in his hands for clues. As he walked, he heard the elevator door open and shut once more, and he turned to see who else was in the basement at this time of night.

Three uniformed men, one from each of the armed services, came toward him, moving like a human barricade through the corridor. Sam swallowed, unconsciously tensing for an attack. Then the man dressed as an Army captain stepped forward from the other two, shifting a briefcase to his left hand and offering his right.

"Dr. Xiao?" he asked. There was a roundness to the man's face that prevented it from looking either old enough or mean enough to be a threat. His eyes were open, direct, and Sam saw an ally; there was something safe in his eyes, despite the lines around them that told Sam his life hadn't been one big party. His brown hair was thinning, but not gray, and Sam guessed he was probably in his mid-forties.

"Can I help you?" Sam asked.

"I don't believe we've met, Doctor. I'm Captain Robert Barrows."

Sam took his hand, trying to keep his expression neutral. "I recognize your name from the list." That seemed to be the right thing to say.

"This is Colonel Jerry Wainwright, and this is Lieutenant Commander Dennis Stern." Sam shook each of their hands. Stern didn't seem to be a threat. But he didn't seem to be a clear ally, either. His handshake was brief and he pulled away quickly and assumed a stance that put him on the edge of the group.

Wainwright was another matter. If Sam had liked Barrows almost instantly, he felt an equal, intuitive distrust of Wainwright. The man's handshake was too tight and his eyes were filled with the kind of determination that told Sam he could be trouble. He was at least four inches taller than Sam and an easy hundred pounds heavier; none of it looked flabby, either.

"I'm glad we caught you before you left," Barrows continued. "We need to talk with Lieutenant Doe." The name was beginning to sound ludicrous.

The three men started down the hallway, but Sam hesitated, his back to the elevator. Wainwright stopped and turned. Barrows and Stern also stopped and waited.

"Is that his chart?" Wainwright demanded, gesturing to the one in Sam's hands.

"Uh, well, yes, it is, but—Captain Barrows, neither of

these men is on the list.'' It was worth a try.

"I have authorization to bring in anyone I deem necessary," he said.

"Well, I'm afraid this—the medical chart is restricted to medical personnel." He didn't want them to have the chart. He couldn't be sure why, but something in this was wrong. He glanced at Stern and saw him hanging back, his hands clasped behind him, watching the other two men with a carefully composed expression that said nothing. As if he wouldn't allow himself to be drawn into the conflict.

"Dr. Xiao," Wainwright said, his voice quieter, "please hand over Lieutenant Doe's chart."

Sam opened his mouth to protest when he heard the Door behind him slide open.

"Give it to them Sam!" Al's commanding voice almost made him turn, but he caught the impulse and stared back at Wainwright.

"Why?" he asked.

"Just do it!" Al insisted.

Wainwright tilted his head to the side.

"Doctor, you *have* been briefed on this operation, haven't you?"

"Tell him yes! Tell him, Sam!"

Sam cleared his throat, wishing Al would move around so he could see him. "Yes, uh, yes, sir, I have. But I don't see why you need his chart. If you want to know—"

"Don't argue with them, Sam! Just give them the damned chart!"

"Please hand over the chart, Doctor. That's an order."

Sam glanced at Stern and Barrows, looking for an ally. There was only silence from Barrows. And a suspicious puzzlement from Stern. He handed Wainwright the chart and shoved his hands angrily into his lab coat pockets.

Wainwright and Barrows glanced through the chart, then looked up.

"You haven't evaluated him yet?" Barrows asked. He looked concerned.

"Well no, I, uh—he wasn't really up to it earlier."

All three men seemed surprised by his answer.

"Dammit, Sam," Al whispered behind him.

" '*Up* to it,' " Wainwright repeated, astonishment saturating the words. "Doctor, did you, or did you not, receive your orders to evaluate this man for psychological fitness?"

"I'm not . . . sure."

"Tell them yes!"

"I mean," Sam backed up, hearing a sound in Al's voice that only added to his discomfort, "I mean I did, I just—well, I guess I didn't realize it had to be done today."

"Look," Stern broke in, "it doesn't matter now. He can do it tomorrow. Let's just get this over with." He turned to Sam. "Sodium amytal," he said.

"*What*?" Sam couldn't help it: he turned around and stared at the hologram. Al stood encased in the elevator door, his form half swallowed by metal, as if he couldn't bring himself to step into the corridor. He looked like he was going to throw up.

Sam turned back to the military trinity before him.

"Amobarbital sodium," Wainwright clarified. "He's not allergic, is he?"

"No," Al whispered behind him, and Sam shook his head mutely.

"Will you get it, please?" Wainwright ordered.

Sam opened his mouth, but nothing came out.

"Eight hundred milligrams. We can use the existing IV line to get it in. Doctor?"

Sam swallowed. "That's too much," he said numbly.

Then reality kicked in. "What the hell do you need amytal for? If you want to ask him questions, just ask!"

"Doctor, this isn't your call," Wainwright said. He turned to Barrows, a peculiar gleam in his eyes. "Captain, would you secure the amytal, please. I don't think Dr. Xiao wants to cooperate."

Barrows glared at the man, then nodded once, silently, and turned to leave.

"Cooperate, Sam! Dammit, cooperate!"

"Uh, wait a minute. You don't have access to drugs in this hospital," Sam started.

"Doctor, we have access to anything in this hospital we want access to."

Sam stared at Wainwright, knowing the sound of an implicit threat when he heard it. He swallowed hard.

"I'll get . . . the amytal," he agreed. He walked toward the elevator, staring at Al, who disappeared into the lift. Sam got in, pressed the first-floor button, and waited for the door to shut.

"Sam," the hologram said, his voice low, "listen to me. You've got to convince them you're Wendell Xiao. They chose Wendell for this operation because he follows orders, he doesn't ask questions, and he does his job. If you don't cooperate with them, they'll get suspicious and they're not gonna trust you. And if they don't trust you, they'll pull you off this operation. It'll ruin Wendell's career, maybe worse! These people are in a different *league*, Sam."

"These people? Who *are* these people, Al?"

"Look, just play along with them," Al said, not directly answering the question. "Do what they tell you. Everything turns out fine, right? So don't try to change anything!"

The elevator stopped at the first floor and Sam stalked toward the pharmacy. He showed the pharmacist on duty his identification and requested the drug. It took a couple minutes before the man returned. Al paced around him, silent, staring at the handlink, his face unshaven, his hair ruffled by having run his hands through it too much.

As Sam took the drug back to the elevator and pressed the button for the basement, Al followed, hovering along with him as he dropped to the bottom of the building.

"Just don't ask any questions, Sam." His voice was much quieter, almost defeated, Sam thought. "And when they tell you to leave—for God's sake, please leave!"

"Leave? Al, if they use even half this amytal, I can't leave!" Sam hissed.

"Yes you can! Look, nothing happens. Nothing a doctor has to be there for."

"Al—" The admiral disappeared and the elevator deposited Sam back in the forsaken corridor. The three men stood where they had been and waited until he produced the hypo before moving.

"We can take it from here," Stern said. There was a tone in his voice that, given Al's warning, made Sam feel uneasy: they weren't sure he could be trusted.

He closed his eyes briefly, hoping that one day he could forgive himself.

"I'm the doctor," he said. "If anyone's going to administer this, it's going to be me." His stomach curled into a tight knot.

Lieutenant Al Calavicci was pacing the room, looking, Sam thought, remarkably like the future image of himself that had just left. The radio Lieutenant Farraday had brought him announced from the bed tray that they were listening to a program called "The Sunday Night Thing of the Past."

Al finished his pace, pulled the IV pole around, turned,

and saw the crowd that had entered. He backed away from them as they stepped in, his eyes moving from one face to another, finally locking on Barrows.

"Al," the man said quietly. Sam stood just behind him, watching, waiting.

"What's going on, Bobby?"

They knew each other! Sam felt the first ray of hope all day; maybe this wasn't going to be as bad as he'd thought.

"We need to ask you some questions."

"What questions?"

"Lieutenant." Wainwright moved forward, and Al's eyes locked on the moving target. "We're going to give you something to help you relax, and then ask you some very simple questions."

Fear turned to terror as Al saw the needle Sam was trying to hold unobtrusively at his side. Al shook his head, violently waving them away.

"No! No more drugs!"

"It's just a mild sedative," Wainwright lied soothingly. "No!"

A clap of thunder and the sound of rain came from the radio. Wainwright stepped closer, and all hell broke loose.

As "Raindrops" pounded the overcrowded room, Al launched himself from the corner where he'd backed, arms outstretched to attack. He punched Wainwright, barely fazing him, and tried to rush past him, oblivious to the IV still attached to his arm. Stern was in the way, blocking Al with his own body, grabbing his arms and forcing him back as Wainwright grabbed Al's ankles.

Together, as Al twisted and tried to wrench himself free, they picked him up and placed him on the bed, Stern pinning his arms, Wainwright his legs. The line in Al's arm came loose and blood oozed from the site.

Al was screaming. He screamed in Italian, he screamed in English. He screamed in Vietnamese.

"Doctor!" Wainwright yelled.

Sam moved forward, standing between the two uniformed men. He shoved the amytal into his lab pocket and retrieved the dangling IV line. He looked around helplessly for a fresh needle.

"Just put it back in," Wainwright ordered. Al was becoming more violent, struggling for his life.

"I can't, it isn't sterile!" Sam objected.

"Reattach it, Doctor, or I will," Wainwright said. Once more, his look told Sam he had little choice in the matter; he tried to find a vein.

"He's moving too much," Sam choked on the words. The unbridled terror of his patient made his own hands shake.

Barrows moved forward and leaned across the bed, grabbing Al's right arm above and below the elbow, wrapping his hands around the limb to still it.

Sam got the needle in, then pulled the amytal from his pocket and began the slow injection through the line. They waited until it took effect and the screams diminished to an occasional whimper. The three men finally relaxed their holds on Al as he slipped into a stupor.

"You can leave now, Doctor," Wainwright said quietly. Sam wiped a hand over his face.

He glanced at the naval commander who, once again, was distancing himself from the activities in the room. He leveled the ugliest look he dared on Wainwright, wishing he had the courage to say what he thought of the man.

Then Barrows pulled a tape recorder from his briefcase and started setting it up on the bed tray, turning down the radio and pushing it aside. Sam watched him, appalled that a friend of Al's could have been part of this. Then, for a second, he locked eyes with the man, and realized he and Barrows were in the same sinking boat.

"The pit is lovely, dark and deep, but I have promises to keep . . ."

The words weren't quite right. He'd changed them years ago. He'd made them tell the truth. In 'Nam, the *woods* weren't lovely; they were jungles. Horrible, uncertain things.

But the pit! The pit was safe. Safer than an A4. Safer than his own thoughts. Safer than the hootch. There, in the cold, wet darkness, he might have to fight leeches and dysentery, but he was alone. Completely alone. No one could hurt him in the pit.

He wasn't sure how long he'd been staring at the Imaging Chamber door, but the silence behind him told him it had been too long.

He turned around and walked down the ramp, slapping the link on the console as he passed through the room. He didn't look at anyone. He couldn't.

He got into the elevator and shut the door. He had to be alone.

Don't make a sound, the voice in his mind commanded.

Admiral Calavicci took a deep breath and sank back against the wall of the elevator, closing his eyes.

He didn't want to think about it. He didn't want to remember.

Maybe, if he tried hard enough, he could *not* remember. And then he'd be safe again. Safe. And alone.

Don't make a sound . . .

DAY 2

Monday, June 16, 1975

CHAPTER
SIX

"Well," Tess Conroy murmured to herself, "this just gets better and better."

Having long ago come to the conclusion that while she could easily live in a cluttered, unorganized apartment, Tess could not work with unorganized material, the first thing she set about doing with Kelly Fulham's file of information was to put it in some sort of order. Tess poured herself a large, cold Coke, grabbed a fresh pack of cigarettes and an ashtray, and sat down at her flaking Formica-topped dining-room table to spread the information out and begin putting it into some kind of workable order.

She had quickly discovered that, appearances aside, Kelly Fulham was a meticulous woman. Every shred of paper, every photograph, every interview and article in the folder carried a small penciled date at the top right corner. Some of the items—newspaper clippings, for example—were already dated, but Kelly's hand-branded date appeared anyway. Sometimes, the two dates coincided. Sometimes they didn't, and Tess began to realize that Kelly had dated each piece of information as she had gotten it.

Over the next eight hours, the chronology of Kelly's search for the truth of Margaret Dawson's death had come into focus as Tess worked through two bottles of Coke, two packs of Camels, and nearly four years of documents she'd sorted into dated piles.

The search began, apparently, by accident. In April, 1971, for the anniversary of Maggie's death, Kelly had written an article eulogizing the photojournalist. The article existed in two forms in the file she'd handed over to Tess: one, published and clipped from *Cavalcade*, bore little resemblance to the unpublished, typed version that had obviously died an obscure, double-spaced death.

Tess had already read the published article as part of her own research. Now, she read the original version, the one that Kelly's notes indicated had been pulled at almost the last moment, and despite the fact that the article didn't actually accuse the Army or Navy of a cover-up. Kelly's research had clearly drawn doubt about the official story surrounding Maggie's death. Copies of the AP and UPI versions of Maggie's obituaries were also in the folder, and those, too, Tess had read and kept copies of.

The official story would have gone unchallenged if Kelly Fulham hadn't been determined to see that Maggie Dawson receive the credit a woman in her position, in the journalistic world, deserved. She outdid herself, tracking down an Army colonel from MACV Saigon who had been at the base during the sapper attack that reportedly took Maggie's life. Colonel Deke Grimwold, just returned from 'Nam the week before Kelly found him, was reluctant to talk about the incident.

Working on her fifth cigarette, Tess read through the transcribed interview.

> GRIMWOLD: *It's a damn shame anyone gets killed over there, Miss Fulham, and it's a worse shame when someone innocent gets killed. Maggie was a hell of a woman, and we're all sorry she's gone.*

> FULHAM: *Colonel, I appreciate that you might not be able to tell us much about the specific circumstances of her death, but could you tell me what mission she was planning to cover.*

[Seven-second pause. Note that.]

> GRIMWOLD: *I'm sorry, Miss Fulham, what do you mean by—mission?*

> FULHAM: *I mean that Maggie's forte was covering assault missions. If she was at a SEAL base in the Delta region, I'd bet my last pencil she was there to accompany your boys on a mission. Can you tell me—*

> GRIMWOLD: *Miss Dawson was there to do a story on the men and officers at the base. A story on the SEAL unit itself. Day-to-day lives, that sort of thing.*

The transcript of Kelly's phone interview with the colonel left even Tess with the impression that there had been something the man didn't want to say. But considering the situation he was in, Tess thought, she wouldn't have jumped to any conclusions about it having to do specifically with Maggie Dawson.

And, to give her credit, even Kelly hadn't immediately concluded that a cover-up had taken place. Her scrawled note at the bottom of the last page said, "Check it out later. Might be another story here."

Kelly continued to track down those who were there the night Maggie died, and within a day had located three men from the SEAL unit. The first, the lieutenant in charge of the unit, was on leave in Indiana with his family. He was interviewed by phone, as well.

FULHAM: *Then you dragged her back into the bunker?*

BECKETT: *Yeah. She was so damned determined to get a story. I—I mean, I tried to drag her back. That's when she was shot.*

FULHAM: *How long was the attack?*

BECKETT: *I'm afraid I can't discuss those details, Miss Fulham.*

FULHAM: *There were no other injuries? No other casualties?*

BECKETT: *No. [chuckles] Should have been me. April the eighth, that was supposed to be my day to die.*

FULHAM: *Excuse me?*

BECKETT: *Just—my kid brother thought I was gonna die over there. He even thought it would be on April the eighth.*

FULHAM: *I thought the attack took place late on the evening of April the seventh.*

BECKETT: *Uh—yeah, that's right. Right, April seventh.*

FULHAM: *Not the eighth?*

BECKETT: *No. Uh, listen, I'm busy. I've gotta go milk some cows . . .*

The conversation ended quickly after that. Two subsequent attempts to reach him at home in the next two days failed.

Kelly also reached two other men who had been at the base. One of them mentioned that *"If she hadn't run off like that she'd still be alive."*

When Kelly asked what he meant by "run off," the man backed up and said, *"I mean, run out. Of the bunker,"* and that interview also was drawn to an abrupt close.

The last man to speak to Kelly Fulham mentioned that *"She'd have done anything to go on that mission. You know what I mean?"*

Kelly had baited him with an implied question: *"Oh, the one you went on the next day? That was to, uh—"*

"Yeah, the POWs. God, that was a disaster."

Fate and timing being as whimsical as they were, Tess thought, reading through the notes that followed, the announcement of the Pulitzer Prizes for 1971 was made the following day. And the now-famous photograph of two POWs stumbling through the Vietnamese jungle was plastered once more on the cover of every newspaper and magazine for days. The photograph purportedly taken by an anonymous Army Intelligence agent.

It was only the coincidence of the photograph's renewed notoriety and the previous day's phone call that helped Kelly Fulham begin to put the pieces together.

She called Grimwold again, and for another two days, and received no response from him or his office. She called other contacts as well, and then, frustrated by the apparent blackout, she went to a source she would not, even in her own folder, identify, and got hold of the original photograph. Where and how and when it was analyzed, she didn't document, at least not here. But the results of that analysis she did.

The photograph itself was taken by the type of camera standardly used by civilian journalists in the field. It used a standard film, designed to withstand hot, humid conditions. It was not, the unnamed analyst assured Kelly, the type of camera or film the military used.

The analyst, apparently working within the military structure himself, added two other pieces of information. The man who had turned to face the camera had been identified as Lieutenant Albert M. Calavicci, U.S. Navy. Kelly noted in a marginal scrawl, "No fam. Wife div. & remarried. U.S.N. won't release info."

The second man, the analyst told her, had been almost positively identified as First Lieutenant Robert Barrows.

It wasn't until Tess got to Kelly's notes for the year 1973 that she realized how honest Kelly had been in her conviction that she was "too close to the story." The newspaper coverage of Operation Homecoming that spring included a list of local men who were returning. One of them was Lieutenant Barrows: Kelly Fulham's husband. Miss Fulham was quoted as saying that "I always knew he'd come back. I'm just glad it's over."

But, as Tess knew from story after story, the homecomings of the men from Vietnam were rarely easy. Kelly's case was no different. In the pile of material from 1974, Tess Conroy found a copy of the court order finalizing Kelly's divorce from now Captain Robert Barrows on the grounds of irreconcilable differences.

It was as if, for Kelly, the end of her marriage were somehow related to the Pulitzer story, Tess thought. Kelly's research into the apparent cover-up of Maggie's death, and the "stolen" Pulitzer, dwindled after that. An occasional, halfhearted phone call, a periodic note or interview. Nothing that led any further than she'd already gotten.

Tess rubbed her eyes and glanced at her watch. "Oh, man!"

Two empty packs of Camels lay by the ashtray, two empty bottles of Coke sat on the floor by her chair, and her stomach growled. She'd spent the entire night getting through the documents. She stretched and got up from the table, headed for the kitchen, and looked through her cabinets and refrigerator for something to eat. In addition to the laundry and the dishes, she realized she hadn't done any shopping in the last week, either.

She finally settled on her old standby and smashed a tablespoon of mayonnaise into a bowl of tuna, muttering, "Something fishy going on here."

And then it hit her.

For proof that Maggie Dawson had taken the Pulitzer Prize photograph, Kelly Fulham had only to ask her own husband: he, after all, had been there. He would have seen her. Or, at the very least, his fellow POW, who had turned to face the camera, would have.

But there was nothing to indicate Kelly Fulham had ever asked her husband. Given her compulsion with the story, given her closeness to it, given her meticulous recording of every lead and interview and question and innuendo, Tess would have expected some mention that she had at least *asked* one of the two eyewitnesses who could have answered her doubts.

Tess went back to the table with her sloppy tuna sandwich and another glass of Coke, and started back through the papers again. Sure enough, not a hint.

For a professional like Kelly, that didn't make sense. Whether her husband confirmed her hunch or not, she should at least have asked him. And recorded his response.

A moment later Tess began to feel suspicious. What if Barrows *had* answered the question? What if he had disproved the theory that Maggie Dawson had taken that picture? Or lent enough doubt to its validity that Kelly had let the story die.

As theories went, Tess thought, it almost made sense. The only question left in her mind, then, was why resurrect the story now?

And as she murmured the question out loud, she looked through the open door to the study at her right. She looked at the picture on the wall above her typewriter. The picture of a young blond woman at a podium at Georgetown University, speaking to an excited, if small, group of female journalism majors on the importance of journalistic integrity.

"Why now, Maggie?" she whispered again. The woman in the picture smiled at the camera and offered no answers.

Admiral Calavicci stood in the cool evening air of the New Mexico desert, staring at the sunset through the smoke from his cigar. He felt, more than heard, someone behind him, and half turned. Donna Elesee moved quietly closer, hugging her shawl around her, her hair loose in the gentle breeze that swept around them.

It was rare for Donna to seek out his company. Without having ever said it, Donna had always given him the oblique impression that she blamed him, at least in part, for the fact that her husband had stepped into the Accelerator before it was ready. Their relationship, begun years ago at the Star Bright Project, had never been an easy one. For the last four years, it had been even less easy.

Al turned back toward the horizon and waited. For several minutes the physicist said nothing and he grew uncomfortable.

"How's it goin'?" he asked at last.

"Weitzman refused the last proposal I sent in." She

stood next to him, following his gaze into the sky. "Said there wasn't sufficient proof that the upgrades I suggested for Ziggy would do any good." She drew a deep, reluctant breath and turned to him. "Think you could pull some strings?"

Al narrowed his gaze and puffed on his cigar. "Love to." He tilted his head. "You could have sent me E-mail for that," he pointed out, not convinced this was her reason for being here.

The shadows of dusk settled over Donna's face. "I had lunch with Verbeena." He waited. "She's concerned."

" 'Bout what?"

"You." She hesitated, staring into the darkening sky. "And Sam's current Leap." She turned to him, the wind still blowing her hair around. "What's going on, Al?"

"You tell me," he returned a little sharply. "Verbeena's had Ziggy 'behind closed doors' all day."

He suspected that Verbeena, unsatisfied with his conviction that Sam's Leap had nothing to do with him, had done some investigating on her own. While Ziggy hadn't admitted to it, Al had noted Verbeena's higher-than-average use of the parallel computer through most of the day. Fortunately, Al knew, whatever records may have ever existed would have been destroyed long ago or be impossible to track down. He'd been assured of that.

"Alright," Donna confessed with a deep breath, "Verbeena did some digging." She finally looked at him, her eyes searching his for a reaction. "But all she's come up with are a lot of contradictions. And a few questions."

"And you've been sent to find out the truth, is that it?" Al asked, almost amused. Verbeena knew *she'd* never get anywhere.

"I haven't been 'sent,' " Donna objected. And then,

with a wry smile, she added, "I volunteered."

"Hmm." Al sucked on the cigar and waited.

"According to your military record, you returned from Vietnam with the rest of the American POWs in spring, 1973. Operation Homecoming."

"Yeah. So?"

"And you went to Balboa Naval Hospital with several other former POWs to recuperate for a month."

He waited.

"And in April of 1973," she continued, turning back to the sand that sifted in the wind beyond the Project's boundaries, "you were sent overseas to France with Special Operations for two years, engaged in counterintelligence against the governments of Laos and Cambodia."

"The reason I was there is classified," he said. After twenty-five years of repetition, the routine protest came out without thinking.

"Ziggy thinks it's unusual," Donna mused, "that of all the POWs returned before, or during, Operation Homecoming, you're the only one who was reassigned overseas within a month of his return."

Al shrugged. "Just like the Navy. You get liberated from a POW camp, and they send you right off on another mission." He added a smile for good measure.

"That's not all," Donna said as if she hadn't heard him. She pulled the shawl around her more tightly. "According to Balboa's records, other than your preduty physical before you shipped off to Vietnam, you were never a patient there."

"Records get misplaced."

"To Bethesda Naval Hospital?" she asked.

Al felt the smoke from his cigar writhe like a snake in his chest. It shouldn't be this easy. It shouldn't be this easy

84

to put this much together, now, twenty-five years after it had happened, years after the last record should have been destroyed.

"There's a record at the Pentagon that confirms you were at Bethesda in June, 1975," Donna said, "to determine your physical and psychological fitness for continued active duty." In the near dark, Donna's eyes appeared almost entirely neutral. He couldn't read her at all, and that unnerved him.

"And the records of the French counterintelligence unit you were supposed to have been attached to? The only indication they ever heard of you was a record, dated June 16, 1975, that praises your contributions to their efforts, signed by someone who joined the team only a week before."

"Now *that's* what I call damning with faint praise," he tried, and waved the cigar for emphasis. Donna didn't smile.

"There's more."

"There always is," Al muttered, and turned away.

"Seems one record led to another—like a string that ties your whole career together."

Al ground the cigar; just how much *had* Ziggy put together?

"To begin with, there's your meteoric rise to the Admiralty," Donna said, a half smile on her lips taking some of the sting from her words.

"Hardly that." He looked down at her with a self-deprecating grin that tried to resemble a moot invitation.

Donna cleared her throat and looked back into the distance. "You returned from 'Nam in 1973 as a lieutenant. You were promoted to admiral in 1980?"

"I got a lot of merit badges for POW camp."

85

"And then there's your miraculous record of getting complete funding for every project you've been involved with since you returned from . . .'*France*.' "

Al puffed on the cigar and Donna looked back.

"Including·Quantum Leap."

He met her eyes evenly for several seconds. "So I'm good." He spoke with the cigar between his teeth.

"Good, yes," Donna agreed, the uncharacteristic compliment setting Al's nerves on edge. "Extraordinary?" She shook her head. "I don't know about that." A cold shiver made her pull the shawl closer. "Whatever happened in '75 has left just enough of a trail to make it look like—" She stopped, closed her eyes, and sighed. "It looks like the Navy bought your silence, Al," she said at last. "Or maybe you blackmailed someone?"

"The Navy isn't in the position of buying off lieutenants," Al snapped, a little too harshly. Donna reacted, a flash of surprise in her eyes. "And *I'm* not in the blackmailing business. Not really." He smiled slyly, remembering an exceptionally successful manipulation of Senator Weitzman four years ago.

His eyes narrowed and he tilted his head upward so he was looking down on her. "Don't you think Ziggy's theory is just a little bit in the Twilight Zone?"

"Tell me we're wrong," she invited casually. "Tell me Ziggy doesn't know what she's talking about."

He said nothing. Second by second, the world around them grew darker.

Twenty-five years! For twenty-five years he'd said nothing. For twenty-five years, drunk or sober, celebrating or angry, he'd never talked. Not even to Sam.

And if he talked now? If he told them what he'd done?

If he told Donna the truth? What would happen? What *would have* happened?

Before he could decide the question, Donna broke the silence for him. "You *were* in Vietnam for two years after the last American POW was returned, weren't you, Al?" she said. "You hadn't just come back from France; you'd just come back from Vietnam."

He stared at her for a second, suddenly speechless. He rubbed a hand over his face, trying to buy enough time to come up with a good answer. She didn't give it to him.

"Were you the only one?" She stared at him, unblinking, a hint of something buried in the tight lips and clenched jaw. Something familiar, frightening. Betrayed.

"The only one?"

"They said all the POWs came back in '73," Donna continued. "*You* didn't. You were there! Were there others, Al? Still alive?"

Don't make a sound.

Al looked away and bit the cigar with his teeth. "Donna—" He knew where this was going, and there was nothing he could do to stop it.

"Did you ever try to do anything to get them back, Al? Did you ever think that if you hadn't stayed quiet all these years the government might have looked harder for them?"

"That was twenty-five years ago."

"It might have helped! Maybe back then, it would have helped!" Donna's face twisted with cold pain. "But you were all tied up in some political blackmail scheme, weren't you?"

Al waited and said nothing.

"Didn't you ever think about anyone else who might have been left behind?" She paused and gulped air, gathering her shawl tightly over her bare flesh. "Maybe if you'd said something back then, they'd have looked harder for my father!''

She didn't wait for an answer. She strode back to the complex, and Al watched her flash her ID badge at the Marine guard before she went inside.

He turned away and looked up at the sky. It was clear, cold, cloudless.

Like a night twenty-six years ago.

Don't make a sound.

Don't make a sound.

CHAPTER
SEVEN

Gunfire. Lots of it. All around him.

"Why can I save strangers, and not the people I love?"

"I dunno."

"Well, I'm not doing it anymore!"

"Sa-am!"

"Just—just tell me what I have to do."

"All Ziggy's come up with so far is a code name, Operation Lazarus . . ."

"I don't give a damn about the mission, Al—"

"Two, maybe three, American POWs."

"I told you it was Pulitzer material."

". . . All I care about is saving my brother."

Gunfire. All around him.

"Sam! I found the POWs! They're right over there! Sam, you can free them!"

Gunfire. Behind him. In front of him.

"Takin' this road got us here ahead of the squad, but not by much," said the voice. "So you'd better get on

89

the horn to Colonel Custer, 'cause we're gonna need the
cavalry!''
"What do I say to 'em?''
"Help!''
"I told you it was Pulitzer material.''
"It's not fair, Al! It's just not fair!''
Gunfire. And he was shooting, and yelling.
"Hoo ya!''
Staccato bursts of gunfire poured out of his rifle, throw-
ing men onto their backs. Dead. Wide astonished eyes
staring up at him.
"Hoo ya!''
"Why can I save strangers, and not the people I love?''
". . . going to be repatriated in '73.''
"It's just not fair!''
"April the eighth, 1970.''
"Why can I save strangers, and not the people I
love . . .''
"What the hell? I get repatriated in five years.''
"You could have been free . . .''

Sam shot up, covered in sweat, and tried to breathe. The
panic receded and he wiped his face with his hands to remove the lingering images, the sounds, the strange battle-
cry he didn't understand now that he was awake.

It was only a dream. Only a dream.

Wasn't it?

The gunfire continued in the background until Sam realized it was only thunder.

He glanced at Wendell's clock: 4:45 A.M. There was no
chance he was going to be able to get back to sleep. He
stretched and went to the bathroom, turning on the hot water in the shower.

And then he remembered. The sour taste in his mouth
reminded him of the nightmarish scene he'd taken part in

last night, and his stomach threatened to turn over. He stood over the sink, trying to remember other details of this Leap, trying to keep his mind from what he'd done. After a while the nausea receded and he stepped into the shower. He still felt dirty when he stepped out half an hour later.

The early-morning summer storm had broken by the time Sam left for Bethesda. Driving from Wendell's apartment in Arlington to the hospital took almost an hour, even at 5:30 in the morning. And Wendell's 1972 Vega, which threatened to overheat as he sat in traffic, didn't help matters. But the drive helped him clear his thoughts, gave him the opportunity to collect the details of this Leap that he'd concentrated on earlier in the bathroom.

He pushed one of Wendell's many Beatles tapes into the car's tape player and listened as he sat on the congested beltway.

He had to stop some kid from killing himself. He had to convince everyone he was a psychiatrist without messing up anything permanent in their lives. And somehow, *somehow*, he had to find out what was going on with Al and make sure another scene like the one last night didn't happen again.

He hoped Ziggy could help. He hoped Al returned before he started his rounds. And, at the same time, he dreaded facing the future version of the man he felt he'd betrayed last night.

The hospital, when he got there, seemed to be sleeping. The morning shift started at 0700, and he was about a half hour early. He went up to his office and began going through the charts, reminding himself of people he was supposed to know.

"Good morning."

The bright greeting pulled his attention away from the chart he was studying and he looked up to see Lieutenant

Farraday, two large cups of coffee in her hands, come in. She put one of the cups in front of him, took a seat, and drank from the other.

Please, let it be black, Sam wished. "Thanks." He was moderately surprised. Nurses *didn't* get coffee for doctors, that much he was sure he remembered.

"I've got the donuts outside, but I thought you'd want to line up our schedule first."

Sam tried not to seem surprised; her tone indicated this was routine. He could learn to like this. A lot. The day was already looking better.

"Right. Uh, let's see . . ." He rummaged through the charts and pulled out a chart at random. "Let's start with him," he said, handing it across the desk.

"You want to start with Campbell?"

"Uh, yeah. That a problem?"

"Well, if you start with Campbell, what are you going to do until ten?"

"Have breakfast?" He drank some of the coffee; it *was* black.

She laughed. "The psych ward doesn't really wake up until ten," she reminded him as if he should have known.

"Well, they're all in the psych ward."

She smiled tightly. "Not all."

Sam turned away and sighed. He pulled Al's chart from the stack on his desk and flipped through it. He hadn't noted the amytal injection from last night, and that wasn't something he could afford to leave out. He recorded it, the dose and time, and saw Farraday watching him.

"What're you doing?" she asked.

"Captain Barrows," he started. "You met him?"

She looked him over carefully. "Once."

"He and a couple others came by last night." He stopped

92

and rubbed his eyes. ''They interrogated 'Lieutenant Doe' under sodium amytal.'' He shut the chart angrily. ''I guess I should check him first thing.''

Farraday watched him and said nothing.

They went through the rest of the stack. Sam's stomach was growling audibly by the time they'd finished.

''How about a donut?'' he asked. He got up and walked to the elevator with her. Her purse was sitting on the table where she'd hastily dropped it, along with a tempting little brown bag.

She pulled out an enormous cruller and handed it to him, followed by a napkin. She'd gotten herself a Bavarian cream.

''Did Dr. Jansen say what kind of meeting he'd be at today?''

''Oh, that's right!'' She swallowed the food in her mouth and reached into her purse. She pulled out a set of keys. ''I've gotta go get those charts. I forgot about his patients.''

She was in the elevator and gone before he could groan. At least he wasn't *supposed* to be familiar with Jansen's patients.

Monday, June 16, 1975, 8:16 A.M.

Sam knocked quietly on the basement door before opening it. He stepped in, last night's anguish still reverberating through the darkened room.

''Mind if I come in?''

Lieutenant Calavicci sat on the edge of the bed, his head cradled in his hands. He looked up as Sam entered, then closed his eyes and turned away.

''Would it make a difference?''

Sam was tempted to turn on the light, but he resisted.

''Have you had breakfast?'' he asked awkwardly. Al didn't respond. ''Sodium amytal'll leave you feeling kinda sick for a couple days,'' he explained. He leaned against the wall, waiting, but Al just cradled his head.

"Lieutenant?" It sounded strange: "Al" or "Admiral," that's what Sam had always called him. But "always" seemed to be wearing thin right now.

Al looked up; in the shadows, Sam couldn't make out the expression in his eyes, but he could guess, based on memory, what was in them.

"What happened—after I left?"

Al stared for a moment, then fumbled for a cigar. Sam saw one on the bed tray just out of Al's reach. He crossed the room, bringing it to him.

"I could have danced all night," Al said. Sam could see his eyes, now, and he turned away. "What the hell do you mean, 'what happened'?"

"Why—*why* did it happen?"

Al stood unsteadily and made his way across the room, the lit cigar giving off a smoky glow. He sucked on the cigar and lifted his chin until he was looking down at Sam. His eyes held an unfamiliar bitterness in them.

"You really don't know what's goin' on, do you? They keeping you in the dark, or what?"

Sam grimaced and shrugged. "Well, I sort of . . . came in at the last minute."

"Then I'll give you a piece of advice, Doc, and you can do what you like with it." His voice wasn't much steadier than the hand that took the cigar from his mouth. "Be careful who you trust. Be careful who you believe." He punched the air with the cigar, a subdued anger in the smoldering gesture. "You wanna know what last night was all about? It was about trustin' the wrong guy."

Then his gaze shifted down and to the left, and back into memory. And almost as an afterthought, he chuckled and looked back, half shaking his head. "I just trusted the wrong guy."

94

CHAPTER
EIGHT

A hesitant knock interrupted Sam's study of the latest patient chart. He was surprised at how grateful he was for the interruption. He had decided he didn't like psychiatry; he didn't like dealing with so many distortions of human minds and emotions.

"Come in," he called and closed the chart. A young man in an ensign's uniform stepped in.

"Dr. Xiao, sir, I'm Ensign Davalos."

"Have we met?" Sam asked, hoping . . .

"No, sir," the young man said. He looked uncomfortable. "I understand you're working with Dr. Meyers, sir?"

Sam nodded. "Yes."

"You have a patient, sir, um, one who came in yesterday? I drove him here?" He was giving Sam hints, hoping Sam would figure out the riddle. Sam nodded mutely, not sure what the ensign meant.

"Uh, I forgot to give these to Dr. Meyers yesterday, sir," he said, and held something out for Sam to take: a thin, silver chain with two small pieces of metal dangling from the loop.

Dog tags. Al's dog tags.

"You know the lieutenant?" Sam asked, wondering suddenly how the ensign had gotten past Farraday.

"Well, sir, I drove him here from the airport." It seemed to Sam that the kid was fairly bursting, either with information or questions, he couldn't tell. But the opportunity to fill in some of the holes in this Leap wasn't to be missed.

It hadn't been easy extricating himself from Al's room earlier. After his initial caution to Sam that he should trust no one—at least, that's how Sam interpreted the dire warning—he'd refused to say anything further. Thanks in no small part to the episode last night, Al's natural paranoia where psychiatrists were involved had only intensified. Convincing Lieutenant Calavicci to tell him what was really going on was going to be next to impossible, Sam realized. So was convincing *Admiral* Calavicci.

But maybe, with *some* information, he could act more convincingly like Wendell Xiao and less like a quantum physicist whose mind had been magna-fluxed. Maybe, with more information, he could at least bluff his way into Al's confidence.

"Sit down, Ensign," he invited. The ensign sat. "Do you, um, understand the situation here, Ensign?"

The young man shifted in his seat. "Only what I was told, sir? May I ask why, sir?"

"Well, I got—well, sort of—called in at the last moment," Sam said, tiring of the explanation. "And no one's been around to brief me. So, I thought, maybe, if you knew the situation . . ." The ensign looked confused and a little wary. "The plane he came in on," Sam said, switching gears. "Where was it from?"

"Paris, sir," Davalos said.

"Paris?" It wasn't what Sam had expected.

"Well, that's where they landed first, sir. And then they transferred him to a military flight home?"

"Where who landed first?"

"The French POWs, sir. He was on the plane that brought them home."

A fragment of memory came to the surface: the last French POWs had been repatriated by Vietnam in 1975. A vague picture began forming in Sam's mind.

"He wanted to know about the Beatles." The kid reached into his jacket pocket and pulled out a tape. "I told him they'd broken up and he seemed kind of disappointed, so I thought I'd leave this for him."

Sam looked at the tape: "Sgt. Pepper's Lonely Hearts Club Band." The gesture of kindness was too sharp a contrast to the atrocity last night.

"Would you like to give it to him yourself?" Sam ignored the warning bell that only he could hear and saw Davalos light up.

"Oh, yes, sir, I would. That'd be real nice."

Sam led him to the door and around the corridor to the elevator. Wherever Lieutenant Farraday had been when the ensign had arrived, she was back at her station now. She looked up as they came into view and he saw concern on her face.

"I'm going to check on a patient. I'll be back in a few minutes," Sam said, stepping with Davalos into the waiting car. The door closed on Farraday's suspicion.

Sam wasn't sure where the nurse would come down if she knew he was breaking a rule: Davalos *wasn't* on the list of approved personnel in Al's chart.

But hell, all the kid wanted to do was give Al a Beatles tape. What possible harm could come of that?

The elevator stopped at the basement, and Dr. Xiao held the door open as he told Mark how to find the room. "I'll be back in about ten minutes," the psychiatrist said. Mark smiled and nodded and started down the hall.

He knocked on the lieutenant's door and opened it, peering around the edge before entering. "Sir?"

Lieutenant Calavicci sat lengthwise on the bed, legs crossed at the ankle, watching the smoke of his cigar twirl around him. He turned, saw who it was, smiled, and swung his legs over the edge of the bed. He looked dizzy.

"Well, whaddya know?" he said quietly. "A friendly face." He walked on unsteady legs toward the ensign.

"I wasn't sure you'd remember, sir." Davalos shook the offered hand.

The lieutenant looked awful. What Mark had expected to pick up at the airport yesterday, and hadn't—a haggard, tortured man—now met his gaze, the handshake too weak, the interior trembling that consumed him making it obviously difficult for him to remain standing.

"I just wanted to see how you were, sir," Mark said, releasing the hand as the lieutenant backed toward the bed and collapsed on it. "You—you don't look well."

The lieutenant managed a harsh laugh. "They threw me one hell of a homecoming party last night," he said. "Should've been here, kid. They pulled out all the stops."

"Sir?"

The lieutenant shrugged. "Never mind." Then he looked at him, suddenly alert. "Do they know you're here?" There was concern in his voice, and Davalos nodded quickly.

"Dr. Xiao said I could have a few minutes."

"Xiao." The lieutenant looked away.

"Sir?" Mark Davalos began to sweat. This was wrong. This was all wrong. This wasn't what they had told him was going to happen; and whatever *had* happened, it wasn't good.

"Does anyone else know you're here?"

"Uh, probably not, sir."

"Then you'd better leave. If they find out Xiao let you in here, all hell's gonna break loose."

Mark moved a step closer to the bed. "I brought you this." He handed the lieutenant the tape and was surprised and embarrassed by the reaction. The lieutenant cleared his throat and made a pretense of removing something from his eye before looking up.

"Thanks."

"Oh, you don't have a tape recorder," Mark said, looking around the bare room.

"Well, until now, I didn't need one." The lieutenant cocked a halfhearted, wry grin, and Mark smiled hesitantly back.

"I could get you one, sir, leave it with Dr. Xiao?"

The lieutenant clenched his teeth and nodded. "That'd be nice, Ensign. Thanks."

He looked around again. "Is there anything else you'd like, sir, something I could pick up for you?"

"A couple brunettes," the lieutenant suggested. Mark chuckled and felt his face flush. "You smoke?"

"No, sir."

"Good, don't start." The lieutenant reached back into the bed tray and pulled out a fresh cigar. "Here."

Mark accepted it, puzzled.

"If you don't smoke, I wouldn't want to trust your memory. Take that to a tobacconist, match it up, and bring back a box.''

''Yes, sir.'' He hesitated, putting the cigar in his breast pocket. ''Sir—?''

The lieutenant looked at him, waiting. Mark dropped his gaze and shifted his weight from one leg to another. ''Sir, is there . . . something else . . . I could do?''

The lieutenant didn't pretend to misunderstand. He shook his head and sighed. ''Thanks anyway, kid. Just don't get yourself in the middle, OK?''

Mark looked at the lieutenant and wanted to ask more, but the look in the man's eyes prevented him.

''Everything'll be fine, you'll see.''

There was nothing in his words that believed it, Mark thought as he left.

Monday, June 16, 1975, 12:01 P.M.

The reason for Sam's Leap was on the fifth floor, in the orthopedic ward. Sam found the chart at the nurses' station and read through it. The accident had killed Terry Martin's wife, Cheryl, on impact. There was some small relief in that, Sam thought. Terry, twenty-four years old, had suffered minor contusions to the right leg and arm, various cuts and abrasions to his neck and face, and a rotation fracture to his left arm, which had been twisted through the steering wheel as the car swerved.

Ensign Martin lay in his hospital bed, staring at the ceiling. He looked younger than twenty-four, Sam thought, his round face and boyish features something he'd probably war against his whole life. He had thin, straight brown hair and a wiry body that didn't quite sit with the round face.

He was hooked to an IV that, Sam discovered, was simply dextrose in water, a standard precaution in case they needed a vein later.

"Ensign Martin?"

Terry swiveled his head on the pillow in Sam's direction, but his eyes didn't really focus on him.

"I'm Dr. Wendell Xiao," Sam said, moving closer and extending a hand. Terry stared for a moment, then took the hand reluctantly, returning a very slack handshake.

Sam sat in the chair near the bed. "I'm a staff psychiatrist here," he said. He heard the Door open and close, and the familiar wailing of Ziggy's handlink behind him. "I thought we could talk about what happened."

Terry focused. "I talked to Dr. Jansen yesterday," he protested. "Why do I have to talk to you?"

"Well, Dr. Jansen's at a meeting today, and he thought it'd be a good idea if you saw someone once more before you leave the hospital."

"Why?"

"You know, he looks familiar, Sam." Al finally moved around in front of Sam, looking down on the kid in the bed. Sam could see concern in Al's eyes for their latest charge, but there was puzzlement, too. "Like I've seen him before."

"Well, sometimes, when things like this happen," Sam said, turning to his young patient, "and you feel . . . badly about them . . . sometimes it helps to talk about it. With someone you trust," he added for the hologram's benefit. Al looked at him, narrowed his eyes, and took a drag on the ever-present cigar.

"Look, I talked to the police, I talked to the doctor, I talked to Jansen. Why do I have to go through it again? Why don't you just leave me alone and let me be."

101

Terry turned away from Sam, his eyes bright with tears he was obviously embarrassed by.

"Terry, it's okay to cry. You lost someone you love, anyone would cry. But the pain won't leave right away, and it can be hard to go through something like . . . what you've been through . . . alone."

"That's good, Sam," Al commented, looking at the handlink prediction.

"So I'm supposed to talk to a shrink? How will that look on my record, huh?"

"I don't think you need to worry about that, Terry."

Al watched him with growing suspicion, catching Sam's double intention.

"Look, just leave me alone." Sam looked at Al for help. The hologram gave the link a shake and a slap and shrugged.

"I don't think you want to be alone," Sam said gently. He risked putting his hand on the young man's arm, trying to draw his attention to him. Then, without thinking, he said, "I think you want to have your wife back."

Terry turned. He gulped back the sudden rush of pain that the words had released. "But I can't have her back!" he yelled. "I can't ever have her back! She's gone! And it's all my fault!"

Sam moved forward and held him, feeling this might be the first positive sign so far. He looked over the young man's head for confirmation from Al, but the hologram was staring at Terry as if he'd seen a ghost.

And then Sam realized that, this time, words he hadn't intended to have a double meaning had had a devastating one.

"I'm sorry," he whispered, but Al was transfixed, lost in thoughts Sam could imagine only too well.

"No. I'm sorry," Terry said, pulling back from Sam and wiping his arm across his face. He sniffed and Sam looked around for a tissue box; there was one across the room.

He got the tissue and brought it back, risking a glance at Al. The man took a deep breath and punched the handlink in his hand.

"Chances are . . . looking better, Sam," he supplied. His voice was raw.

"Better?" Sam asked, knowing he could get two answers from one word.

"Yeah," Terry said, wiping his face and blowing his nose. "I guess."

"Ziggy says—there's only a 58 percent chance he's gonna try it now." Al kept his eyes on the handlink.

Sam turned to Terry. "I know it hurts," he said, "but sometimes, talking with someone—not being afraid to face the pain—that's what'll get you through."

"Through?" Terry repeated numbly.

"The pain will never go away, Terry. But it'll get better. A lot better. It just takes time. You've got to give yourself the time . . . to feel better."

"Why did she have to die? I mean, why her? Why couldn't it have been me?"

Sam chewed his lips.

"I don't—I don't know if I can stand to go home tomorrow. You know what I mean?"

Glancing at Al, Sam knew exactly what he meant.

"You should have someone with you. Is there someone who can go with you, help you?"

Terry shrugged. "My sister, Diane, I guess. She's been here every day. My folks, they live in Texas, but they're . . . flying out for . . ." He stopped.

"I know."

103

Terry stared at his sheets, twisting them in his hands.

"Why don't you try to get some rest," Sam suggested. Terry nodded, and managed to smile as Sam got up to leave.

"Thanks, Doc," he called.

Alone in the corridor outside the orthopedic ward, Sam waited for Al to give him the latest figures.

Al punched Ziggy's extension. "Damn, that kid looks familiar." He waited for a response from his link. "Ziggy says the chances were dropping there for a while, Sam, but now—now they've gone back up. He still kills himself."

"But why?"

Al shrugged. "Dunno. Maybe you said something that—"

"That convinces him to kill himself?" Sam demanded, lowering his voice just as a pair of nurses passed by. To his dismay, Al didn't even seem to notice them.

"Or maybe he's just rethinking it again. I dunno."

"Look, Al," Sam said, "I don't know how to help someone who's going to commit suicide."

"Well, you've done it before, Sam," Al insisted. "Remember Gloria Collins?"

"Gloria?"

"Yeah, Samantha Stormer's roommate. You talked her off the ledge, remember?"

Sam stared at him; he had an image of a terrified woman standing in the rain, hugging the thin edge of life as she stared down at imminent death.

"She was going to jump," he said, more to himself.

"Yeah, she was gonna take a dive onto an asphalt swimming pool," Al added, gesturing the action with his hands. "You talked her off the ledge, Sam. You can do the same thing with Terry."

104

"Al," Sam interrupted, "it's bad enough having to deal with all these other . . . abnormalities," he said, waving his hands around the hospital, vaguely indicating the other patients. "But I—I can't relate to this kid. I mean, I've never been desperate enough to try to kill myself, have I? I don't know what he feels like."

Al looked at him steadily and put the cigar between his teeth. "No," he agreed. "*You* don't."

"Well, at the very worst," Sam said, ignoring the implication in Al's words, "if I can't talk him out of it before he leaves here, I'll just have to make sure I'm around when he tries it."

He moved to the elevator and pressed the button. The door opened almost immediately, and Sam got in. "So where and when does he . . . try it?"

Al was boxing with the handlink, the squeals and cries and flashing colors protesting the battering. "At his home, in . . . *two* days? Sam, you've changed history. He doesn't wait for a week, now he kills himself in two days!"

Sam leaned against the elevator door and closed his eyes. "Great! Now I'm Dr. Death!"

"Don't whine, Sam," Al lectured.

"I'm not—where's the kid live?"

"It's coming up—2343 Drummond Court. A part—a part of?—oh, apartment 410."

"Drummond Court?" .

"It's in Chevy Chase. You've got a map!"

The elevator door opened and Sam stepped out; once more, Al wouldn't follow. This time, Sam didn't press the issue.

"Al," Sam said, moving back and holding the door to the elevator open. "About . . . what happened last night . . . here, I mean."

Al looked past him, staring down the corridor. "You did what you had to do," he muttered. Then with an automatic, unthinking gesture he punched out.

The lock was broken. The Imaging Chamber was empty.

"Admiral?" Ziggy's voice broke through the silence, but Al didn't answer. Maybe they wouldn't find him this time. Maybe if he was very quiet . . .

"Admiral, are you going to leave the Chamber?" Ziggy asked.

Don't make a sound, the voice ordered. He leaned against the wall and slid down until he was on the floor, his knees pulled up against his chest, his arms wrapped around them.

"Admiral?"

They were going to find him. They always did, even in here. And when they took him out, they'd be angry that he'd tried to hide from them.

And Charlie wouldn't help. Charlie didn't care what happened to him now.

He heard a noise.

Don't make a sound.

"Al?" Verbeena's soothing voice broke through his memories. He stood quickly as the Door shut behind her.

"Uh—I dropped the link," he said, pretending to retrieve the colorful box. He shook it, punched a few buttons, and managed not to look at her.

"Talk to me, Al."

If you scream or cry out, we'll make it so bad . . .

" 'Bout what?" He shrugged. He started for the door.

"About this Leap," Verbeena said, grabbing his arm as he passed her.

106

He glanced at the hand, then looked at her. He pulled away.

"What about it?" Verbeena looked genuinely concerned, but he couldn't think why.

"Al, you're not yourself."

He chuckled. "Really? Then who am I? Sam Beckett?" He left the Chamber, tossing the link onto Ziggy's console.

And Beth was there.

He stared at her for a long minute, wondering where she'd come from.

"Al, honey?"

He blinked and swallowed hard.

No. Not Beth.

Tina.

Beth was gone. Beth had left him.

Beth hadn't believed he could survive what they'd done to him.

But he *was* a survivor, right? Rule numero uno: whatever it takes to survive.

And right now, Al knew what it was going to take.

He had to stop remembering. He had to stop thinking, at least for a while.

"I'll be in my quarters," he said, walking to the lift.

He needed a drink. Or three or four.

CHAPTER NINE

Monday, June 16, 1975, 12:35 P.M.

Kelly Fulham had disappeared from the face of the earth. That was the conclusion Tess Conroy reached when, after four calls to her office, she had failed to talk once to the woman who, just yesterday, had surrendered the story that had obsessed her for more than four years.

"I'm sorry, Miss Fulham is in a meeting all morning."

"I'm sorry, we don't expect Miss Fulham until this afternoon."

"I'm sorry, Miss Fulham is out of the office today."

"I'm sorry, we haven't heard from Miss Fulham this morning."

Four different calls, four different answers. Something was going on. And whether Kelly was involved or not, her absence from the *Washington Life* office this morning had certainly not been expected by the staff there. Everyone was covering, either because they knew something they didn't want to say, or because they were in the dark and didn't want to admit it.

Half an hour ago Tess had finished a well-organized, typed summary of the information Kelly had given her, packed it into the very professional briefcase she'd bought last winter, and headed for Arlington.

Parking at the Pentagon was a sweltering, crowded, time-consuming affair. By the time she'd found a spot and walked nearly a mile back to the world's largest office building, Tess was half soaked with sweat from the humidity, her carefully pressed gray suit wrinkled, her neat white cotton blouse sticking to her back. And her feet, corrupted into high-heeled shoes a half size too small, were burning with pain.

"Tess Conroy. I have an appointment with Captain Barrows. I called this morning."

It had taken nearly an hour to verify her credentials, check her possessions, call three other security posts, and pass her through the front door. Compared with this, the gas lines she'd sat in a couple years ago were expresses. The Pentagon was on alert status; Tess remembered the routine from her trips here in '72, right after Watergate broke wide open. And right about the same time of year, she thought, watching the attractive black woman scan through Robert Barrows's day on her desk.

"Conway," Barrows's secretary muttered, smacking gum between the syllables.

"Conroy," Tess corrected gently.

"Conroy," the secretary repeated. "With a 'K' or a 'C'?"

"A 'C.' Tess Conroy."

The gum popped again as the woman shook her head and looked up. "Nope. Sorry."

"I'm sure it's there. I spoke with him—is he in? Maybe you could—?"

"He's gonna be late today," the secretary said. Then she glanced at her watch. "Well—he should be in soon. You could wait?"

Being able to wait, Tess thought, nearly another hour later, was one of the first prerequisites to being a good journalist. When, finally, the outer door to Robert Barrows's reception area opened and a man wearing both the uniform and the name badge of her prey stepped in, Tess stood from the chair against the plain wall and said, "Captain Barrows, I'm Tess Conroy." She stepped forward, extended her hand, and added, "*Cavalcade* magazine."

In lying to the secretary about her appointment with Barrows, Tess had taken little risk: only that she get to the punchline before the secretary said anything.

Barrows took her outstretched hand as the young civil servant informed him, "Says she has an appointment, sir? Talked to ya this mornin'?" A loud, pink bubble exploded from her mouth.

"Yes," Barrows said. Warm green eyes, hollowed into sleep-deprived shadows, met Tess's. He swallowed, released her hand, and sighed sadly. "Hold my calls, Bonita," he ordered, and gestured Tess into his office.

Captain Barrows's office sported a typical array of wood-framed military decorations, pictures of himself with various presidents, a small oriental rug between the door and his desk, and a window that faced an unimpressive view of Washington, D.C. A mountain of papers and folders surrounded the coffee cup on his desk. An ugly gray filing cabinet towered in the corner near the window.

"What can I do for you, Miss Conroy?" he asked, slipping off his uniform jacket and hanging it on a coat rack by his desk.

Tess sat in the chair he gestured her to. "I'm doing a

story for *Cavalcade*. I thought you might have some information for me.''

Barrows took a seat behind his desk and rubbed his eyes, sighing. ''What story?''

''*Cavalcade*'s Fourth of July issue is focusing on the POWs and MIAs from Vietnam. A kind of—salute to unsung heroism.''

''Dammit to hell!'' Barrows grumbled. ''Kelly's up on that damned high horse again?''

Tess cleared her throat. ''Captain Barrows—''

''You want some coffee?'' the man interrupted her, grabbing his cup and starting around the desk.

''Uh, no, thanks.''

''Well, I do.''

It was two minutes before he returned, this time not as unprepared as he had been when he'd first come into the office.

''What's your story?''

Tess pulled the Pulitzer picture from her opened briefcase and put it on his desk in front of him. ''That,'' she announced, ''is my story.''

Captain Barrows pulled his teeth together so tightly she heard the snap of enamel on enamel. He stared at the photograph and said nothing.

''What can you tell me?'' Tess asked. The captain was suddenly so pale that his shadowed green eyes turned into black holes in his face.

''God,'' he whispered. Or prayed.

Tess felt a trembling moment of weakness as instinct started calling to her. ''Captain Barrows, did Miss Fulham—did your wife—ever ask you about this picture?''

The transformation was subtle and startling. Human coloring replaced the morguelike paleness his face had taken

111

on and his jaw unclenched as if someone had pried it apart. A quick, furtive glance at her from the photo was followed by a desperate swill of coffee.

"The . . . picture?" he repeated, almost incredulous. "*That's* what your story—you want to know about . . . the *picture*?"

"Yes," Tess said, and at the same moment instinct screamed, "*No!*"

Captain Barrows let out a half sigh and leaned back in his chair. He took a deeper breath and let it out. He picked up the photo, gingerly, by the bottom edge. As if he were afraid of touching it, Tess thought. Then his forehead wrinkled and he turned it over. The light in the room had allowed the words on the back to shine through. The man read the paragraph, then looked at her. "Did you write that?" he asked, destroying Tess's theory that Barrows himself might have.

"No."

"Who did?"

Tess shrugged. "I don't know." He put the glossy photo back on the desk. "What can you tell me about that picture?" Tess asked.

"I'm sorry, Miss Conroy, I have nothing to say about it."

No, Tess thought. *But you've got something to say! What?*

"But you do recognize it?" she asked. She pulled a pack of Camels from her purse, noting the pipe on Barrows's desk. "Mind?"

He shook his head. Then, answering her first question, he said, "You know I recognize it. So?"

"Who took it, Captain?"

Barrows pushed his ashtray toward her. "I don't know."

"Was it Army Intelligence?"

"So they tell me."

Tess took another puff on her Camel and sat back in the chair, crossing one leg over the other. "I think that was taken by a woman who—"

"Maggie Dawson," Barrows supplied. He folded his hands together on the desk. "*Kelly* thinks it was taken by Maggie, and she's sent you out on a quest to prove it, am I right?"

Tess said nothing.

"You're tilting at windmills, Miss Conroy. Kelly and Maggie were close friends. When Maggie died, Kelly just had to find some reason in it all. Even if there wasn't one."

"Are you saying she didn't take that picture?"

"I'm saying Army Intel says *they* took it. And I can't say differently."

"But you were there! You must have seen—"

"Miss Conroy," Captain Barrows interrupted, "I was tied at the neck to another POW. We were being force-marched through the jungle, beaten with rifles to keep us going. We were wet, and tired, and scared. And we were just trying to stay alive. I didn't notice a damn thing except the elephant grass that whipped my legs and the bugs that crawled on my arms and the fact that when the guy I was tied to faltered, I thought I'd choke to death."

"He didn't falter, he looked back," Tess heard herself saying. "He saw something. *Someone!*"

Barrows reached for his pipe, then pulled a small plastic pouch of tobacco from his desk. "Maybe he did." He stuffed the pipe bowl, pulled a lighter from his shirt pocket, and puffed until the fragrant smoke filled the air.

"Maybe? He never said?"

Barrows didn't answer.

113

"According to my information, the man in that picture with you is"—she checked the notes in her portfolio—"Lieutenant Albert Calavicci. He was listed as MIA in '67 when his plane went down. In 1969, at the request of his wife, he was declared 'presumed dead.' The woman remarried two months later. A year later, this picture was declassified, and his status was changed back to 'confirmed POW.' Then, late in '72, it went back to MIA." She looked up. "Seems like a hard man to keep track of," she tried to joke. Barrows seemed unamused. "My sources tell me—"

"Your sources!" Barrows pulled his pipe from his mouth. "My wife—my ex-wife—is your source, Miss Conroy. Face it: Maggie Dawson, and my marriage to Kelly, were both casualties of that war, and Kelly wants to put some meaning to it."

"My sources," Tess continued calmly, ignoring the outburst, "indicate that you and Lieutenant Calavicci were together for several months after that picture was taken. Is that true?"

Barrows rubbed his eyes again, then his head. "Yes. So?"

"Did he ever tell you what he saw when he turned?"

"No."

"Never?"

Barrows looked up, defeated and tired. "No."

Tess took a deep breath, uncrossed her legs, and leaned forward in her seat in semiattack mode. "Let me get this straight," she launched. "A man hears something in the grass while being led, at gunpoint, through the jungles of Vietnam as a POW. He turns around. He's tied at the neck to another man, who thinks he's being choked to death. And he *never* told that man what he saw that made him turn?"

Barrows stared at her. "Charlie didn't let us talk to each other very often."

"But when you did?"

Barrows put his pipe in the ashtray and picked up his coffee, staring at it. "There were other things to talk about."

"Didn't it occur to you," Tess pressed on, "that it might have been a rescue attempt?"

Barrows drank from the black pool he'd stared at. "What *'might have been'* was too dangerous to think about, Miss Conroy. Suicidal." His green eyes locked on hers. "You only think about that moment, that day. You don't even think about the future, not if you're smart. And you sure as hell *never* let yourself think that you were that close to being rescued—and it failed."

The eyes that stared into Tess's were tormented. He held her gaze for a long moment, as if debating with himself.

"Hell," he finally breathed. He closed his eyes and shook his head. "Okay, he—mentioned it once," he confessed. "That night, on the way to the next camp. He was trying to keep both of us awake. We were wet and cold, and I'd lost a lot of blood. If we'd fallen asleep, we'd have probably died of hypothermia." His eyes shut again and Tess realized she'd tumbled onto a very private pain.

"Al sat up all night, telling me stories, asking questions, making me talk back so I wouldn't go to sleep."

Tess listened carefully as the tone of the man's voice changed, became deeper. His eyes began to flick away from hers, not quite dropping his gaze, but obviously having trouble holding hers. And, Tess noted, it was the first time he'd actually referred to the man by name.

"Far as I could tell, the whole world was nothing but a

115

long, dark tunnel of pain I wanted to escape from. And Al knew that.

"So he said, 'Bobby, they know we're here. I saw one of them. They're going to get us home.' "

The glassed-over look that had overtaken Barrows's face faded as he focused on her. He cleared his throat. "I believed him. We waited all night in that jungle. I was sure we'd hear gunfire, hueys, *something*. All night, we just waited, and Al kept saying, 'Don't worry, Bobby. The cavalry's coming.' "

Barrows closed his eyes and wiped a hand across his face. He looked very tired, Tess thought, as if he hadn't slept at all the night before.

"The next day," he continued, his voice back to its normal timbre, "Charlie whipped us up and kept us marching. Al never mentioned it again."

Barrows sucked hard on the stem of his pipe while Tess fidgeted uncomfortably in her chair.

"I figured it was just another one of Al's stories," the captain said. His mouth crooked upward without much amusement. "He was famous for them in the camps. Always had a story to keep us going." He chuckled then, and a hint of bitterness went into the sound. "One day, someone'll collect them into an anthology called *Al in Wonderland*."

"Did Lieutenant Calavicci return home?" Tess asked. The captain's sad sarcasm was infectious.

"I couldn't say."

"I understand I can get an official list of all the men who returned in '73 from your office?" Barrows nodded once, resigned. "And a list of those who are still MIA?"

The man almost grinned. "I can get you a list," he said,

"but so can the Navy. The Air Force. Congress. And none of them will match exactly."

"It would be a start," Tess said. The man across from her stared without blinking, but his eyes weren't focused. "Well," she said, standing, "thank you for your time." She held her hand out, and as if only then remembering she was in the room, Captain Barrows stood and took her hand.

"Miss Conroy, if you don't mind my asking—why are *you* after this story?"

"I beg your pardon?" The question startled her and she pulled her hand back.

"I mean—what's in this for you?"

Tess raised one eyebrow and felt a moment of anger. "Why, Captain? Are you intending to make it more worth my while to drop this story than to pursue it?"

A flash of surprise in Barrows's green eyes seemed to confirm her theory. Then he shook his head and rubbed his eyes again. "No, Miss Conroy. I just wondered how Kelly managed to get someone who's obviously pretty bright to chase after her windmills."

Tess wasn't sure how to answer the question; the same sweeping sadness she'd noted earlier when the man had detailed his experience in Vietnam returned now as he spoke of his ex-wife.

"Do you still love her, Captain?" *Damned brash*, Tess thought. But the question paid off. Barrows held her eyes for a long moment.

"I don't think either of us ever stopped loving the other one, Miss Conroy. But Vietnam changed things." He paused. "You haven't answered my question."

It seemed only fair, Tess thought. She pulled herself back a little, hefting her briefcase and shifting the shoulder strap

117

of her purse. "If I can prove Maggie Dawson took that picture," she said, "it'll make the cover story."

Barrows considered her response, sucking for a second on his pipe. "I guess I know how important something like that can be when . . . you're just starting out."

He was fishing, Tess thought. And her defenses rose. "I'm not exactly 'starting out,' " she said, thinking of her worn furniture, the scraping efforts to always keep five or six articles going at once, the sometimes desperate weeks when money ran out . . . "But the cover story of the Fourth of July issue of *Cavalcade* is nothing to sneeze at."

"No, it certainly isn't," he agreed, a half smile of pride on his face.

"The MIA and Homecoming lists," Tess said a few seconds later. Barrows sighed. "When can I get copies of them? I'm sure you understand I'm working under a tight deadline. Wednesday, to be exact."

He nodded and looked around his office. He went to the filing cabinet and searched through the top two drawers. "I'm sorry, I don't have copies here," he apologized, sliding the second drawer closed and standing in the middle of the office. "But if you stop by tomorrow—sometime after noon?—you can pick them up. I'll be gone most of the day myself, but I'll see that Bonita has them for you out front."

"Thank you."

The man nodded, shook her hand, and opened the door for her to leave. She started for the door but Barrows stepped in front of the opening as if a sudden thought had come to him. "Miss Conroy, have you—spoken to anyone else yet about this?"

Instinct again screamed a warning in Tess's mind. "I might have."

"Well," Barrows continued, "there's a guy named

Grimwold. Colonel Deke Grimwold.'' Tess remembered the name from Kelly's file. "He was there when Maggie died. And I think he knows a lot more than he ever said about it.'' Barrows tilted his head back. "Kelly tracked him down once, then he was transferred.'' There was a glimmer in his eyes. "You could probably find him on your own, but you'd probably miss your deadline by then.''

Tess heard in Barrows's words an opening bid. "I'm waiting,'' she said quietly, and cursed the advertisement that had promised her deodorant wouldn't fail her under stress.

"Kelly won't take my calls at the office, and she has an unlisted number at home. I'd like to see her. Talk to her.''

Tess took a deep breath. This wasn't at all what she'd bargained for.

"Captain, Miss Fulham is giving me a big chance here to—''

"She's your meal ticket, I know,'' Barrows interrupted. "All I'm asking is that you tell her. Tell her we talked. Tell her whatever you want. But—let her know I want to see her. Just to talk to her.''

Tess nodded, and her mouth went dry. "Alright,'' she agreed. *Assuming she ever surfaces again* . . . "So where's this guy Grimwold?''

"Fort Belvoir RDT&E Center.''

"RD—?''

"Research, Development, Test and Engineering,'' Barrows translated. "And without knowing that, you'd have never tracked him down. At least,'' he added with a grin, stepping aside to let her pass, "not in time for a story this year.''

119

CHAPTER TEN

Donna Elesee wandered idly through the sleeping Project. It was late, but she couldn't sleep, so she headed for her office.

She dropped into her chair and stared at Sam's picture; he was so young, so hopeful, so promising. She hadn't had time to get a new picture when he'd come back for one night last year. Less than a night, really.

Accidentally switching places in time with Al had brought Sam back to the Project. Then Ziggy's voice stole their time together with the prediction of Al's imminent death.

She had known, watching Sam climb into the stark-white Ferme-suit, that she was going to lose him. He was going into the Accelerator Chamber; he was going to Leap. He was going to leave her again.

He had to save Al.

And she couldn't blame anyone else for not stopping him. This time, when Sam stepped into his timeless sanctuary, Donna herself put out her hand, and the light from a thousand shooting stars grabbed her husband and filled the Accelerator Chamber and the Control Room. And Sam was gone.

"Why, Sam?" she asked for the thousandth time. "Why don't you come back to me again?" It wasn't a question she expected an answer to.

She turned to the picture of her father, then picked it up. One night. She'd had only one night with her father, too, before he'd gone. One night after all those lost years.

"Feeling sorry for yourself?"

Donna looked up, surprised to see Verbeena Beeks leaning in the doorway. "You're up late." The psychiatrist looked tired, Donna thought, but not as tired as she normally would, given the hour.

"I'm on Leap Time," the woman joked wryly. "Grabbed a nap earlier this evening when things were quiet." She moved into the room. "You didn't answer my question."

Donna smiled. "No, I'm not feeling sorry for myself." She cocked her head to the side, an unpleasant hunch playing at the edge of her mind. "Why? Should I?" she asked carefully.

Verbeena never came down here to chat. They met for lunch or breakfast, sometimes after work. But never here. The feeling that bad news was coming gripped the pit of Donna's stomach.

But Verbeena seemed calm, unconcerned. She shook her head and took the seat across the desk from Donna. "You really ought to do something to make this room more livable," she commented, looking around the bare walls. A solitary computer terminal, one of Ziggy's orb-shaped monitors, and a bookcase were the only other furnishings in the room.

Donna shrugged and played with the proposal in front

of her. "Maybe I will," she acquiesced. But there was no agreement in her voice. "You didn't come down here to talk about decorating my office."

Verbeena leaned back in the chair. "What did Al say when you talked to him?"

Donna sighed. "He *was* in Vietnam until '75, you were right. But he wouldn't tell me what was going on at Bethesda."

Verbeena nodded. "Ziggy came up with some answers. Partial ones, anyway," she started. "According to her, there was *another* history. One where Al came home in '73. Somehow, he and Sam changed that."

"They changed—" It wasn't the sort of news Donna wanted to hear. "Did Ziggy say how?"

Verbeena shook her head, her eyes locked on Donna. "She's never traced the changes to find out what made the difference. And until now, she never knew Al *didn't* come back in '73. Not only did this operation cover its trail pretty well, but apparently Al never even told Ziggy the truth."

Donna turned and stared at the proposal on her desk. "You think he told Sam?"

Verbeena shook her head as if she'd already considered the question. "From the way he's acting, I'd say Al never told a soul." She rubbed her eyes and stifled a yawn. "And from what Ziggy's found out about the people on that operation, I can see why."

"What do you mean?"

Verbeena leaned forward. "I mean that if I'd been 'rescued' by that bunch, I'd wonder if I hadn't been better off in Vietnam. They're trained intelligence operatives, Donna. You can't tell the good guys from the bad guys without a script. They play with human lives like pawn pieces and then find themselves on the pages of a Tom Clancy novel.

The stakes in this game are bound to be pretty high. And— I guess, that explains at least some of Al's nervousness. I wouldn't want to think about what could happen if something went wrong.

"And," she continued, sighing and leaning back, "it seems, after all, that Sam is at Bethesda Naval Hospital to keep some ensign from killing himself. So, I guess Al was right in trying to keep Sam out of whatever was going on. I'd say that operation was loaded with land mines, and it'd be real easy for Sam to step on one."

Donna held the dark eyes that didn't blink, reading the warning in them. "Something else was going on," she said, reminding Verbeena of her own suspicions earlier. "All those questions Ziggy raised about Al's Midas touch with funding, his record of promotions—"

"It's none of our business."

Donna turned away and realized, for the first time, the disadvantage of not having decorated her office: there was nothing in the room to stare at in order to avoid Verbeena. Except the pictures. Sam. Her father.

"There were others, Verbeena," she said, quiet anger edging her voice. "Other POWs, still alive over there. It just isn't fair!"

"What? That Al came home, and your father didn't?"

Donna didn't appreciate the psychiatrist's phrasing it quite like that.

"Best case scenario." Verbeena leaned forward again, this time for emphasis. "Could your dad still be alive over there? He'd be—what? Seventy-something?"

Donna chuckled without humor. "Thanks for reminding me how old that makes me!"

"Could he have survived that long over there?" Verbeena pressed.

"That's not the point."

"Then what is?"

Donna looked at the desk and ran her fingers along the edge of the bound volume. "If Al had gone public about being repatriated in '75, there'd have been a lot more pressure to get the others out."

"I don't know," Verbeena said. "That was a paranoid operation."

"So?"

"Have you ever heard of Bobby Garwood?" Verbeena lowered her voice as if she were afraid of being overheard.

"Who?"

"Robert Garwood. He came back in 1979, claimed he'd been a prisoner of war since '65. The Army claimed he wanted to stay in Vietnam. He claimed he didn't."

"What happened to him?" she asked.

"He was accused of aiding the enemy. He faced a court-martial," Verbeena added, her voice still barely above a whisper. "And although he claimed there *were* other American POWs still alive over there—in 1979—he didn't have much credibility after he was court-martialed."

Donna twisted the ring on her finger, extrapolating Verbeena's theory in her own mind: what would have happened to Project Quantum Leap if Al's credibility had been destroyed in 1975? After all, like it or not, it *was* Al who had secured the funding for Sam's dream.

"Last he was seen, he was pumping gas in rural Virginia," Verbeena concluded, and it took Donna a second to realize the psychiatrist meant Bobby Garwood, not Al Calavicci.

She shivered.

"You have to let go of your father, Donna," Verbeena insisted gently. "You can't bring him back. You can't—"

"Change the past?" Donna challenged. She rose from the desk and grabbed the shawl that had fallen over the back of her chair.

"No." Verbeena shook her head and met Donna's determined stare. "You can't change the past.

"It's convenient to have someone else to blame, Donna," Verbeena said. Donna turned and watched the woman head for the door. "But it isn't Al's fault your father didn't come back from Vietnam. And," she added, her eyes very serious, "it wasn't his fault Sam stepped into the Accelerator before it was ready."

Donna felt a stone slide through her stomach. "I never said it was."

"You never had to," Verbeena said, and lifted her hand in a quick wave as she left.

Monday, June 16, 1975, 5:12 P.M.

Mark Davalos drove to his apartment debating with himself. It was a losing battle, but as he listened to the Bee Gees "Stayin' Alive" and tried to keep part of his mind on the traffic, he knew in his gut what he had to do.

He hadn't been told much about this assignment. He had the feeling he wasn't supposed to be any more than a very minor player. The captain from Army Intelligence had told him only a little about the returning POW. He'd said even less about why the man was only just returning home.

But Davalos watched enough TV to know that if the press found out a living American POW was coming home two years after the nation had been assured that all their sons and fathers and brothers and husbands were back or accounted for, the proverbial something would hit the proverbial fan.

The Army captain had explained that they were bringing him back this way to keep the press from mobbing him. It was going to be hard enough returning after all this time without being assaulted by a news-hungry horde that wanted to sensationalize an ordeal that no one should have had to go through to begin with.

It had all made sense to Davalos. He'd been in the Navy long enough to know there was a lot that went on that no one ever talked about. He didn't have a problem with that.

What he had a problem with was what had apparently happened last night. When he had gone to the airport to pick up Lieutenant Calavicci, he'd fully expected a man who looked like he'd just returned from a POW camp. But, then, it had taken three months for the final "negotiations," as they were called, to be finalized. Mark figured the Vietnamese must have tidied him up for the trip home. And three days in France in the hospital before he made the final leg of the journey back to the States had apparently done him some good.

But all that seemed to have been undone last night. Lieutenant Calavicci's "homecoming party" had been a surprise to him; it was sure a surprise to Mark. He'd been told very little about what would happen after the man was dropped off at the hospital, but he'd been given a clear impression that a hero's welcome of some sort—even if it was just on the part of those who were involved in the operation—awaited him.

Whatever was going on with Lieutenant Calavicci, it wasn't a hero's welcome. Or a desire to protect the man from the press.

He reached his apartment building, checked his mail, and

climbed the two flights of stairs to his floor. He felt an idiotic fear that someone would be waiting for him, but his apartment was empty.

He tossed his mail on the table in the dining room and went to the bedroom. He sank down onto the bed and put his head between his hands.

For a long time he just listened to the traffic outside the building, waiting for sirens to pierce what was left of the day. The sun had set low enough for his room to have darkened. He got up finally, turned on a light, and started to change into civvies for the party he didn't feel much like going to tonight.

Lieutenant Jackson Fellows could throw a party in honor of the earth's rotation, Mark thought. He always had *some* reason to celebrate. The first day they'd worked together a few months back, he'd invited Mark to join him after work for a drink, and Mark had had more fun that night than he'd had since high school.

The guy wasn't afraid of the rules, either, wasn't intimidated by "the powers that be." In fact, he seemed to have some pretty good connections, being as how he worked at the Pentagon full-time and all.

Mark hadn't fully made up his mind about telling him anything by the time he left to go to Jackson's apartment. But he was considering it very strongly. Jackson had always seemed like the kind of guy you could trust.

Monday, June 16, 1975, 5:24 P.M.

Determined not to let Maggie Dawson's story ruin her health, Tess Conroy stopped off for her first meal of the day at a Burger King on her way home from Fort Belvoir.

The trip to the post had been a waste of time; she'd arrived too late in the day for anyone to be able to help her, and, after pleading, cajoling, insinuating threats of unwanted publicity—and finally, begging—Tess left with nothing more than she'd gone down there with. After Burger King, she stopped off at *Cavalcade*'s office on her way home and asked for Kelly Fulham.

"Have you got an appointment?" the young man who intercepted her asked.

With an ease borne from the day's frustrations, Tess lied and said, "Yes. My name is Conroy, and I have a story she's waiting for."

The man waved her back to the half-hidden office and Tess knocked on the closed door.

"Come in."

She did, found the room filled with smoke and Kelly Fulham looking years older than she had the day before. She also looked surprised to see Tess.

"You've got the story already?" Kelly demanded without introduction, stamping her current, half-finished cigarette into the overflowing ashtray and pulling out another.

"Not exactly," Tess said. And as she had the day before, she sat without invitation across from the senior editor. Kelly lit up her cigarette and leaned back in the chair. "I talked with Captain Barrows today," Tess started, watching carefully for the reaction. Kelly snorted and smoke blew from her nostrils.

"How is the bastard?" she asked, only half interested. It was on the tip of Tess's tongue to give her Barrows's message, but the story came first.

"Why didn't you follow up with the story after your divorce?" she asked. *God, I've become brazen in the last twenty-four hours! she thought. Almost as if Maggie Daw-*

son's own spirit had taken control.

"I had more important stories to follow up. Now, are you sitting here asking me questions because you've hit a dead end or because you're just nosy?"

"Neither." Tess bristled with the accusation. "But I guess being nosy is what makes a good reporter, right?"

Kelly didn't answer. She turned back to red-lining an article that lay on her desk, the marks she'd made on it almost obliterating the original text. Tess winced.

"Did you get my messages from this morning?" she asked.

"Mm-hmm." The woman waited another moment, then blew out a cloud of smoke and looked up. "Is there something you want, Miss Conroy?"

"I made a deal with your ex-husband for some information about that picture."

The words tore Kelly's attention from her mutilation of the article on her desk. Her head snapped upward, true surprise, bordering on shock, in her eyes. Then, almost as soon as it appeared, it dissolved and the woman's eyes were once more tired and wary.

"Good for you," she said, trying to sound congratulatory. The cigarette trembled between her fingers. "What kind of information?"

Interesting, Tess thought. *Not "what kind of deal?"*

"Information about Colonel Grimwold. You interviewed him a couple years ago about Maggie's death, remember?"

The half-smoked cigarette met its doom among the ashes as Kelly nodded and reached for the pack of Benson & Hedges. "He was a real ass," she volunteered. As she lit the next smoke, Tess waited. "So," the woman exhaled, "what about Grimwold?"

"Your—Captain Barrows," she said, deciding not to

keep reminding the woman of the terminated relationship, "said he was at Belvoir's RDT&E Center. He indicated I'd have a difficult time tracking him there on my own."

Kelly smiled knowingly. "They must have him stashed in some hush-hush project," she guessed. "So, did you talk to him?"

"Got there too late," Tess confessed. Then she took a deep breath, determined that if she were going to become the kind of journalist who engaged in tit-for-tat information exchanges, she was going to damn well keep her side of the bargain.

"Miss Fulham, in exchange for telling me where Colonel Grimwold was, Captain Barrows asked me to relay a message to you."

Kelly's eyes flashed and she stood roughly from her chair, half toppling it. "I don't want to hear any messages from *him*," the woman said. And if she hadn't known better, Tess would have interpreted the violent reaction as fear rather than loathing. "I do *not* want to hear it!"

"Miss Fulham—"

"I'm very busy, Miss Conroy. Now, I don't expect to see you in here again until you've got a story for me. And in case you don't get it here by Wednesday night," she continued, a hint of what really sounded like a threat in her words, "I've got a backup. So if I were you," she added, moving around her desk to open the door and usher Tess out with her arm, "I'd get back to work."

Tess stood grounded to her spot for a few seconds, her mouth half opened in protest. Then she moved to the door and slid past Kelly Fulham to stand in the doorway. But as Kelly let go of the door to let it slam shut under its own weight, Tess reached out and stopped it with her palm.

"He just wants to see you, Miss Fulham," Tess called

into the room. Kelly had already returned to her desk, but she hadn't sat down. A cigarette hung from her lips as if forgotten. "He just asked me to tell you he wants—"

"Get out, Miss Conroy," Kelly ordered, her eyes darkening with anger.

Tess took a deep breath.

OK. I've done my part. No need to make an enemy, right?

She left the *Cavalcade* offices and went back to her car. A half-finished hamburger and cold fries sat on the passenger's seat, a Coke sweated in the heat and humidity, and another storm seemed to be building in the distance. She drank some of the warm Coke, munched a couple of fries, and started the car.

It was well past six when Tess made it back to her apartment, hot and sweaty and tired and aggravated. And her feet burned like hell. She kicked her shoes across the room, stripped off the gray suit and the rest of her things, took a long, cool shower, and changed into jeans and a T-shirt. Rain pounded against her windows, the thunder clouds having finally broken open to unleash a typical Washington summer storm.

It was past eight when the phone rang. She picked it up, reluctant to let the interruption stop her work. She wasn't much further ahead than she had been this morning, but she had begun to put together a list of questions for Grimwold in anticipation of hunting him down tomorrow morning.

"Conroy."

"Hey, babe, where are you?" Jackson Fellows's voice was loud and he sounded a little drunk. In the background, Jethro Tull's electric flute was overlaid with occasional wild shrieks and laughter, most of it coming from the upper range of the scale. Tess sighed; she'd completely forgotten about the party.

"Jackson, I'm sorry, I—I can't make it after all." There was silence, so she rushed on to explain. "Look, I got a story yesterday, from the editor of *Cavalcade*. And I'm under a real tight deadline."

"I thought you were working on that story a month ago?" he demanded, a little angry. Jackson Fellows, as Tess remembered, did not make a good drunk.

"This is another one," she said, deciding not to explain that the story she'd spent the last month on had been scrapped. "And I really have to work on it. I'm sorry."

"Yeah." A second later she heard the muted sounds of someone murmuring half-garbled promises to him. From the few words she could hear clearly, Tess didn't think Jackson Fellows was going to be suffering much from her absence. "Look, I'll call you later, okay?" he said, suddenly distracted.

"Okay. Sorry, Jackson."

She hung up and went back to her questions for Grimwold.

CHAPTER

ELEVEN

Monday, June 16, 1975, 6:35 P.M.

Lieutenant Commander Dennis Stern's official title, when he was working on official business, was Interagency Coordinator for the Assistant Director of Naval Intelligence. But he wasn't working on official business now, and neither was the man who drove him to Andrews Air Force Base.

"You really think this is going to do any good?"

Bob Barrows broke what had been nearly an hour of complete silence with a dejection that seemed to seep through the world tonight. The storm that had threatened most of the afternoon was now a full-blown monster. Wind-whipped rain pelted the car, stalled traffic on the beltway, made it nearly impossible to see, and turned the world a soggy, polluted gray.

Dennis glanced sideways at Bob, noting the tightened jawline. "Do you want to leave it so Wainwright's the only one who's talked to our 'friends' in France?" he countered. "Calavicci as much as damned himself with what he said last night, Bob," he reminded the captain. "And thanks to Wainwright giving Blackwell the transcript, your hero goes up against the wall tomorrow. Ten to one, he'll be staring at a firing squad by the end of the week."

Bob gripped the steering wheel. "Did you give a copy of last night's transcript to Joe?" he asked. Dennis shook his head.

"Just summarized it." He sighed. It had been a long twenty-four hours already, and he doubted he was going to get much sleep in the next two or three days, either.

"We didn't ask the right questions," Barrows insisted, repeating a refrain he'd kept up since he'd first reviewed the transcript from last night.

"Or maybe," Dennis considered, "the other POWs are agreeing with the Vietnamese and Wainwright to cover their own butts."

"Blackwell's promised them immunity," Bob reminded him grimly. "He's after Al, not them, and they know it. They have nothing to lose by telling the truth, no matter what that truth is."

Dennis turned again, glancing at the older man out of the corner of his eye. "What would you say the chance is that every other POW in that camp maintained complete military discipline in the last two years?" he asked. Barrows shook his head. "I'd be willing to bet that somewhere along the line, everyone over there did something he was ashamed of."

"Everyone over there did," Barrows muttered, staring out the front window. Dennis looked at him sharply. The lights from the other cars on the road reflected through the drops of rain on the windows of their car and covered Barrows's face with spotted shadows. After a moment the captain shook himself free.

"Sorry," he apologized quietly. "Sometimes, when it rains like this—"

"I understand." Dennis cut off his apology, eager both to get back to the business at hand and to pull Barrows from the rain-triggered flashback. "If Calavicci wasn't the only one who screwed up, then Wainwright's going to have a hell of a time touching him," he concluded.

Barrows nodded, still not quite free of his own demons, and Stern left him alone. By the time they got to the base, they arrived at the airport with barely ten minutes to spare. Dennis reached down and grabbed the single satchel he'd brought with him.

"Listen, Dennis," Bob started as he idled the car in front of the terminal, the windshield wipers swishing a quiet rhythm in the background. "Something happened today I think you should know."

Dennis stopped, his hand on the handle, the door half opened. He had a feeling, from Bob's tone of voice and hesitance, that he wasn't going to like what came next.

"A reporter from *Cavalcade* came to see me today—"

"Shit!" Dennis exploded and abruptly pulled the door shut. "Dammit, Bob, you talked to Kelly? I can't believe—"

"No! Now, just wait!" Barrows was clearly distressed. He shifted in his seat to turn to the naval commander. "First of all, it wasn't Kelly. And secondly, she's working on another story. A story Kelly gave up on about a year ago."

"*What* story?" Dennis demanded.

As Bob summarized Tess Conroy's quest, Dennis listened, suspicion still quivering in the pit of his stomach when Barrows finished.

"I don't like it," he said. "It's too damned coincidental." He held Barrows's eyes seriously. "And while *I* believe you haven't had any contact with Kelly since this operation started, I doubt Blackwell's going to."

Bob glanced away and lightning slashed the sky.

"Oh, hell, you didn't talk to her?"

"No." Bob swallowed convulsively and twisted his hands around the steering wheel. "No."

Dennis waited, but Bob wasn't volunteering any more. "Bob, you're the one who made the choice to stay on this operation. You made the decision—"

"I *haven't* talked to her," he repeated quietly.

Dennis glanced nervously at his watch: four minutes. "This Grimwold you sent her to."

"He's at Belvoir," Barrows repeated. "I thought that as long as she's on the trail of the *picture*, her focus won't be anywhere near us. I tossed her to Grimwold to keep her busy. She's got to finish the story by Wednesday. Kelly likes to have a two-week lead on her deadlines."

"Will Grimwold talk to her?"

Barrows met Dennis's eyes. "I was hoping he would." The way he said it made Dennis's flesh crawl. He shook his head, not understanding.

"It's an Army Intelligence matter," Barrows explained. "Up 'til now, it's been considered too hot. I think someone should drop the word that there's something hotter that should be kept out of the papers.

"I want Grimwold to talk. I want him to lead her to anyone else who can talk. Anyone except Al."

Stern ground his teeth and shook his head. He sighed and stepped out into the downpour. "Ask Joe tomorrow," he suggested. "Tell him I concur. For what it's worth."

"Have a good flight," Bob called as Dennis shut the door and dashed for cover.

Then, despite how close he was cutting it, Dennis ran quickly back alongside the car just as Bob began to edge from the curb. He pulled the door open and Bob stepped on the brake.

"The paperwork?" Dennis called over the thunder.

Bob grinned and gestured to the back of the car. A garment bag hung on the clothes hook behind him.

"Good going. That'll mean a lot," he called, shutting the door again and racing back inside the terminal.

As he ran for his plane, listening to the overhead page for the last call on his flight, he thought about Calavicci. Dennis didn't believe he was guilty. At least, not any guiltier than anyone else who came back from Vietnam alive. And as far as he was concerned, the United States Navy owed Calavicci *something* for all those years.

And Senator Joe Weitzman had agreed.

One. Two. Three. Four. Five. Six. Seven. Eight.
Turn.

"Albert M. Calavicci," the lieutenant whispered to himself. "Lieutenant. United States Navy. Serial Number B-21-23-29."

Rain pounded the walls as he paced the small basement cell and sucked on his cigar, no longer hearing the music that came from the radio on his bed stand.

One. Two. Three. Four.

Without warning, a bamboo pole slammed against human flesh and the sound reverberated through the walls of the hospital, down to the basement. Lieutenant Calavicci stood still, braced, waiting for the screams.

Then he realized it was only thunder he'd heard.

He shut his eyes and forced his breath out.

Don't think about it. Don't think about it.

137

Five. Six. Seven. Eight.

Turn.

He continued the pace.

Think about something else.

Think about being home.

You're home, you lucky bastard, remember? Home sweet home.

New job waiting. Navy ought to owe you a hell of a lot of back pay for all those years, huh? Play your cards right, you probably won't have to worry about money for the rest of your life.

One. Two. Three.

Wonder if they'll ever let me fly again?

Another bamboo slap of thunder intruded and Lieutenant Calavicci tried to steady his breath.

"Albert M. Calavicci," he recited, a little louder. "Lieutenant. United States Navy. Serial Number B-21-23-29."

Four. Five. Six.

Home. You're home, Allie-boy.

Seven. Eight. Turn.

Sure as hell doesn't feel like home.

One. Two. Three. Four.

Everything's changed. Nothing's like what I remembered. Not like what I thought I'd come home to. Not even—

Beth. Oh, God, Beth. Why'd you leave me? Why?

Lieutenant Calavicci cleared his throat and rubbed a hand across his face.

No. Don't even think about it. Don't think about it.

Five. Six. Seven. Eight.

"Don't make a sound . . ."

"Why the hell should we take the word of a traitor, huh?"

I'm not a traitor!

Am I?

Was it really my idea to begin with? Eddie came up with some of it, right? Eddie knew what I was going to do with the information he gave me.

He knew!

"Don't make a sound."

"If you scream or cry out . . ."

"Shut up!" Another crack of thunder cut through his concentration. "Just shut the hell up!" He waited. And the world was silent again.

One. Two. Three. Four.

Think of something else.

Davalos. Yeah, there was something safe to think about.

Problem was, the kid was too nice to last long in this man's Navy.

Too nice. And too trusting.

Just like that corn-bred farmboy they'd dumped into the camp two years ago.

Five. Six. Seven. Eight.

A kid like that should never have been thrown into that godforsaken hell.

He should never have been there.

Thank God he was.

One. Two. Three. Four.

I should have gotten that kid home. Damn!

He should have been the one to come home! He had a whole family waiting for him: mother and father, and brother and sister.

Why the hell did they have to kill him?

Five. Six. Seven. Eight.

Rain pelted Bethesda Naval Hospital and thunder sliced a sharp incision through Lieutenant Calavicci's memories.

He choked and shut his eyes and rubbed a hand across his face.

Don't think about it.

Turn.

One. Two. Three. Four.

There had to be something in the universe that was safe to think about. *Something*.

"Albert M. Calavicci. Lieutenant. United States Navy. Serial Number B-21-23-29."

Name, rank, serial number. Yeah. That worked.

Five. Six. Seven. Eight.

Turn.

Monday, June 16, 1975, 7:18 P.M.

As far as Senator Elwood Blackwell was concerned, briefings and debriefings could take place just as easily in a civilized setting as in a cramped, hot office. He poured a glass of Cabernet Sauvignon and handed it to his guest, then returned to the massive cutting board to finish chopping garlic for dinner.

His apartment at the Colonnade in Northwest Washington was considered, by many in his circles, to be a more elegant alternative to the somewhat brash Watergate, where even television personalities lived. And the Colonnade didn't suffer the public stigma still attached to its counterpart, a fact that gave its residents more freedom from the press.

"So all the pieces are in place," Elwood started. The garlic went into the blender.

"Just about." Jerry Wainwright, dressed in a well-

140

tailored Brooks Brothers's suit, watched his host cook the gourmet meal.

He gestured Wainwright to the small table against the kitchen wall, where a plate of caviar, cream cheese, and crackers waited. "Help yourself, don't stand on ceremony."

It was only the second time he'd had Wainwright come here for a debriefing, and he knew the colonel was uncomfortable with the informal arrangement. The man was too "by the book" sometimes for Elwood's taste. But Wainwright was just what he needed in every other regard. As Elwood turned the heat up on a large pot of water that was not quite boiling, Wainwright helped himself to the caviar.

"I need a favor," Elwood said, sipping his own wine as he spoke. "There's a colonel stationed at Fort Belvoir. He heads up some R & D projects."

Wainwright took a seat at the small table and put his glass down. "And?"

"I'd like him moved. Tomorrow. Early."

Wainwright coughed on the wine, surprised. "That's an Army matter," he protested.

Elwood grinned. "No. It's a Phoenix matter."

"What does a colonel at Belvoir have to do with—"

"He's a decoy," Elwood explained. He checked the oven, made sure that the small, new potatoes weren't overcooked. "Barrows's decoy."

"Barrows?"

Content that everything was progressing as it should, Elwood joined his companion at the table, helping himself to the appetizer. "You remember I told you I convinced Fulham to do an MIA issue? Well, Barrows has the reporter out hunting up leads on the Dawson picture. I want her focusing on the *man* in the picture. If she's wandering around Belvoir, she's going to miss the target. So I want Grimwold moved.''

''The decoy?''

Elwood nodded, smiling. ''Moving him tomorrow will be very important.''

''It'll make the reporter suspicious,'' Wainwright concluded.

''Exactly.''

Elwood returned to the cooking area and checked the pot of water. In the sink next to the stove sat the main course, waiting to be plunged into the pot. The lobsters's claws were still taped shut.

''I'll do what I can,'' Wainwright sighed.

Elwood watched the colonel for a few seconds; there seemed to be a hint of regret, or hesitation, in his manner.

''Remember the original plan, Jerry?'' Elwood asked quietly. ''Repatriate one or two—even three—men at a time? And each time, we work out a few quiet little deals on the side for the Vietnamese.'' Wainwright nodded and downed another caviar-laden cracker.

''Well, from sterilizing each procedure, to contacting the families, to arranging new identities for those who *have* families, to making sure the operation isn't compromised after each batch—it's going to take too long. Decades. The whole point was to get this over with rapidly so we could normalize relations.

''Aside from that,'' Elwood added, ''let's take a look at the quality of the lives we're saving. Most of them have been there so long they're quite . . . unstable. Like the French that just got back. Hell, I wouldn't want any one of them still on active duty after what they've been through. They're a loss to the military. They're probably all walking time bombs!''

142

"So we . . . cut our losses." There was still hesitation in Wainwright's voice.

"We bring the press in now, and the whole thing shuts down. We move to Plan B and all our men are accounted for in five years. Maybe six. That's a hell of a savings in time, and money, and risk, right?"

Without waiting for an answer, he turned to the pot of boiling water. He pulled off the lid, lifted the first lobster from the sink, and turned back to Wainwright. "Not only that," he added, almost waving the lobster in the air as he spoke, "but it gets the whole government off the hook with this MIA issue. Think about how much money we waste every year on *that*? Placating families, issuing statements, creating special investigations . . . It's a service to the whole country to get this over with."

Wainwright lifted his wine to his lips, took a drink, then stood and walked back to the sink. He watched as Elwood held the lobster above the boiling water, the steam burning both it and his own hand.

"You see," Elwood observed, half smiling as the lobster struggled to avoid the heat, "it's much kinder to just get rid of them quickly. Put them out of their misery." He plunged the creature into the pot and reached for the second. Wainwright stopped him, met his eyes, and took the lobster from him.

"I'll take care of it," he said quietly, and dropped his lobster into the boiling water.

CHAPTER
TWELVE

Monday, June 16, 1975, 8:15 P.M.

Sam was back. Back in the corridor from hell, facing the dingy white hallway that led to the one person who could shed the most light on this whole bizarre Leap, and who wouldn't.

Almost five hours ago, Lieutenant Farraday had left to brief the next shift and, as she put it, "get myself dolled up for Jackson's party.

"Want to join me?" she'd asked.

Sam had the feeling, not something he really wanted to dwell on, that Farraday had some feelings for Xiao that the man was not reciprocating. But unless he had guidance from Ziggy to do otherwise, Sam wasn't going to move Wendell into a relationship he had no idea would work.

He'd backed out of the invitation with the legitimate excuse that he had a mound of records to finish before leaving. Lieutenant Farraday seemed only marginally disappointed.

Sam completed his rounds alone and finished making his

notes in all the records. Stifling the desire to immediately drive back to Wendell's apartment and collapse into bed, he decided to check on Al once more. Maybe Davalos's visit this afternoon had cheered him up.

He knocked on Al's door, but a several-second pause didn't bring an invitation, and Sam finally opened the door and stepped in.

Al was pacing. Again. At least, Sam thought, some of the effects of the sodium amytal had worn off.

"Uh, Lieutenant?" As usual, Al fulfilled his self-imposed, eight-step ritual before allowing the interruption. He turned at the end of the room and pulled the cigar from his mouth.

"I just . . . wanted to see how you were," Sam started awkwardly, standing just inside the door. "Before I left for the night."

Al tilted his head back. "Gosh, all this attention! I'm overwhelmed." The acid in his voice was unmistakable.

"Look," Sam started, not used to the sharpness, "I'm sorry about . . . what happened last night."

Al resumed his pace.

"Look, I don't know what's going on here, I'm just—" Sam stopped. He was once more talking to Al's back. "I'm supposed to evaluate your fitness for continued active duty," he tried, falling back on a Wendell-sounding plea. "I've already gotten in trouble once for not doing it yesterday, so—well, maybe we could—talk now?"

Al paced toward him, not looking at him. "I don't talk to shrinks," he said.

"Why not?"

"Looks likes crap on your record." Then he looked at Sam, shrugged, turned, and paced away.

Sam sighed with frustration, wanting to grab Al and hold

145

him in place so he could at least talk to a stationary object. But after last night, Sam resisted the urge and thrust his hands into his lab coat pockets. "I don't think any of this is going on your record," he pointed out.

Al didn't respond to that, so Sam pressed on. "Look, I—I tried to stop them from using the amytal. They wouldn't—I guess, they didn't think they had any other choices."

Al snickered and the sound made Sam cold. "We *all* had choices." He turned burning eyes to Sam when his pace to the other end of the room was completed. "Take Bobby. *He* sure as hell had a choice."

Sam swallowed hard and ground his teeth. "Did you two know each other—in Vietnam?" he asked carefully. Al stared at him, a long, evaluating stare.

"Charlie introduced us," he said simply, and continued his pace.

Sam was about to ask about that, deciding that the answer signaled a small crack in the layers of suspicious distrust Al was using to keep the world at a safe distance. But a knock at the door interrupted the conversation.

Cautiously Sam opened the door, noting out of the corner of his eye that Al had stopped pacing and was backing slowly toward the far corner of the room.

"Dr. Xiao! I—didn't expect you to be here so late."

Speak of the devil, Sam thought. He hesitated a moment before gesturing the rain-drenched Captain Barrows into the small room. He glanced at Al, standing uncertainly near the corner of the room, his eyes flicking from Sam to Barrows and back, his muscles tensed for attack.

"I've brought you something, Commander," Barrows said, breaking the tense silence. He beckoned Sam away from the door, half shut it, and hung a dripping garment bag on the hook over the back of the door.

" '*Commander*'?" Al's voice was full of suspicion, as he spoke around his cigar, as it had been earlier. "What the hell—?"

But Barrows broke him off. "You were promoted to lieutenant commander in 1968," he said as he unzipped the garment bag to reveal the dress white uniform inside. Sam glanced at it and noted several rows of medals over the left breast pocket.

"Of course," Barrows continued, "the paperwork couldn't be completed while you were in Vietnam—"

"Kinda hard to promote a dead man?" Al interrupted sharply. Sam held his breath.

"—but it's been completed now," Barrows finished, ignoring the remark. "Retroactive to August 12, 1968. Congratulations." There was a sad apology in his voice.

Al continued to stare in turn at the men and the uniform hanging on the door, as if he weren't sure any of them were real. Sam waited, not sure what was going through Al's mind.

Al narrowed his eyes in a familiar, contemplative gesture and slowly stepped forward, toward the uniform, toward the men.

"Why?" he demanded.

"Why what?" Barrows asked. Al reached out, pushed aside the flap of the bag just enough to actually see the bars on the epaulets. Then he dropped his hand.

"Why the hell should it matter?" he asked quietly. He turned away and paced the eight-step pattern of helpless captivity.

"You'll be expected to wear it," Barrows explained reluctantly. "Tomorrow."

The word caught Sam's attention and Al's. Lieutenant

147

Commander Calavicci stopped pacing and waited, chin lifted for the right cross he obviously anticipated.

"Tomorrow?" Sam asked, when Al wouldn't.

"Tomorrow morning—at the hearing."

"Hearing?"

Barrows was distinctly unhappy. "Hearings begin tomorrow morning at 1000. I'll be by to pick you up at 0900."

Sam watched Al carefully. The man looked steadily at Barrows, and an instant later a naval officer was resurrected from the tomb of Vietnam. He squared his shoulders and pulled himself to attention.

"I'll be ready. Captain."

Al's formality signaled an obvious distance from whatever friendship might have existed between him and the man who always seemed to bring tidings of bad news.

Barrows nodded once and left without another word.

"Excuse me," Sam said and followed him out. A thunderclap penetrated the walls of the hospital basement as he closed the door behind him. Barrows was a few feet down the hall. He stood there, breathing as if it were hard to get air into his lungs.

"Sorry, Doc, I probably should have told you first," Barrows said. Then he took a deep breath and cut off Sam's imminent questions. "I'm afraid I've got some more news you're probably not gonna like."

Sam decided to wait.

"Nathan Meyers is off the operation." Barrows crossed his arms over his chest. "His wife had twins yesterday. Real premature. He's been granted a compassionate leave of absence."

"How are they?" Habit, Sam thought.

"They'll be okay." The captain shrugged. "Thing is, we

148

don't have anyone else cleared for this operation right now, so—I'm afraid you'll have to double as his physician until we can bring in someone else."

Sam stared in disbelief and swallowed several times. "His physician?"

"Someone has to." Barrows watched him carefully for another minute, then lowered his voice. "Doc, just between you and me—Nathan never briefed you, did he?"

Sam considered the question, Al's warnings, and the risks.

"Just between you and me, would you remove me from the operation if I said he hadn't?"

Barrows shook his head. "Dennis and I pretty much had that figured out. Just don't let Wainwright or Senator Blackwell get wind of it, OK?"

Sam's forehead wrinkled. "Senator Blackwell? Uh, yeah, OK." No one had said anything about any senators, Sam thought.

"Look, Nathan never had a chance to give Al a physical. Right after they got him out of the elevator—"

"Elevator?" Sam interrupted, glancing down the hall to the single-door lift. "What elevator?"

Barrows paused. "That's not in the chart?" Sam shook his head. Barrows looked away, stared at the ceiling, the exposed air-conditioning ducts, and the pulleys between the laundry rooms. Finally, he shut his eyes, cleared his throat, and looked back. "Al was pretty upset when Nathan told him about his wife," he started. "He got into the elevator before anyone could stop him and—jammed it between floors. It was almost an hour before maintenance could get him out. And he was still huddled up on the floor in the corner."

It was an image Sam could never have pictured before yesterday.

"How do you purposely jam an elevator?" he asked.

Barrows looked amused. "In these old things, it's pretty easy. You punch a button for another floor and as soon as it starts to move, you punch the button for the floor you're on. Guess it confuses the machinery. Al used to say that any plebe who's ever wanted to be alone with a girl knew the trick."

"Figures," Sam muttered, drawing a puzzled expression from Barrows. "I mean—he just . . . seems like the kind of guy who'd . . . know that." It was a lousy cover, Sam realized.

"Anyway," Barrows continued after a moment, "Nathan's wife went into labor right about then. Al got a cursory physical in France, but all we know from that is that he can walk, talk, and stand upright. Given what Charlie likes to do with POWs, I'd bet there's a hell of a lot more needs to be taken care of. And—" he paused, looking uncomfortable, "I thought that—if you found anything that would do it, we might be able to delay the hearing until Dennis can—" He caught himself apparently about to say too much. "So Al can get another couple days' rest," he finished.

Sam took a deep breath. "It's after dinner, Captain," he protested. "I mean, everything's shut down except for emergency treatment. There's not a lot I can do."

"It's the perfect time. You can run him through every damned department in the hospital without a lot of people around."

Barrows had a point, Sam agreed reluctantly. It *was* the perfect time to do a barrage of tests on a patient who wasn't supposed to be there.

"Well, since Dr. Meyers didn't brief me, you want to tell me how I'm supposed to explain him to all those departments?"

Barrows smiled thinly. "You haven't been at Bethesda

long, have you? John Does come through here all the time, Doc. Everyone here's used to it. All you do is use the name, and give the orders, and no one asks any questions.''

Sam glanced back at the closed door to Al's room, then shut his eyes, wondering how the future Al was going to react to this development in light of his drastic pleas for Sam to stay as far away from this as possible.

But since nothing Sam had done could have been responsible for Meyers's wife giving birth prematurely, he suddenly thought, and since that was the reason Meyers was off the operation, it occurred to him that it had probably been Xiao all along who'd done the workup on Al.

So why hadn't Al told him that? And how could he possibly expect Sam to remain uninvolved?

He shook his head, recognizing only another string of questions he had for his friend.

"OK, um, what—what do you need in order to stall?"

Barrows hunched his shoulders. "Anything that says he's not fit to testify tomorrow morning. Look for parasites: something that'll make the guys on the Hill squeamish," he advised.

Sam grimaced, and felt suddenly very tired.

"I'll call your office later, say around ten? See what you've got."

"A lot of the blood work won't be back by then," Sam protested.

"Well, if we're going to stop that hearing, we need something before nine o'clock tomorrow morning." He punched the elevator door and waited. "Do your best."

Monday, June 16, 1975, 9:40 P.M.

The party was in full swing, a roaring, rousing, abandoned success, Jackson thought.

151

Even if Tess *hadn't* shown up.

Half a dozen men and women danced to the music of Jethro Tull, living in the past, drinking, munching popcorn and chips, smoking joints. A couple of them had bottles of 'ludes, but what the hell? It was their life, right?

"Hey, Jackson, you got any more beer?" The attractive and oh-so-tempting Lynn Farraday sidled over to him, half drunk, and flicked her tongue against his ear.

"Maybe," he said, "but it'll cost ya." He grabbed the nurse, tipped her backward, and kissed her hard, leaving her reeling with alcoholic dizziness when he was done.

"What do I have to pay for a glass of wine?" She laughed. He pointed her in the direction of the kitchen and watched her backside as she stumbled off.

Across the room, Mark Davalos, whom he had only half expected to actually show up, sat on the sofa, nursing his third beer. Mark was a straight arrow, the kind of kid whose idea of taking a risk was to try to make an illegal U-turn without getting caught. And that's exactly why Jackson had invited him to this party. Mark was so straight that, despite his junior rank, he'd been assigned to a couple of very sensitive operations in the last year, Jackson discovered. Just the kind of guy Tess would want to meet: completely clean and completely trusted. She'd have been grateful for *that* kind of contact.

Grateful, ha! The woman was an ice maker!

But Mark Davalos, Jackson thought, watching the ensign through the largely illegal smoke that filled the room, wasn't the kind to sit in the corner and down three beers in near isolation in the middle of a roaring good party. Granted, you had to talk him into doing something dangerous so that he'd have an excuse for his wild, abandoned behavior. But even if you couldn't talk him into anything really "risky," he still knew how to have fun at a party.

Tonight, Mark clearly *wasn't* having fun.

Jackson swaggered over and sank onto the couch next to the kid. "How ya doin', bud?" he greeted.

"Jackson."

Davalos was well on the way to a drunk. His eyes weren't focusing well and his voice was just a little slurred.

"So, what gives?" Jackson asked. Lynn Farraday sauntered past and he reached out, pinching her as she passed with a provocative wiggle. She squirmed away and looked distressed. *Good act*, Jackson thought.

He turned back to Mark.

Davalos licked his lips and put his beer on the end table. "Well, there's a kind of a—a situation." He looked around the room nervously. "Look, before I say anything, I gotta know you won't tell anyone I said anything, right? I mean, *no one*!"

Jackson nodded and smiled and thought about Tess. "No one," he agreed, his voice taking on Mark's exaggerated tone of conspiracy. "So, what is it? KGB after you?"

Davalos pulled back and watched his friend. "Look, if you won't take me seriously—"

"I'm taking you seriously, OK?" Jackson protested, putting on his best wounded look.

Davalos sighed. "OK." He picked the beer up, took a swig, and wiped his lips with the back of his hand. "I pulled detail to pick this guy up at Dulles and take him to Bethesda, right?"

"What guy? Some VIP?"

Davalos hesitated while he looked anxiously around the room again.

"Hell," Jackson said, trying to reassure the kid, "the whole place is so high, no one's paying any attention to you."

Nevertheless, Mark lowered his voice to a whisper. "He's a returning POW, Jackson. From Vietnam. Just now coming back."

He had Jackson's attention. Fully.

"You serious, bud? A POW? *Now?*"

Davalos nodded. "But they were bringing him in real quiet so the media wouldn't be all over him right away, you know?"

Jackson chuckled without humor, Jethro Tull's "Bungle in the Jungle" sounding strangely appropriate just then. "Man, if you bought that, you're simpler than I thought. Hell, they're not protecting him, they're covering their own butts." He lit a cigarette, puffed on it, and watched the smoke curl up to the ceiling. *Oh, Tess . . .*

"How are they gonna keep something like that quiet?" he probed carefully.

"Well, see, that's what I was wondering. Something's happening with him, something they didn't tell me about. After I dropped him off at Bethesda, I wasn't supposed to see him again, right? But this Dr. Xiao at the hospital, he let me take him a Beatles tape." He stopped, watching Jackson.

"A Beatles tape. So?"

"So when I got down there to see him, it was—this is gonna sound crazy, Jackson, but it—well, it was like they'd tortured him, or something."

Jackson snickered. "Torture? Come on, kid! Hell, whatever's going on, it's not torture."

"He looked awful, Jackson," Davalos insisted. "And when I asked him what had happened, he said something about them throwing him a 'homecoming party,' only there was nothing about it that was a party."

Davalos took another nerve-calming drink of his beer.

"Maybe they gave him an enema," Jackson suggested, shrugging.

Davalos shook his head. "No, it wasn't—Jackson, look, I know what I saw!"

"You've been watching too many late-night movies, kid, you're even sounding like one now." *Tess, my darling, you will be eternally grateful . . .*

"Will you listen!" Davalos licked his lips again. "Something's going on with this guy, right? I mean, he's locked in this horrible little room in the basement of the hospital, he doesn't have a window or anything, and he's not allowed to see anyone. I mean, that's not right."

"So what do you want me to do? Picket the hospital for better accommodations?"

"You're not listening," Davalos said.

"Wait a minute, buddy," Jackson said, grabbing his arm. "OK, let's assume there's something fishy here, right? Let's say you're right; what do you think I can do about it?"

"Well, could you just—I don't know." Mark seemed suddenly lost and Jackson's eyes wandered to Lynn Farraday, dancing with another of his guests across the room. He gave her a long, lingering look. She smiled back, knowing just what the look meant.

"Look," he said, turning back to Mark. "I have some . . . friends who might be able to do a little snooping around tomorrow. I'll see if I can find anything out, OK? But look, don't worry. I'm sure you've got this all wrong and everything's fine."

Davalos looked puzzled by his reassurance. "Thanks," he muttered. "But remember—"

"We never had this conversation, I know. What's the POW's name?"

"Calavicci. Al Calavicci."

155

CHAPTER
THIRTEEN

Monday, June 16, 1975, 10:15 P.M.

She was gorgeous. Unbelievably gorgeous, Sam thought, stepping off the elevator on the third floor and facing the night-duty nurse sitting at Lieutenant Farraday's desk. The woman looked up and smiled as the elevator door opened.

"Can I help you?" she asked.

Oh, good, Sam thought. *At least I haven't met her yet.* He stared at her, the thick black hair that fell to her shoulders in waves, her large, round eyes and olive complexion indicating perhaps a Filipino background. And in the close-fitting nurse's uniform, there was no hiding her incredible proportions.

"I'm—" he stopped, clearing his throat and the thoughts that rose unbidden in his mind: *playing doctor* . . . "I'm Dr. Sam . . . I mean," he tried again, "I'm Dr. Xiao. Wendell Xiao."

She took his hand and he found his eyes drifting below her neckline. He pulled them up, suddenly realizing what an advantage she could be after all.

"Lieutenant Sharon Mulcahy," she returned. Irish, Sam thought, probably black Irish. She sat back at the table. She was on the list, Sam remembered. Thank God!

"Lieutenant Mulcahy, you're working with me on the 'Lieutenant Doe' case?" he asked, trying to confirm what he prayed was true.

"Yes, sir."

"Have you met the lieutenant—actually, he's a lieutenant commander now. Have you met him?"

She shook her head. "He's been asleep each time I've checked him."

Sam found himself grinning and tried to appear serious as she watched him with apprehension. He explained the new developments to her quickly.

"So, what's first?" she asked, accepting the news with equilibrium.

"Well." Sam shoved his hands into his lab coat. "I thought I'd start with a basic physical and then you can run him through radiology and hematology and all the rest, if—if that's alright with you."

She waved her hands in a sort of shrug. "You're the doctor," she said cheerfully.

"I'll go get his chart," Sam said, walking toward his office.

Al was there, waiting for him, just lighting a cigar. Sam closed the door to his office quickly behind him.

"Al! Why didn't you tell me?"

"What?"

Sam wasn't in the mood for twenty questions. "That in addition to poking around in your mind, I'm also supposed to go poking around your body!"

Al made a face. "Sam, *please*!"

"Sorry. At least it's more familiar ground." He walked

around Al to his desk and searched for Lieutenant Commander Calavicci's chart. "I just—I wish you'd have given me some warning, that's all. I mean, you've been telling me to stay out of this, and I keep getting drawn more and more into it."

He looked up, waiting for some response, and saw a familiar *unfamiliar* look in the admiral's eyes. A redness, narrowness that he'd seen before, years ago, when Al had still been drinking.

"I hoped we'd figure out what you were here to do, and you'd do it, and be outta here by now." Al moved closer to Sam, waving his cigar in the air. "Look, instead of going back down to the Black Hole of Calcutta there, why don't you just send me off to radiology to take some X-ray-ted pictures with Nurse Long Legs, and go back and talk to Terry Martin. Maybe you can convince him this time."

"I just came from trying to talk to him, Al, he won't listen to me." Al sucked on the cigar. "I don't know what else to say to him."

Al gave Sam a long look and pulled the cigar from his mouth. "You could try listening," he suggested. "You *used* to be pretty good at that."

Sam winced at the accusation and sat in his chair. "What's going on with you, Al? I mean—aside from the fact you just got back from 'Nam," he added. "I mean all the rest of this." He waved helplessly at the chart in front of him. "False identities, amytal interrogations, a room in the basement!" He glanced up and saw wariness in Al's eyes. "And hearings?"

"It's just a debriefing, Sam," Al said, staring at the handlink. "SOP."

"Then why does Barrows want to postpone it?"

Al shrugged, still paying a lot of attention to the squealing box in his hand. "Like he said. Give me a couple days' rest." He wouldn't look up.

"So why do *you* want me to stay out of it?" Sam demanded.

Al sighed. "Because you're not Wendell Xiao!" He looked up then. "Sam, in the original history, Wendell stayed pretty much out of this. He did his job—he did what they told him to do. That's it!"

"So?"

"So, Sam Beckett isn't known for following orders," Al snapped. "And if Sam Beckett makes these guys nervous, or changes anything that happened in the original history, who knows what they might do? This is a secret operation, Sam. *Everyone's* jumpy, okay?"

"Alright, okay, then just—cut to the chase for me, okay? Do we find—*did* they find—anything that postponed the hearing tomorrow?"

Al puffed on his cigar, shook his head, and muttered a nonverbal negative. "After the negotiations to get me out were finalized, the VC sent me off to one of their hospitals before shipping me back. They did the basic surgery and got rid of the little creepy crawlies that had made their home in my gut."

"Surgery?" Sam asked. "In 'Nam?" He glanced through the chart on the desk, shaking his head. "There's no mention of any surgery in here."

Al looked impatient. "Well, there isn't a hell of a lot that *is* in that chart, if you'll notice."

"Is it in your official records?"

"Sort of."

"Sort of?"

Al narrowed his eyes. "Do you have to repeat everything?"

"Do I have—what do you mean by 'sort of'?"

Al shrugged. "The details are in there, but they scrambled up the dates."

Sam considered asking him the fifteen questions that instantly came to his mind, but he decided against it. "What kind of surgery?"

"Reset a couple bones, that's all." But he wasn't looking at the physicist anymore and Sam waited, detecting the lie. Al finally looked back. "What?"

"Anything else I should know about before I do an exam?" Sam asked, his voice sharp. He was losing his patience.

"No." It was a flat response, intended to stall any further questions.

Sam turned to the chart on the desk and asked, "Did you receive any blood transfusions?" He was trying to sound clinical.

"Why don't you ask *him*!" Sam looked back up. Al took a deep breath. "I'm sorry, Sam, I—I just wish this whole thing were over with."

Once more, the hauntingly familiar, almost forgotten expression of a man who'd had too much to drink transformed Al's face.

"So do I," Sam said. He swallowed, his throat constricting. "Look, is there any change with Terry Martin?"

Al perfunctorily punched a button on the handlink, waited a second as it cried out, and then shook his head. "Nope. He still kills himself day after tomorrow."

Sam stood back up, pulling Al's chart with him. "Well, go see if Ziggy's got some ideas, OK? I mean, she's got access to the greatest psychiatrists in the world, right? So— have her dig something up I can use."

He passed Al, not waiting for an answer, and halfway

160

down the hall, he realized there might have been something to Al's accusation after all.

Verbeena Beeks's vertebrae cracked against each other as she stretched her neck back and to the side. Although it was just past lunchtime chronologically, it had been a long day already in "Leap" terms.

Leap days took a toll on all key personnel, especially those who had to adjust their natural circadian rhythms around a past that was often out of synch with the present. Verbeena usually dealt with it—when she had to—by catching short naps throughout the first twenty-four to forty-eight hours, slowly adjusting herself to the "days" and "nights" of Sam Beckett. In the early days of Sam's journey through time, the key personnel had all learned tricks for dealing with the need to be on-call at any time. Mostly, they slept when Sam slept, and woke when he woke, under the often-reliable premise that very little was likely to happen while Sam was snoring.

The psychiatrist stood up from her desk, shut off her computer, turned off her light, and left the room. Having an office at the edge of the Control Center, the hub of Project Quantum Leap, had its advantages and disadvantages. The biggest disadvantage, Verbeena thought, was that everyone in the Control Center knew who came to, or went from, her office. That wasn't a problem for many of the personnel on the Project, the majority of whom were civilians raised in a generation that accepted the occasional need for psychological help just as they accepted the occasional need for an antibiotic.

But for the military types? For them, it was hard enough to admit they might need help at all, harder still to ask for it. And to get one of them to walk through the Control

Center to talk to her was a feat in itself.

Take, for example, Admiral Calavicci. Typical of the military mind-set, Verbeena thought. She stood just outside her office and watched him, standing as he had so often since this Leap began, staring at the closed door to the Imaging Chamber. Staring as if the image of God Himself were emblazoned on it. Or, she thought, moving silently up behind him, the image of the devil.

Gushie and Tina were working at the console, doing whatever it was they routinely did after contact with Sam was broken and Al stepped out of the Chamber. They'd tried to explain their jobs to her, but the technical jargon that surrounded their explanations had left her more confused than before.

Now, they glanced nervously at the back of the admiral, unwilling to intrude on his thoughts, but obviously sharing Verbeena's increasing concern. Gushie watched her as she crossed the room, then nervously turned away, busying himself with Ziggy's needs.

She put a hand on Al's shoulder and felt him flinch from the touch. He didn't, however, pull away.

"You can tell me it's none of my business," she started quietly, "and maybe it isn't. But whatever was going on in '75, Al, I don't think you've really come to grips with it yet."

The muscles beneath her fingers cringed. But he still didn't move away.

"It might help to talk about it."

"I don't talk to shrinks," Al said finally. He ground out the words as if he were having trouble speaking. "Not back then. Not now."

"Why not?"

"Looks like crap on your record."

162

"Your record?" Despite the seriousness of the moment, Verbeena couldn't help laughing. "Al, don't you think, at this point, that's absurd?"

He didn't answer.

"Tell you what," she began, lowering her hand. And when she did, he turned around. The look in his eyes was something she wasn't prepared for. The normal, lively glint of attempted seduction was gone. The usual jaunty, self-assured leer was replaced by a glassy, haunted look. And Verbeena could smell the alcohol on his breath. She swallowed her surprise.

"Instead of talking to a shrink," she suggested, "maybe you should talk to a friend?"

Al seemed to consider her invitation. To her right, Gushie and Tina tried to ignore them, not very successfully. But Al seemed oblivious.

Then he focused, and seemed to remember the cigar that hung in one hand, the handlink in the other. He took a shaky breath and punched several buttons on the handlink; Verbeena doubted there was any real purpose to the gesture.

"Good idea," he muttered. "I know just the guy. Good ol' Jack Daniel's."

He stepped around her and tossed the handlink on the console. Neither Tina nor Gushie even tried to meet his eyes. He headed for the elevator and Verbeena started after him.

"Admiral!" she called, using her best authoritative voice. "Don't you think you've had enough to drink?"

Al stepped into the elevator and shook his head. "Not as long as I can still remember."

DAY 3

Tuesday, June 17, 1975

CHAPTER FOURTEEN

Dennis Stern rubbed his eyes and tried to stay awake. He was going to suffer from jet lag for the next ten years, he was sure. But the man in the barren, soundproofed room with him was having no such trouble. For him, the jet lag of flying to France from the Vietnamese jungle camp where he'd spent the last two years of his life was a distant memory.

"Can you be more specific?" Stern asked. The man across the table lit his cigarette and smoke filled the room.

"He's a damned traitor. The bastard."

The emotional accusations had been consistently free of facts for the last hour. Stern watched the slow winding of the tape in the recorder on the table between them, not sure if he should be frustrated by the lack of any substantive accusations or grateful for it.

"Please be specific," he said again. "What did he do?"

"We got him good," the man said quietly. His gaunt face was suddenly alive with the memory. "We got him for what he done to us."

167

"What—exactly—did he do?" Dennis repeated. Exhaustion was taking its toll. Six hours in flight, two hours to the safe house. And the time change. Despite the bright sunlight pouring in through the window of the house, his body told him it was the wee hours of the morning.

Once he'd gotten here, the colonel had refused to talk to him, but the colonel was refusing to talk to just about everyone, Stern discovered. The sergeant, on the other hand, seemed only too happy to talk. And that's what he'd done for the last hour.

Dennis glanced at his watch, still purposely set for Washington time. He had two hours to finish the interview, get on the phone to Bob so he could transcribe it, and hope to hell there was something in it Barrows and Weitzman could use in the hearing against Lieutenant Commander Calavicci.

Unfortunately, keeping Sergeant Young on the subject at hand wasn't easy.

"You know he was the one made sure we were left behind?" the sergeant informed him. The burly man tipped his cigarette into the ashtray and grinned. "But we got him. Yessir, we got him."

Dennis swallowed. "How?" The other questions weren't working; the sergeant seemed intent on describing his vengeance, and Dennis decided to let him talk. He knew that those who were suspected of collaborating were often shunned by the other men in the camp, and in a place where survival depended on the support of your fellow prisoners, that had sometimes proven deadly in itself.

"Just a game," the sergeant said. His eyes darkened. "But he lost."

"A game?" Stern leaned forward. This didn't sound like shunning. "What game?"

The sergeant grinned. " 'Judas's Judgment.' That's what the colonel called it. And Judas confessed real fast, then." He puffed on the cigarette. "Believe me, that bastard's guilty as sin."

Tuesday, June 17, 1975, 6:00 A.M.

It had been a long night. Long, frustrating, tiring, and depressing. Sam drove to the hospital, watching the Vega threaten to overheat again.

Al had been right: the barrage of tests Sam had compiled for Lieutenant Commander Calavicci had revealed a relatively fit man, somewhat undernourished, but in generally good health. They had also revealed an eight-year history of abuse and neglect that Sam couldn't remember having faced before.

Sam wasn't sure, but he didn't think Al had ever talked to him about Vietnam. He was pretty certain Al had never told him what had happened to produce the results Sam saw on the X-rays last night. Admiral Calavicci would never have told a farmboy from Indiana—even one with seven degrees—of acts committed in a POW camp that would leave still-healing wounds in 1975.

But Sam Beckett was a lot more than a farmboy, now. He was more than the MIT whiz kid who had won a Nobel Prize, more than the physicist who had built a time-machine. He had lived other lives, gained insights into other people's pleasures and pains. He had no trouble, now, interpreting the causes of those wounds.

He did have trouble sleeping.

He made it to the hospital just before seven and found Lieutenant Farraday waiting for him, her eyes a little red and puffy, but the coffee and donuts were present again, for which Sam was grateful.

"Good party?" he asked, taking the cruller from the brown bag she held out for him.

A low growl came from the nurse's throat. She eyed Sam's breakfast with loathing, then swallowed dryly, sank her teeth into the edge of the plastic cup in her hand, and gulped hot coffee.

"Any excitement *here* last night?" she asked.

"Not as much. We need to rearrange my schedule for the day, though." As they walked toward his office, he updated her on the most recent changes and ignored her occasional groans when he spoke too loudly.

"That hearing could go all day," she protested. "And with Jansen out—"

"Dr. Jansen's still gone?" Sam asked. He sat at his desk, a familiar, exhausting workload now looming ahead of him, distracting him from Farraday's hangover.

"Yeah. Said he had another meeting. And no, he didn't say what kind." She picked up Al's chart, hefting it; it had gained weight overnight.

"Whew! Is there any test you *didn't* run on him?"

"Pregnancy," Sam said without humor. Lieutenant Farraday chuckled.

"Did you have to do it all in one night?"

"Well—" Sam hesitated. He didn't like the idea that he'd actually been looking for evidence that Al was unfit to attend the hearing today. "I just thought I'd take advantage of the opportunity. Never know what might come up later." Close enough.

They spent the next hour and a half rearranging Wendell's schedule for the day. Sam expected he'd be back to the hospital by lunch, and would start his rounds then. That gave him three hours before discharge to see Terry Martin and try, once more, to get through to him before he was released. Barring that, he'd just have to hang around Chevy Chase tomorrow until Terry tried to kill himself, and make sure he prevented it.

They worked out Farraday's schedule for the morning, and he promised to call her at one if he thought he'd be delayed. Then he headed for "The Corridor," as he had begun to think of it.

Once more, the hologram met him at the elevator. Al was dressed in a somber and unusually restrained black suit, shot through irregularly with silver threads. Under the jacket, a deep purple shirt glistened with colorful rhinestones arranged over the left breast pocket. Punctuating the outfit was a black tie with semicircles cut out around the edges.

"What are you doing, Sam?" The look on his face was positively threatening and his eyes reminded him strongly of Lieutenant Farraday's.

"I'm going down to the basement."

"Sam, you're not going to that hearing!"

Sam met his eyes defiantly, then turned and stared at the elevator door. "Yes, I am."

"Sam, in the original history, Wendell Xiao did *not* go to that hearing!"

"Well, in case you haven't noticed, Al, I'm not Wendell Xiao."

"Sam, you've got patients to see! You've got to go talk to Terry Martin so—"

"I'm *going* to see my patients, Al," Sam hissed. "But I'm going to that hearing first. *You're* one of my patients, too, remember?"

"Sam, I'm not the reason you're here! You're here to save Terry Martin!"

Sam was glad no one else could hear Al, because his voice, in Sam's ears, had risen dramatically.

"I'm going to save him, Al, don't worry."

"Sam, if you talk him out of killing himself now, you could Leap!" He was practically begging. For a moment it almost stopped him.

Almost.

"Al, Ziggy says this Leap has something to do with you, doesn't she?" Al hesitated, a desperate look in his eyes. "Answer me, Al. Truthfully."

The door to the elevator opened, and Sam stepped out, knowing Al would not walk through this corridor, even as a projection. He turned and held the door, waiting several seconds.

"You're here to save Terry Martin," he said. His voice was flat, defeated.

"What *else* does Ziggy say I'm here to do?"

Al closed his eyes. "She isn't sure," he admitted.

Sam took a deep breath and started down The Corridor as both doors shut behind him.

Tuesday, June 17, 1975, 8:58 A.M.

Tess was just drying herself off from her shower when the phone rang. She raced to the bedroom, lunging for the phone, pulling it onto the floor in her haste.

"Conroy."

"Hey, Tess! How's your story coming?"

Tess sighed heavily and sat on the edge of the bed, toweling off her feet as she cradled the receiver between her neck and shoulder.

"Jackson. It's fine, thanks. Look, I'm in kind of a hurry right now, I've got—"

"I don't think you'll be in too much of a hurry when you hear what I've got to say," Jackson teased, his voice lowering seductively. "Tess Conroy, how would you like to get your hands on something bigger than Woodward and Bernstein ever had?"

Tess shook her head. "You forget, I've seen it. It isn't that big."

"I meant a story," Jackson explained, ignoring her intended insult.

Tess dropped the towel on the floor and stood, rummaging through her dresser. "A story that's bigger than Watergate?" she asked. "Come on, Jackson!"

"I'm serious, Tess. Look, I can't talk about it here, but— how about lunch?"

She pulled on her underwear and started bunching a pair of stockings, working them up her legs, glancing again at the clock. "I don't know, Jackson. Look, I have to get to Fort Belvoir this morning . . ."

"Tess, trust me, this is one story you *don't* want to miss out on!"

She finished with the stockings, shoved her feet into a pair of pumps, and sat back on the bed.

"Okay, why not? I'm picking something up at the Pentagon anyway. How about one?"

"Great. But not at the office. Meet me at that little Italian place in Rosslyn. Luigi's, remember it? Where we first met?"

"I remember." Tess sighed again. "Okay, I'll see you then. And this had better be good, Jackson, 'cause what's happening with the story I'm working on now is going to be hard to beat."

"I'll beat it," Jackson promised. "See ya."

She hung up, went to the closet, and found a short-sleeved cotton dress to wear. Something that wouldn't leave her sweltering as the day went on. Then, packing her notes and Kelly's research into her briefcase, she headed off in search of Colonel Deke Grimwold.

Tuesday, June 16, 1975, 9:05 A.M.

Sam stepped out of the elevator and walked through the basement corridor, mentally comparing it to death row.

Death row? What do I know about death row? Never mind, probably better not to ask.

He dodged the sacks of laundry, crossing the ceiling on the conveyor belt, the heavily laden cotton bags swinging through the air. Blue-clad men and women dragged the bags down, opened them, and dumped their contents into waiting bins. He walked on, wondering if any of them ever questioned what went on down here, right under their noses.

He reached Al's door, knocked, and, as usual, received no reply. He opened the door and stepped in.

Al was pacing, but this time he paced in uniform. It did a lot for his appearance, Sam thought. He looked hardly as battered as he had yesterday morning, and not at all as if he really needed another couple days' rest.

Once again Sam wondered about Barrows's excuse for the barrage of tests Sam had subjected his patient to. He had been on the phone with Barrows through the night, as each test came back with nothing significant enough to delay the hearing.

From Sam's perspective, the most disappointing part of the night had been that Al had never once made a pass at Nurse Long Legs, a fact Sam verified with her after explaining that he was hoping Al would.

"Too bad, really," she'd mused. "He's kind of cute."

Lieutenant Commander Calavicci interrupted his pace when Sam stepped in, a fact that didn't go unnoticed in the physicist's mind.

"Where's Bobby?"

Had Al still been wearing the hospital gown, Sam might have heard mild panic in the words. But coming from a man in a crisp white uniform, the question snapped like a command and left Sam feeling irrationally derelict in his duty by not assuring Barrows's promptness.

"Uh, I don't know," he stammered. "I . . . guess he's . . . running late."

Al stepped forward, not quite a steady step, but a very sure step nonetheless. "Late?" he demanded, looking up at Sam and down on him at the same time. "A captain in the U.S. Army is running *late* for a Senate subcommittee hearing?"

Sam cleared his throat. "A—*Senate* subcommittee?"

Al's eyes narrowed. "They really *are* keepin' you in the dark, aren't they?"

"Uh, well—" He grimaced and cleared his throat. Then a flash of inspiration came to him. "Well, maybe that's just as well, right? I mean—that way, it's not like—it isn't like I'm on *their* side," he tried, shamelessly playing on Al's paranoia.

Al stared at him through the smoke for a few seconds. "Yeah?" he asked. "Then whose side *are* you on?"

Sam shrugged and added a half grin. "I don't suppose you'd believe me if I said yours?"

Al turned on his heel and strode briskly across the room. "Damned right I wouldn't." He pushed the bed tray open, half tipping the radio as he did, and pulled several cigars from the compartment. Three of them disappeared somewhere in his jacket, and the fourth he unwrapped and started to light.

Sam waited, watching the man whose uniform seemed to have imbued him with a renewed sense of authority and self-assurance.

"Have you had—"

"Breakfast?" Al interrupted impatiently, snapping his lighter shut and putting it in his jacket. "Yes." He began again the pace that filled his days and nights. But this time he locked one arm at a stiff right angle behind his back and strode with his head up, facing Sam as he walked toward him. "Am I feeling better? Thanks, I feel just great," he continued sarcastically. "Is it past 0900? Yes." He glanced at his wrist, then held his clenched fist up so Sam could read from the standard-issue watch. "It's seven past, and we have a hearing—"

As he began his repeated assault, there was a quiet knock on the half-opened door behind Sam and Robert Barrows stepped in. Despite himself, Sam breathed a sigh of relief.

"Where the hell have you been?"

Al's verbal attack took Barrows off guard. The captain stepped back.

"I had some business to take care of at Fort Belvoir," he explained. "I got held up."

"Belvoir?" Al narrowed his eyes. "You had to go to Belvoir? What the hell for?"

Barrows didn't answer. Instead, regaining his own composure, he looked Al over, a critical inspection that started at the spit-polished, white shoes and ended at the perfectly aligned rows of medals on the jacket.

"Funny," he murmured. "You don't *look* like a horse's ass."

Sam opened his mouth to object to Barrows's implied insult. But a glance at Al told him that some inside joke had just been shared. The lieutenant commander's anger dissolved into a narrow gaze that admitted a reluctant concession.

"Yeah, well—don't feel much like one, either," Al muttered. And a smile laced his expression.

Barrows grinned back and checked his watch. "Ready?"

Without a word, Al started for the door, and Barrows moved aside to let him out first. Sam followed them down the hall and through a maze of hallways to a door that opened onto a small parking lot cluttered with trash bins.

It was only then that Barrows seemed to notice Sam was still with them. "Dr. Xiao?"

"I'm going with you to the hearing," Sam explained, crossing his arms over his chest to reinforce his statement.

He had deliberately not broached the subject earlier, especially with either of them alone. If there was an objection from one of them, he hoped the other might counter it. And if they both objected, he now had ample reason to push his point: he was Al's doctor, physician *and* psychiatrist. He had a right to be there.

Al concentrated on his cigar. But Barrows looked uncomfortable.

"There's really no reason for you—" he started.

"I'm his doctor," Sam explained. He had rehearsed this last night, and again this morning. "I'm supposed to evaluate his fitness for continued active duty, right?"

"You're supposed to have already evaluated him," Barrows reminded him.

"Well," Sam pressed, "this is—part of my evaluation." He caught the skeptical look in Al's eyes and turned back to the captain. "How he deals with . . . the hearing. I mean, he's been closed in that room for two days, he hasn't had a chance to . . . interact . . . with many people, yet, and I think—"

"Let him come," Al interrupted. He'd been studying Sam with a narrowed gaze. "Wouldn't hurt to have someone on *my* side there, right?" He looked pointedly at Sam, and Barrows winced.

"I don't know how long it'll take," the captain warned. "What about your other patients?"

"I've taken care of them."

Barrows sighed. "OK. Then let's go."

CHAPTER
FIFTEEN

Tuesday, June 17, 1975, 10:12 A.M.

The drive took nearly an hour. When he asked, from the back seat of the car Barrows drove, Sam discovered that Wainwright "and the others" would meet them there.

"There" turned out to be the Senate Office Building. They walked unchallenged through the basement hallways as Barrows led them through a labyrinth he was obviously familiar with. Outside a set of gray metal doors, Barrows stopped and looked at Al.

"Commander?" He was all military, a convention that seemed to be holding Al together for the moment. Al nodded once and Barrows pushed open one of the doors.

The underground room was lit by fluorescent lights hanging from the ceiling in long rows. The pale blue glow they gave off made everything in the room seem unreal, unearthly. The room was nearly empty, except for a few ugly pieces of bureaucratically inspired furniture. In the center was an oblong folding table, the kind Sam remembered from his school days. At the table, facing the far wall, were three equally ugly folding metal chairs. Colonel Jerry Wainwright stood up from one of them as the door behind him opened, and the look he shot Barrows across the room was filled with what looked to Sam like gloating victory.

To the right of the table, a small cluster of chairs was set up, as if for an audience. At the far end of the room, at a small raised dais, sat two men.

The man on the right was probably in his mid-sixties, Sam guessed. But he chewed nervously on a pencil, like a bored teenager in school. His hair had probably been black at one time; now, dark gray, it was combed back from his forehead to cover a bald spot. His round face and too-full lips made him look just a little self-indulgent. Or maybe, Sam thought, that was only because of the contrast between him and the man next to him.

Then, as Sam actually looked at the second man, he felt his breath shoved from his body.

"*Tall, skinny guy with a stovepipe hat . . .*" recited the voice in Sam's mind. "*He's got a Lincoln fixation, and he wants you declared non compos mentis.*"

"Weitzman!"

Senator Joseph Weitzman had been on the Committee that approved the funding for Project Quantum Leap; he had been on the Committee that *ran* the Project.

And he was here.

Lieutenant Commander Al Calavicci walked alone through the emptiness of the room, toward the table where Wainwright waited. But Barrows held back, hearing Sam's unguarded reaction. He let the door close and moved closer, concerned.

"You know him?"

"Uh—" Sam gulped for breath and shook his head. "Uh, just—I've heard of him," he struggled. He stared at

180

the man, the long, lanky figure a full head taller than the pencil-chewer next to him, even seated. He *wasn't* wearing a stovepipe hat, but his resemblance to Abraham Lincoln was still unmistakably cultivated.

"The other one's Senator Elwood Blackwell." Barrows gestured with his chin to the man gnawing the pencil. "He's not exactly sympathetic to our position."

"Our position?" Sam repeated dully. He was still staring at Weitzman, trying to gather his shredded memories of the man into some cohesive impression. Aside from a few un-flattering sentiments of Al's, Sam couldn't recall him; had he been one of those who'd opposed or supported Project Quantum Leap?

Sam couldn't remember.

"Blackwell chose Wainwright for this operation," Barrows explained. "Weitzman chose Dennis. That should tell you something about where we all stand on this."

"Where you stand?"

Barrows shrugged. "In case you haven't guessed, Doc, this isn't exactly the Peace Corps. If Al's really guilty, Blackwell will be more than happy—"

Sam turned from the haunting image of Abraham Lincoln. "Guilty?" he demanded, a little too loudly. "Guilty of what?"

The four men in the room all turned. Barrows seemed embarrassed.

"Excuse me, Mr. Senator," he said quickly, addressing Blackwell, "but I need a moment before we begin."

Without waiting for an answer, he grabbed Sam's arm, pulled open the door, and hustled the quantum physicist back into the hallway.

"Damn," he whispered, once they were alone outside. "I keep forgetting you haven't been briefed." He took a deep breath and crossed his arms over his chest. "Look, so I don't waste my breath or your time—what *do* you know about this?"

"Assume nothing." It had gotten very cold all of a sudden, Sam thought, staring at the closed doors to the chamber they'd just left.

Barrows scratched his fingers through his hair and took a deep breath. "We got out three of the POWs we wanted," he began.

"Three?" Sam repeated. "There are others?"

Barrows met his astonished gaze with suspicion. "Someone had to have told you at least *that* much! You're going to evaluate them when we fly them back."

"Uh, well, I—I guess, I've been so concerned with A . . . uh, Commander Calavicci, I forgot—" He didn't finish his excuse; Barrows wasn't buying it, in any case.

"They're still in France," Barrows explained. "They're flying in tomorrow night. We didn't want to take them any farther at first, they . . . weren't in as good condition as Al."

"The Vietnamese fixed him up before they sent him back," Sam protested.

Barrows stared hard at him. "Did *he* tell you that?"

"Yes," Sam answered, before he remembered that it had been the future Al who had told him, not the lieutenant commander.

"Damn."

"What?" The coldness of the corridor was seeping into Sam's bones. He shivered.

"Well, that only makes things worse." Barrows looked at him steadily. "The VC didn't 'fix up' the others, did they?"

Sam wrinkled his forehead, not sure he understood the implication in Barrows's words.

"We had information before Al came out that he'd collaborated with the VC while he was there," Barrows explained. "I didn't believe it, neither did Dennis or Senator Weitzman. And the information we had was, well, from questionable sources.

"So we sent Wainwright to France to question the other two. And according to Wainwright, they confirmed it."

"No," Sam whispered. He could feel the blood leaving his face, rushing to his stomach. He felt sick and weak and leaned against the wall. "No, he wouldn't—I *know* he wouldn't."

"That's how I felt," Barrows agreed, a slender smile of common belief on his lips. But it quickly left. "That's why Dennis is in France now. So he could talk to them himself. See if maybe Wainwright . . . offered them something. Or threatened them."

"He wouldn't collaborate," Sam repeated.

"Look, Doc, he admitted to it," Barrows confessed. Sam stared at him, his face twisted with disbelief. "Under sodium amytal."

He pulled away from the wall, suddenly angry. "I told you it was too much to use! He was probably responding to questions without really hearing them!"

"Let's hope so," Barrows said. "In any case, Dennis and I were on the phone most of the night. And we think we've got something that, well, maybe it mitigates what happened." He gestured to the doors behind him. "Coming?"

A second later the Door to the future opened behind Sam and he half turned at the sound.

"Yeah, in—in a minute." Sam nodded, trying to swallow without the pain of every muscle in his throat tightening at once. Barrows disappeared into the room and Sam whirled on Al.

183

"Sam. I *asked* you not to come here." Admiral Calavicci, in full-dress uniform, got the first words out.

"Well, *Lieutenant Commander* Calavicci wants me here."

"Well, *he*—" Al stabbed the air at the closed doors behind Sam, "doesn't know it's *you!*"

Sam hesitated, then said quietly, "Maybe not. But at least *he* trusts me."

Al stared at him, his mouth opening for a response that never came. Then, slowly, Al took a deep, defeated breath and tilted his head in a gesture that Sam recognized.

"Al, Barrows said that—" Sam closed his eyes. "Did you—did you collaborate with the VC?"

It was a horrible stretch of time and breath and hope from the question to the answer. Sam opened his eyes. Al met his gaze, the first second's hesitation already telling Sam to expect the worst.

"Yeah. I guess I did."

"You *'guess'*? What do you mean, you *'guess'* you did?"

"I helped them hide other POWs." Al's voice was quiet and monotonous, as if he were reciting a script. His alcohol-reddened eyes glazed over as he spoke. "I helped them camouflage the camps in the jungle so our reconnaissance wouldn't find them. I kept at least a dozen men from coming home. And that's just from the camp I was in."

"Why? Why would you—*Why*, Al?" Even from his own mouth, Sam couldn't believe, not deep within him.

"Whatever it takes to survive?"

Sam looked at his holographic guide and saw an unfamiliar look of self-loathing in his eyes. Sam shook his head.

"No, I don't—I can't believe you'd do something like that, Al."

184

The admiral's gaze shifted, as if he were repeating Sam's protest to himself. "Me either." He looked back and shrugged halfheartedly. "But I guess I did. Right?"

The question wasn't completely rhetorical.

Sam looked away, pressing his fingers tightly on the bridge of his nose. He turned back suddenly.

"No," he said, his hands gesturing denial. "No, if you'd really—if you'd done something like that, you'd never be an admiral now."

"In a game like this, kid, you don't go for the court-martial. Then the press gets involved and blows the lid off your nice little secret, *unauthorized* operation that involves two senators and a dozen upper echelons in all three branches of the service. And you don't make his life unpleasant, because then he might think he's got nothing to lose by going to the press himself. So you make him happy, keep him quiet, and tuck him away somewhere where no one will ever find him."

"Make him happy?" Sam repeated. He looked at the stars on the admiral's shoulders, at the rows of medals pinned to his jacket.

Al tilted his chin up at Sam's implication.

"Your whole career is a lie? A fake?"

"I wouldn't say that."

"Then what would you say?" Sam demanded. "You've only been home for two days and already you've been promoted! How long did it take you to make admiral?"

Al's face was emotionless.

Sam took a deep breath. "They made you happy," he said quietly. "So you'd keep quiet—about what? The fact that you came home in '75?" Al looked away, toyed with the box in his hand. "Or the fact that there are still other POWs alive over there?"

Al's silence was its own damning answer.

"Oh, Al!" Sam closed his eyes, the significance of what he'd stumbled onto suddenly overwhelming him.

"I didn't have a choice, Sam," Al protested.

The response slammed into Sam's memory and brought his thoughts back to the purpose for this Leap: Lieutenant Commander Calavicci, Sam thought, just might not agree with the admiral.

"Well, maybe you do now," Sam suggested. Al looked up, his forehead wrinkling in puzzlement. "Maybe—maybe you weren't supposed to keep quiet," Sam explained. "Maybe—maybe you should have—"

"No!" Al began to wave his hands in a frantic, repetitive circle. "No, Sam!"

"Ask Ziggy."

"No!" Al began pacing; the familiar idiosyncracy took on a pathetic twist in Sam's mind, now.

"Ask Ziggy what the chances are—that I'm here to make sure you talk to the press."

"No, Sam." Al let out a frightened breath and stopped pacing. "If the press gets hold of this, a lot of heads will roll, including, probably, Wendell's. I told you. This operation is unauthorized. The president doesn't know about it; Congress doesn't know about it. And if the press gets hold of it, you'll bring down a lot of people who only wanted to do something good and were willing to break the rules to do it."

"If this is against the rules, then how do you explain Weitzman's involvement? I seem to remember that *he* doesn't break the rules."

"No. He rewrites them." Al lifted the almost-abandoned cigar and took a puff. "You're not here to get the press involved, Sam."

186

"Ask Ziggy."

Al met his eyes for a second, then punched the handlink and waited. He shook his head and looked back. "Ziggy agrees with me."

For a moment the two men locked gazes; Sam wasn't sure he trusted Al's translation of Ziggy's data.

"If you're goin' to that hearing, you better get in there," Al finally said, breaking the silence and his unblinking stare at the same time. "They started without you."

Sam glanced at the doors behind him. "I thought you didn't want me there."

Al shrugged and punched the opening sequence on the link. "Well, I don't," he agreed. He looked up, met Sam's eyes for a second, then turned to the closed chamber doors. "But you're right," he added as the silver lining of the future engulfed him. "*He* did."

Sam watched the Door to the Imaging Chamber shut, then turned and opened the door to the chamber.

Captain Barrows had taken the seat to the left of Lieutenant Commander Calavicci, who sat between him and Colonel Wainwright. Both Blackwell and Weitzman watched Sam as he took one of the spectator seats, but neither man questioned his presence.

Al's expression was difficult to see. Sam had a better view of Wainwright, who sat closer; the man looked awfully pleased with himself, Sam thought.

"Commander," Blackwell asked, removing the pencil from his mouth, "how many other POWs were in the camp with you?"

Al leaned forward, speaking into a microphone set up on the table. It seemed silly to Sam; the room was small enough to hear Al's answer without a microphone. "Eight in the end, sir," he said. "However, there were four others

187

who passed through the camp.''

''And what happened to them?''

''Three of them were transferred out. The other one . . . died.''

''Commander,'' Blackwell continued, flipping through a pad of paper in front of him and apparently reading from his notes, ''while you were in the hands of the enemy in a time of war, did you, at any point, and without proper authority, act in a manner contrary to law, manner, or custom, to secure favorable treatment by your captors, to the detriment of your fellow prisoners?''

''Commander Calavicci,'' Weitzman interjected, cutting off any response Al might have made, ''did the VC tell the other prisoners that you had collaborated?''

Sam saw the ghost of a nod from Barrows in response to Weitzman's swift, almost unnoticeable look in his direction.

Al cleared his throat and looked uncertainly from one to the other. Then, speaking into the microphone, he said quietly, ''Yes, sir, they did.''

''You haven't answered my question, Commander,'' Blackwell pointed out.

''Military protocol, sir,'' Al explained. ''Follow last orders first.''

Despite himself, Sam grinned at Al's subtle defiance.

''And what was the response of the other prisoners to that information?'' Weitzman pressed.

''Answer my question, Commander,'' Blackwell ordered.

The tall, lean senator sighed quietly. He folded his hands in front of him and, without quite looking at Barrows, communicated his regret just as well.

Al hesitated before he leaned forward again. ''I acted under the authority of the senior ranking officer in the camp.''

"Did those actions include providing the enemy with information designed to aid the Viet Cong in hiding their prisoners from American intelligence forces?"

Sam watched Al carefully. Al said nothing. He leaned back in his chair, the muscles in his throat visibly distended as he swallowed.

"How did the other prisoners respond when they were told you'd collaborated?" Weitzman asked again.

Al took a deep breath. "I beg your pardon, Mr. Senator." He sounded tired. "I don't understand the question."

"Commander, I was a POW in Korea," Weitzman said.

Sam felt a moment of surprise at Weitzman's admission; he glanced at Al, and saw, instead, a far stronger look of shock on Barrows's face.

"Neither of us up here," Weitzman said, glancing at his colleague, "is an idiot. How were you treated by the other POWs after they were told you'd collaborated?"

Even from the distance at which he sat, even from the oblique angle of his view, Sam could see Al pale.

"I was under the impression, sir, that I was here to testify to my own actions. Not those of the other prisoners."

"You're here," said Blackwell, a glimmer of pleasure in his silver eyes, "to answer our questions, Commander. All of our questions. Would you like Senator Weitzman to repeat the last one?"

Al shook his head. "That won't be necessary, sir." His voice was no longer quite as steady. "The other prisoners . . . engaged in the usual forms of . . . ostracism. They'd stop talking when I was near; they developed codes I had no access to, for communication among themselves. That sort of thing."

Weitzman leaned forward, a long, languid motion. "I said that no one up here is an idiot, Commander." He waited, but Al said nothing. He opened a slim bound volume, one of

189

which lay in front of each of the senators. "According to one of the two men who returned with you, he and the other POWs, *under the authority* of the senior ranking officer," he added deliberately, "engaged in—and I quote—'a game called "Judas's Judgment." ' " He closed the volume and looked at Al. "Would you elaborate on how that game was played, Commander?"

Al's uniform was suddenly darker than his face. He leaned forward and spoke into the microphone.

"Begging the senator's pardon, sir," he said, "but go to hell."

Without warning, he was out of his seat and covered the distance to the door before anyone could react to what he'd said.

Barrows shoved his chair back and stood, moving toward Sam as they started to follow Al from the room.

"There goes breakfast," the captain predicted.

"It's the amytal," Sam said.

"Yeah, if hell froze over."

Sam hesitated a moment and met Barrows's eyes.

"Captain Barrows." They both stopped and turned at Blackwell's call. "I thought Commander Calavicci had agreed to cooperate." The senator was clearly exultant.

"He has, sir," Barrows answered tightly, "but I believe he was . . . unprepared for this line of questioning."

"This hearing is adjourned for the rest of the day," Blackwell said. "We will reconvene tomorrow morning at ten."

Sam opened the door and followed Barrows out, a half step behind him. Then, stopping just outside the chamber, Barrows took a long, sad breath and shook his head.

"*Now* you look like a horse's ass, Al," he whispered.

Less than a dozen feet away, Lieutenant Commander Calavicci leaned against the wall and retched on the floor of the Senate Office Building.

CHAPTER
SIXTEEN

No one spoke on the drive back to the hospital. Al leaned his head back against the car seat and closed his eyes. Barrows turned on the radio, and Sam, in the back, was just as happy no one felt like talking. *He* certainly didn't.

As hard as it was for Sam to believe that Al had collaborated with the enemy, after his examination of Lieutenant Commander Calavicci last night, he could understand it. Sam doubted *he* could have survived what Al had, much less retained his sanity.

But he wasn't convinced that Al *himself* believed he'd collaborated. The admiral had listed his crimes with well-rehearsed phrases that didn't ring true. And he seemed uncertain of his own motivations for what he'd admitted to, as if the memory weren't clear in his own mind.

Knowing Al as he did—or, at least, as he thought he did—Sam could imagine the returning POW shoving whatever had happened in Vietnam into a well-guarded corner of his mind and never thinking about it again.

Maybe never asking himself what really *had* happened. Or why.

And from what he knew of the real Wendell Xiao, Sam was willing to bet that Al had originally made it through Bethesda Naval Hospital without ever having the opportunity to talk about what *had* happened. Not, Sam admitted to himself, that Al would have been likely to take advantage of such an opportunity, even if it had presented itself. Not, at least, with Wendell Xiao on duty.

But this time it wasn't Wendell Xiao who was assigned to the operation; it was Sam Beckett. And Sam had seen the consequences of not facing the demons now; Admiral Calavicci had started drinking. Again.

Sam couldn't talk to the future Al. By now, the future Al probably didn't even know what was bothering him.

But this Al, who sat in his own self-imposed isolation, knew.

At the hospital Sam left Barrows to the task of seeing Al enclosed in his basement room, sensing that the captain might want a moment alone with the commander. But Barrows came back out almost immediately, shaking his head and stalking toward the elevator.

"I *knew* I should have warned him!"

"What happens now?" Sam followed him down the hall.

Barrows slammed his palm against the wall near the elevator and turned. "Now? I go try to smooth Blackwell's feathers. And Wainwright's."

"I mean—with the hearings."

Barrows shrugged. "They resume tomorrow."

Sam sighed. "What will happen if they think he's guilty?" he pressed.

Barrows gave him a long, suspicious look. "You're awfully interested in this case."

Sam cleared his throat and realized he wasn't acting like the real Wendell. "Well, it *is* . . . unusual," he tried.

"He won't be court-martialed, if that's what you're wondering. They couldn't do that without the press getting involved."

Since Barrows brought it up, Sam thought, he might as well get a second opinion about that. One that didn't come from the inebriated interpretation of a box of colored cubes.

"Well, what if they did? I mean, what if someone leaked it to the press?" Sam asked carefully.

The look in Barrows's eyes was as clear an answer as Sam could have hoped for. Between panic and anger and shock, the man's expression was too convulsed to misinterpret.

"My God, man, you didn't!"

"I didn't—? No!" Sam answered, realizing Barrows had assumed the worst. "No, no, I didn't—"

"Let me tell you somethin', Doc." Barrows ran a hand through his hair and shook his head. "I was married to the senior editor of *Cavalcade* magazine. This operation is so sensitive, I had to leave my wife so I could stay on it!"

Sam took in a sharp breath. "You left . . . your wife?" he repeated, disbelieving. "You left your own wife so you could—" The physicist felt a dull ache in the pit of his stomach.

"I wanted to make sure Al got home," he said, looking away, almost as if he were embarrassed. "If I hadn't stayed on this operation, they wouldn't—he wasn't going to be one of the ones we brought out."

When he finally looked back, he searched Sam's eyes. "He saved my life over there, Doc. Several times." The man shrugged. "I owe him.

"But all it would take is one reporter, and Blackwell will pull out all the stops," Barrows continued. The words pulled Sam's attention away from the inexplicable throbbing in the back of his mind. "Wainwright has a file on Al," Barrows continued, and held up his thumb and forefinger about two inches apart. "This thick."

"What kind of file?" Sam asked. His mouth felt dry.

"Nasty stuff. The kind of stuff that makes the press drool. The kind of stuff most of us have somewhere in our pasts, but wouldn't want made public." Barrows sighed. "We call it 'Plan B': Blackwell will make the media believe that we were approached by the government of Vietnam because of their humane desire to let a collaborator return home when he asked to. They court-martial him, and send him away to Leavenworth. Or, best case, just make sure he's publicly disgraced so no one would ever believe his side of the story. And then they let him crawl away into some little hole."

"How could they court-martial him for hiding POWs, and then deny there are POWs still alive over there? I mean, if the press finds out POWs are still alive and our government knows about it—"

"Wait a minute!" Barrows interrupted the barrage with a hand on Sam's arm. "Just because there *were* POWs alive over there early in '73, that doesn't mean there are still any alive now—two years later."

"But Al—Commander Calavicci is alive, and—"

"And collaborators get special treatment," Barrows finished, his tone of voice reminding Sam of the circumstantial evidence that only confirmed Al's confession.

"But—what if he told them there were others over there?" Sam pressed. "What if *he* went to the press and told them—"

"And told them he and two other POWs just came back and now he wants the government to get the others out?

Well, first of all, with no proof of any other POWs—"

"But there *is* proof," Sam interrupted. And as he said it, the expression in Barrows's eyes told him he'd made an error in logic. "You'd—you'd lie about it, wouldn't you?" Barrows said nothing.

Sam closed his eyes. It wasn't right: all the deceptions, the lies, the fabrications. The sacrifices.

"Al won't talk," Barrows continued. "If this operation shuts down, it'll be damn near impossible to ever start another one. Not only will the Vietnamese be less willing to agree, but, well, if this blows open, there won't be much incentive for them to keep our men alive any longer."

"They'd kill them?" Sam whispered, horror dropping the volume in his voice.

Barrows took a long moment to answer. He wouldn't look at Sam when he did. "Yes. And all their remains are repatriated. Blackwell makes sure the official autopsies reveal the men died years ago. And poof! No more POW issue." His eyes flashed for a moment, then lost their focus as he stared into his own grim prediction. "Gets rid of the major problem in the way of normalized relations." He looked at Sam again, and the physicist shivered involuntarily from the expression in Barrows's eyes. "Al won't talk," he repeated. "Not as long as there's a chance in hell of getting the others out."

And Sam understood. Al's silence had been protective: not so much for himself, but for all the others who still had a chance.

"Will A . . . Commander Calavicci, and the other two— will they ever know if you get the rest of them out?" Sam asked quietly.

Barrows almost chuckled. "You mean, are we going to

put out a monthly newsletter announcing how many alumni we have? Not likely.''

"They'll never know if—if any others come home?''

Barrows didn't answer the question. He didn't really need to, Sam admitted. "How are they supposed to explain where they've been for the last two years?''

"They each have a different story. Al's is that he was in France with Special Operations, engaged in counterintelligence against Laos and Cambodia. His records are being changed to reflect a tour of duty there, and the records of the operation he was supposedly involved in are going to be adjusted. We'll brief him on the details in the next few weeks.''

"And he agreed to this?''

"They all agreed to it, Doc. It was part of the understanding. On both sides of the fence. Besides,'' he added, "we've worked out nice deals for all three of them; they should be pretty happy with their lives, once they get past the readjustment.'' He glanced once more at Al's closed door, then started down the hallway. "Look, I have a couple senators I've got to talk to,'' he explained. "I'll see you in the morning, Doc.''

Sam watched him leave and turned, eyeing the door to Al's room for a long minute.

"*Once they get past readjustment . . .*'' More than twenty years from now, Sam thought, something about this "readjustment'' still didn't sit right with Admiral Calavicci.

Sam stared at the closed door another minute, then went back and knocked.

Lieutenant Commander Calavicci was changing out of his uniform when Sam came in, pulling the white jacket over the hanger lying on his bed. He didn't give Sam much attention.

"Feel any better?''

"Just great.'' He stripped to his underwear, then grabbed

196

the hospital robe and wrapped it around him. He already had a cigar lit, sitting in the ashtray, and he continued to ignore Sam, turning instead to the radio. He played with the dial, trying station after station, listening for a minute, then turning the dial again.

"What are you looking for?" Sam asked.

"That new music," Al answered, concentrating on the sounds coming through the small box. "What did he call it? Disc-something?"

"*Disco?*"

The tone of Sam's voice must have pulled Al's attention. He looked up.

"Don't like it much, huh?"

Sam winced and shook his head. "No."

Al went back to running through the stations. "What kind of music you listen to?"

Sam thought back and remembered the collection of tapes in Wendell's house; he and the psychiatrist had something in common. Maybe something in common with Al, too.

"Beatles."

Al snorted. "The Beatles?"

"And—well, rock and roll in general."

Al turned back to him, something in his eyes Sam didn't understand.

"Yeah, well, rock and roll is in the past." He stood there, waiting, not saying more, not yet returning to his quest. Sam was supposed to say something, maybe he was supposed to *know* something, and Al was waiting.

"And disco is—here. Now."

Al gave him a familiar, sardonic look. "Yeah."

Close enough, Sam thought.

Al finally succeeded in finding the horrible music and

197

turned to see Sam's reaction. He chuckled. "You really don't like it, do you?"

Sam remembered why he hated it; it seemed so fake, so superficial. The seventies had been a time of all-consuming me-ness, of mood rings and polyester suits. Disco never seemed significant, never important.

Then, looking at Al, he began to understand why he would find such attraction there; Al needed something that wasn't "important," something that demanded nothing more of him but enjoyment. Something that would give him time to heal, to forget, to create a new Al Calavicci, one who could face life again.

"You have anything to wear besides your uniform?" he asked suddenly, inspired by a memory and an idea.

"What?"

"Do you have anything—"

"Yeah, a couple shirts and some khakis. Why?"

"Get dressed."

"What?"

"Just do it. I'm going to check another patient and I'll be back here in about fifteen minutes. Be ready."

He left before Al could ask anything further. He took the elevator back to the fifth floor and found Terry Martin, dressed and packed and ready to leave. Sam glanced at his watch.

"I thought discharge wasn't for another three hours," he said, entering the room and catching Terry by surprise. The young man turned from his efforts to force his small suitcase closed.

"Oh, hi, Doc. Yeah, well, the doctor said I could leave. Said there was no reason to keep me. And it was easier for my sister to meet me now."

Sam walked in and sat on the edge of the bed, trying to meet Terry's eyes.

"How are you feeling about . . . everything?"

Terry shrugged and swallowed tightly. "Well, it still hurts, but—like you said—I guess it's just gonna take some time, right?"

The words were right, but the tone wasn't. And neither was the fact that he wouldn't look at Sam.

"Terry, I read the accident report. You swerved the car to avoid hitting a kid on a bicycle. You did what anyone would have done. You weren't drinking, you weren't on any drugs, you have nothing to feel—guilty about."

Terry looked at him then. "Except maybe killing Cheryl." He said it quietly. There were no tears in his eyes now. He picked his suitcase off the bed with his good arm and turned to leave.

"Terry, you didn't have any choice! You can't blame yourself for what happened. It was an accident."

"Yeah. Thanks, Doc. I know." Terry left, and Sam considered following him. But he'd closed up, and Sam knew, even without training, that they weren't going anywhere right now.

He stood, took Terry's chart back to the nurses' station, and made his final note.

The man looked at him oddly.

"Are you sure this is the brand you want?" he asked.

Mark Davalos compared the cigar in his hand with the one in the box, very carefully, checking for the third time.

"Yeah," he said. "That's the brand. See?" He held out his sample for the tobacconist's inspection.

"These are pretty pricey, son," the man warned.

"That's the brand!"

It wasn't the man, or his attempt to keep Mark from spending too much on a box of cigars that bothered him, Mark admitted to himself. It was his own guilty conscience.

He paid for the cigars and took them out of the store, wandering through the mall, not really concentrating on anything in particular.

He hadn't slept worth beans last night, and he'd woken up with a headache from the beers that hadn't made anything clearer. So he'd called in sick and headed for the mall to keep his promise to a man he had already probably betrayed.

In the four years since he'd worked in the Special Security Division, he'd *never* done anything like he'd done last night. *Never* broken security.

Not that he hadn't been in worse situations, right? Like two years ago, when they'd brought in the spy from Russia? And that trade with Nicaragua, the year before that?

But there was something different about this one. Maybe just 'cause he got to see the guy's face. Got to really see him. Look him right in the eye.

It was a real human being this time. Not a case number, not a name.

That made things different.

He rearranged the packages under his arms: a tape recorder and a few more tapes, and a box of cigars.

Maybe he should call Jackson, see if he'd found anything out. Maybe he should call him off, tell him to leave it alone.

But he wasn't sure, now that he was sober, how much he'd actually told Jackson. Maybe he hadn't said too much after all.

Maybe he'd only hinted at—

For the hundredth time, he churned through the faded memories.

He went back to his car and loaded his bags in, and decided that maybe it'd be a good idea to just keep his mouth shut from now on.

CHAPTER

SEVENTEEN

Twenty-eight hours.

Twenty-eight hours before the deadline that would make her career. And in July her name would be scorched across America with the cover story of *Cavalcade* magazine.

Tess Conroy sat in the small Italian restaurant on the edge of the Potomac River, smoking a Camel and waiting for a man she barely liked to show up for lunch. So far, the day had been less than promising, but not quite disappointing.

The drive to Fort Belvoir had been a waste of time from one perspective: Colonel Deke Grimwold, purported witness to Maggie Dawson's death, was no longer stationed at Fort Belvoir, she'd been told. And a two-hour, bureaucratic whirlwind of being shuffled from office to office, from the Welcome Center to the public relations bureau, had finally yielded limited information: a suspiciously timed transfer of Colonel Grimwold had taken place early that morning.

From another perspective, though, the visit *had* been useful. The helpful information specialist, who suspected nothing, volunteered the fact that a Captain Barrows had also been by earlier looking for Colonel Grimwold. Funny, the young man mused: no one seemed to have been notified of the colonel's reassignment, except the colonel.

Tess had smiled thinly, thanked the man for his help, and left the base. Her next stop was Captain Robert Barrows's office. There, once past security, she had found the lovely Bonita in full bubblegum glory, ready to hand over the promised lists of men who were still MIA, and those who had returned during Operation Homecoming.

"Is Captain Barrows in?" Tess asked, hoping against hope. It was after noon, and she glanced at her watch to indicate her impatience.

"Nope. Said he'd be in this afternoon, though." Pink gum snapped between the women.

"I'll come back later," Tess promised.

Now, Tess waited for Jackson Fellows in the restaurant where, three months ago, they'd met.

By the time he arrived, Tess had ravenously consumed two baskets of bread sticks and three glasses of Coke. She wasn't hungry any more.

"Hi, honey," Jackson greeted her, leaning over to plant a kiss on her cheek before she could protest. He sat across from her in the booth she'd taken and looked around for their waitress. "Sorry I'm late," he apologized, leaning closer, his hands folded in front of him.

In his uniform, he was actually a very handsome man, Tess admitted to herself. He was a little on the slender side for Tess's ideal, but his hair was dark and wavy, his eyes were a very deep brown, almost liquid brown, and his square jaw balanced a broad forehead. He had nice hands, too, Tess thought, looking at the long fingers clasping themselves on the tabletop.

If only he weren't so pushy about getting into bed! If only he'd listened when she'd said "no."

Oh, well. Water under the bridge. If Maggie Dawson had to sleep her way to a Pulitzer Prize–winning story, Tess thought, maybe *she'd* have to, too.

"So?" she prompted, after Jackson had waved down their waitress and ordered a small pepperoni pizza for himself; Tess declined anything more to eat. The bread sticks were already bloating her stomach.

"Before I say anything, we need a few ground rules."

"Ground rules?"

"Hey! All informants get something in return, right?" he joked. Tess grimaced. "Including a certain amount of confidentiality."

Tess breathed hard. "What do you want?" she asked as piped Italian music filled the restaurant. *Oh, solo mio . . .* She drummed her fingers on the table.

"A date with you," Jackson said. She looked up. "No pressure," he promised, fanning his hands in the air. "You don't have to do anything you don't want to."

"You've said that before," she reminded him.

"Well, I mean it this time." He reached across the table and took her hand. "Honest, honey, I really mean it. You can draw the lines."

She sighed and glanced around the packed restaurant. "Alright," she agreed. He smiled, a devilish, seductive smile that had once turned her loins to butter. Once. "If the story's real," she cautioned, and pulled her hand away. "And only after I get the story I'm working on finished."

"It's real," Jackson promised. The waitress brought him a beer and he took a sip, waiting for her to leave before he

203

leaned forward again and lowered his voice.

"I've got a friend, works for one of those intelligence divisions no one's supposed to know exists," he started, and Tess began dismissing the story immediately. "I invited him to the party last night, 'cause I though he'd be the kind of guy you'd want to meet. He works out of NAVINT, usually down in Crystal City, but sometimes he's stationed at the Pentagon. That's how we met."

On the other hand, Tess thought, she'd pursued this relationship with Jackson because she had word from a reliable source that he himself was involved in one of these "divisions." Maybe it was worth listening, at least.

"What's his name?"

"Mark. Davalos, but—you can't talk to him. I mean," he added, hastily taking another sip of beer, "you can't let him know *we* talked. Ground rule, okay?"

She nodded, not yet interested. She was still thinking about Grimwold being transferred from Belvoir this morning. She wanted to get this lunch finished so she could catch Barrows in his office and ask him about it.

"Mark's a straight shooter," Jackson continued. "He's never lied in his life, probably. He's the kind of guy who's so sweet and nice you immediately suspect him, right?" Tess smiled and took a drink. She knew the type. "Well, in Mark's case, it's not a cover. And I'll tell you, the Chief of Naval Operations himself would probably trust this guy to shave his balls!"

Tess choked on her Coke; Jackson could be crude, but she'd never heard *that* before. Maybe it was Navy slang, or something.

"That's why I believed him."

"Okay, so what did he say?" Tess prompted, wiping up the spilled Coke and glancing at her watch.

"He's involved in some kind of operation to bring home MIAs," Jackson whispered. "And the first one is at Bethesda Naval Hospital right now."

In her mind, disjointed pieces of information—Kelly's research, her own work, her meetings with Barrows, and her instinct—began to form a picture.

"Are you sure?"

"Mark says he's in a room in the basement. He's got a doctor named—damn, what was that name? Something Chinese, I think."

Tess waited as he downed more beer.

"Chow, I think," he finally told her. "Yeah, Chow."

"How do you know he's an MIA?" Tess asked, lowering her own voice. Not that anyone else in the restaurant was paying attention.

The waitress arrived with the pizza and Jackson pulled a slice from the tray. "Mark picked him up at the airport. He's been briefed on the details, but he didn't tell me."

"Why did he tell you about it all?"

Over the next three pieces of pizza, Jackson summarized his conversation with Davalos, who, Jackson guessed, had just come face-to-face, for the first time, with the person around whom one of his operations centered.

"Tell you the truth, I think this is the first time they took him out from behind the desk, you know? I think he was surprised at what really goes on."

Tess thought she probably would be, too, but didn't ask any more about that aspect of Jackson's tale. Her mind was still busily digesting the information Jackson had given her, putting it together with everything else.

A POW just returning from Vietnam. A story about Maggie Dawson just resurrected. An Army captain, paling at the sight of a five-year-old picture. And a colonel at Fort

Belvoir transferred the morning she was going to talk to him. The morning *after* she'd prowled the post looking for him.

"I don't suppose," she tried, starting her first cigarette since Jackson had arrived, "that you've got a name for this POW?"

Jackson shoved half a piece of pizza in his mouth, and grunted. "Yeah, he told me. Damn, what was it?" He chewed the pizza and took another swig of beer. "Some Italian name," he said at length. Then he smiled and looked around him. "That's why I thought of coming here, huh?"

"Right. So?"

Jackson thought hard for a moment, his forehead wrinkling with the effort. He shook his head. "Sorry, honey, I was . . . a little drunk, I guess. What the hell—Cal? Al. Al, that was the first name."

Tess waited, her palms sweating, her mouth dry. She swallowed some more of her Coke.

"Cala-something. Like that flower," he muttered, and picked a piece of pepperoni from his teeth.

"Cala lily?" she whispered. That would be close. Damned close.

"Calavicci!" Jackson crowed. "That was it! Al Calavicci."

Tuesday, June 17, 1975, 1:15 P.M.

"So what kind of car is this?"

Sam drove Wendell's car through the growing heat of mid-June. For the moment, he was risking the air-conditioning, but the temperature gauge was beginning to creep up.

"It's a '72 Vega. And I have no idea why Wend . . . um, I mean, why I bought it. It overheats all the time."

Since they'd sneaked out of the hospital fifteen minutes ago, Al's attention had been riveted by nearly everything he saw. He asked endless questions, trying to fill in the gaps, the missing years of his life. Sam answered as well as he could, but his own memory had holes in it, and some things he just didn't know.

Being out of the hospital, out of the clutches of the operation he'd found himself suddenly thrust into, Al had perked up. At one point, Sam even caught him eyeing a woman on the street, a long-absent, appreciative gaze just beginning to reappear; Sam had never thought he'd be glad to see *that*!

"So. Where you taking me?" he asked at last. Sam had driven down Wisconsin Avenue, taking a direct—if tedious—route back to the city.

"I'm trying to remember how we got there," Sam muttered to himself.

"How we got—you're taking me back to the hearing?" The sudden hostile suspicion grabbed Sam's attention. He turned.

"No," he said, trying to recapture the calmer man who was disappearing by the second. "No, just relax. It's just been a while, and I'm trying to remember how to get there."

"Where?" Still cautious, Sam heard.

He smiled. "You're gonna love this place, Al—" He stopped, realizing that, for a moment, he had forgotten: this Albert Calavicci wasn't yet his friend. "Uh, Commander."

He waited, but Al said nothing. "Look, would you mind if I . . . call you Al?" he asked quietly, watching the road.

"Why not? The way things are going, I don't think the

uniform's gonna last much longer.''

"You might be surprised," Sam muttered.

"Not anymore." The bitterness had returned, and Sam waited, wondering how to draw him back out.

He didn't have to. A minute later Al took a deep breath. "You didn't answer my question. Where are we going?"

"You'll see."

Al was quiet, having exhausted his need for information. At least, for now. He leaned forward and turned on the radio.

"You mind?" he asked.

"No, go ahead."

He scrolled through the dial until the disco sound that captivated him blared through the car. Sam risked a glance at him, remembering better times. Commander Calavicci stared out the window, still watching the world intently as it passed them by. But he was relaxing again, his face less pinched. Then Tony Orlando and Dawn tied an ugly yellow ribbon around the moment.

Sam lurched forward, not quickly enough, shutting off the horrible song and winning a long examination from his passenger before Al leaned forward and turned the radio back on.

"I wanna hear it," he growled. He sat back and stared out the side window.

Sam gripped the steering wheel tightly, ground his teeth, and said nothing. But his memory returned to San Diego, to a warm April night and the sound of "Georgia" filtering from the bungalow across the street.

Would it have been so bad after all? he wondered. *Would it have really been so bad just to tell her he was alive?*

When the song ended, Al took a deep breath, still looking

away. "God, I hope—she's happy," he whispered sincerely.

They drove without a word for another forty minutes before Al finally spoke again.

"You're lost, aren't you?" He seemed to have regained his equilibrium.

"I know it's here, somewhere," Sam protested, looking at every building as they drove through the crowded city. "I just can't remember—" He stopped, a horrible thought suddenly crawling through his mind. "What if it's not here yet?"

"Yet?"

"Still," Sam corrected. "It's . . . been a few years since—No. It is here!" He shifted in his seat, relieved by the sudden memory: they had last come here, he and Al, for its twenty-fifth anniversary.

Just before he Leaped.

He stared out the window, eyeing every building they passed until, finally, he saw it.

"There! There it is!" He gestured out Al's side of the car and Al followed the direction.

"Looks like a lot of fun," he said dryly.

"Don't judge it too soon." Sam found a parking spot half a block away, and they walked back.

By day, the Harbor Light was a hole-in-the-wall restaurant that barely kept one waitress and the owner busy. But by night, it was one of the best-known secrets in town, a place where everyone from construction workers to lobbyists could be found.

At night, even long after the height of the disco fever, the Harbor Light turned off its lights, turned on the rotating globe, and cranked out enough disco to keep John Travolta in business for the rest of his life. Twenty years after disco had hit its peak and then plummeted to become what Sam considered a well-deserved cliché, die-hard fans of the music could still find one small alcove where the music reigned. Sam had always believed the owner had a peculiar fascination for the seventies, but then, it did keep him in business.

Whenever he and Al had come to Washington—for congressional meetings, appropriation hearings, technical reviews—Al had insisted that they come here at night, at least once each visit.

They stepped into the nearly deserted restaurant, Al looking around him with mild curiosity. "Geez, of all the places to go, *I'd* have picked this one," he said.

Admittedly, the place looked like a dive, Sam thought: worn, dark red plastic-covered booths, old linoleum on the floor, and fluorescent lights. But Sam knew the magic of this place, and he smiled at Al.

"Go grab a booth. I'll be right back," he said, and turned toward the bar in front of him. Al stared after him, then went to the nearest booth and slid in.

The left side of the restaurant was for patrons who wanted to eat; the center was devoted to those who wanted to drink; and the right was for those who wanted to dance. The dance floor never opened before six, Sam remembered, but as he approached the bar and saw the familiar face of the owner, he knew an exception was about to be made.

"Excuse me," he said, "are you Pete?"

The bartender looked up from his newspaper, oblivious to the fact that anyone had entered his establishment.

"Yeah," he said. "Help you?"

Pete had been a POW, Al had once told Sam. He'd lost a leg in the camp, and was one of the first POWs traded back to the United States. Sam had never discovered whether Al had known the man in 'Nam or had just struck up a casual friendship with him after he'd discovered the Harbor Light, but whichever it *had* been, Sam now knew how it was *going* to be.

"My name's Wendell Xiao," Sam said, shaking Pete's hand. "A friend of mine told me about this place."

"You want lunch?"

"No, actually—I hear you've got a great dance floor."

"Yeah, well it don't open up 'til six-thirty. But come on back, OK?" Gruff, but not unfriendly. He turned back to his paper.

"See that guy over there?" Sam asked, gesturing to Al sitting in the booth: aside from the commander, only four other people were in the restaurant, and two of them were at the bar with Sam. Pete looked up.

"Yeah."

"He's a buddy of mine. He was a POW in Vietnam, and he's been . . . in the hospital since he came home. Just got out. And I was wondering," Sam added, pulling a twenty out of Wendell's wallet and laying it surreptitiously on the counter, "if maybe you could open up the floor a little early."

Pete eyed the twenty, then looked back at Sam. "POW, huh?"

"Yeah."

"There long?"

"Too long."

Pete glanced back at Al, who fidgeted and looked at Sam, and gestured with his hands: *what are we doing here*?

"You think he'd like to rock and roll?" Pete asked.

"Disco," Sam said firmly. "He wants . . . disco."

Pete picked up the twenty and said, "This'll buy you enough beer to get both of you drunk." He turned around and called to the woman who sat alone in a booth near Al. "Christy!"

She looked up from studying a book in front of her, and Pete gestured her over. Al was watching, suspicion growing in his eyes again.

Christy was an attractive young woman, probably in her late twenties, and her dark eyes looked Sam over appreciatively as she came over.

"Christy, do me a favor, hun," Pete said, leaning forward. "Take your nose outta your books and go light up the floor."

"You're opening the dance floor at this hour?" she asked, glancing at her watch.

"Special request. Hell, why not?"

The young woman was either a regular or a friend, Sam thought, and she shrugged good-naturedly.

"And after that," Pete added before she turned away, "take this guy out on to the floor so he can show his buddy how to boogie."

"Sure," Christy said, obviously liking that idea.

Sam grinned, watching her departing figure as she crossed behind him. Then he pulled his eyes away, cleared his throat, and turned to Pete.

"Thanks," he said. "You have no idea how much this means."

"Don't get mushy," Pete ordered.

Sam went back to the booth and took Al's arm. "Come on."

"What's all this about?" Al asked. He was beginning to lose his interest, his enthusiasm, even his desire to find out what Sam had planned. Sam just smiled at him and led him through the darkened bar, past the man and woman who sat there, taking him to the floor.

And suddenly the magic happened. The lights went down, the music came up, and the globe above them began to rotate, showering them with a storm of shooting stars.

Al beamed. "Oh, hey! Lights! That's great!"

"It isn't disco without the lights," Sam said. Christy was waiting for him on the floor. "I'm only gonna show you once," Sam said, "so pay attention."

It was almost fun this time, Sam thought, dancing the ridiculous movements that had captivated a decade. Christy moved with him as if they'd practiced the steps for weeks. Sam paid attention only to trying to remember the swings, the turns, the hip thrusts, the hand gestures. He felt like an idiot. But when he glanced at Al he saw renewed joy in his eyes, a smile creeping onto his face almost against his will.

When the song ended, Christy left Sam and walked toward Al, her hips wiggling just a little more than necessary.

"Your turn," she said, grabbing his hand.

"Oh, no, no, I—I haven't danced in years," he apologized, and pulled away.

Sam crossed the floor and saw that the other patrons in the bar and restaurant had left their places to stand near the floor, watching the demonstration.

Christy lowered her voice and said, with a look that made Sam's mouth water, "Something tells me you used to be a dancing king." There was no mistaking the tone of her voice, either. Sam cleared his throat, embarrassed by the disconcerting thoughts that were creeping through his mind.

"And there are some things," she added, moving her face very close to Al's, taking his hand again, "you never forget how to do."

And then, Sam saw it: Calavicci was back! The look Al turned on Christy would have scared him if Sam hadn't known he was essentially harmless. And Christy seemed completely unconcerned. Al followed her and Sam waited by the side, smiling.

Al caught on fast and didn't seem to mind the audience. There were times when he winced with pain from the moves, but nothing was going to stop Calavicci.

By the time the "Hustle" ended, Al seemed comfortable with the basic steps. Sam grabbed the hand of the woman who'd been sitting at the bar and took her onto the floor. When the bar opened officially, nearly four hours later, everyone but Pete was out there, dancing and sweating and laughing. Sam's partner couldn't dance to save her life, but she was willing to go through the motions of trying, and she'd had enough to drink to keep anything from embarrassing her.

Sam watched Al, never forgetting the purpose for all of this, never forgetting his charge. The bruised and battered lieutenant commander was recovering, Sam thought; he was learning to laugh again, to trust again. To have fun. And once, when he caught Al's gaze across the floor, the lieutenant commander gave him a grateful smile and a familiar wink.

But as the crowd grew to fill the room, a change came over Al; the press of people seemed to bother him. The look of growing terror in Al's eyes told Sam it was time to go.

He pushed his way through the people, grabbed Al's arm, and took him off the floor, waiting to say anything until they were in the bar.

"You don't want to overdo it too soon," he said. Al took a deep breath, recovering from the sudden claustrophobia, and closed his eyes, trying to catch his breath.

"Dammit," he whispered.

Sam waited until Al's breath became regular again. "It'll get better," he said quietly. He wasn't sure at first if Al could hear him over the music. But the terror slowly ebbed and Al looked at Sam and smiled.

"Yeah," he agreed. "It will."

CHAPTER
EIGHTEEN

The phone rang, startling Lynn Farraday from her novel. She grabbed the receiver, put a bookmark in her paperback, and said, "Floor Three, Nurse Farraday."

"Hey, honey, it's me. Jackson!"

Lynn smiled, the memory of last night's party now pleasant enough without the hangover she'd battled this morning.

"Hi, Jackson. Didn't expect you to *actually* call."

Jackson Fellows was, by definition, an irresponsible, childish, lecherous man for whom life was a party or nothing at all. A night with Jackson was just that: a night. Lynn knew what Jackson was and wasn't capable of, and she rarely expected more from him than she got. So, sometimes, like now, she got more than she expected. That was the beauty of setting low expectations for the man.

"Well, I said I would," he responded, sounding mildly wounded. "Listen, honey, I'm calling to ask a favor."

"I knew it."

"Listen, I've got a friend, she's been invited to a costume party. Spur of the moment thing, but—well, her boss expects her to be there."

Lynn listened as Jackson wove a tale she wasn't entirely sure she believed. In the background, she could hear Italian music, and she knew where Jackson was: that little Italian place where she and he had met some months ago, out in Rosslyn. She knew that's where he was; it was the only Italian joint he'd go to.

"So? How do I fit in?"

"Well, it's more like—*what* you fit in."

"What?"

"Well, honey, I kind of . . . suggested she should go to this shindig as a nurse. Make some points with the boss, right? He could play doctor . . . Anyway, you're about the same size, so I thought—could I borrow one of your uniforms?"

Lynn felt her mouth hanging open as the door to the elevator in front of her slid in the same direction. Captain Robert Barrows, identified by his name badge, stepped out and stood over her, his face dark and gaunt, his eyes not at all near civil.

"Yeah, sure," she said hastily. She had to get off the phone. Having summoned Barrows, she'd damn well better be prepared to talk to him. "Look, I'm off at three-thirty. Come by my apartment around four, okay?"

"Honey, you're a dream!"

"Yeah. Look, Jackson!" she called, just before he hung up. "I need it back by Friday. Cleaned and pressed, got it? No stains, or you pay for a new one."

"You got it, honey. Thanks a million!"

She put the receiver down and stood. "Captain Barrows, I'm—I didn't mean to be—"

"Where is he?"

Farraday gulped. Maybe, after all, she shouldn't have called him. But she hadn't known what else to do.

"I don't know. No one saw them leaving."

"Them?"

She inhaled. "Dr. Xiao hasn't been back, either. Well, he *did* check one of Dr. Jansen's patients, but that was all. No one else has seen him or Commander Doe since this morning."

Barrows scoured his face with his hands. "Let's go."

Without really waiting for her to follow, Captain Barrows led her back to the elevator and down to the basement. They checked John Doe's room, a perfunctory search giving no indication that he didn't intend to return: the radio, the novels, his cigars, uniform, clothing, everything he'd had was still there.

"Damn!" Barrows, Lynn thought, could be intimidating when he wanted to be. Not, she guessed, that he usually was; he just wasn't the type. "Any idea where Xiao would have gone? Any idea at all?"

Lynn shook her head, and Barrows tilted his to the side, as if he didn't believe her.

"Look, Lieutenant, I'm one of the good guys, alright? I know you and Dr. Xiao have been seeing each other. Unofficially."

"We haven't exactly . . . been seeing each other," she protested, feeling her face and neck grow hot with embarrassment. "We just . . . went out. Once or twice."

"Well, did he mention anything—once or twice—that would give you a clue—"

Farraday, shaking her head as he asked, cut him off. "He's one of those really closed-up people, Captain. I never found out a thing about him. Still haven't."

The man laughed quietly. "That's the first thing I've heard so far that seems consistent with the man we chose."

217

"Excuse me?"

Standing in the middle of the dark basement room, Barrows crossed his arms and evaluated her. She waited, hands clasped behind her back, almost at attention.

"Have you noticed anything—odd, or different—about Dr. Xiao since—well, since Commander Doe arrived?"

Lynn swallowed nervously, not sure what to say. "Anything—like what?"

Barrows shrugged one shoulder. "I don't know, anything that—might not be in keeping with his character."

Lynn looked away. Actually, she had. Unfortunately, she liked this new Wendell Xiao more than the old one. For the first time since she'd known him, he really seemed to care about his patients, not just about his work. He really seemed to care about a lot of things.

"Well," she said, watching Barrows's eyes, "he does seem . . . more involved than usual."

"More involved?"

"She gestured to the radio and the half-read novel lying open on the bed. "He asked me to get those for Commander Doe," she explained. "And I'm pretty sure he sneaked that ensign back down here yesterday. The driver, remember him?"

"Davalos?" Lynn nodded and Barrows mirrored the wrath of God on his face. "Are you sure about that?"

"Um—well, no, not exactly. But he came back here, and Dr. Xiao took him—I assumed he came down here."

Barrows gnawed the inside of his cheek and nodded. "Great. Our security's been compromised, our only doctor is AWOL, and Commander Doe has vanished. Dammit!"

After a few more minutes, Barrows decided there was nothing, at this time, that they were going to do except wait. Lynn suggested that, given Dr. Xiao's uncharacteristic concern for his patients—especially, Commander Doe—it was likely that wherever they had gone, they'd gone together.

When she finally left, Barrows had taken up a watch in the basement corridors, making the rounds of the two entryways Xiao and Commander Doe might use to return. He told Lynn to brief her replacement and have her check down here every half hour.

"Should I call anyone else, sir?" she asked as she headed back for the elevator. "Colonel Wainwright or—"

"Hell, no!" Barrows caught his own panic and laughed harshly. "Lieutenant, all we need is for *him* to get wind of this and all our asses are in the sling. Got it?"

"Got it. Sir." She left, sinking her finger heavily on the elevator button, then leaning back against the wall.

Sometimes, she was glad she listened to her instincts. Colonel Wainwright had told her to call *him* in the event of any unusual activities regarding the "John Doe" case. And Captain Robert Barrows, separately, had told her the same thing.

Well, Captain Barrows's name was listed in the chart, and Wainwright's wasn't. So if push came to shove and she had to defend her decision not to call Wainwright, she could always fall back on what was written.

She didn't have to explain that Wainwright scared the hell out of her.

Tuesday, June 17, 1975, 4:00 P.M.

She was cutting it close, she knew that. It had taken Tess longer than she'd hoped to confirm the few pieces of information she needed about Albert Calavicci's ex-wife. And one piece of information was still missing: she wasn't sure how she'd bluff her way through this without knowing the woman's new married name.

And, of course, the detour to Captain Barrows's office, a stopover she'd indulged in right after lunch with Jackson on the off chance that his information didn't pan out, had taken longer than she'd expected, too. Security was still tighter than a drum.

Barrows's appearance had gone downhill. If he'd looked bedraggled yesterday, today he looked ''cat dragged in.'' His eyes were sunken into pale caves of flesh. His hair was ruffled, as if he'd been running his hands through it too often. And his lips were dry, cracked, as if he had given up drinking water for the last thirty days.

He'd looked up from his desk when she came in, the resignation in his eyes promising a breakthrough for Tess.

''I got the lists,'' she started. ''Thank you.''

The man stood and crossed the room as Tess pulled the papers from her briefcase and looked through the alphabetically arranged records.

''But I don't see Lieutenant Calavicci here.'' She handed him the homecoming list. He took it and glanced over it quickly, as if he knew what he was looking for.

''No.'' He took the second list from her hand and checked it over. ''There he is,'' he said quietly. ''Still MIA.'' He handed the pages back to her. Then something else caught his eye, and he took them back, chuckling. ''Damn. I told you these weren't accurate.'' He held his finger against one of the names higher on the page. The small print was hard to read. ''Look at that.''

She read aloud: ''Lieutenant Robert M. Barrows, U.S. Army, captured June 8, 1969.''

Barrows seemed amused. ''Don't let the clerks who cut my pay see that,'' he ordered. ''Took me long enough to get my checks started when I first got back. All I need is

220

for them to decide I'm not really here."

Tess smiled. "Why did you send me to Fort Belvoir?"

Barrows looked momentarily caught off guard by her change in subject and turned away. He rubbed his face with both hands, sighing into his palms.

"To talk with Grimwold. Did you see him?" he asked innocently. He picked up his coffee cup and tilted it. It was empty.

"You know I didn't. You went down there this morning."

He leaned his head to the side. "You're not bad."

"All it takes is some kid who doesn't know when to shut up."

"The truth?" he asked. "I wanted him to talk to you." He sat back at his own desk and stared at the empty coffee cup in his hands. "It's been five years," he murmured. "And I thought if I—" He looked up and sighed. "Well, it doesn't really matter, does it? He wasn't there."

"No, he wasn't. He was transferred this morning."

"As I understood it, he hasn't really been transferred," Barrows explained. "I was told they were having problems at one of the labs, and he had to go check it out. New Mexico, somewhere. Coffee?"

"No, thanks. Don't you think the timing's a little suspicious?"

Barrows's smile, though warm, was decidedly strained. "Coincidental, yes, suspicious, no. Miss Conroy, you're already tilting at windmills; don't go off chasing wild geese at the same time."

"Thank you for the advice." She shifted the lists back to her briefcase and said, "Captain, in case I *can* get this story in time, I'd like to add in a few details about the man in that picture. Lieutenant Calavicci? I wonder if you could tell me something about his background—''

''Kelly has a lot on his background already, Miss Conroy,'' the captain snapped. He took a deep breath and let it out slowly. ''If you've got her notes, you've got enough in there to write a story, I'm sure.''

Tess shook her head. ''Miss Fulham's notes only include a few facts, dates, that sort of thing. Nothing to lend any human interest, if you know what I mean.'' Barrows waited warily, not quite refusing to answer her questions, not quite agreeing to. ''For instance, did he go to Annapolis?''

Barrows smiled then; she must have asked the right question. ''Yeah.'' The man's eyes had drifted out of focus. ''He wanted to fly. I think he surprised himself with how well he did.'' He looked back. ''He was born for the Navy. One of the few men I've ever met who was made for military life.''

''Including you?'' she asked, not really interested.

''Including me.''

''So after the Academy—'' she prompted.

Barrows gazed at the empty cup, then turned to the stacks of paper on his desk. ''Said it scared the hell out of him when he got promoted to lieutenant.''

''Why?''

Captain Barrows's eyes had lit up; for the first time he hadn't looked like a man on the edge of disaster. ''He told me he thought anyone with a rank above lieutenant was a horse's ass.'' And whatever amused him about that, Tess couldn't quite fathom.

She never had the chance to find out what the joke was, though. Barrows's intercom beeped and he pressed the button.

''Captain,'' Bonita's bubblegum voice said, ''there's a Lieutenant Farraday on the phone, sir. Said it was urgent.''

Barrows's eyes lost the gleam of humor they'd had a

moment before, and disaster loomed in them once more.

"Excuse me, Miss Conroy." He picked up the receiver. "Barrows." He listened for a moment, and as Tess pretended to interest herself with the various pictures hanging on his walls, she listened carefully.

"Damn! When? How long has he—alright, just sit tight, I'll be there in twenty minutes." He hung up, standing up from his desk and grabbing his jacket from the coat stand. "Miss Conroy, I'm sorry, but I have to go."

He walked with her out of the office, and as they parted on the way to their cars, he said, "I hope you get this story, Miss Conroy. I sincerely do."

Now, on her way to Crystal City, Tess realized that the chance was just as good that, as Jackson had warned her, Ensign Mark Davalos was at the Pentagon, or the hospital, or who knows where, engaged in any number of other operations.

But fate and timing seemed to be on her side—mostly. And Tess intended to stay in their favor.

She found a parking spot and made her way through the futuristic, underground walkways that connected the skyscrapers of Crystal City. She'd only been here a couple times, and she wasn't sure she liked the idea: a self-contained cluster of buildings that, in theory, a person who lived here would never have to leave. A kind of space station, with work, entertainment, shops, and apartments all within walking distance. The idea was that you could move in here and never have to leave the three or four blocks that made up the city. Just like prison.

The idea made Tess's skin crawl.

She found the satellite office where Jackson said Mark Davalos was normally stationed. It was in one of the buildings that, like an iceberg, was mostly below ground.

She prepared herself for the Pentagon-level security she anticipated the offices here would demand, and was surprised to find herself unchallenged at any level. By the time she'd introduced herself—not by her real name—to the first half-dozen clerks who asked her to sign in and take a badge, she had gotten quite used to her assumed identity. No one ever asked her to prove who she claimed to be; there wasn't even one request for as much as a driver's license.

That would make a great story, she thought, clipping the fourth of what, in the end, were five visitor badges to the belt on her dress. *How secure are we? What if some terrorist country wanted to plant a bomb here? What if a spy wanted to gather information?*

Probably too implausible.

She knocked, finally, on the door identified as "E-267," and waited. A very young voice beckoned her in and Tess took a deep breath, preparing for the most important acting role of her life.

The door swung open into a small, cold room lit by a single fluorescent light that hung from the ceiling. But the room was warmed by memorabilia and knickknacks. There were scores of pictures clustered on the walls: baseball pictures, family pictures, graduation-from-Annapolis pictures, and various awards and commendations. Personalized paperweights and pen holders, a Naval Academy mug, and a still-wrapped cigar cluttered the desk.

And within five seconds, Tess Conroy knew exactly how to play her role.

"Oh, uh—I'm sorry," she stammered, seeing the young, round face looking up in puzzlement from his desk. The ensign stood quickly, a gesture born of manners his mother had obviously instilled in him long before.

Tess appeared as hesitant as she could. "Are you—I was looking for Mark Davalos."

"I'm Mark Davalos," the young man said. "Can I help you?"

Tess glanced nervously at hands she twisted together. "I . . . don't know." She looked back up, forced a glistening of tears into her eyes, and added, "I don't—I'm looking for someone— Maybe this wasn't such a good idea."

She half turned toward the door and Mark Davalos rounded the desk. "No, wait a minute!" In a very gentle move he took her shoulders and said, "Look, ma'am, I don't know if I can help you, but—why don't you tell me who you're looking for, okay? Maybe I can find someone who *can* help you."

She shook her head and sniffed. "If anyone can, it'd be you. That's what—he said."

"Who said, ma'am?" he asked, and urged her carefully toward the chair on the other side of his desk.

Tess timed her silence, her hand-wringing, her hesitant glance at the young man in front of her, very carefully. "I got a phone call," she whispered. "Someone who said— he said he was calling—unofficially."

Mark nodded, encouraging her, as he sat against the edge of his desk.

"Maybe—maybe it'd be easier if I just . . . told you who I was?" she suggested. He waited, very patiently. "My name is Elizabeth. My last name—well, it probably wouldn't mean anything to you." She covered her lack of information and looked him full in the eye. "I've remarried now, but . . . I used to be . . . Mrs. Albert Calavicci."

The look in his eyes said it all. And Tess looked quickly down at her lap so she wouldn't betray herself with the glorious excitement coursing through her.

CHAPTER
NINETEEN

Tuesday, June 17, 1975, 7:00 P.M.

They sneaked back into the hospital through the basement, as they'd left. Sam scanned The Corridor first, making sure Wainwright and his minions weren't around, then beckoned Al to follow him.

"This is like being back at the Academy on Saturday night," Al mused, obviously enjoying himself. Sam closed the door behind him and leaned against it; *he* wasn't used to pranks like this.

Al collapsed on the bed, chortling. "God, that was fun," he said. He looked at Sam. "Thanks."

Sam shrugged. Al pulled out a fresh cigar and lit it, kicked his shoes off, and let them fall haphazardly on the floor.

"You're doin' it again," Al accused a moment later. Sam pulled himself up.

"Doing . . . what?"

"Givin' me that 'shrink-patient' look," he said, narrowing his eyes. "You've been doin' it since I got here." He paused, a wry grin on his face as he tilted his head. " 'Cept when we were on the dance floor!" He sat up, swung his legs over the side of the bed, and chuckled. "That Christy was pretty groovy, huh?"

"Groovy?" The slang was just dated enough by '75 for Sam to wince. "Yeah, she was."

Al rubbed his hand across the back of his neck, still smiling. "Haven't used some of those muscles in years." He grimaced happily. "Probably be sore as hell tomorrow."

"Couple aspirin before you go to bed might help," Sam suggested. He was feeling suddenly awkward. The wild abandonment of the afternoon was behind them, and they were once more in the grim surroundings of the "Bethesda Naval Interrogation Center."

"No thanks." Al shook his head. "No more drugs." He met the physicist's eyes and shrugged. "Might go for some dinner, though," he suggested. Sam smiled.

"Yeah, I guess you've worked up an appetite." He opened the door. "I'll be right back," he promised.

It took Sam less than ten minutes to find the kitchen, order two plates of greasy meat loaf and cold, crusty mashed potatoes, with green beans cooked to a slimy scum on the side. And the kitchen personnel were happy to give him his selection of soggy bread pudding or lukewarm Jell-O for dessert. Sam chose one of each, a glass of water for Al and a cup of instant coffee for himself.

When he returned, Al was sitting lengthwise on the bed, still dressed in his khakis, the smoke of the cigar coiling around him. Between that and the expression on his face, he looked just like a mafia don waiting to be served an elegant meal. Despite himself, Sam grinned.

"Your dinner, sir," he said, affecting an accent to go

227

with his flourished gestures. He put both meals, still covered, on the rolling bed stand, pushed the radio aside, and pulled the table to the bed. Al chuckled.

"Room service? Not bad. Two days home, and already I've been promoted and I'm being waited on hand and foot." He put the cigar down in the ashtray and lifted the top off the food tray.

"You ought to make admiral any day, now," Sam muttered. He grabbed the top tray and went back to the orange chair.

"Somehow, I don't think so."

"I thought I'd . . . join you. If you don't mind the company?" Sam settled into the chair and Al watched him suspiciously. Then, a moment later, the commander sighed and picked up his fork.

"What the hell?" He sliced off a piece of meat loaf and waved it at Sam. "Guess I owe you for this afternoon, huh? Okay," he said as Sam tried to follow his train of thought, "you get one freebie. Your choice: ink spots or Freudian slips."

And then Sam understood. He had intended just to keep Al company. But he must have been giving him the "shrink-patient" look without realizing it.

And Al had capitulated.

"Uh, well," he said, caught off guard by the swift surrender, "I'm not real good at ink spots myself," he admitted. "Maybe we could . . . just talk."

Al looked much less happy. "Talk. 'Bout what?" He spoke around his mouthful of food as easily as he spoke around his cigar.

"Well—anything." Sam tried the first bite of meat loaf, then spat it out. "This is—oh, this is awful!"

228

All laughed and continued eating. "Depends on what you're used to."

Sam looked up and Al's amusement slowly dwindled. He turned away.

"Yeah, I guess it does." Sam washed out the vile taste in his mouth with his coffee. "I'll bet—I'll bet it'll be a while before you're in the mood for rice again, huh?"

Al had the grace to chuckle. "Yeah." He looked back, his composure once more in place. "Even longer before I'm in the mood for those little slugs we used to catch. Course, if you hid them in the rice, it wasn't so bad."

"Slugs?" Sam whispered. "You ate . . . slugs?" He began to feel distinctly queasy.

"Nice thing about them is, they don't have any bones, so you don't have to worry like you do with sardines. You know, that you'll get one of them stuck between your teeth."

"Al!"

"Course, some of those little suckers are real juicy. So you gotta watch who you're sittin' across from when you bite into 'em, so you don't squirt—"

"Al!"

Al started to laugh. And he continued to laugh. He laughed so hard, and for so long, that Sam became a little concerned. Sam waited until the near hysteria stopped and Al wiped his hand over his face: the laughter had brought tears to his eyes. But a small safety valve had opened, Sam thought, to release some of the pent-up emotions.

"You know, Doc, I got a feeling I'm gonna like you after all," he admitted.

Sam winced, wondering if that meant he was going to be subjected to more grisly stories of life in the jungle.

"Why don't we talk about something else," Sam suggested. He covered his tray and put it on the floor. His appetite was thoroughly destroyed.

Despite the fact that Al held his fork a little awkwardly, he'd packed away most of his food by the time he answered.

"Yeah, OK. Whaddya wanna talk about?"

Sam had hoped he'd choose his own topic, but given the opening, Sam said, "How about what happened earlier today."

Al looked up as he mashed the last of the potatoes and green beans between his teeth. He swallowed. "Yeah, that place was a lot of fun. I liked the lights. Maybe we can go back there again, huh?"

"I wasn't talking about the Harbor Light," Sam said, knowing Al had understood that very well.

"Oh." Al stared at him a moment, then he looked away. "You're talkin' about me barfing all over the floor of the Senate Office Building." He looked up, a devious humor in his eyes, and shrugged. "Think of it as a political statement."

Sam had a hard time *not* smiling.

But he wanted to get Al to talk about what had happened in Vietnam. He wanted him to face it, whatever it was, so that he wouldn't still be trying to anesthetize it twenty-some years from now.

But Lieutenant Commander Calavicci didn't seem in the mood to face it. And Sam sighed with frustration.

"No, huh?" Al pushed his empty tray aside. "Well," he said, picking up his cigar and sucking on it, "I can see the report now. 'Lieutenant John—Lieutenant *Commander* John Doe,'" he corrected himself with a cold grin, "'made it successfully through three questions before telling the senator to go to hell and vomiting on the floor. In

230

this professional shrink's opinion, Lieutenant Commander Doe is no longer qualified to remain on active duty.' End of report.'' The bitterness had returned to Al's voice.

"I haven't seen anything so far that disqualifies you for active duty," Sam protested.

"No? Well, how 'bout treason? Now *there's* one hell of a disqualifier!" He stood up from the bed, cigar in hand, and began his pace.

"I don't believe you're a traitor, Al," Sam said quietly, watching the man move rhythmically through the room.

"Well, maybe you *would* if you'd hung around on Sunday night instead of taking off as soon as you'd drugged me and leaving me alone with those bastards!"

Sam sucked his breath in; Lieutenant Commander Calavicci was angry that he hadn't stayed!

"I was told to leave," he said lamely.

"Well, you seem to be pretty selective about the orders you follow!" Al stabbed the cigar at him, his anger growing.

Sam screwed up his courage and took a deep breath. "Were *you*?"

Al whirled, interrupting his pace, and glowered at Sam.

"You said you acted under the authority of the senior ranking officer in the camp," Sam reminded him. "Did he . . . order you to give information to the enemy?"

This time, there was no humor in the chuckle that crawled from Al's throat. "There's a big difference between following orders and acting under your CO's authority," he explained. He dragged the cigar through his teeth, then released it and sent a cloud of smoke into the air. "Eddie never *ordered* me to do anything."

"But he—knew what you were doing?" Sam asked.

"Yeah. He knew what I was doin'." Al looked down

on him. "*He* gave me the information."

"Did he know what you were going to do with it?"

For a long moment Al just stared at him, his chin lifted, his cigar smoking unnoticed in his hand. "Yeah," he said at last. His voice was harsh. "He knew." He turned away and resumed his pace. "Change the subject, huh?"

"What happened to him?"

That stopped Al's ritual. He didn't, however, turn around. "Eddie?"

"Yes." Al didn't answer, so Sam prompted him. "Did he—was he—was he the one who died in that camp?"

"No." The answer was almost too quiet to hear, even in the soundless room. "Woulda been better if he had." Al took in a long breath, then he turned. "As luck would have it," he said, waving the cigar, "he's in France right now, waitin' to come back. Him *and* Young," Al added, as if that information had some meaning to Sam. "Talk about the trip from hell. Six hours in flight from Saigon, stuck between those two . . ." His voice faded off and his gaze drifted away.

He shut his eyes and ran a hand over his face. "Okay, so—" he faced Sam again. "Are we even, now?"

"Even?"

"Yeah. You got me out of this little hell for an afternoon, and I told you about another one. We done, now?"

He'd closed up, Sam realized. He was back to the bitter captive who was caught in yet another prison. Another cell.

And with another set of captors.

"That's not why I took you out today."

"Really? Then why *did* you take me out?"

A sharp defense of purely humanitarian motives came to mind.

Then Sam remembered the wisecracking admiral who'd

never let *him* get away with the kind of self-pity Al was on the verge of.

So he smiled and said, with a well-executed example, "So you could shake your booty!"

The shock that showed on Al's face quickly burned through his anger and left, in its place, the reluctant laugh of a man whose sense of humor had survived eight years of hell.

"Try to get some sleep, OK?" Sam suggested, realizing that Al had probably talked more about Vietnam in the last ten minutes than he'd ever talked about it in the next two decades. He opened to the door to leave.

"Not unless you've got more amytal."

Sam turned back to him, his hands still on the doorknob. He saw Al waiting for him to understand.

"You haven't been sleeping?"

Al shrugged; having made the confession, he now seemed uncomfortable with it.

Sam let go of the doorknob. "But Nurse Mulcahy said you were asleep when she checked you."

Al put on a mischievous grin. "Did summer stock when I was a kid. Besides, it's kind of fun when they lean over to check you, and they don't know you're awake."

Sam wasn't sure whether he was more relieved by Al's resurrected interest in women or concerned that he hadn't been sleeping. He glanced around the room, then remembered something he'd read long ago.

"Here. Look out," he said, moving past Al to the bed. He tossed the pillow on the floor, then grabbed the top sheet and blanket and pulled them free.

"What're you doin'?" Al asked.

"Guessing that you probably didn't sleep on a boxspring and mattress for the past eight years."

233

"Charlie must have saved 'em for the more important POWs."

Sam glanced at him, then pushed the bed flush against the wall, leaving the rest of the room bare and empty.

"How . . ." Sam asked, gesturing to the floor, the blanket and sheet in his hands. It took Al several seconds to understand.

"In the corner. Against the wall."

Sam laid the sheet on the floor where Al directed, then put the blanket on top. He picked up the pillow, considering it.

"No," Al said. His voice was quiet and Sam looked up into eyes that made him suddenly think twice about his idea.

"Isn't this a little sick?" Al asked. "I mean, reproducing the hootch to help me *sleep*?"

Sam took a deep breath. "You reproduced the tiger cage when you jammed yourself in the elevator."

Al looked down on him, puffing on the cigar. After a minute, still meeting his eyes, he said, "No. Not the cage. The pit." He looked away then, his eyes traveling to the makeshift pallet on the floor. He swallowed tightly. "It was the only safe place. Pretty horrible, but—safe."

Sam didn't speak. He waited until Al shook himself free of whatever memory had grabbed him.

Al tried to smile. "What the hell?"

Sam smiled a little. "Well, if it works, you get some sleep. And if it doesn't—you get a great view of the nurses as they walk away."

Sam started back for the door.

"You know," Al said, contemplating the pallet on the floor, "I'm startin' to like the way you think."

At that moment the door opened, and Robert Barrows, in full military dress, stormed in.

"Where the hell have you two been?" he demanded, his

234

blustering fury catching Sam completely off guard.

He glanced at Al, expecting him to back himself into the corner, as he had the last two times Barrows had arrived unexpectedly.

Instead, Al wrinkled his face into a grin and looked at Sam conspiratorily. ''We've been busted,'' he said quietly, almost as if he found the situation amusing. Captain Barrows, Sam realized, clearly didn't.

''Busted?'' the man fumed. ''You two are damned lucky Wainwright didn't come down here while you were out playing whatever games you've been playing! You could have been seen!''

''Well, actually—''

''Uh, Captain,'' Sam interrupted Al's intended confession, ''look, I just—I thought it might do him some good to—get out for a couple of hours.''

''A couple hours?'' Barrows slapped his fists against his hips.

''Wendell took me dancing,'' Al said, his eyebrows moving up and down in a wicked pantomime of Groucho Marx.

''Wendell?''

''Well, see, actually—''

''Yeah, Wendell,'' Al repeated defensively, moving closer to the captain. ''And *my* name, in case you forgot, is Al. Al Calavicci. *Not* John Doe!''

Barrows, his mouth half open for another assault, stopped short of delivering it. He met Al's eyes for a second, then turned to Sam. ''According to Farraday *and* Mulcahy,'' he said, ''you haven't checked in since the hearing this morning.

''And I can personally vouch for the fact that *you*,'' he added, turning back to Al, ''haven't been here for at least four hours.''

Al shrugged, stuck his cigar between his lips, and said, "We got lost."

"Dammit, Al, will you be serious!"

"No." Al pulled the cigar from his lips and stabbed it at Barrows. "No, I won't be serious! Not now, not anymore. Dammit, Bobby, I've been serious for the last eight years! Far as I'm concerned, it's time to have a little fun."

Sam held his breath as Al stared Barrows down.

"I need to talk to you," the captain said after a long silence. "Alone." He turned to Sam. "If you'll excuse us."

Sam pulled his shoulders up. "No. I don't think I will."

Al grinned. Barrows didn't. He looked, if possible, angrier than when he'd walked in. And more dangerous.

"Dr. Xiao," he said quietly, "you were chosen for this operation because of your exemplary record of following orders without question. Now, do you want to ruin that record?"

"Or worse?" Sam asked, picking up just a fraction of Al's defiance and tossing it into his response. "I'm Al's doctor—"

"'Al'?" Barrows turned again to the khaki-clad cigar smoker.

Al shrugged. "It's good for all that deep, intense shrink-patient stuff," he explained, not believing a word of it. But Al was enjoying Barrows's discomfort.

"Alright, look," Sam started, sensing that at least half of what was going on in the room was the painful Ping-Pong match of emotional betrayal Al felt from his friend, "I'll—I'll go check my patients."

Al watched him carefully from the corner of his eye.

"Yes," Barrows agreed, sighing. He looked Sam directly in the eye. "You don't want anything like dereliction of duty to show up on your impeccable record, do you?"

Sam glared at Barrows, then left the room.

CHAPTER
TWENTY

There weren't many patients Sam could check at that hour. He returned to Wendell's office and ground through the charts, trying to make his final evaluation of the lieutenant whose ''behavior unbecoming an officer'' had turned out to be an incident involving a lot of alcohol, some women's underwear, and a charge of homosexuality. The man wasn't a homosexual, but he was, as far as Sam could tell, not the kind of guy who would ever fit comfortably in a uniform.

The sound of the handlink behind him as he concentrated on how to phrase his recommendations startled him. He half jumped, gasping his surprise, and turned. Admiral Calavicci stood in a smoky shroud, his eyes still rimmed with the aftereffects of indulgent self-destruction.

''You're here late,'' the admiral started. He didn't look at Sam, but played with the box in his hand. Nervously, Sam thought.

''Well, I had to . . . finish up some work here,'' he explained, as if Al were unaware of the afternoon's activities that had kept him from doing this earlier. "Al, what am I supposed to put down in this guy's record?" he asked, hoping for a clue to Al's current state of mind. He tried to keep his voice light as he ran his hands through the recorded history. "He went to a party and woke up the next day in a pair of women's underpants and stockings. And they put him in a psych ward!"

Al half glanced at Sam and shrugged. The story should have been cause for at least three crude, suggestive comments, Sam thought.

"He's not happy, Sam. Ziggy says he's in and out of trouble with the Navy for the next four years, finally settles for a discharge."

"Maybe he should be discharged earlier," Sam suggested. "Although I can't justify that on the basis of a pair of misplaced women's stockings."

Again, Al let the opening slip and just shrugged.

Sam decided against the subtle approach and put his pen down, closing the chart without making a decision about the inadvertent transvestite. "Why'd you come home so late, Al?"

The admiral, who had started to punch the link in his hand, looked up. "What?"

Sam took a deep breath. "Something happened when we saved Tom, didn't it?" he asked. "Something . . . changed. And—instead of coming back in '73, you were—"

Left behind. . . . He couldn't bring himself to say the words.

"You didn't come back until now." Al chewed his cigar and wouldn't look at him. "What happened, Al? How did saving Tom—"

"It wasn't . . . saving Tom," Al interrupted. "Not exactly." He seemed sober now, Sam thought. Sober. And very unhappy. "It was . . . the Pulitzer that did it." He ran a hand across his face.

"Maggie Dawson's picture?" Sam asked incredulously. It wasn't what he'd expected.

"You remember that?"

"*I traded a life for a life . . .*"

Sam nodded. "She died."

"Not in the original history," Al reminded Sam. "In the original history, Maggie didn't go on that mission." He put the cigar in his mouth. "She never took the picture."

"But I convinced Tom . . . to bring her along," Sam murmured. "So that she'd file a story on the mission, and we'd be able to know what to do—how to save Tom." He swallowed tightly. "But she died—"

"*. . . a life for a life . . .*"

He waited for Al to acknowledge his memory as real, waited for Al to confirm that his memory could be trusted.

Al's expression *was* the confirmation. "She went off on her own," he said. "She got the picture." He paused for a deep breath before continuing. "It made the cover of all the magazines. It was in all the papers. It was even published overseas. And—the VC got hold of it." He looked at Sam. "But in 1970, the U.S. sure as hell wasn't going to admit that a female civilian, even a journalist, was killed on a hot mission. So the Army claimed the picture was taken by an intelligence officer. And the VC figured American intelligence on the locations of the POWs was better than they'd realized. They thought it was better than it actually was."

"*I wish she'd have won the Pulitzer," Sam's brother said.
"She did. For her last photograph.*"

239

"But you told me *Maggie* got the Pulitzer," Sam protested. "I remember that, Al!"

Al shrugged. "The picture won a Pulitzer. And Maggie took the picture. Same thing, right? I mean, it wasn't like Maggie was around to care."

Sam looked away: for some reason, he felt irrationally angry at the small lie.

"You could have been free."
"I was free . . ."

Sam ran a hand across his eyes and looked up again, and suspected the truth in those words, too. But Al had lost two years of his life by helping Sam save his brother. His own irritation over who got credit for Maggie's picture faded in that light.

"So the VC thought it was a reconnaissance photo?" he asked.

"Yeah." Al's face had turned a cold, ashy color, Sam noticed. The memory couldn't be a good one. He shrugged, trying to appear casual. "They changed their tactics and started moving us around. A lot. They kept us moving so no one would find us."

He paused again, and Sam waited. "First time—in the original history—I stayed in one camp from '71 to '73, and came home with all the others. But then we changed things. And I was moved around. And late in '72 I escaped." His voice retreated to the well-rehearsed sound of a practiced script.

"You escaped," Sam repeated. "And?"

Al shrugged. "I was recaptured." He tried to smile and made a halfhearted gesture with the cigar. "Missed the last

240

plane home.'' Then, he gave Sam a familiar what-the-hell? shrug.

And without warning, without another word, he punched out.

Tuesday, June 17, 1975, 7:57 P.M.

''So? How do I look?'' Tess Conroy examined herself in the full-length mirror that hung on the back of her bedroom door, then stepped around for Jackson's opinion. The man looked her over appreciatively.

''I always had a thing for a woman in uniform,'' he said, liquid brown eyes dancing with suggestions.

Tess cleared her throat and adjusted the outfit. The woman who owned this was much more well endowed than Tess. ''Must be built like an ox,'' she muttered, not intending to be heard.

''Yeah, Farraday's got a good set of hooters, that's for sure,'' Jackson agreed. He sat—actually, squirmed—on the sofa in her living room, still eyeing her with open intent.

''Farraday?'' Tess asked, stepping closer, her pulse beating harder in her neck.

''Yeah.''

''*Lieutenant* Farraday?''

''Yeah.''

''She works—at Bethesda?''

''Yeah.''

Tess laughed, not believing the beauty of it all.

''What?'' Jackson demanded. ''Why, you know her? I didn't tell her it was you, so—''

''No,'' Tess interrupted. ''No, she called Barrows's of-

241

fice while I was there. She's on this operation, Jackson. She's part of it.''

Jackson looked a little pale, then. He stood up from the sofa and grabbed her arms. "Tess, you're not—you aren't going to talk to her, are you? I mean, look, I gave you this—''

"Don't worry." She pulled free of his grasp and cocked her head. "Look, if Calavicci's there, he's the only one I'll have to talk to, right?"

Jackson wasn't breathing steadily. "But if you expose this—Tess, you can't *ever* tell anyone where you got that uniform!"

And then it hit her. "Jackson Fellows," she said, lowering her voice for the attack, "you've got a thing for this Farraday woman, don't you?"

"No!" The protest resounded too loudly and came too quickly.

Tess laughed. "Well, don't worry, Jackson," she said, feeling suddenly much less anxious about the payment she was going to make for all this information. "It'll be our little secret."

She gathered her purse, headed for the front door, and waited for him to follow. "So—" Jackson said, clearing his throat against the embarrassing truth that she'd exposed, "where're you and Mark meeting?"

"*Our* little secret," she said, locking the door behind them. "For his protection, as well as mine."

CHAPTER
TWENTY-ONE

It had already been one hell of a day, Bob thought. First, the news that Grimwold had been transferred from Belvoir to some unknown destination; the timing on that was too coincidental, despite what he'd told Conroy.

Then, the hearing this morning.

And his efforts to placate Blackwell and Wainwright, convincing them that Al *would* cooperate tomorrow, something he wasn't at all sure of.

And then the visit from Tess Conroy, confirming that the noose was tightening around Al's neck, even if Al didn't realize it.

And on top of all that, the call from Farraday, telling him Al was missing, and that Xiao had never shown up to see his other patients.

The only bright spot in the day had been his brief talk with Weitzman at the Watergate, confirming what two shreds of information and his own intuition had told him.

Kelly knew. She knew why he had gone through with

the divorce. She knew why he had left her. And if Weitzman was any judge, she was willing to hold out hope that when this operation was over, things might work out for them after all.

If Weitzman hadn't mentioned being in Korea today, Bob thought, he'd have never known. But the typed paragraph on the back of the Pulitzer picture, the one Tess Conroy had brought to his office yesterday, had compared Vietnam with Korea. And so had Weitzman, this morning.

"I never wondered why you were on this operation, Captain," the senator said, sipping from a glass of wine as he finished his lunch. *"Did you ever wonder why I was?"*

Sitting comfortably in the man's elaborately decorated dining room, Bob smiled. "Because I asked you to help me," he said, and took a drink of coffee.

The Lincoln-ite senator stroked his beard and said, "You wanted to stay on the operation and Blackwell wanted you off. He wanted an excuse to go to Plan B."

Barrows waited.

"That bastard never served one day of active duty in his life," Weitzman concluded quietly, his words pulled slowly into the air as he spoke. Weitzman was never in a hurry, Barrows noted. *"He's never been in combat. And he's never been a prisoner, in the hands of the enemy, in an undeclared war."*

And at that moment, Barrows saw something more to the man than he'd seen in the last year and a half. Bob had always believed that Weitzman had kept him on the operation to give himself a full hand. Now, he considered the other motivations that might have been at work.

Weitzman admitted that he'd told Kelly her husband was working on an operation that required "extraordinary sanitized credentials.'' And he had urged her to consider their separation as an ''extended tour of duty.''

According to Weitzman, Kelly had agreed that she would.

Now, alone in the room with the man he'd sacrificed his marriage for, Bob found himself wondering once more about motivations.

His own.

And Al's.

The man had confessed to having betrayed the men in his camp. He'd confessed to helping the Vietnamese hide them. And his confessions rang with details Bob couldn't ignore: details like the locations and appearances of the camps he said he'd helped to hide. Bob, who had received every aerial reconnaissance photo from Vietnam since 1973, knew Al was telling the truth.

Al knew those camps. He knew where they were. He knew the specifics, the layouts, the number of men. He'd even named some of the men he'd seen when he was there, men who'd begged him to remember their names, to tell someone they were still alive.

He'd known the codes, the signals, that someone at those camps had set to catch the attention of Army Intelligence in their routine surveillance of the areas. Signals Bob himself had first seen on a photograph in 1974. Signals that hadn't even existed when Al was captured in '67.

So there was no doubt in Bob's mind that what Al had confessed to under sodium amytal was true. For him, the question was no longer *whether* Al had helped the VC: the question was why.

The man he'd spent seven months in hell with would have never willingly betrayed his men. He'd have never willingly surrendered intelligence to the enemy, or broken the Code of Conduct. Not without a reason strong enough to overwhelm everything else Al Calavicci valued most.

Al had started pacing the moment Xiao left. But now he stood in the center of the room, saying nothing, waiting for Bob to start. Barrows glanced around; the bed had been pushed to the side and the sheet and blanket lay in the corner, a makeshift pallet.

"Hard to sleep in a real bed?" he asked. Al said nothing. "I did that, too," he said, gesturing to the floor, "when I first came back."

Al blew smoke from his cigar. "How long?" he asked finally. It was an opening.

"Three months," Bob confessed. "Drove Kelly crazy."

Al lifted his chin. "How is she?"

Bob looked at the pallet again. "We're divorced." Al watched him sadly for a moment, then turned away.

"I'm sorry about . . . Beth." He waited, but there was no acknowledgment from Al. "I looked her up when I came home," he offered quietly, not sure if he should pursue the topic.

Al turned around, but it was obvious that he couldn't bring himself to ask.

"She was . . . fine," Barrows answered him anyway. "She—"

A small gulping sound filled the room and Bob decided to change the subject.

"Did you tell her I was home?" Al whispered, before Bob could think of something else to say. It was the last question he wanted to answer.

He took a deep breath and pulled his pipe from his jacket. "Did you ever wonder what you had in common, Al?" he asked. "I mean, the three of you we brought back."

Al narrowed his eyes and shook his head. "Figured we all agreed—" He stopped and let out a heavy breath. "To follow the rules," he finished reluctantly.

"The sergeant had no family," Bob said. He drew a plastic bag of tobacco from his back pocket. "And the colonel was divorced. Hadn't even seen his kid since she was six."

"Yes he has."

Barrows stuffed the bowl of his pipe. "Once in twelve years doesn't really count when you're giving out paternity awards," he observed. He held the lighter to the tobacco and lit it. "Besides," he added, "she's not even listed as a dependent. No reason to notify her." He sucked twice on the pipe before pulling it from between his teeth. "And you—"

"Had no one," Al finished. Bob knew the look in Al's eyes. Seven months, tied together in the jungles of Vietnam; some things you learned the hard way.

"The operation didn't want to bring back anyone with families at first," Barrows explained. He wanted to ignore the look in Al's eyes; he wanted to make it go away. But he couldn't. And he couldn't make the rest of this any easier, either.

"They aren't going to inform your families that you're home."

"So Davalos and Meyers . . . they just lied, huh?" Al concluded, his voice tight.

Bob stared at him and couldn't think of a thing to say.

Al shook his head and a low, bitter rumble came from his throat. Then he turned his back to Bob and started to pace.

Barrows watched the ugly, familiar routine, and finally said, "I told her."

Al didn't stop his pace. He walked, head down, one hand lifted to the cigar at his lips, the other shoved into his pants pocket, his eyes locked on the floor.

"Al, I told her! I went behind their backs, and I told her!"

"Did you tell Eddie's kid?"

It was the last question Bob had expected. He pulled his pipe from his lips and wrinkled his face. "What?"

Al stopped pacing and looked at Bob. "Did you?"

"No. No, she's—"

"Are you going to?"

Barrows shook his head. "I wasn't planning on it."

Al ran the back of his thumb across his upper lip. "Then don't."

Bob took a deep breath and shoved his pipe back between his lips. "Okay," he agreed. "Why not?"

Al looked at the pallet on the floor and shrugged. " 'Cause you're right," he murmured.

Bob left him to his silent contemplation for several minutes. He smoked his pipe and Al sucked on his cigar. A smokescreen fell around them and neither of them spoke for a long time.

"Okay," Bob said at last. "Let's hear it."

Al turned to him. "Hear what?"

"The truth," he said. Al's face turned to stone and Bob pulled the pipe from his mouth. "Tell me what happened to you over there. What happened in '73?"

"You know what happened," Al said. "That's why I'm here, right? That's why we're having 'fun with sodium amytal and secret hearings.' " He snapped the cigar out of his mouth. "That's why you came up with all those damned conditions I agreed to."

"I'm not asking what you did, Al. I want to know what happened to you."

The expression in Al's eyes told Barrows he wasn't getting through to him.

"Late in 1972, during a transfer between camps, I managed to escape my captors," he began. He was reciting a well-rehearsed script and it made Barrows angry.

"Dammit, stop that! I know the facts, Al! I know them inside out. I've worked with them, eaten with them, slept with them, and bathed with them for over a year. So save your sterilized speeches for the shrinks!"

He paused, seeing the look in Al's eyes.

"I put my butt on the line to get you out, Al. I think I deserve to know what the hell happened to you over there." He closed the distance between them. "Not what *happened*; what happened to *you!*"

Al pulled back instinctively as Barrows came toward him and stared at the captain over the cigar. After a few seconds, he turned his back to Barrows. It was several seconds more before he spoke.

"It was a transfer in the jungle. One of me, two of them. They'd been careless, hadn't tied my hands very tight. I worked them loose as we went. The guard in front of me tripped. I grabbed a rock and hit him over the head while he was still down. The other guard—he was just a kid, maybe fifteen. He was still struggling with his gun. I grabbed it and shot him. Then I ran.

"I hid in the jungle. Survival training came in pretty handy. So did the occasional isolated VC: I got some extra ammo, sometimes even some rations."

He took a deep drag on the cigar before continuing. Barrows waited.

"One morning I woke up and there was a fire in my gut,

like someone was pulling my stomach out a piece at a time. It got worse. At first, I thought it was something I ate, but I was real careful about that. By the end of the day, I knew I was in trouble.

"I don't remember too much after that, I guess I was delirious. Next thing I know, I wake up in this hootch in some village and there's this little old lady talking to me a mile a minute in Vietnamese and there are kids and dogs and chickens running in and out. I had no idea where I was or how I'd gotten there or how long I'd been sick.

"They took care of me for a couple days. Guess I was damned lucky. Then Charlie showed up. Started blasting the village. Killed almost everyone there before they found me."

Al turned around and looked at Barrows, sour amusement on his face.

"I think I was a surprise to them. They didn't know I was there; they were after a South Vietnamese squad they thought was hiding out in the village. They didn't really know what to do with me. So they ended up taking me with them. I didn't know where we were, I still don't remember how I got to the village.

"We marched for about three days before we got there."

"There?" Barrows asked.

"POW camp. Big one. Set up for scores of prisoners." Al swallowed audibly. "Only the place was empty. Deserted, except for a few French the VC were still holding there.

"That's when they told me: all the other American POWs had already gone home."

Barrows heard the barest hint of a crack in the last word, but the cigar seemed to be working well to help Al maintain control.

Barrows considered breaking in, but decided against it. He had to hear Al's version, all of it, without his own input.

"They threw me in a pit at the edge of the camp." Al chuckled. "All those empty hootches and they threw me in a pit. They said I was technically MIA again. I was expendable. My country didn't want to bring back another POW after they'd promised America they were all home. That's what they said."

The ash on Al's cigar dropped to the floor, but he seemed oblivious. His hand shook as he lifted the cigar to his mouth, and his eyes lost their focus.

"It got bad then. There was jungle all around, and the trees blocked most of the light from the pit, even at high noon. And there were"—he swallowed tightly—"all kinds of things in there with me. I guess, maybe, if I was a biologist I'd have tried to figure out what they all were. But I really didn't wanna know. They crawled on me and slid up my legs and flew around my face . . ." He closed his eyes and let out a harsh breath. When he looked back, he wrapped a wan smile around his lips. "Too many to eat," he tried to joke. Bob couldn't bring himself to laugh.

"I was in the pit for two weeks. The only time they let me out was to work me over in their little shop of horrors." Al's voice broke then and he shook his head. He said nothing for a while, and Bob waited in silence.

"I don't know which was worse at the time: the torture or the pit. When it rained, the pit filled with water. You couldn't sit down, your feet were always wet, and at night it got so cold—and everything hurt from what they'd done to you during the day.

"The only thing warm was your own blood, and the piss running down your legs; you couldn't even move to the can, the pain was so bad. All you could do was huddle

251

there and wait and try not to breathe too hard.'' His hands gestured through the air as he spoke, small bits of ash flying off the end of his cigar.

"I guess that's when I realized—they were right. They didn't give a damn if I died 'cause my country didn't give a damn about getting me back. And I guess—I guess, for a while, I didn't give a damn about my country.''

Barrows stared at the floor. And Al looked away, shifting his gaze down and to the right. He puffed nervously on his cigar.

"Anyway,'' he said finally, "I guess at that point I'd've told them anything they wanted to know. Then *they* screwed up. I was in the pit, and I heard noises. I couldn't see anything, but I could hear. It was English, an American voice. There was another American POW in the camp with me.'' He wiped his hand over his face, removing any hint of tears that might have betrayed him. He let out a harsh breath and grunted.

"I wasn't alone. Not completely. If I'd been left behind, so had someone else.''

He took a deep breath. "That's when I started thinking clearly again. At least, it seemed clear at the time.'' He shrugged, not meeting Barrows's eyes.

"I figured, maybe it wasn't as easy to write off two MIAs as it was to write off one. And if there were two, there might be others.''

For a long minute, staring again into the empty room, Al said nothing. "I thought,'' he whispered finally, "being with another American would be better than being alone.''

The cigar, Barrows saw, was taking quite a beating between Al's teeth.

"I told them, maybe they could use us as a bargaining chip. You know, get concessions from the U.S. I don't think I expected we'd ever get home, but I guess I figured being alive and used as a hostage was better than being expendable.'' He looked at Bob. ''Rule numero uno, right?''

Bob nodded silently.

''Charlie had already started to use the MIAs as leverage. But they took advantage of my willingness to help. I told them I'd use my knowledge of our aerial reconnaissance to help them camouflage the camps. *If* they'd keep us together and treat us decently.''

It was quite a while before Al said anything more. He paced two full circuits, the cigar burning between his lips. When he spoke his voice was quiet and angry. ''It wasn't until later that they told me.''

''Told you what?''

Al swallowed loudly, painfully, Barrows thought, as if his throat had suddenly closed up. ''They said it was April. I *thought* it was April. I know the rain should have clued me, but God, I was so disoriented from being sick and tortured and stuck in that hole—'' He turned around then. Barrows wanted to look away, but he didn't.

''Dammit, Bobby, it was only February! My God, it was February! They might have come home. We *all* might have come home.''

CHAPTER
TWENTY-TWO

It was taking longer to break free of the images. Longer to break free of the memories. The fear. The pain.

Don't make a sound.

Sam was getting too close. And he—Lieutenant Commander Calavicci—was going to talk too much. He knew it. He just knew it.

Don't make a sound.

Admiral Calavicci finally turned from the Door and strode through the Control Center, not breathing until he was safely enclosed in the elevator. Then, leaning back against the wall, he tried to break away from the days Sam's Leap was making him relive.

"Albert M. Calavicci," he whispered. "Lieutenant—*Admiral!*" He shut his eyes. "United States Navy. Serial Number B-21-23-29."

The door opened three repetitions later and he walked to his quarters.

He needed another drink. Badly.

Don't make a sound.

If you scream or cry out . . .

Eddie! For God's sake, Eddie, make them stop!
Tell them what we did! Tell them the truth!

It was hard being this close to his past, reliving a history Sam had already managed to change here and there.

Like letting Davalos bring him that Beatles tape: "Sgt. Pepper's Lonely Hearts Club Band."

Damn, that had been nice.

Such a little thing shouldn't have meant so much. But it had.

And that one song . . . How'd it go? Somethin' about a little help from his friends? And singing out of tune.

He liked that song, always had.

Ever since he'd first heard it . . .

He pushed the button on his door.

"Al."

He jumped at the voice as the door slid open.

"What the hell are you doing in here?"

Verbeena Beeks stood up from the chair at his desk, but didn't move toward him. "Pulling rank," she said simply. "Everyone on this Project depends on you, Al. *Especially* Sam." She lifted the nearly empty bottle of Jack Daniel's from his desk and held it out to him. "You want a drink, fine," she said quietly. "But you're going to tell me what this is all about before you get one."

He stared at the bottle, embarrassed and angry. And scared.

Don't make a sound . . .

It was hard to breathe. Hard to remember how those muscles were supposed to work, the ones that forced the air out of your lungs. They were supposed to work on their own, weren't they?

Then why the hell couldn't he breathe?

Don't make a sound.

He ran his hand across his face, trying to wipe away the

images that cascaded through his mind.

New memories—just little things, so far—were already taking hold.

But you learn how important little things are when the difference between life and death is nothing more than the look in a man's eyes.

Or a song.

Don't make a sound.

A song could make the difference between life or death over there.

"Al?"

Life or death.

He'd already begged enough.

He eyed the bottle in Verbeena's hand.

Time to confess . . .

"Okay," he said. The word was half intelligible. "You wanna know what this is all about?" He moved a step closer, but Verbeena pulled the promised anesthetic back, away from his outstretched hand. He chuckled bitterly and shook his head.

"God." He shut his eyes tightly, and choked. And then, very soberly, he faced the psychiatrist. "It's about Donna's father," he confessed.

And Verbeena handed over the scotch.

He was tied to the stakes, spread-eagled on the ground.

It was Young's turn; the sergeant stood between his feet, looking down on him, holding the bamboo pole horizontally in both hands. It was all part of the game. Around him, the others watched, waited, blood-lust glistening in their eyes.

"Say it, Judas," Young commanded. "Say it!"

"I didn't . . . betray anyone." It was hard to talk. They had left him in the sun most of the day, without water,

waiting until the pain in his muscles from being tied in that position was intense enough to drive him to capitulate.

"Come on, Judas. Admit it, and this ends." He heard the voice, but he couldn't turn his head to look. "Confess! You collaborated, you betrayed us. You set it up so we could never go home!"

"No. I didn't. God, why won't you listen to me?" Almost a prayer.

"You bastard!" Young moved a half step closer. "Why the hell should we take the word of a traitor, huh?"

Somewhere, standing just out of sight, Eddie was watching, as always. He wanted to look at him, plead with him to stop this, but he couldn't move his head. And he had already begged enough.

"Remember the rules, Judas." Young raised the pole over his head. "Don't make a sound. Until you're ready to confess." He grinned. "If you scream or cry out, we'll make it so bad . . ." He didn't finish the threat.

There was an agonizing second before it started: this game was only a week old, and he already knew they were going to win. He just wasn't sure how much he was going to lose before they realized that.

And then the pole came down, hard, in the same place it always did. Again, and again, and again.

An unbearable five minutes later, it was over.

Not before he screamed.

Not before he confessed.

Tuesday, June 17, 1975, 10:01 P.M.

It was raining again. Summer thunder pounded Sam's ears as he stepped out of the elevator in the basement of Bethesda Naval Hospital.

"You could have been free."

He started down The Corridor, lost in thought, wondering if Al would ever have told him the price of saving Tom's life if he hadn't remembered on his own.

And then he heard it: above the thunder, a scream tore through the hallway. And then another. And another.

Sam raced down the hall to the room where the horrible sounds came from. He threw open the door, reached for the light, and turned it on.

"Al!"

Lieutenant Commander Calavicci was curled on the floor, trembling, his eyes wide and glazed. Sam dropped down and reached for him. But Al pulled back, huddled in a tight ball, shaking his head.

"No! Get away! Get away!" His voice was terrified and his breath shook, and his eyes were wide with some remembered horror.

"Oh, Al."

Sam's voice broke and he fought to control his emotional response. He was supposed to be Wendell Xiao, a psychiatrist, someone who could handle this situation with professional detachment. That's what Wendell was famous for, right? Detachment.

He pulled his hand back and waited. But the trembling continued; Al was drenched with sweat. Sam stood up, pulled the fitted sheet from the hospital bed, and draped it over his patient. Then he sat back down, watching him, waiting for the terror to leave.

"It's alright," he said quietly. "You're free, Al. You're home."

He wasn't sure when Al started to hear him; Sam repeated the mantra for more than half an hour before Al moved. He uncurled slowly, gingerly, as if the motion would call back the pain. He looked at Sam and opened his mouth, but nothing came out.

"You're free," Sam repeated. "No one's going to hurt you." He could have been talking to a child; the look in Al's eyes was one Sam never wanted to see again.

Al's breathing eventually calmed and he took several deep, controlling breaths and wiped a hand across his face.

"Oh, God."

Sam wasn't sure what to say, so he said nothing. *Try listening*, he heard in his mind. *You* used *to be pretty good at that.*

"Sleeping's damned overrated," Al whispered after another minute. It was a surprisingly hopeful response.

"Maybe—you just shouldn't be alone."

Al looked at him and snickered. Then he swallowed what might have been a sob. "*You* gonna stay?" he asked sharply.

Sam smiled. "Yeah."

Al watched him suspiciously for a very long minute. Then he closed his eyes and took a deep breath. "Leave the lights on," he ordered.

Sam settled back against the wall and watched him.

After several minutes, Sam thought he had fallen asleep. Then Al opened his eyes and looked at Sam, a strange embarrassment on his face.

"What?" Sam prompted quietly.

Al shifted his eyes to the blanket he was clutching in his fist and slowly released his grip. "There was this kid," he whispered. His face was wrinkled with pain. "Plucked right out of a cornfield and dropped into the middle of a POW camp." Al stopped, swallowed, and gripped the blanket again, his gaze drifting to the harsh industrial-strength woolen cloth. "He was the only one . . . He tried to help me. Kinda like Davalos,'' he added. He looked back at Sam. "He brought me a tape, you know?"

Sam nodded.

"Beatles." Al swallowed a gulp. "Just like Ronnie. Couldn't believe I was guilty, even when I confessed."

"What happened to him?" The moment Sam asked, he knew he shouldn't have. The distant, emotionless look that came over Al told him the answer.

"They killed him." He swallowed and rolled on his back, flinging one arm over his face. "Know what he did?" Al whispered after a minute. He didn't wait for Sam to answer. He wiped his face again and tried to take a breath that didn't shake. "He came into the hootch after they'd finished. And just sat there. And sang . . . Couldn't carry a tune . . ." Al's voice trailed off.

"What kind of songs?"

Al made a gesture that if he'd been standing would have been a too-careless shrug. "Beatles."

Then he looked at Sam, and waited. A horrible, trusting wait, hoping Sam would understand a request he couldn't quite bring himself to make.

After a few seconds, he closed his eyes, turned on his side, and put one arm under his head for a pillow. Sam leaned back against the wall and wondered why, when he really needed to think of a song, he couldn't.

He looked around the room. Not much to look at: a stripped hospital bed, the tacky orange chair, the bed tray . . .

And Sgt. Pepper.

He stared at the unopened cassette on the bed tray, not wanting to disturb Al by moving from his position. But a faded, Swiss-cheesed memory made him want to check the list of songs on the back of that box.

There was that one song, right after the introduction . . .

And Sam smiled as the lyrics slowly came back to him. Yeah. A little help from a friend . . .

He sang the song slowly; line by line, the words sifted into his memory.

Halfway through the first verse, he glanced at Al, the lieutenant commander's face twisted into a knot as he fought to retain his composure.

Sam's voice faltered, a little off-tune for a couple lines. The last time he'd seen Al this close to tears had been in San Diego—in 1969.

He risked a cautious touch on the hand that lay loosely on the floor. And Al took hold, his grip tight, his body suddenly wrenched by deep, painful sobs.

The dam had broken. Finally. And Sam didn't try to stop it.

But as he tried to ignore the nails that dug into his hand, he found himself choking on the words. And wishing again that he knew what really *had* happened to Al over there.

The distorted picture of Al's alleged—*confessed*—collaboration just didn't make sense. There had to be another explanation.

And Sam was determined not to Leap until he found it.

Then the door to the room opened and a young nurse, probably Mulcahy's shift replacement, stood hesitantly in the doorway, astonishment in her eyes at the picture that met her: Commander Calavicci, curled on the floor under two sheets and a blanket, and Dr. Wendell Xiao sitting next to him, singing.

Sam signaled the nurse to silence and gestured her to leave. Her expression told him she was only too happy to do so.

But Al didn't seem to notice. He was too far away.

Back in Vietnam, in the pain he couldn't forget.

And the memories that still wouldn't let him turn out the lights.

CHAPTER
TWENTY-THREE

Tuesday, June 17, 1975, 10:15 P.M.

"Did you see him?"

Mark Davalos's anxious question came before Tess had climbed back into the car idling outside the back of the hospital. She shook her hair free of rain and took a deep breath.

"Well, in a way," she said. The excitement she was battling was stronger, more thrilling, than anything she'd ever felt in her life. She really didn't want to share the moment with a stranger. But she didn't have much choice.

She tried to stay in character, a difficult act to pull off while her heart was pounding with the quicksilver beat of the story that was going to make her as famous as Jackson Fellows had promised. She felt dizzy, drunk.

"He was asleep," she said. *Did her voice really quaver?* "And—that doctor was still there, so I—"

"Oh, no." Davalos had moved them out of the garbage area at the back of the hospital, and they drove toward the beltway. "Did he see you? Dr. Xiao, I mean?"

"Yes, but—well, he probably thought I worked there."

She gestured to her uniform. She'd explained to Davalos that she—Elizabeth, formerly Calavicci—was a nurse. That much she'd confirmed from Kelly's old notes. And, as she explained, "It might be helpful in case anyone *does* question what I'm doing there. I can always say I'm new and got lost."

Actually, her cover had reassured the nervous young man. While he was eager to bring some cheer to Calavicci, he was equally terrified of being found out.

"So—what are you going to do now?" he asked after they were back on the beltway. Traffic was light now, and only the rain made their drive slower than usual. It was pouring.

"Well, that depends on you," she said. This much of her plan she'd worked out in the forty-five seconds after she'd closed the door on the bizarre scene in that basement room. *Sound hesitant*, she reminded herself. *You're not sure of anything, remember?* "Do you think—if I called you tomorrow—do you think—well, maybe he'd see me? If you asked him, I mean?"

Davalos took in a long breath and let it out just as slowly. "Gosh, Mrs. C., I don't know." She'd let him call her that, not wanting him to question her about her last name. "I mean—I don't know if I can—" He ran his hands back and forth over the steering wheel. Then he glanced at her and she put on her best desperate look. "Okay, look, I'll—I'll try."

She beamed at him. "Mr. Davalos, I knew I could trust you. My husband used to say," she added, just for good measure, "that you could trust an ensign or a lieutenant, but anyone above that rank was a horse's ass."

The young man chuckled, and dimples actually appeared in his cheeks. Tess tried not to think how young he must be. *Too young to be on an operation like this*, she decided.

He dropped her off at the hotel she told him she was

staying at in Arlington. "I'll call you tomorrow," she promised. "Around ten?"

"OK."

"Mr. Davalos," Tess added, standing under the porte cochere of the Hyatt, "you have no idea how much this means to me."

The ensign smiled at her, a hesitant, hopeful smile. "I hope he'll see you, ma'am."

She closed the car door, and as he drove away, she murmured, "Oh, he'll see me. One way or the other."

She went into the lobby of the Hyatt and looked for a pay phone. She found a row of them across the lobby, near the entrance to the small bar from which disco music was loudly pulsing. She had to cover her other ear when she made the call.

"*Washington Life*."

"This is Tess Conroy. Is Miss Fulham in, by any chance?"

"Please hold." She waited, and a moment later was rewarded with the familiar, brusque voice that promised a very bright future for Tess.

"This is Fulham."

"Miss Fulham," Tess said, "I think I have a story that's bigger than Maggie Dawson's." She waited, but there was no sound on the other end. "There's a covert operation to bring home MIAs from Vietnam. And," she rushed on to fill the silence, "I've seen one of them. And it's the man in Maggie's picture. And—your husband is involved. I think."

She finally stopped, waiting for some reaction from the editor of *Cavalcade*. When it came, Tess could imagine the smoke that wrapped around the woman as she spoke.

"Where are you now, Miss Conroy?"

"I'm at a hotel in Arlington," she explained, looking

around herself. "But—the man I saw is at Bethesda Naval Hospital," she added.

For a long time—long enough for Kelly Fulham to smoke half a cigarette and then smash it into her ashtray—the editor said nothing.

"I told you I wanted the story on Maggie's picture," she said at last. "Now, if you want to pursue this . . . other story you think you have—that's your choice. And if you're right, well, I'll publish it. But if you're wrong," she added, "and you don't have the story on Maggie—that's the risk. You'll have to decide what you want to do, Miss Conroy. But one way or the other, you'd better have a story here tomorrow night. By the time I leave. And that," she added, and Tess heard the soft click of a lighter in the background, "is usually much earlier than this."

"I understand." Tess swallowed, not sure now how secure success really was. Maybe, like all dreams, it was too elusive to become real.

"And Miss Conroy," Kelly added. "Captain Barrows is my ex-husband. Please remember that." The woman hung up without another word, but by now Tess wasn't put off by the abruptness. She ran her fingers through her rain-dampened hair, ignored the looks from the men behind the front desk, and walked back out into the rain to her car, half a block away.

Tuesday, June 17, 1975, 10:54 P.M.

Senator Elwood Blackwell hung up the phone near his chintz sofa and settled back on the seat, swirling the liquid in his snifter. He looked across the room at Jerry Wainwright and smiled.

"The final piece just fell into place," he explained. The

larger man nodded, not, apparently, savoring the moment quite as intensely as Elwood himself was. It didn't matter; what mattered was the mission, not that those who worked with him enjoyed their jobs as much as he did. He drank some of the cognac.

"How are you controlling her?" Wainwright asked, breaking out of a long, pensive silence. Elwood smiled tightly.

"Actually, I had help," he said. It was almost amusing the way other people's good intentions could be used so easily against them, he thought. "Weitzman felt—well, he wasn't pleased with the deal we struck to let Barrows stay on the operation. So he went to Fulham himself. Hinted broadly at her husband's motives for ending their marriage." He grinned, feeling the warmth of the liqueur seep through him.

"It wouldn't take much to convince her," Wainwright agreed. "After all, Barrows has been in intelligence since before he went to 'Nam."

"Exactly," Elwood agreed. Then, unable to resist sharing the one secret he'd kept from everyone on the operation, even Wainwright, he stood. With success so close, he wanted someone else to enjoy that first, small victory with him.

He crossed the room and opened the top drawer of the Federal-style desk that sat beneath a walnut-framed mirror. He pulled out a photograph, looked at it, and turned back to the sofa.

"All I had to do after that," he said quietly, returning to his seat, immersed in the photographic memory in his hand, "was to convince Fulham that by cooperating with *me*, her husband wouldn't meet an untimely death."

Wainwright looked up from his own snifter of brandy, his expression devoid of any perceptible emotion. "She bought that?"

"I explained to her that it was easier to eliminate her

266

husband than it had been to eliminate a POW in Vietnam.'' He handed over the picture. "Remember him?''

Wainwright's jaw clenched as he took the picture. He put his brandy on the Queen Anne end table next to his chair and stared at the photograph without blinking.

The image was admittedly grainy. But aerial reconnaissance photos always were. This one captured on film the image of PFC Ronald Martin, a twenty-six-year-old draftee, being executed in a rice paddy outside Camp 69.

"He practically cost us this whole operation,'' Elwood explained. "Remember when we first heard the stories of Calavicci's activities?'' Wainwright looked up from the picture, his eyes distant. "I realized then what a gold mine we had. A perfect excuse to shut this down and invoke Plan B. Then Calavicci started his humanitarian charade and the Vietnamese *almost* let him stay. They liked the idea of having him there to take the pressure off them. But,'' he added, reaching forward to recover the precious memento, "I convinced them it would be much better for Calavicci to be *here*, where he could be publicly tried for treason.'' He smiled at Wainwright. "Of course, that meant getting rid of anyone who stood in the way.''

Wainwright should have looked happier than he did, Elwood thought. "You have a problem with this?'' he asked quietly, and picked up a pen from the table next to him. He chewed it absently. Wainwright smiled halfheartedly.

"No,'' he said. Then he lifted his snifter. "To Plan B,'' he offered. And Elwood smiled; it was nice to find a common spirit in the middle of smothering bureaucracy.

He lifted his own glass in return. "To normalized relations with Vietnam. Before reelection.''

The storm had delayed every flight coming into, or leaving, the Washington metropolitan area for the last two hours. It had crept up from the coast, catching air traffic in its paralyzing grasp all along the East Coast. Robert Barrows, whose day had not begun well, found himself in a foul mood by the time he and Dennis Stern finally left Andrews Air Force Base.

"I'm telling you, Bob," Dennis started, "those two are—they're way over the edge."

Barrows was too tired right now to really care. It had been two days since he'd really slept.

He wanted to go to bed.

He wanted to go to bed with Kelly. He wanted to see her, talk to her.

He wanted the damned rain to stop!

"They didn't shun Calavicci," Dennis said, his animation borne, no doubt, of the adrenaline surge of anger he still felt. "They didn't ostracize him. They tortured him, for God's sake!"

"Yeah, we figured that out."

His lack of interest in a topic that had consumed the last year of his life must have shown. For a moment Dennis said nothing. Then, shifting in his seat, he turned to Bob. "Okay. What happened?"

Barrows filled him in on the events of the day—from Grimwold's transfer to Al's confession. Dennis listened without comment as Bob recounted a day he'd just as soon forget, and drove to the Watergate for the late-night debriefing Weitzman had insisted on.

"Do you believe him?" Dennis asked, staring out the window. "You've been there. Could what he described—being sick, being in the hole—could that have really disoriented him

268

that much? So that he didn't even know what month it was?''

"Yes.'' He considered not saying anything further, and lost the battle. "There were times,'' he explained, gripping the wheel of the car for control, "when it got so bad— you'd wake up and not even remember your own name.'' He tried to laugh, but the sound came out twisted and harsh. "You ever had that happen?'' he asked, shooting a quick glance at his passenger. Dennis shook his head.

"It's scary as hell. The couple times it happened to me, I was lucky. There was someone around to tell me who I was. Usually Al,'' he added bitterly. "But even then, sometimes, I couldn't tell you *where* I was. Or what day it was.''

Lightning flashed ahead of them, and a second later thunder echoed through the night. Bob winced, despite himself.

They drove in silence the rest of the journey, found a spot in the garage, and took the elevator to the lobby. There, they checked through the newly tightened security and went to Weitzman's apartment.

The senator had opened the sliding door to the balcony to let the sounds and smells of the night seep through their conversation. It was a habit Bob had become used to in the past year; the man loved the heat, even the humid, stifling heat that Washington suffered through. In the summer, he only turned on the air-conditioning for the sake of his guests. And in the winter, the apartment sweltered. Until this morning, Bob had always attributed the idiosyncracy to the senator's natural leanness.

But Korea was a damned cold place to be a prisoner of war.

And the sound of the rain still sent Bob's mind back five years to a long march and the hopeless wait for a cavalry that never came.

Over coffee, Bob repeated his tales of Tess Conroy's visit and Al's version of what had happened in '73. Dennis

269

volunteered his opinion that when the colonel and the sergeant returned to the States, Xiao's evaluation would leave no doubt that they were both emotionally unstable.

"I couldn't get to the colonel," Dennis apologized. "He won't talk to anyone. But I did get the preliminary results from his physical." He handed over a slim document, three pages of information typed in French.

Weitzman took the papers, then handed them to Bob. "You're the translator," he said, and stroked his beard thoughtfully.

Bob read through the medical report, not bothering to translate the entire thing. He skimmed it, skipped to the final diagnosis, and read aloud.

"While a definite diagnosis cannot be made at this time, the patient's symptoms, history, and test results strongly suggest frontal-lobe carcinoma." Bob ran a hand over his very tired eyes. "Damn."

"He's dying," Dennis interpreted. "I talked to the doctors. They said it's probably been growing in there for a long time."

Weitzman's face darkened. He didn't look at either Bob or Dennis for quite some time. He stood and walked over to the open balcony door. A few drops of rain, whipped by the wind, landed on the carpet just inside the door.

"Was anyone with you when you talked to Commander Calavicci this afternoon?"

"No. Not when he told me what had happened in '73." Weitzman turned back and lifted a dark, questioning eyebrow. "Xiao was there when I arrived," Bob explained. "But then he left." He'd very carefully *not* mentioned the psychiatrist's "abduction" of Al from the hospital. It wouldn't go over well, he was sure of that.

"Why didn't he tell us that this morning?"

"We didn't ask?" Bob offered halfheartedly. He replayed

the conversation with Al in his mind, then shrugged. "I don't know," he admitted. He drank some of the freshly made coffee he'd been given, grateful for the small consideration.

"He collaborated. The other POWs found out. They tortured him for vengeance." Weitzman had a devastating way of summarizing the facts, Bob thought. He glanced at Dennis, who stared at his lap. "Unfortunately, that doesn't improve his position, does it? He still gave information to the enemy. Intelligence designed to aid them. Intelligence that may have prevented some of those men from returning home *before* Operation Homecoming." The man turned back to the wet balcony. "It would have been different if he'd done it *after* the operation," he mused.

"He thought it *was*," Barrows reminded him.

"He was wrong." Weitzman stared into the rainy night. "He'll take a disability retirement."

The verdict came without warning, and Bob felt his stomach lurch. "What?"

The senator didn't turn around. "We'll need the psychiatrist's concurrence." Then Weitzman turned around. "He'll be entitled to a lieutenant commander's retirement pay. He's still young enough to find another career. It might even do him some good to take some time off. And he has skills—"

"You can't!" Bob shot from the seat, slammed his coffee onto the end table, and ignored Dennis's attempt to keep him from ruining his own career. "Dammit, the Navy's his life! You can't make him retire!"

"If he doesn't, it's a court-martial," Weitzman said softly. "You and I both know Blackwell wants a public circus so he can shut this operation down."

"I don't—I don't believe Al's told us the truth."

Weitzman's astonishment reached his eyes and the left side of his mouth, which crooked upward with amused irony.

271

"I think—he's protecting someone. Maybe—I don't know, maybe someone who's still over there."

"The only person Calavicci ever indicated any concern for was that kid he said he wanted to give his place to," Dennis reminded him. "And he's dead," he added, glancing at Weitzman. "Brought his remains home this week. Navy's supposed to have notified his family by now."

Bob winced. "Al's not telling us the truth."

"You interrogated him under sodium amytal—quite a heavy dose, from what I hear—" Weitzman began. Bob sighed. "And you talked to him yourself—alone, without any pressure from anyone else. And you *still* don't believe he's telling the truth?"

"Not the whole truth," he said carefully.

Weitzman glanced at Dennis, and Bob followed the gaze, waiting.

"You're too close," Dennis suggested. He, too, stood. "I think Joe's right. The best we can hope for is that Blackwell will agree to letting Calavicci take a disability retirement. Not push the issue. Let him—"

"Crawl away into some little hole?" Bob snapped. "Dammit, no! He doesn't deserve that!"

"If he's a traitor, it's more than he deserves," Weitzman said. His voice was no longer friendly. "Bob, I have personally put my own career on the line to try to help you. And I did it because I know what it's like to owe someone your life. But things change. People change," he said philosophically. "And you're going to have to accept that."

Bob glanced at Dennis for help and found none. He closed his eyes, rubbed them, and then sighed. "That wasn't part of the deal."

Outside, thunder cracked in the air.

"Neither was treason," Weitzman pointed out coolly.

DAY 4

Wednesday, June 18, 1975

CHAPTER
TWENTY-FOUR

Wednesday, June 18, 1975, 6:32 A.M.

Lieutenant Commander Al Calavicci was just coming out of
the small bathroom, zipping his uniform trousers and tucking
his shirt into the waistband when he heard the knock on his
door. He ran his fingers through his wet hair, called "Come
in," and hoped against hope that it was that tall, good-looking
nurse with the incredible legs and great kazooms. He sat on
the edge of the bed and pulled on a pair of socks.

"Sir?"

He looked up and smiled, despite his initial disappointment. "Well, whaddya know?" After last night, there was
something reassuring about seeing Mark Davalos today.

"I brought you something," the ensign said, crossing the
room to hand over his package.

"This the tape recorder?" he asked, taking the brown
paper bag and settling it on his lap. He looked inside.
"Hey!" He pulled out the box of cigars, grinning broadly.
"You got it right!" Under the cigars sat the tape recorder,
and rattling loosely in the bag were several tapes. "Boy, a

whole collection.'' Al chuckled, removing each item from the bag and putting them on the bed. There were half a dozen tapes in the bag, three of them Beatles. But the other three were groups he didn't know.

''Bee Gees?'' he asked, turning a questioning gaze on the ensign. ''Village People?''

''Well, in case—well, they're more current. Disco,'' Mark explained. ''Good dance music.''

Al couldn't stop smiling. ''I think I'll listen to *these* right now,'' he said. While Mark opened the box the recorder was in and began to set it up, Al tore the wrapper from the Bee Gees tape. He popped it into the tape recorder.

A second later the sound of the new world he'd returned to filled Al's ears, a fast-paced, happy sound that was a universe away from the jungles of Vietnam.

He looked at Mark and nodded approval. ''That's great,'' he said and tried to keep the emotion from his voice.

''I'm glad you like them. Sir,'' the kid added, a little hastily.

''You almost forgot, huh?'' Al laughed. He bent down and pulled his shoes from under the stripped bed and put them on. ''Well, in case you manage to forget completely,'' he said, concentrating on his shoelaces, ''the name's Al.''

He glanced up and saw the kid debating the wisdom of taking a senior officer up on the offer to call him by his first name.

''Uh, sir, I was wondering—?''

Oh, well, Al thought. *Can't win 'em all.* ''Yeah?''

''Would you—would you want . . . to see your . . . wife?''

The simple, happy world of the Bee Gees tumbled down. Al tried to breathe, tried to take a breath that didn't hurt, and couldn't. ''Beth?'' he whispered. He looked in Mark's

276

eyes, trying to decide if this were a sick joke.

"She—she said someone contacted her—unofficially," Mark explained.

Al nodded and ran a hand across his face. "Bobby." He took a long breath and stood from the bed. "Where is she?"

"She's—she asked me—she wanted to see you, sir, so I—I brought her down here last night—"

"Last night?" Al interrupted, thinking back. "No one came down here last night."

"Well, you were asleep, sir. She saw Dr. Xiao, but—well, she was in uniform, so he probably thought—"

"Uniform?" The vision of Beth in her uniform danced through Al's mind, a strong, clear image that wiped out all other thoughts.

"Yes, sir. She . . . said she was a nurse?"

"She is." He closed his eyes to wipe away the image.

"She was going to call me," Mark continued, and Al was aware that the kid was watching him as he had when he'd picked him up at the airport. Waiting for him to fall apart. "To see if . . . you'd want to see her," he finished.

Want to see her? She was life and sanity and . . . "You sure it's her?" It was hard to believe. Bobby had said he'd told her, but he hadn't said she'd come.

"Well, if you've got any pictures of her, I could tell you for sure, sir."

Al tilted his head upward, just a fraction. "Yeah, I got lotsa pictures of her," he said quietly. Then, gesturing to his temple, he added, "Up here."

Mark looked at him sadly. "I'm sorry, sir."

Al turned away, angry at himself for having maneuvered Davalos into offering sympathy. "Well, who else would it be, huh?" he asked, and tried to smile. "Yeah," he finally said. "I'd . . . like to see her."

Mark beamed. "Okay, I'll tell her—"

"Not here," Al said quickly. Barrows had gone behind the backs of the others on this operation to tell Beth; if she showed up here, he had no doubt the ca-ca would hit the fan. And Bobby. And the kid. "Tell you what," he said, pulling a fresh cigar from the box Mark had brought, "there's a place Xiao took me to yesterday. Harbor Light. It's in D.C., you know it?"

Mark laughed. "Yeah, my friends and I go there all the time. Sir," he added belatedly.

"Bring her there," he said. Al lit the cigar and took a puff and exhaled; the cigars they'd given him in France had been stale. Better than nothing, but stale. These, however . . .

"Now *that*," he told Mark, holding the cigar out and surveying it, "is a great smoke!"

Mark smiled happily. "Uh, what time should I tell her—?" He glanced at his watch for emphasis.

"I'll be tied up this morning," Al said. *Better not to think about that too much. Just get through it when it happens* . . . "Let's say noon. If I'm a little late—wait for me, okay?" Mark nodded. "And—well, I guess I'll have to take a cab," Al explained, and waited.

Mark nodded. "Okay."

Al cleared his throat, embarrassed. "Well, kid, the thing is—they haven't exactly started my checks comin' yet, so I—"

"Oh!" The light of understanding flashed across the young face, and without hesitation Mark pulled out his wallet and handed him ten dollars.

Al shook his head. What did the kid think he was going to do? Call the White House escort service? "I said a cab, kid, not—"

"Oh, right." Mark *added* to the money in his hand. Al stared at it.

"You're kidding, right? It's gonna cost that much for a cab?"

Mark grimaced. "Guess prices have gone up since—" He didn't finish.

"Since I was captured," Al said. He looked the kid in the eye and smiled. "Guess I've got a lot to catch up on, huh?" Al shoved the money into his pocket and pulled the cigar from his mouth.

"So what do you do when you're not involved in all this cloak and dagger stuff?" he asked, wondering how the hell a kid like this could possibly survive in this world.

Mark shrugged and looked uncomfortable. "Well, mostly I'm involved in . . . cloak and dagger stuff," he said. And then laughed. "Gee, I never thought of it like that before."

Al laughed with him. And the raw pain of last night and the agonizing hope of seeing Beth today disappeared into the happy sound of "Stayin' Alive."

Wednesday, June 18, 1975, 7:18 A.M.

Sam stared at Wendell Xiao's face looking back at him in the bathroom mirror and turned on the water in the sink. He looked like hell. But then no one ever said that spending the night on a hospital floor, cramped into one position for several hours, was likely to improve your appearance. He splashed his face to try to wake up, and winced as the cold water stung the four small gouges on the back of his hand.

He hadn't slept much, dozing fitfully from time to time, afraid to move in case he woke Al. An hour ago he'd finally

279

given up his watch when the commander woke, at first confused, and then embarrassed. And that was *before* he noticed the marks his anguish had left on the back of Dr. Xiao's hand.

Sam left him to regain his composure in solitude, promising to return before Barrows arrived to take them to the hearing.

He showered and dressed and left for the hospital, his tired thoughts torn between the knowledge that he had to save Terry Martin sometime today, and the desire not to Leap until he'd fixed *whatever* was wrong in Al's life.

This time, Sam decided, the rules be damned; even Ziggy had indicated Sam *was* partly there to help Al.

He parked Wendell's overheating car and stepped out into the hazy, hot, humid morning, glad that he'd be spending most of the day inside air-conditioned buildings. He went straight to the elevator and took it to the basement, wanting to speak with Lieutenant Commander Calavicci before Barrows showed up.

"You plannin' on goin' to that hearing?"

Admiral Calavicci, dressed in shockingly bright yellow slacks and an iridescent red and blue shirt, stood in The Corridor as the elevator door opened, flourishing a half-finished cigar in the air as he spoke.

"Al!" Surprised delight twisted Sam's mouth into a broad, open grin, and he stepped forward, arms half extended to grasp the man with friendly relief. "You look great, Al."

The admiral shrugged and winced with the gesture. "Got one hell of a hangover," he confessed.

"But you're—well, I mean, you're—"

"Sober?" Al finished, cracking a guilty grin of apology. *More than that*, Sam thought. Admiral Calavicci had left the elevator—and the pit—behind. Maybe a small victory to some. But for Sam it was a lot.

Al met the physicist's steady gaze, as if he understood what Sam *hadn't* said, and cleared his throat.

"Depending on how long this hearing goes," he started, dropping his gaze and the subject at the same time, "you may have to leave early so you can save Terry. So, you'd better take Wendell's lemon, just in case." He worked the handlink, drawing out squeaks and whistles.

"What do you mean, depending on how long it goes? Wasn't there a hearing the first time through?"

Al shrugged, still studying his palm. "Yeah, but—Ziggy's not sure how long it'll go this time."

"Why not?"

Al looked up reluctantly. He took a puff on his cigar and narrowed one eye. "Things change," he said simply. Sam wrinkled his face into a question. "Well, it kinda made a difference having someone—well, not bein' . . . alone . . . last night," he mumbled. Then he shrugged, embarrassed.

"Wendell wasn't there the first time through?" Sam asked, starting down the hallway. He ducked a swinging laundry bag that traveled overhead; Al walked through it.

"No. Course, *he* didn't have to stay late 'cause he was out playin' hooky all day at a disco joint," he pointed out sharply. But the glance Al shot him held the gratitude his words didn't.

"So—what does Ziggy say about Terry?" Sam asked.

"Still the same." Al elicited a long, low wail from his electronic Legos and shook the box. "Looks like sometime around one . . ." His face wrinkled in concern. "Huh," he grumbled. "Damn thing!"

"What?" Sam stopped and turned to the hologram. "What, something wrong?"

Al smacked the small box against his palm and read from the tiny screen, shaking his head. "Ziggy says—she says you changed something, Sam. Something's different."

"You mean, Terry's not going to kill himself?"

"No, no, he still—no, Ziggy says—" He stopped and looked up, clearly unhappy with the prediction. "She says I'm gonna have to retire, Sam!"

Sam grimaced and shrugged. "Well, it was bound to happen *some* day, Al!"

"No, I don't mean now! I mean—in 1975!"

Sam stopped and pushed his hands into the pockets of Wendell's lab coat. "Why?"

Al had turned back to the gloomy prediction, shaking his head. "She doesn't know. Not enough data." He turned back, his eyes beginning to register desperation. "She says I have to take a disability retirement!" He spat the words out as if they were vulgar. "I am *not* disabled, Sam! I am perfectly fit for—"

"Al, Al!" Sam interrupted the indignant barrage with his hand, once more half extended to the image. "I know you're not disabled, okay?"

Al began a small, circular pace in the hallway, sucking on his cigar, his eyes locked on Sam's. "What did you say to them, Sam? Did you tell them I wasn't fit for duty?"

"I told them I'm still doing the evaluation, Al," Sam reminded him. "And I have no intention of saying you're not fit for duty, so relax, okay?"

Al took a heavy breath and winced again from the hangover. "Then what happened to change this?" he demanded, waving the handlink at him. "What did you change, Sam?"

"I don't know! I mean, I couldn't have changed much, could I? I've been with you mostly." And then it came to him. "Wait a minute!" Al stopped and faced him eagerly. "That's it!"

"What's it, Sam?"

"Well, you said—it made a difference . . . not being alone last night," Sam reminded him, a little awkward with the memory. "So—maybe that changes what happens at the hearing today."

Al was punching the question into the handlink. After a moment's wait and the painful cry of the cubes in his palm, he shook his head.

"Ziggy says—she doesn't know. But there's a 93.4 percent possibility that I won't say the same thing today that I said the last time." He shut his eyes and dragged on the cigar.

"So—what *did* you say the last time?"

Al looked up and narrowed his gaze. "Nuthin'."

The grinding sounds of the machinery that carried dirty laundry from room to room filled the silence as Sam debated his next question. He turned it, instead, into a statement.

"Then you never told them that you only gave the VC that information because you broke."

Al tipped his chin upward. "Who told you that?"

Sam shrugged and grimaced. "Well, it just—it seems pretty obvious," he explained. This wasn't an issue he'd expected to talk to *Admiral* Calavicci about. There was something about the mature Al that made Sam realize it was a forbidden subject.

"Well, it may *seem* obvious," Al snapped, "but Charlie never broke me!" He was defensive, angry, insulted by the conclusion.

"Then what was last night all about?"

And then Sam saw the remote glaze that had come over

Al's expression in the hallway of the Senate Office Building.

"When you're captured by the enemy," he started, his voice husky, "you expect *them* to work you over. You don't expect it from your fellow prisoners." He looked at Sam carefully, waiting for understanding to come without further explanation.

And it did.

"Judas's Judgment?" Sam gasped and stared at the closed door behind which Lieutenant Commander Calavicci was, no doubt, pacing. When he looked back, Admiral Calavicci had started the familiar series of codes that signaled his imminent departure.

"Eddie wanted me to confess," the admiral said quietly. "And I did." The glowing future engulfed him. "I'm gonna—check with Ziggy on this retirement thing, Sam," he said. Then the Door shut and the elevator, a dozen feet away, opened and deposited Robert Barrows.

Wednesday, June 18, 1975, 9:18 A.M.

"Aren't you finished yet?"

Senator Elwood Blackwell caught Jerry Wainwright by surprise as he walked silently through the Senate hearing chamber. The man looked up as Elwood walked up to the raised platform and glanced over the edge of the table.

"I don't want anything to go wrong," Wainwright explained, looking like he'd been caught with his hand in the proverbial cookie jar. "Without this, it's our word against his."

Elwood smiled thinly with his fleshy lips. For today's hearing, he'd dressed exceptionally well: a perfectly tailored two-piece pinstripe with a conservative blue tie. Within hours of handing the tape over to Tess Conroy, he would call a press conference and he was sure it would be televised. He wanted to look his best. Appearances, he knew, could make all the difference when reelection came around.

"Well, his word isn't likely to convince too many people. After all, two U.S. senators and three intelligence officers are likely to have more credibility than a broken down lieutenant who's been missing for eight years and whose record even before then was not spotless." Elwood tried to control the growing thrill of approaching victory; it was always dangerous to count your eggs too soon.

Jerry nodded absently, and placed the tape recorder back in its niche where no one, not even Weitzman, would detect it. When he looked back up, his attention was diverted from Blackwell.

Elwood turned and saw Joseph Weitzman looming in the doorway behind him. The lanky man moved catlike into the room, his slow pace measured and rhythmic and unhurried.

"I'd like a word with you before the hearing," the man said, his attempt to imitate the great humanitarian grating on Elwood's nerves, as always.

"Of course." He met the senator halfway between the door and the dais and ushered him into the hallway. They took the elevator to the fourth floor where Elwood's office was.

"I assume," Elwood said as soon as the door to the small room was closed, "that you're here to plea bargain."

Weitzman helped himself to a seat across from Elwood's desk and stretched his legs forward, crossing them at the ankles. He laced his fingers together, elbows resting on the arms of the chair, his grasp hanging in midair.

"I'm here to explain my plan to you," the man said quietly. "And I expect your cooperation."

Blackwell sat in his own chair and picked up a well-chewed plastic swizzle stick from the blotter on his desk. "Go ahead."

"I think we should offer Calavicci a disability retirement."

Elwood had trouble not smiling. He leaned forward, pulling the stick from his mouth. "Why? Does the psychiatrist say he was physically or mentally incompetent in Vietnam?"

"He will," Weitzman promised. "I'd prefer it to be a physical disqualification."

Elwood sank back in his swiveling chair and rolled it back so he could stretch his own much shorter legs in front of him under the desk. "I'd prefer he be declared *non compos mentis*. Just in case he ever decides he *does* want to talk."

Weitzman reached one hand up and stroked his beard, considering the bargain carefully. His eyes never left Blackwell's. "Will you call off the hounds?"

Elwood chewed on the plastic straw. "I can't call off all of them," he said, not exactly grinning. "But . . . I'll contain the damage, if that's what you mean."

"If even one reporter gets wind of this—"

"Calavicci's a collaborator. He's been treated well by the Vietnamese, but he's obviously insane. So—" He shrugged. "He won't be believed. And the press can do whatever they want with him, it won't affect our operation. I'll reassure our . . . 'friends' . . . across the sea, and we can continue with the repatriation efforts as planned."

"I don't trust you."

Elwood gnawed the swizzle stick. "You're questioning my integrity?"

"I'd question your existence, if I thought it would do any good." His adversarial colleague leaned forward, hands once more clasped in front of him. "I want you to call off Tess Conroy. I want you to let go of Kelly Fulham."

Elwood leaned his chair back, hearing the familiar, reassuring creak of the hinges as he folded his hands behind his head and stared at the ceiling. "And in exchange—" he began lightly, "I get Calavicci?" He laughed quietly. "I'm not impressed."

"There's no reason to kill them all," Weitzman said firmly. His voice dropped an octave. "We can bring them home alive and *still* normalize relations. They returned Ronald Martin's remains this week. It was a gesture of goodwill, an indication that they want the MIA issue resolved," he said tightly. "There's a vote on Friday. I'll support lifting the embargoes on that basis." He pulled his fingers apart, then clasped them again so they were next to his palms, almost making a fist with both hands.

Elwood considered the bargain. *"Non compos mentis,"* he insisted, "and you've got a deal."

Jerry Wainwright watched the two senators leave the chamber and let out a groan of relief. He couldn't believe that fate or timing had worked so well in his favor.

In *his* favor? Or in Calavicci's?

He removed the tape recorder from its hiding place under the table and pulled the plug on the recorder very slightly from the socket, leaving it just intact enough to appear connected, in case Blackwell checked it during the hearing. Then he put it back and stood up from the dais.

The image that had kept him awake all night—the picture of Ronald Martin's execution—flashed again through his mind.

Being responsible for the deaths of enemy agents was one thing; being responsible for the brutal execution of a twenty-six-year-old American who'd been drafted against his own will was something else.

And responsibility for the deaths of every American POW still alive in Vietnam was something Jerry had decided he didn't want on his conscience.

"Once I hand the tape to Conroy, she'll have everything she needs to 'break the story,' " Blackwell explained. "But once she does, the press will crawl all over us. So we cover our hides with the collaboration story, and the press is satisfied. And," he'd added, sipping from his drink, "our 'friends' in Vietnam can take whatever measures they feel are necessary to protect themselves."

Blackwell tossed the photograph onto the coffee table between them, face up. Wainwright stared at it.

"All we need is Calavicci's uncoerced, freely given confession," the senator explained. "And the story's closed."

Jerry ran his hand over the microphone on the table where Calavicci would sit, and glanced at the dais where the hidden, useless recorder sat.

He took a heavy breath; changing sides wasn't an easy matter, he realized. And he felt a pang of sympathy for Calavicci.

CHAPTER
TWENTY-FIVE

Wednesday, June 18, 1975, 9:56 A.M.

Tess Conroy sucked on her Camel, doubted that she'd actually walk a mile for one, and stared at the telephone on the brick and board shelf unit next to her sofa. She'd been staring at it, staring at the picture of Maggie Dawson at Georgetown University, and staring at the picture of an American POW in Vietnam for nearly an hour. She'd pulled Maggie's picture off the wall, brought it out to the living room, and put it on the coffee table next to the black and white glossy.

"This is what you'd do, isn't it, Maggie?" she asked her mentor. "Whatever it takes to get a story?" *Especially one this big*, she thought. But it didn't help.

The exultant thrill of victory last night had slowly dissipated in the hours since. She hadn't slept at all, hadn't even tried. She started writing the story, writing what she knew so far, disguising her sources, covering the trail that had led her to Bethesda Naval Hospital to protect those who'd helped her. Fellows, Davalos, Farraday, Barrows.

But by three this morning she wasn't feeling as happy about this as she had when she'd started. Nowhere near as happy as she wanted to. Somehow, writing the story of the man she'd seen on the floor of that basement room last night had changed something inside her. And the idea of trapping him into an interview by pretending to be his ex-wife was actually beginning to turn her stomach.

And in the gray, predawn hours of the morning, when she went to the bathroom to wash her face and try to stay awake, she'd looked at herself in the mirror and didn't at all like what looked back.

Now, having just confirmed the time and place where she'd meet Calavicci this afternoon, the debate with herself had grown to paralyzing proportions. She stared at Maggie Dawson's vibrant face staring back at her. She stared at the haunted face of the man in the jungle. And she smoked the Camel to a nub.

Then she picked up the phone and dialed the *Washington Life* office.

"I'm meeting the POW this afternoon at the Harbor Light," she told Kelly Fulham, once the woman got on the phone. "I won't be able to finish writing the story until after that, so—is six o'clock alright?"

Kelly Fulham was silent for a long time. "That's fine," she said, sounding nearly as enthusiastic as Tess felt. "Miss Conroy," Kelly asked, "out of curiosity—how'd you get him to agree to talk with you?"

Tess stared at the pictures on her coffee table. "I don't think you want to know," she said, and abruptly hung up.

Wednesday, June 18, 1975, 10:06 A.M.

"I trust, Commander, that you're prepared to cooperate with this committee today?"

Senator Blackwell's opening volley was designed to put Al on the defensive. But as Sam took the spectator seat next to a tired-looking Dennis Stern, he saw a change come over Al that Blackwell had probably not counted on. He was ready for whatever they threw at him today. He seemed more in control of himself, more confident, than he had yesterday.

At his seat between Barrows and Wainwright, Al leaned forward, once more folding his hands on the table in front of him. "Yes, Mr. Senator, I am. To the extent I agreed to before I was repatriated."

"Meaning what?" Blackwell kept his voice calm, soothing, and chewed nervously on a ballpoint pen cap.

"Meaning, sir, that I agreed to full disclosure of my activities in Vietnam, specifically from the end of 1972 until I returned. However, I will not discuss the activities of other American POWs in any of the camps."

Senator Blackwell glanced at Weitzman, and then at Bob Barrows. "And why is that, Commander?"

"Because they have no bearing on my activities."

"Commander." Weitzman leaned forward. "I'd like to remind you that these are serious charges; this is your career we're discussing. I'd think you'd be interested in bringing to light *any* mitigating factors in your own defense."

Al studied the man for a moment, then shot a quick glance at Barrows to his left. "I was under the impression, sir, that this was a debriefing. Not a court-martial." His voice was dangerously quiet.

Blackwell grinned; an ugly sight, Sam thought. "This *is* a debriefing, Commander. But in light of the charges—"

"Excuse me, Mr. Senator," Al broke in, leaning toward the microphone. "You say 'charges' as if I've been formally accused of wrongful activities. I wasn't aware that

291

any of the allegations against me had been substantiated, nor that any 'charges' had been brought.''

He was angry. Angry and willing to fight for himself, Sam thought. A far cry from the scared, defensive man who'd stormed out of this room yesterday.

''No, Commander. *Formal* charges have not yet been brought.''

''Damn.'' Dennis Stern's quiet exclamation pulled Sam's attention. He turned and saw the commander exchange a quick, half-hidden glance at Barrows. Neither of them looked happy.

''How long were you in the pit, Commander?'' Weitzman asked, his first question so far.

Sam turned to Dennis. ''What? What's wrong?''

Before Dennis could answer, the blaring sound of the handlink pierced Sam's ears. He started, then caught his reaction and managed to catch a glimpse at the hologram who hovered in a panic just to his right.

''Sam! Sam, they're gonna court-martial me!''

''I beg your pardon, Mr. Senator,'' the calm but angry Lieutenant Commander Calavicci said, ''I don't recall ever mentioning a pit.'' He threw an angry look at Barrows.

''Court-martial?'' Sam whispered. Dennis looked at him and nodded.

''That's what it looks like,'' he agreed grimly. ''Weitzman wanted him to take a disability retirement,'' Dennis explained. ''It looks like he couldn't talk Blackwell into it.''

''Sam, we've gotta talk!'' The admiral's desperate voice sliced the air and Sam struggled not to respond to him directly. ''Ziggy says there's a 78.8 percent chance I'm gonna be court-martialed!''

''We understand from the others that there was a pit in

Camp 69 where you spent a lot of time," Weitzman said. "Is that true?"

"Sam!"

"I'll be right back," Sam whispered, and stood up from his seat. Admiral Calavicci disappeared and Lieutenant Commander Calavicci watched with barely concealed disappointment as Sam left the room. Then he turned away and answered the question Weitzman had directed at him.

"There *was* a pit." His voice sounded suddenly defeated. "I wouldn't say I spent a lot of time in it."

Sam's hologram waited for him in the hallway, pacing frantic steps, his eyes locked on the handlink, a look of growing disaster in them.

"What's happening, Al?" Sam demanded.

The admiral shook his head, confusion and anxiety warring for control of his features. "You've changed something, Sam. Blackwell—Ziggy says Blackwell goes to the press this afternoon and tells them they brought out a collaborator. They buy the story, Sam! They're gonna court-martial me and send me off to—"

"Alright, alright, now calm down!"

Al took a deep breath and started his eight-step pace.

"Ask Ziggy—ask her what the chances are that we can stop Blackwell—if you tell the truth in there."

Al pulled the cigar from his lips and glared at Sam. "What *truth*?"

He sounded suspicious, Sam thought. And scared. Sam swallowed tightly and met his friend's gaze for several seconds.

"You *didn't* collaborate, did you, Al?" he asked quietly. The hologram lifted the cigar to his lips and regarded Sam for a long moment, his head tilted back. Then he looked away.

" 'Til yesterday, I wasn't sure," he admitted. He sucked in a deep breath and closed his eyes, running a hand across his face. "No,' he said, his answer hesitant. Then, looking once more at the physicist, he shook his head. "No. I don't think I did."

"Ask Ziggy—if you're going to tell *them* that."

For a moment Sam would have sworn Al didn't want to know the answer. His gaze drifted to the door, a glazed, puzzled look. Then he turned to the box in his hand and punched a button and sighed at the result. "Ziggy . . . can't predict *what* I'm gonna say this time around, Sam." He looked up and shrugged apologetically.

"Can we stop Blackwell if you tell them?" Sam demanded again. He glanced back at the door, wondering how he was going to get Al to do it, even if Ziggy said it was the thing to do.

And Ziggy did.

"Sam!" A glimmer of hope appeared in the holographic eyes. "Ziggy says—if we can keep the press out of this—the chance that I'm court-martialed drops to . . . less than ten percent!"

Sam headed back into the chamber.

"Sam! Where're you going? What are you gonna do, Sam?"

Sam shot the older man a reassuring look. "I'm going to go convince Lieutenant Commander Calavicci that he's not a traitor," he explained, sounding far more certain of himself than he felt.

The hologram didn't follow him back in. Sam heard the squealing carol of the handlink and the low thump of the Door sliding open and shut. Then he took a deep breath, shot a frantic glance at the ceiling for help, and opened the door to the chamber.

"Non compos what?"

Lieutenant Commander Calavicci's explosion coincided with Sam's return. Al shot up from the table, tipping over the metal chair. Barrows leaned back, nervously retrieved it, and set it back up.

"It's your alternative to a court-martial." Senator Weitzman leaned back in his chair and spoke quietly, as if to counter the rising intensity of Al's anger.

"You're sayin' I'm nuts?" Al demanded.

The situation, Sam realized, had definitely deteriorated.

"I'm saying that you're no longer mentally or emotionally fit for continued active duty."

"You son of a bitch!" Al's anger boiled over and he slammed his fist onto the table, actually tipping the microphone onto its side from the reverberation. Barrows rose to try to calm him, reaching for him to urge him back down to his seat. But Al wrenched himself away and strode toward the door.

"Al! Al, wait a minute!" Sam stood in the way, blocking Al's exit. The lieutenant commander fumed in front of him, looking nervously for a way around Sam, a way to escape. "Al, just wait, okay."

"Wait? Why? You gonna take off again, like you have every *other* time things started to heat up?"

"Listen to me," Sam tried. At the moment Al was not making a strong case for his own rationality.

"Listen to *you*?" Al demanded. His face was reddening. "*You* told them I wasn't fit for active duty! *You* told them I was a nut case, didn't you? You bastard!"

"Al, I didn't—"

"You're as bad as Eddie, you know that? Got me to trust you. Made me believe you were on my side. And then you told *them*"— he gestured violently back at the group of

men who waited for Wendell Xiao to control his patient—
"that I'd turned!"

Sam sucked his breath in. Al trembled, his muscles
tensed, his hands crushed into tight fists of barely controlled
rage, his eyes glazing over as he lost himself in the thun-
dering memory that, finally, wouldn't be ignored.

"What happened, Eddie, huh?" he demanded. "What
happened? You forget our plan? Is that it? Did you just
forget what it was like in that pit, huh? Or the fact that *I*
was the one who kept you alive all those weeks!"

"Al—"

"Did you, Eddie? How could you forget that, huh? How
could you forget how we felt when we found out there were
others still left behind with us? You remember that, don't
you? Remember when we heard Charlie talkin' about the
other camps, Eddie?" Al's voice broke and tears started in
his eyes. "God, we couldn't believe it! After all that time,
thinkin' we were the only ones!" He stared into the face
of Wendell Xiao and saw another man. Sam waited, not
breathing, barely aware of the audience Al had already long
forgotten he had.

"*You* gave me the new information, Eddie. Mine was
too old, you said. I'd been over there so long, no one back
home would believe I was still alive. So I used *your* codes
to set the signals in the camps. Dammit, don't you remember? I told Charlie I'd help them so we could get to the
other camps. And it worked! It was working, dammit! I set
those codes so someone—someone back home—would
know we were still alive!"

"Oh, my God."

Sam glanced over Al's shoulder at Barrows's exclamation. He looked pale. So did Weitzman. And Stern. Even
Wainwright looked distinctly uncomfortable.

Only Blackwell seemed unmoved by Al's revelation.

"And then they brought in the others," Al whispered. He didn't seem to have heard Barrows. His eyes reflected only memories, darkening his unfocused gaze. "And you—you told them I'd turned!" Even when he focused, Sam knew he didn't see the man in front of him.

"Dammit, Eddie, why? Why the hell didn't you tell them the truth? Why did you tell them I was collaborating, huh?"

"Al—" He reached out, but the man backed away, violently, his arms waving in the defensive gestures Sam remembered from Sunday night.

"No! Get away! Get away, don't touch me!" Sam dropped his hands and stepped back. "You bastard!" Al swore. "*I'm* the one who bargained with Charlie to get you out of that pit, remember? I got them to put you in a hootch! And you turned our own men against me! You told 'em they could do whatever they wanted to—" He stopped, his eyes wide with the memory, his mouth open in what Sam imagined was a scream he couldn't force from his mouth.

"Oh, God, Eddie." The final exhalation of betrayal whispered from his lips after a long silence. "I trusted you! I trusted you, dammit! You were the only thing I had left and you turned against me! Why? You bastard, why? Why did you set me up?"

Sam let out a long, sad breath and shook his head. "I don't know," he whispered sadly.

"He has . . . a brain tumor."

Sam turned to the captain. And Al seemed, finally, to realize where he was. And who was around him. He closed his eyes and wiped a hand across his face, removing any trace of the emotional display. He took in a deep breath through his nose and turned around.

297

"It's inoperable," Barrows said, crossing the room. "He's dying." The Army captain held Al's gaze for a long moment. "Yes, Al, he probably did . . . forget. Doctors in France say it's affecting his memory, his reasoning, his judgment—everything." Al swallowed convulsively, but didn't say a word. And he didn't blink.

"And in case anyone in the room missed the punchline," Barrows continued, turning deliberately to Blackwell, whose self-satisfied look had finally started to fade, "it was the colonel's personal SOS we first saw in '74 that got this operation under way to begin with. A signal Commander Calavicci set." He glanced at Weitzman, then at Dennis. "Not only is Al *not* a collaborator," he added quietly, looking back at Al, "but he's actually responsible for bringing home every POW this operation gets out."

It took a moment for the meaning in Barrows's words to sink in, Sam saw. And for the terrible memories to fade. Then, as they did, Al Calavicci snickered bitterly and almost smiled.

"Ain't *that* a kick in the butt?"

CHAPTER
TWENTY-SIX

Al said next to nothing on the drive back to the hospital. Barrows, Stern, Wainwright, and both senators had stayed behind, obviously to talk; that was one conversation Sam was glad he didn't have to sit in on.

"Would you . . . like some company?" Sam offered, once they were back in Al's basement room. The lieutenant commander, looking a little ragged, smiled.

"You got other patients besides me?" he asked, starting a fresh cigar. Sam nodded, feeling a little awkward. "Then go take care of them for a change," Al instructed, waving him out.

"Are you sure—you're alright?"

"Tell you the truth, I'd rather be drunk, but—" He shrugged casually. He was almost a little too eager for Xiao to leave, Sam thought.

"Maybe—maybe later we can . . . go back to the Harbor Light," he suggested. Al narrowed his gaze and smiled guiltily.

"Yeah," he agreed, and turned away.

Sam took a deep breath and opened the door. "Okay, well—I'll check on you later."

And then Sam noticed the tape recorder and the small stack of tapes on the rolling bed tray. "Where'd those come from?" he asked, moving back into the room and eyeing the collection. "And cigars?" he added.

Al looked more than guilty, now, Sam thought; he looked anxious. "Well, Doc, see, that kid—aw, hell, he just wanted to help!"

"What kid—Davalos?"

In response, Al lifted his chin, a belligerent, defensive gesture. But the memory of last night was still fresh in Sam's mind, and even if it hadn't been, he wouldn't have been likely to bring the violation to anyone's attention.

"Relax." Sam smiled and looked at the tapes again. "I'm the one who let him down the first time, remember?"

Al let out a long breath, almost a sigh, and nodded. "Yeah, I guess you were." Sam started for the door and as he opened it, Al called, "You know, Doc? You might just change my mind about shrinks."

Sam laughed and closed the door behind him. The hologram, hovering just outside the door, wasn't laughing.

"Come on, Sam, you gotta get to Terry!" Admiral Calavicci, once again in uniform, gestured him down the hallway.

"Now?" Sam asked, disbelieving. "You said he didn't try it until around one." He glanced at the watch on his wrist. "What happened, has history changed?"

"Uh, yeah, it . . . must have changed," Al agreed rapidly, as if Sam had just given him the answer to a test question. Sam stopped walking and stared at the hologram.

"You're hiding something, Al," he accused. Al

wouldn't look up from the handlink. "What is it?"

"What, me? No, Sam, I'm not—" He finally met Sam's eyes. "Okay, the thing is—see, well, Ziggy thinks that—if you get to Terry *now* you can talk him out of it."

It sounded reasonable, Sam thought, so why didn't he buy it?"

"What's going on, Al?"

"Nothin' is going on, Sam, now come on! Let's go talk to Terry, huh? Keep him from screwing up his life?"

He wouldn't hold Sam's gaze, but Sam wasn't up to pressing the issue. Maybe Al was just uncomfortable around him right now. That would make sense. Lieutenant Commander Calavicci had told Sam Beckett a lot more than Admiral Calavicci ever had.

But leaving the basement of Bethesda Naval Hospital wasn't as easy as Sam expected. As he reached the elevator, the door opened and Barrows, Stern, and Wainwright all poured out of the small enclosure. A sick feeling of déjà vu swept over Sam and he whirled on the hologram.

"What the hell is going on?"

"Dr. Xiao," Wainwright said. Sam braced himself against the team, waiting for an answer from the future.

"I—I don't know." Al looked puzzled. And a little uncertain of the situation. He began punching the handlink that, until this moment, he *hadn't* consulted.

"Doctor, we have a . . . situation," Wainwright explained. Sam's mouth dried and he pulled himself up.

"Sam!" Al shouted. "Dammit, Sam, he *is* gonna try it earlier! Damn, I didn't check—"

"What?"

"This operation is about to be exposed," Dennis Stern explained, moving forward slightly. He glanced at his companions. "We need to talk to Commander Calavicci."

"Sam! Sam, come on!" This time, Sam believed the look in Al's eyes: fear.

"What do you need to see him for?" He wasn't about to let Sunday night repeat itself.

"Sam, leave them, alright! Whatever's goin' on here, it's not the reason you Leaped. Ziggy says Terry's gonna swallow about a half-dozen quaaludes and wash 'em down with scotch. Come on, Sam! Maybe you can stop him! At least keep him from screwing up his life!"

Sam swallowed hard.

"Captain Barrows, what's going on?"

"Al's going to talk to a reporter from *Cavalcade*," he explained. "I can't imagine why—but he's agreed to meet her and talk to her."

Sam's stomach turned over and he stared hard at the hologram who hovered behind Barrows's back: Al looked gray.

"It's . . . supposed to be . . . Beth," he whispered, staring down the corridor.

And then, Sam understood; Al had wanted him out of the hospital *now* so Lieutenant Commander Calavicci could make his escape. And go see Beth.

"She's been on our tails this whole time, but I—well, we tried to throw her another story," Barrows explained.

"Why didn't you tell me?" Sam asked, not talking to Barrows.

Al shut his eyes. "I was afraid you'd . . . try to stop him," he mumbled miserably. Sam swallowed the metallic taste of guilt and turned away from the admiral.

"Frankly, it didn't concern you," Barrows said, also answering his question. "Now, if you don't mind, we need to talk to Al."

They didn't have to force the issue. Lieutenant Commander Calavicci, expecting the hallway to be empty, stepped out of the room at the far end of the corridor. And the moment he did, he saw the crowd waiting for him.

"Al," Barrows started, moving forward. The others started to follow him, but Sam put his hand out.

"Just—hold on, alright?" he ordered angrily. He'd seen the growing panic in Al's eyes. "Just give him a minute."

Barrows walked alone toward the younger man, and Sam shot a quick glance at the admiral; he didn't like what he saw in *his* eyes, either.

"Sam!" The hologram took a ragged breath and his voice cracked. "Come on, you gotta help Terry!"

"How are you going to keep the reporter from blowing this story?" Sam demanded, turning to Wainwright. The man shook his head.

"We haven't got a plan yet."

"Oh, yes you do," Sam said, his anger finally uniting with enough courage to say what he'd wanted to say from the beginning. "It's called 'Plan B,' and it involves throwing Al to the wolves to save your own skins!"

"Actually," Stern interrupted, "until this morning, that *was* the plan. But now—" He glanced at Wainwright for permission before he went on. The enormous man nodded once. "As long as we had a confession, Blackwell's plan would have worked. But there's no way in hell Calavicci's going to go quietly to a court-martial now. And frankly, I don't know that we could discredit him enough to convince the press anyhow.

"It's our butts in the sling, now, Doc. And all the guys still in 'Nam."

"Then—we'll just keep him from going . . ."

"She's got enough to do the damage already," Wainwright admitted quietly. "At least enough to keep us all

303

ducking the press long enough for those grass-roots MIA groups to start believing it.''

''And that could prove disastrous for the men still in 'Nam,'' Dennis Stern added pointedly.

Sam felt sick and looked away. He watched as Barrows and Lieutenant Commander Calavicci walked back to the group. The odd sight of both Als standing so close to each other was disconcerting.

''Sam, you gotta get outta here now. Ziggy says if you leave now, you can make it in time. Maybe still keep him from ruining his career. If he actually tries to kill himself, his career's gonna be over! Even if he lives, he'll be washed up! You've *got* to get there now!''

Admiral Calavicci wouldn't look at his younger self at all.

''What's the plan?'' Commander Calavicci asked. The shock of disappointment that it wasn't Beth he was going to see was still clearly visible in the younger Al.

''We haven't got one,'' Wainwright admitted. Al looked down on the much taller man and narrowed his eyes.

''Wait a minute,'' Sam interrupted. ''The reporter from *Cavalcade*. You said you tried to get her interested in another story?''

''Sam!'' the admiral interrupted. ''Sam, come on!''

''Damn.'' Barrows's eyes lit up. ''That might work.'' He turned to Al. ''A female journalist got killed taking a Pulitzer Prize–winning photo in 'Nam,'' he explained.

Sam shot a quick look at the hologram, who seemed just as surprised. He punched the handlink in his palm.

''She was out with a SEAL team on a rescue mission. In the delta,'' he added, looking very deliberately at Al. ''In 1970.''

"So?" Lieutenant Commander Calavicci asked, barely interested.

"You saw her."

And then he *was* interested. He pulled his cigar from his mouth and stared at Barrows, a hard, penetrating look. Admiral Calavicci was giving the man an equally unhappy stare.

Barrows looked uncomfortable.

"He owes me an apology," the hologram explained, his chin tilted back, waiting.

"I guess—I owe you an apology . . . for not believing you," Barrows admitted.

The admiral smiled grimly. "Damned right," both Als muttered in unison. But while the admiral seemed pleased, no one else did.

"So what's the story?" the lieutenant commander asked.

"Army claimed credit for the picture. Didn't want anyone to know the journalist was on that mission when she got blown up."

Lieutenant Commander Calavicci chortled. "Yeah, well, introduce me to the nozzle who decided to take a woman along on a mission like that, and I'll—"

"Al," Sam interrupted, not wanting to hear the threat. The lieutenant commander turned to him, looking at him quizzically.

"*You* could give her the proof she needs," Sam told him. "And," he added, glancing hastily at Admiral Calavicci for confirmation, "you're supposed to have been in France for the last two years, right? So—"

"Won't work," Al said gloomily. "She was down here last night." He shot a meaningful look at Sam.

"The nurse," Sam whispered. The strange nurse who'd

appeared in the doorway last night. He remembered the scene she'd walked into.

"You really think she's gonna believe I just got back from France?" Al asked.

For a moment, Sam had to agree. Then, looking back at the holographic projection, he smiled. "Al," he said, very certainly, "I'll bet if you put your mind to it, you could come up with a story about last night that Woodward and Bernstein would buy."

"Who?" the commander asked.

"Woodward and—never mind. You can do it, Al."

"Sam!" The hologram looked up, a very restrained hope in his eyes. "Ziggy says that there's a 73.3 percent chance it'll work."

Lieutenant Commander Calavicci looked from one to the other, his gaze lingering a little on Barrows. "Well, none of you better show up there or she's gonna know somethin's goin' on," he pointed out. "I'm supposed to be expecting to meet—" He took a shaky breath and let it out heavily. "Course, she already saw you," he said, turning to Sam. "And well, if I came back from France and was havin' some physical problems, well, it might explain . . ."

Sam grinned. But the handlink in Admiral Calavicci's hand squealed. "Sam! You can't go with *him*, you gotta save Terry."

"Wanna come along?" Lieutenant Commander Calavicci pressed. Sam heard the plea for help. The meeting Al was going to, on top of everything else, was looking to be the last straw, Sam thought. And if the reporter asked the wrong question, touched the wrong nerve . . .

He shut his eyes; he *couldn't* let Al down again.

"Sam! You gotta save Terry!" Admiral Calavicci ordered. "It's *important*, Sam!"

Sam looked from one to the other, his glance on the insubstantial future version of the man swift and unnoticed.

"Sam." Admiral Calavicci's firm voice broke into his conflict. "That kid doesn't deserve to die."

Sam looked at the projection and saw more than he'd expected to. And then he understood.

He turned to the lieutenant commander. "I have a patient—" he started. "I have to—I need to make sure he's alright."

Lieutenant Commander Calavicci chuckled dryly. "Figures. Things startin' to heat up again?"

Sam took a breath, prepared to respond to the bitter assumption. But the commander spoke before he could.

"Guess I better go catch a cab." He shot a final, disappointed look at Sam, then walked through the group to the elevator.

"Come on, Sam," Admiral Calavicci urged him. But Sam waited until the elevator had closed and Lieutenant Commander Calavicci was gone. Then he turned to the three men in the hallway and glared at each of them in turn before he opened his mouth.

"Don't say it," Al warned. But the gleam in his eye showed appreciation for Sam's intent.

Frustrated and angry, the physicist turned away and strode quickly through the hall to the back exit, where he'd parked Wendell's car. As he started it, he prayed that it didn't overheat on the way to Terry Martin's house.

CHAPTER
TWENTY-SEVEN

For the first time since he'd come home—actually, since a lot longer than that—Lieutenant Commander Calavicci had finally begun to feel in command of a situation again. In fact, he admitted secretly, he was actually looking forward to this.

The sharp depression he'd felt over not seeing Beth was gone now. The quick moments of panic as he'd braced himself for a new threat had dissolved. And the adrenaline surge of walking back into the ring for a roaring good fight had taken over.

Again.

And it felt *damned* good!

Mark Davalos was waiting outside the Harbor Light when Al stepped out of the cab. He waited for change from the driver, remembered to hand him a tip, and crossed the street to where the kid was standing, looking at least as excited as Al should have felt.

"She's inside, sir. I thought I'd wait out here for you—"

308

"That's not my wife," Al said. His voice was dangerously quiet, and the ensign heard the tone very clearly. Panic drenched his features, and sweat began to pour down his sides.

"What?"

"She's a reporter, and you're in deep ca-ca."

Davalos gasped and glanced hurriedly inside the Harbor Light. "Oh, shit!"

Al tried not to smile. "Yeah, that about summarizes it," he agreed. Then, as Davalos turned back to him, he said, "Now. You're gonna come in there with me, follow my lead, and keep your mouth shut unless I kick you under the table. Got it?" Davalos nodded nervously. "And if we get ourselves and this screwy operation out of this in one piece, you and I are gonna have a nice long talk about loose lips and sunken ships!"

Davalos gulped and nodded silently, and tried not to look like he was going to wet his pants. Al just hoped he didn't. That'd definitely give them away. He took a deep breath, smoothed his jacket, and looked down on Mark Davalos with a narrow gaze. "Okay, kid. It's show time."

"What happens at the Harbor Light, Al?"

Admiral Calavicci hovered at Sam's side as they drove at breakneck speed along the beltway, hoping a police cruiser didn't stop them. He shrugged and punched the handlink, still checking the prognosis for saving Terry Martin. "Dunno," he muttered. "Hasn't happened yet, has it?"

Sometimes, Al thought, Sam Beckett could be a stubborn fool! Hanging around as long as he had at Bethesda had been damned dangerous.

And if they didn't save Terry . . .

He didn't want to think about that.

Sam took a deep, frustrated breath. "Look, don't worry about it, okay?" Al continued. "Once he—I mean, I—get a look at Tess Conroy, it'll all fall into place." And then, just out of curiosity, he punched up the latest figure and smiled. The chance of convincing Tess Conroy to drop this story in favor of the Dawson one had already risen to nearly eighty percent. When it came to dealing with women, Calavicci was *never* at a loss.

"Oh, no!"

In her usual unpredictable manner, Ziggy had volunteered more information than Al had asked for, and the admiral's stomach turned over as he read it.

"What?" Sam demanded. "*What?*"

"He's done it, Sam," Al reported dully. He let his hand drop to his side. "He's . . . taken the 'ludes." He shut his eyes and wiped a hand over his face. "His career's gonna be over now. Even if we—" A sense of utter failure gripped his whole body.

That kid didn't deserve to die . . .

"Okay, okay, just . . . is this the fastest way to get there?" Sam asked.

"I dunno."

"What do you mean, you don't . . . Ask Ziggy!" Sam glanced at him, puzzled and desperate, and the look pulled Al back to the present.

"Oh, yeah, um—" He punched in the request and Ziggy came up with an unprecedented, immediate response.

Sam followed Al's directions as he navigated them through the circuitous shortcut Ziggy suggested. "It's right up there, Sam," Al told him, gesturing to an old, four-story brick apartment building. "He's on the fourth floor. Ziggy says he's got maybe ten minutes before he goes into a coma."

310

Sam barely put Wendell's car in "park" before he leaped out and ran to the building, taking the steps two at a time to the fourth floor. Al relocated himself ahead of the scientist.

"It's right here, Sam!" Al gestured to Terry's apartment and glanced at the unpromising prediction in his hand.

Sam knocked on the door, but there was no answer. "Terry!" he called. "Terry, it's Dr. Xiao!" He waited and Al shook his head. "Terry! Can you hear me? Terry, open up!"

Across the small hallway, the door to the only other apartment on that floor opened, and a elderly black woman, wearing a purple muumuu, poked her head out.

"Call 911," Sam ordered. "I'm a doctor, and there's a medical emergency here."

Scared, the woman closed her door and Al heard the latches falling into place. "She's not gonna call them, Sam. Break the door down! Come on, we're runnin' out of time."

Sam braced himself and lunged, kicking at the door. It didn't budge. "Come on, Sam, you can do it!"

Sam tried again. And again. The fourth kick slammed the door off the hinges and it fell into the room.

"Terry!" Sam called, stepping over the fallen door and rushing into the small apartment.

"Over here, Sam!"

Terry Martin was slumped on the kitchen floor, his eyes half shut, one arm hanging loosely at his side, the one in the cast lying heavily in his lap. Next to him, on the floor, were two empty bottles: one of scotch, one of quaaludes.

"Damn!" Sam swore, and hefted the young man. "I've gotta get this stuff out of him."

Al grimaced, imagining what Sam had in mind. Sam

311

propped him against the counter.

"Terry!" Sam called loudly, slapping the young man's face until he got a response. Terry woke marginally and glanced at Sam. Then he turned to Al.

"Admiral," he said.

"He can see me!"

"Must have something to do with the quaaludes and alcohol," Sam guessed. "Terry," he continued, "listen to me. Stay awake, Terry. Terry!" He shook the kid, trying to keep him conscious enough. "You've got to get that stuff out of your system."

"Leave . . . me alone," Terry said, sagging back against the counter. Sam reached around and pulled him back up, then turned him to the sink.

Al watched from behind, turning away as Sam forced Terry's mouth open and shoved his fingers down his throat to trigger the gagging reflex. Al covered his own mouth when the sound of retching began, wishing suddenly that he'd been a little more temperate with his own drinking earlier.

"Stay with me, Terry," Sam coaxed. "Stay with me."

Al waited until the sounds stopped before risking a glance back at the two men. Sam turned the water on and ran the garbage disposal.

"Thank God for small favors," Al muttered. Sam supported the exhausted, semiconscious ensign against the counter and stretched one arm out across the room for the phone. He couldn't make the stretch; the phone was out of reach as long as he held on to Terry.

"Al, talk to him," Sam ordered. Reluctantly he let Terry slide to the floor, then stepped away to grab the phone and call for help. "Talk to him, Al!"

"Yeah, I'll talk to him!" Al said. He stood angrily over

the dying boy. "Ensign Martin, you're a disgrace to your uniform! Look at me, mister!"

Something in Terry still responded to the command. He looked up, his eyes glassy and dazed, trying to focus.

"Admiral?"

"Ensign Martin, your brother was one of the bravest men I ever met! But you?" he said, punching his cigar at the kid. "You're a coward."

"It should've been me." Terry's words were blurred by the drugs in his system. "I should've died, not him. Not Cheryl."

"Yeah, maybe you should've," Al agreed. "Instead, you're sittin' here like an ass, feeling sorry for yourself! Well, let me tell you somethin', kid, your brother never gave up! You think he didn't lose people he cared about over there?"

In the background, he heard Sam giving the address to the 911 operator and describing the nature of the emergency. When he hung up, he bent down to the floor and dragged Terry back up, pulling Terry's free arm around his shoulders and forcing him to walk.

"Al," Sam asked, his voice quieter, "is there something going on here you haven't told me about?"

"Yeah," Al said, not paying much attention to the anger in Sam's voice. "This nozzle thinks that just 'cause he lost his wife and his brother, that gives him the right to give up! Well, let me tell you, kid—"

"Al!" Sam interrupted. Then he turned to Terry. "Terry, when—when did you lose your brother?"

"'Nam," Terry mumbled. "Told me ... today. They just ... brought him back." But his eyes were fixed on Al. "You knew him?"

"Knew him? Kid, if it weren't for Ronnie, I wouldn't

313

even be here!'' The barrage of anger, Al admitted to himself, was only partly to shock the kid into alertness.

"Ronnie?'' Sam repeated. Al met the physicist's eyes steadily for a second.

"Yeah,'' he admitted. And took a deep breath. "Liked to sing. Couldn't carry a tune, though.''

Sam swallowed tightly. "Al!''

"I didn't put it together until today,'' he confessed.

It had been a long time since he'd let himself think about Ronnie. Or anyone else he'd lost in 'Nam.

And Martin was such a common name.

And Ziggy could be such a putz!

Terry's head lolled to the left, and he tried to focus on the man who half carried him out of the kitchen and back to the living room.

"Terry!'' Sam called. "Terry, it's me, Dr. Xiao. Can you hear me?'' Sam called. There was no reply. "Al, keep trying. He . . . seems to be listening to you.''

"Yeah, well, I'm not sure it's gonna do any good, Sam,'' he admitted, glancing once more at the handlink. The box squealed, and the sound pulled Terry's attention from the fog he was diving into.

"Terry Martin,'' Admiral Calavicci snapped, "you're in a hell of a lot of trouble!''

Sam was walking him around the room, trying to keep him awake. There was still enough of the deadly combination in him to drop him over the edge, Al knew.

"Killed her,'' Terry whispered. The neurological depression kept the words from reflecting the pain that had driven Terry to this. He just said it, the calm, sleepy words matter-of-fact.

"You didn't kill her,'' Sam insisted. He sighed from the effort of walking with the half-unconscious man slumped

314

across his shoulder, and glanced at Al for a sign. "You did what anyone would have done, Terry. You swerved to avoid a kid on a bicycle. You saved that kid, Terry. You weren't responsible for the fact that Cheryl died!"

Terry stopped moving, and in the background, Al heard the whine of the ambulance.

"Yes, I am." He tried to look at Sam, then turned to Al, standing in the doorway, still apparently visible. Al punched the handlink, but the only figures it brought up weren't worth repeating to Sam.

"Terry, anyone would have done what you did," Sam insisted.

Terry almost chuckled as the wailing ambulance stopped outside the apartment building. The kid looked at Sam then, focusing for a second as hurried footsteps outside the apartment raced up the stairs.

"Doesn't matter," he whispered. "I traded a life for a life, didn't I?"

The emergency crew was suddenly there, taking Terry from Sam, placing him on the floor, starting an EKG, beginning the routine that might, possibly, save his life.

Sam stared silently over the scene, looking at Al.

Out of the corner of his eye, Al saw one of the technicians turn to Sam. "Are you the doctor that called this in?" the man asked.

Slowly Sam shook himself free of the memory of Maggie Dawson's death and looked down. "Oh, yes, um, Wendell Xiao. He's taken . . . quaaludes."

"How many?"

"'Bout ten," Al answered quietly, reading Ziggy's best guess.

"Ten," Sam repeated.

"And that bottle was full when he started," Al volunteered.

"And a bottle of scotch," he added.

The technician shook his head and turned to his partner. "Get the stretcher." The other man left.

"I got him to vomit about five minutes ago," Sam continued. He ran a hand over his face, wiping away the sweat that drenched him.

"Do you know his name?" the technician asked.

"Terry Martin." Sam bent down to join them. "Have you got any norepinephrine?"

"Sorry, Doc, we're EMTs, not paramedics. We don't carry that kind of stuff."

The second attendant returned with the stretcher and they loaded Terry onto it.

"I'm coming with you," Sam announced. He glanced in Al's direction once more before he followed the others out the door.

Terry Martin's heart stopped beating on the way back to Bethesda Naval Hospital. It stopped beating while Sam was in the middle of giving the ambulance technician a brief summary of Terry's recent medical history. Al, hovering in the ambulance, unseen now by anyone but Sam, stopped his unsuccessful attempt to wheedle information from the hybrid computer as the sound of the EKG flat-lining drew all three men's immediate attention.

"No," Al groaned. "No, Terry, don't!"

Sam acted. He ripped open Terry's shirt and administered a precordial thump, pounding his fist on the young man's chest and watching the monitor.

"Damn!" He repeated the gesture, and the technician

watched the EKG, shaking his head. "Dammit, Terry, don't give up! Live!"

Sam and the technician started CPR and continued it for the next ten minutes as the ambulance crept around the traffic that snarled Wisconsin Avenue in both directions. They rode on median strips, shoulders, and curbs until they reached the hospital. Sam had managed to convince the civilian ambulance attendants that Bethesda was not only closer, but he was on staff there and Terry had just been discharged from the naval hospital. They had capitulated gracefully.

The emergency room was ready. A Dr. Larry Tighe was waiting for them as they rolled Terry through the automatic doors to the waiting emergency personnel. Al followed them, watching the team descend on the unconscious ensign.

"He's in cardiac arrest," Sam told them as he paused in his pumping of Terry's chest for the technician to administer a short breath.

And then medical personnel who were adept at handling emergencies of this type took over, pulling Terry into a waiting cubicle, attaching an IV, transferring him from the stretcher to their own gurney, and preparing a defibrillator, all while continuing CPR without interruption.

Sam and Al waited in the background, watching the physician in charge bark orders to the nurses and technicians around him, a well-rehearsed routine taking place.

Terry's slender form jerked violently under the electrical charge of the defibrillator, but as the physicist and hologram waited, the EKG finally showed a beat.

"Normal sinus rhythm," Dr. Tighe announced. He glanced at Sam. "Dr. Xiao, isn't it?" he asked. "You just happen to get lucky, or what?" he asked, turning almost immediately back to his patient and administering the epinephrine he'd ordered.

"I was . . . afraid he might try something," Sam answered carefully, half glancing at Al. "I did a consult on him a couple days ago."

The epinephrine began to take effect.

"We'll pump his stomach, but it's gonna be a while before he's out of the woods," Tighe said. "He could still slip into a coma, but I think the worst is over."

Sam turned to Al and waited as Ziggy deigned to answer his request for information. He looked up from the answer. "You did it, Sam," he predicted. Then, a small squeal from the link pulled his attention, and he grinned hugely.

"Well—almost. Ziggy says there's still one more thing you gotta do."

Tess Conroy waited nervously in the nearly empty restaurant portion of the Harbor Light, working on a soda and trying not to look as uncertain as she felt. The war she'd been fighting with herself—with the Maggie-like part of herself—all day still wasn't over.

She drummed her fingers on the portfolio of information she'd culled from Kelly's notes, information that mostly focused on the man whose ex-wife she was impersonating. On the off chance that this story didn't pan out, and even if it did, she'd continued pursuing the other one. She'd finally dug up a phone number for Grimwold on the West Coast. And this morning, after suspiciously little prodding, the Navy had coughed up a number for the man who'd been in charge of the SEAL unit when Maggie died.

One way or the other, she *was* walking out of here with a story.

She watched as Mark Davalos and Lieutenant Commander Calavicci came toward her and saw the first glimmer of expectation on the man's face fade into angry suspicion as Davalos pointed her out from across the room. To his credit, after a moment of hesitation, he came over to her table.

"You're *not* my ex-wife," he said, looking, she thought, almost amused. Then he ran his eyes over her, a long examination that lingered lecherously on areas she'd have preferred he ignore. "Can't say I'm disappointed, though," he said at last, his eyes once more meeting hers. "The name's Calavicci," he said, holding his hand out. "Course you probably already know that, don't you, Miss . . ."

"Conroy," she answered. She took his hand. "I'm a reporter," she explained quickly. Calavicci gave no indication that he was going to let go of her hand. "I'm doing a story," she said, and pulled her hand free.

"Really? On what?" He slid into the booth across from her and signaled the waitress, who came over instantly.

"Hi, Al!" the young woman greeted. He leaned up, gave her a peck on the cheek, and let his gaze roam over her as he released her.

"How ya doin', Christy? Listen, get me a beer, huh? And one for my buddy."

"Sure," the woman said happily, and left to fill the order.

Calavicci turned back to Tess. "So, what's your story about?" he asked again.

Tess stared after the waitress; they knew each other! "It's about you," she said, clearing her throat, trying to figure out how Calavicci—who'd been kept locked up in a basement room at Bethesda Naval Hospital—could know this waitress. Even if they'd known each other before he left for 'Nam, surely she'd be surprised to see him now, wouldn't she?

"Me?" Calavicci laughed and leaned back and pulled a cigar from his jacket. "Do you mind?"

Actually, Tess hated cigar smoke, but she smiled tightly and shook her head.

"So, what'd I do to deserve a story in *Cavalcade*?" he asked, as he concentrated on lighting the cigar.

An electric shock of adrenaline surged through Tess's veins with his words; it was more than instinct, now. She leaned forward for the kill.

"You tell me," she said, resting her arms on the table. "You seem to be pretty good at reading minds."

One dark eyebrow tilted upward. "Reading minds?" A near smile struggled through imitation curiosity that might just as easily have looked like fear.

"I didn't say I was with *Cavalcade*."

It took less than a second for the man to recover from the slip. But it *was* a recovery she witnessed. His gaze slipped away, focused backward, then returned with renewed conviction.

"A WAG," he explained smoothly, waving the freshly lit cigar in a circle.

"What?"

"Wild-Assed Guess." He grinned a sly, dangerous grin. "You and I both know who Mark here reports to," he said, tilting his chin and cigar in the direction of the sweating ensign. "Figure anyone who could get to *him*—and get this much outta him—has to work for *Cavalcade*."

Ninety-nine percent of her didn't buy the explanation.

But one tiny little percent wanted to.

The waitress returned and put two frosty mugs of beer in front of Calavicci and Davalos. "Pete says they're on the house,'' she told them, and Calavicci grinned.

''Tell Pete thanks.'' He turned back to Tess after watching the waitress depart. Whatever was going on here, she thought, it was undoubtedly a cover.

That's what ninety-nine percent of her believed.

''You just returned from Vietnam,'' Tess launched.

Calavicci swallowed the wrong way and choked. ''I what?'' he asked. There was no nervousness in the question. Now he actually seemed to be enjoying himself.

''Vietnam. I have a source that says you've just returned home from Vietnam. That you've been a POW until—''

''Hold on,'' he said. ''What source?''

Next to her, Davalos jumped, as if he'd been kicked. ''Well, sir, actually—'' The kid sighed and glanced at her. ''Well, I didn't talk to Miss Conroy, sir, but I did—well, I went to this party the other night, and I . . . had a little too much to drink, so I—well, I guess—''

''You started bragging again about all your 'top secret' missions, huh?'' Calavicci asked. There was real annoyance in his voice and he shook his head. ''You'd better not have that,'' he added, and reached across the table to remove the beer from the ensign's grasp. ''Hell, kid, I keep tellin' you: there are *other* ways to impress a woman.'' He turned back to Tess as he said that, making it very clear that he'd like to demonstrate some of them.

She cleared her throat. ''Then when did you return home, Commander?''

The man hesitated. Just long enough. ''Not until '73.'' He turned to his beer. ''Six years. God!''

''If you've been back since 1973,'' she said, leaning forward, ''then why were you so eager to see your ex-wife?'' It was a low blow, but the man smiled through it.

''Got back in March,'' he explained, ''and they shipped

me off to France in April. As you obviously know, my wife took off with another guy while I was in 'Nam. But if any of my stuff is left anywhere, it's with her!'' He was gesturing with the cigar, waving it around like a baton. ''I've had a bunch of my buddies tryin' to track her down so I can get my things back. Mark was one of 'em.'' He snickered. ''The woman's hard as hell to get hold of. I figured Mark,'' he said, turning a critical gaze on the man, ''got lucky.'' Then he turned back to her. ''Guess instead, maybe *you* did.''

One more try, Tess decided. ''I don't mean to question your honesty, Commander—''

''Call me Al,'' he suggested suggestively.

''—but I went to the hospital last night. I saw you.''

''Yeah? When?'' He looked puzzled at first, then shot her another suggestive look. ''I'd've remembered seeing *you*.''

''You were curled up on the floor. Crying!'' Something inside her cracked open as she pushed the line of decency. And Davalos's facial response to her words confirmed her conclusion. ''There was a doctor with you,'' Tess added.

For another breath, the feigned puzzlement remained.

Then, looking clearly unhappy, the man whispered, ''Damn,'' and sighed heavily and shook his head. ''Xiao. Him and bad news always come together.''

''Bad news?'' Tess prompted.

For a moment clear embarrassment suffused his face. Then he stared at his beer and rubbed his hands around the glass and took another deep breath. ''They brought me back from France early 'cause I picked up some little creepy crawly. They had me in isolation, right, so I wouldn't give it to anyone else. But then—well, then Xiao tells me I caught one of those . . . French diseases, too.'' He shrugged, looking genuinely embarrassed.

"That wasn't the reaction of a man who's just found out he has a venereal disease."

He lifted one eyebrow, narrowed the opposite eye, and said, "It is if you're Italian."

The man was unbreakable, Tess decided. She met his eyes suspiciously. Knowingly.

"Look, sorry I can't help you," he said. "That would've been a damned good story." Then he glanced at the dance floor. "Wanna see if we can get Pete to open up the floor?"

Tess hesitated, then made her decision.

When she'd first started this story, Barrows had sent her to Grimwold. But Grimwold had been transferred the next day. Calavicci, on the other hand, had shown up. And obviously, *not* so the world would know he'd just come home from Vietnam.

Even if he had.

"Maybe you *can* help me." She pulled the Pulitzer picture from her portfolio and laid it in front of him. "Recognize that picture?"

He turned a little pale as he looked at it, and swallowed loudly before looking up. "Yeah, sure," he whispered harshly. "What about it?"

"Did you see who took it?"

Al glanced at Mark Davalos, then closed his eyes and wiped a hand over his face. "That was a long time ago," he said. He looked back up. "Yeah, I saw who took it. I told Bobby—Bob Barrows," he corrected. "He's the other guy in that picture." He took a longer drink of his beer before he continued. "He didn't believe me. And—well, I was pretty sure we were gonna be rescued. And when we weren't—" He shook his head. "It was rough."

"Who took the picture?"

"Some woman. Blond hair. She was wearin' an Aussie hat, but she'd pinned things to it, medals or something. They caught the light. I saw her takin' the pictures. I figured—she wouldn't be out there on her own, right? So I thought—we were gonna be rescued."

"Would you recognize her if I showed you a picture?"

"Yeah, probably."

Tess pulled the deframed photograph of Maggie Dawson from her portfolio and placed it on top of the Pulitzer Prize–winning one. A warm smile came over the commander.

"Yeah," he nodded. "That's her." He blushed. "Spent a lot of time thinkin' about her over the next couple years."

Tess sighed. "Would you let me quote you in my story?" He looked puzzled. "The Army claims they took that picture. It won a Pulitzer, Commander. And Maggie Dawson died right after she took it." She held his eyes. "Winning a Pulitzer was everything to Maggie. Everything."

He looked down at the woman's picture, then moved it aside so he could see the other one. "Sure," he said. "What the hell? I'm not in the Army. No way they're gonna shut *me* up." He sighed, finished his beer, and gave her another look. "So, how 'bout that dance now? Can't catch any French diseases just by dancing."

"Actually," Tess said, gathering her things together, "I'm on a really tight deadline. I need to track down a couple other sources. Is there a number where I can reach you?"

"Call *him*," Calavicci suggested, grinning at Mark. "He can get hold of me. I'm still supposed to be under a doctor's loving care," he added sarcastically.

Tess glanced at Davalos, then nodded and left.

It had started raining again. But as Tess raced for her

car, she felt better about herself than she had in what seemed like a long time.

There wasn't a word of Calavicci's story about France that she believed. And she didn't really care too much whether Maggie Dawson got credit for the picture.

But ten minutes ago, she'd realized she *didn't* want to be like Maggie Dawson. And having decided that, she expected she'd probably be able to sleep tonight. And look herself in the mirror tomorrow.

And maybe even like what she saw.

CHAPTER
TWENTY-EIGHT

Wednesday, June 18, 1975, 3:45 P.M.

Sam Beckett paced the small room that Al Calavicci had called home for the better part of a week, not smoking a cigar, but otherwise enjoying the same helpless frustration of waiting.

Despite Admiral Calavicci's earlier reassurances about the future, Sam was still on edge.

"Don't worry, Sam," Al had said, nudging the belated information from Ziggy's link. "Tess Conroy goes with the Pulitzer story. And get this: in six years, she writes a novel that wins *her* a Pulitzer."

"It wouldn't be about Vietnam, would it?" he asked. And Al had smiled, twitched his eyebrows once, and refused to answer him.

As Terry Martin was wheeled to the ICU, Sam had turned to his holographic guide. "What happens to Davalos?" Sam asked. In his mind—and in Al's, he suspected—Ensigns Davalos and Martin were somehow tied together.

"Oh, he's fine." Al grinned. "I can still get any favor

outta him I want. And these days, he's got clout!'' he added.

Sam and Al followed Terry to the small cubicle in the ICU and watched as the nursing staff set him up in the room. He was still unconscious.

''What I don't get,'' Sam said quietly, trying not to be overheard, ''is why it was so important that Maggie get credit for the picture.'' Despite his own irritation over Al's fudging the truth about it, Sam couldn't find any significance in changing such a little thing.

''Well, it sort of . . . puts a closure on it,'' Al explained. ''Maybe it doesn't matter to Maggie, but it mattered to Kelly.''

''Kelly?''

''Bobby's wife.'' And then Al had explained, some of the information gleaned from Ziggy, some of it coming from memory. ''She and Maggie were friends. And then Maggie died, and Bobby was captured. And when Bobby came back, there were problems. Ziggy says some of Kelly's anger was probably directed at Bobby, even though it was the Army she was really angry at for claiming credit for the picture.''

''And now?''

''Now—'' Al punched the handlink. ''Now, they get re-married, Sam.'' He looked up and grinned widely. ''They live happily ever after,'' he added, flourishing his cigar for emphasis and shoving the handlink into his pocket.

''So getting Maggie credit for the picture—''

''It was her memorial,'' Al concluded. And then his gaze drifted away. ''Maybe that's it,'' he said, and pulled the colored cubes back out, punching them.

''Maybe *what's* it?'' Sam asked.

''Memorials aren't for the dead, Sam,'' Al explained,

sounding unusually philosophical. "They're for the living." He looked up from the link and smiled. "I gotta go— take care of somethin' back at the Project," he said hastily. "So you just . . . do what I told you, huh?" And a moment later he was gone.

Sam stopped his pace in front of the bed tray and looked unhappily at the men in the room with him: Robert Barrows, Dennis Stern, Jerry Wainwright. Three musketeers, Sam thought. Or the three stooges.

He looked at the tape recorder and, on impulse, picked up a tape, tore open the wrapper, and stuffed it into the recorder. "You guys mind?" he asked, and didn't wait for an answer.

Seconds later, Sgt. Pepper's introduction to the world filled the room with its harsh, almost caustic sound. But it was better than the silence. And it was a *lot* better than the Bee Gees, Sam thought, though from the expressions on their faces, he wasn't sure the men in the room entirely agreed with that. But Sam didn't really care.

He turned away and walked the eight-step pace Al had taught him in the last three days.

Then the door to the room opened and a rain-soaked Al stepped in. Sam stopped his pace.

"Well?" Wainwright demanded.

"I'm gonna have to practice that story some more," Al reported. He looked tired. Defeated. And then he sighed. "She didn't buy a word of it."

"What?" Sam gasped with shock.

"I convinced her not to print it, though," he said. "So she's goin' with the Pulitzer story."

Sam wasn't sure, but he didn't think Lieutenant Commander Calavicci was telling the truth.

"Are you certain?" Barrows asked.

328

"Oh, yeah. I turned on the Calavicci charm and she melted like wax!"

And then Sam *was* sure. "You mean she's got a conscience and decided not to blow the story," he interpreted, smiling.

Al looked at him. "Were *you* there?" he demanded.

"No," Sam confessed quietly, feeling a twinge of guilt as he answered.

Then the song Sam had sung last night began to play in the background. And halfway through the first verse, Al grinned at him dangerously.

"Then I mean she melted like wax. Or butter. Or . . . *chocolate*—"

"Al!" Sam interrupted. "We get the picture."

Al cocked an eyebrow at him and smiled.

"Where's Davalos?" Stern asked, rising from the orange plastic chair near the door. Al eyed him critically.

"Before I tell you, I wanna know who he reports to."

Stern looked at Wainwright, who looked at Barrows, who looked at the ground.

"I'm afraid I can't say," Dennis answered at last.

"Figured," Al muttered. He crossed the room, turned off the tape recorder, pulled out a new cigar, and unwrapped it. "Well, here's the deal," he said, looking at each of the men in turn. "I don't know my way around the Pentagon jungle, yet," he started, biting a hole in one end of the cigar. "So I'm gonna need an assistant at my nice new desk job who does." He pulled his lighter from his jacket and held the flame to the cigar. "Someone like Davalos. So when you transfer him out of intelligence—and you will," he added, clicking the lighter closed, "you'll transfer him to *my* office." He looked down at Stern over the cigar. "Got any problems with that?"

Stern glanced at Barrows, then shook his head. "I don't think so."

"Good."

"Well," Wainwright said, moving a little hastily to the door, "I'd better go talk to Blackwell. Let him know what's happened."

"Give him my regards."

Wainwright hesitated, his hand on the knob, and held Al's angry glare for a moment. Then he left.

"Guess we'd better go talk to Weitzman," Barrows decided, including Stern in his gaze. Sam shook his head at the quick exodus taking place in the room.

"Ditto for *him*," Al said, pulling his cigar from his mouth.

Barrows met Al's look steadily, took a deep breath, and said, "You don't know the whole story, Al."

"Yeah? Well, I don't think it'd matter much if I did."

Sam watched Barrows carefully. "I think," the man said, "knowing the *whole* story matters a lot." Uncertainty flickered in Al's eyes. But Barrows and Stern had left before he could respond.

For a moment, left alone in the room with Al, Sam couldn't think of what to say. Or how to broach the topic he was supposed to broach. Then Al jabbed his cigar at him and said, "What are *you* hangin' around for?"

Sam shifted uncomfortably on his feet and jammed his hands into his lab coat pockets. "I want you to meet someone."

Al sank onto the stripped bed and shook his head. "Well, to tell you the truth, Doc, I don't really feel a hell of a lot like seeing anyone right now. Especially a stranger."

"Well, he's not exactly a stranger," Sam tried. Al looked up at him, waiting. "Just trust me. You won't be sorry."

Still clinging to the smoky cigar, Al followed him to the elevator.

"You're going to have to get rid of that," Sam instructed, punching the button for the sixth floor.

"Yeah? Why?"

"Because there's no smoking in the ICU."

"ICU?" Al repeated suspiciously.

"Intensive Care—"

"I know what it means! Why the hell are we going there?"

"Just get rid of the cigar," Sam said. Al hesitated, glaring at Sam as they rode to the sixth floor. Then the elevator door opened and Sam turned to him. Angrily, Al dropped the expensive habit and ground it under his foot.

"There. Happy?"

"Not yet. Come on." Sam led the reluctant commander down the sterilized hallway, through the "Authorized Personnel Only" door, and toward the small, glassed-in cubicle.

"I'm sorry, Dr. Xiao, but—" A frantic nurse moved from the centralized desk as Sam and Al passed.

"It's alright," Sam interrupted. "He's . . . family."

The look of puzzlement on Al's face was wonderful. Sam beckoned the commander to follow, waiting for Al to join him outside the glass cubicle.

"Ronnie!" Al's painful gasp was followed by a quick movement toward the half-opened door to the room. Sam held him back.

"His name's Terry," he explained. "He's Ronnie's brother."

Al stopped and Sam let go of his arm. The commander stared at the unconscious young man, hooked to an IV and heart monitor in the small room.

331

"What happened to him?" It took a long time for Al to ask the question.

"His wife was killed in a car accident this week," Sam explained. "He was driving. He blamed himself."

Al sighed and closed his eyes. "Poor kid."

"And then," Sam continued, "today, he found out about his brother." Al turned, startled. "They just brought his remains back. And—all the hope he'd held out—for his brother to return home—was gone." Sam looked at the too-round face that lay asleep in front of them. "I guess it was just too much for him."

There was another devastatingly long silence before Al whispered, "He tried to kill himself?" His eyes were locked on the kid in the bed.

"Yes."

For a long, long time, Al said nothing and stared at the unconscious form. Then, finally, in a very strained whisper, he asked, "Can I really trust you, Doc?"

"Yes."

It was several seconds more before Al believed him. "The night Ronnie sang—that night, when they—" He cleared his throat. "If Ronnie hadn't been there—I would've—"

Sam almost smiled. "I know," he said.

Al turned to him, tilting his head back in an unspoken question.

Sam shrugged. "You talk in your sleep."

Al narrowed one eye, not quite believing him. Sam turned back to Terry. "His career's going to be over," he predicted. Then he looked back. "Unless someone puts in a good word for him."

"Someone?"

"Someone who could pull some strings?" Sam suggested carefully. "Maybe someone who's got a nice little deal with the Navy?"

Before Al could answer, a movement in the cubicle drew their attention. Terry was awake. At last.

Al swallowed and walked into the room, and Sam followed.

Terry looked at both men, then settled his gaze on Al.

"How ya doin', kid?" Al asked.

"Admiral," Terry murmured.

Lieutenant Commander Calavicci chortled and turned to Sam. "You know," he said, "I like the way this kid thinks!"

And Sam Leaped.

EPILOGUE

Albert M. Calavicci stood outside the door to Dr. Donna Elesee's office, both packages in hand, and knocked. Thanks to a few contacts who still owed him, getting the contents of one package had been easy. Thanks to still *owing* a few others, getting the contents of the other had been a little trickier.

"Come in," Donna called.

Don't make a sound . . .

Al took a deep breath and waited for the electronically keyed door to slide open.

"You workin' on Leap Time?" Al asked as he walked into the barren room and saw a very tired-looking physicist running her fingers through her hair and staring at the computer terminal at her desk. She looked up at him and shook her head.

"These calculations just don't seem to work," she half explained. Without invitation, he crossed the room and glanced at the equations sprawled across her screen. "In theory, they should," she said, and rubbed the back of her neck. "But I can't—"

"Increase the temperature," Al suggested, and put a finger on the screen, "there. And decrease the pressure"—he moved his hand—"over there."

Donna stared at him suspiciously, and he shrugged. "Hey! You hang around Sam Beckett long enough, you pick up a few things. Or die trying," he joked. Then he cleared his throat and backed up. "Anyway, I got you somethin'." He handed her the first envelope and stepped back around her desk.

"What's this?"

"A political statement." She had started to open the envelope before Al answered.

"I don't underst—" Her voice trailed off and Al watched with silent pleasure as Donna read the letter of authorization to increase funding on the Retrieval Program and permit the upgrades to Ziggy that her last proposal had recommended. She looked up.

"That was fast," she remarked. Then she smiled. "Who'd you have to sleep with?"

He tilted his head back. "Don't you mean who'd I have to blackmail?" For a few seconds Donna didn't blink.

"I'm sorry about that," she muttered finally, looking back at the letter in her hand.

"Don't be." Her head shot up, surprised, and he shrugged. He handed over the second package and cleared his throat again. "Here."

"What's this?"

He waited nervously and pushed his hands into his pants pockets; Donna wouldn't let him smoke down here. "I think—maybe it's part of why Sam Leaped into Bethesda."

Donna pulled open the manila folder and slid out the pages. "Oh!"

The half-spoken exclamation sounded very small, Al thought.

Don't make a sound . . .

He ground his teeth and took a shaky breath. "You fell through the cracks of the bureaucracy, honey," he said, beginning his carefully rehearsed explanation. "You weren't listed as his dependent and—well, the Army just screwed up—not tracking you down earlier."

Donna looked up from the death certificate in her hands, her eyes moist, her nose a little red. Her mouth opened, but nothing came out.

"I pulled some strings," Al volunteered needlessly, nervously. "Figured—well, this Leap made me think of a few places I could look that I hadn't thought of before."

"It says he died—in Vietnam. From a brain tumor," Donna interrupted quietly, sniffing and looking back at the certificate. "His remains were shipped back in . . . 1976."

"Yeah. He's buried at Arlington."

Donna stared at the pictures on her desk, pictures Al knew well.

Don't make a sound . . .

"I made a phone call," Al said, running a hand across his face. "Figured his name should be on the Wall." Donna turned to him. "They'll give you a call before they put it up, so you can be there. Hope you don't mind, I just thought—"

He waited a moment, but Donna didn't say anything. Not that he was sure what he expected her to say.

Don't make a sound . . .

He started to leave.

"Al." He hesitated at the door, waiting. "Can I—can I trust this?"

She was staring at him, waiting.

Eddie! For God's sake, Eddie, make them stop!

"Did my father really die over there?"

Don't make a sound . . .

He took a deep breath and forced himself to look her in the eye. "In some ways," he confessed, "I think we all did."

Very, very carefully, Donna put the death certificate back in the envelope and set it on the desk. "Sam's Leaps permitting," she said quietly, looking back at him, "I'd really—I'd like you to come with me when they put his name up."

Don't make a sound . . .

But the eyes of Eddie's daughter held a dawning forgiveness he never thought he'd see there.

And, just for a second, a suspiciously knowing look.

Al lifted his chin, narrowed his gaze, and smiled. "I'd like that, too," he agreed, his voice a little husky. He cleared his throat. "And while we're there," he added, "there's this little disco joint I'll take you to . . ."

POSTSCRIPT

In February 1994, the United States lifted the trade embargoes imposed against Vietnam for more than twenty years. In May, Vietnam and the United States announced their intention to reopen embassies in each other's countries, a move expected to "help resolve the continuing question of MIAs."

When asked his opinion, Senator Joseph Weitzman, who, for nearly twenty years, sat on various Senate subcommittees dealing with the MIA issue, said only, "Personally, I don't believe it's the *Vietnamese* government that's reluctant to give America a full accounting."

Officially, only one American is still listed as Missing in Action in Southeast Asia. Nearly two thousand have never been accounted for.

*When the empire died, they were born—
a new hope for the New Republic. The young twins
of Han Solo and Princess Leia are now fourteen,
and enrolled at Luke Skywalker's Jedi academy
on Yavin 4. Together with friends both old
and new, the future heroes of an already
legendary saga begin their training.*

STAR WARS®
YOUNG JEDI KNIGHTS

__HEIRS OF THE FORCE   1-57297-066-9/$4.99

While exploring the jungle outside the academy, Jacen and Jaina discover the remains of a TIE fighter that had crashed years ago during the first battle against the Death Star. But the original pilot, an Imperial trooper, is still living in the wild. He's been waiting to return to duty...and now his chance has come.

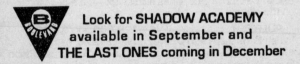

**Look for SHADOW ACADEMY
available in September and
THE LAST ONES coming in December**

® TM & © 1995 Lucasfilm Ltd. All Rights Reserved. Used Under Authorization.
